W9-AOW-633

THE
DELPHI
RESISTANCE

ALSO BY RYSA WALKER

The Delphi Trilogy

The Delphi Effect

The CHRONOS Files

Novels

Timebound
Time's Edge
Time's Divide

Graphic Novel

Time Trial

Novellas

Time's Echo
Time's Mirror
Simon Says

Short Stories

"The Gambit" in *The Time Travel Chronicles*
"Whack Job" in *Alt.History 102*
"2092" in *Dark Beyond the Stars*
"Splinter" in *CLONES: The Anthology*
"The Circle That Whines" in *Tails of Dystopia* (forthcoming)

THE DELPHI RESISTANCE

The Delphi Trilogy
Book Two

RYSA WALKER

SKYSCAPE

SKYSCAPE

This is a work of fiction. Names, characters, organizations, places, events, and incidents are either products of the author's imagination or are used fictitiously.

Text copyright ©2017 by Rysa Walker
All rights reserved.

No part of this book may be reproduced, or stored in a retrieval system, or transmitted in any form or by any means, electronic, mechanical, photocopying, recording, or otherwise, without express written permission of the publisher.

Published by Skyscape, New York

www.apub.com

Amazon, the Amazon logo, and Skyscape are trademarks of Amazon.com, Inc., or its affiliates.

ISBN-13: 9781542047227
ISBN-10: 1542047226

Cover design by M. S. Corley

Printed in the United States of America

This book is dedicated to the many people around the world—past, present, and future—who risk their lives in the ongoing resistance to tyranny, injustice, ignorance, and oppression. Without the candles you light, the world would be a much darker place.

October 30, 2019
Telephone interview with female psychic, age twelve

_____

Q: Okay, just tell me what you remember.

A: It's a bumpy road. Not like potholes, though. Uneven. More like a dirt road. Later, when they opened the trunk, I saw a bunch of tall pine trees. But . . . I think they learned something from Nicki running like she did. The boy who I was in this time . . . his hands and feet were bound. Although he couldn't move much anyway, because he was piled in the trunk with the other four kids.

Q: Do you know which one of the boys you were . . . seeing through?

A: I'm pretty sure it was Hunter, because later when they had the other kids in the building, I could see the two girls really good. One of them was right near these animals—like drawings from a children's book—that were painted on the walls in the room. I never got a close-up look at the two boys at the far end, but I saw their feet once I was inside, and they were bigger. So it had to have been Hunter. And he was a sweet little kid. He . . . he didn't deserve this. No way.

Woman's voice: You okay, sweetie? We don't have to do this. We can call back later if you're too upset.

A: No. I want to, Mom. Like you said, maybe she can get the cops there to listen. Maybe they can find the guys who did this . . . or at least find the kids' bodies.

Q: Take your time. No rush.

A: So . . . anyway . . . I was inside Hunter, and when the car stopped, someone opened the trunk. I couldn't see anything because Hunter was squeezing his eyes shut so they wouldn't see he was awake, but the voices got louder. One was saying nasty stuff about a girl he met at some bar, and the other said he'd better shut that crap up before the boss heard him. Then they start dragging something—the other kids, I guess. Once they were gone, I could see again, because Hunter opened his eyes, and the men, they didn't close the trunk. One of the girls, the younger one, was next to Hunter, but she wasn't moving. He starts thrashing around. I think he was trying to get the tape off his hands and feet so he could run away. But then he hears the men coming back, and he plays possum again.

Q: Your mom said the vision happened last night, but this group of kids disappeared nearly a week ago. Does the boy know where they were holding them before this?

A: I don't know, but it wouldn't matter even if he did. I don't get their thoughts, just what they see and hear. Sometimes smells, but not always. And it's fuzzy sometimes. Blurry. Like it's far away. Anyway, after that, I mostly just saw the ground, because the big guy flung us over his shoulder and went inside. Hunter kept pretending he was still knocked out. I guess he was worried that if they knew he was awake, they'd give him more of the drug and he wouldn't have any chance of escaping. Not that he ever had a chance anyway.

Q: Did you see much of the building? Or the area around it?

A: Enough to know it was the same area where they brought Nicki last week. Same fence, but one section of it was down. One of them had a big flashlight, and once we were inside, I could see crap all over the floors—food wrappers and beer bottles. Even a hole in the floor in one room. They went upstairs, and just before they propped us up against the wall next to the other kids, the flashlight reflected off these big chunks of white . . . what do they call the stuff you make sinks and toilets out of?

Q: Porcelain?

A: Yeah. There was an open pipe right next to them, so I think it was a bathroom. I could see the walls, but only a little, since Hunter was squinting so they wouldn't notice he was awake. But I'm sure about the drawings—paintings, I guess?—on the walls. A couple of dogs. And this one that looked like a rabbit. The walls were crumbling in places, but the drawings were like something from *Peter Rabbit* or whatever. So, I guess kids lived there at some point. And now kids *died* there, too. There was a shot and then another and another. Not loud. Just a *fwap* sound, kind of like when you pull a cork. Hunter opened his eyes when the shots began, and he started screaming . . .

Woman's voice: It's okay, baby. I'm here.

A: After Hunter screamed, the man who was bragging about his sex life before starts cursing and saying the kids were all supposed to be asleep. That he didn't sign on for this. So the third person, the woman, shoves the guy out of the way. She points the gun straight at Hunter's face. I only saw her briefly, but she didn't look angry like I expected. More sad, really. She said, "I'll make it quick for you." Hunter squeezed his eyes tight, and I heard another *fwap* noise. And after that, I didn't see or hear anything else.

CHAPTER ONE

Somewhere in Ohio
October 31, 2019, 5:20 p.m.

I wake to music, barely audible over the hum of the road. At first, I think I'm still in the truck with Porter. But it's Aaron's hands tapping on the edges of the steering wheel this time as he sings along with Arctic Monkeys about Arabella and her interstellar gator-skin boots.

"I'm sorry," I say, my words punctuated by a yawn. "I was supposed to be keeping you company."

Aaron smiles but doesn't take his eyes off the road. "Your job was to keep me awake, and you did. You were snoring right in time with the music."

I give his leg a half-hearted swat. "I do *not* snore."

He catches my arm and squeezes it briefly, then his hands go right back to the wheel. Even though he's been towing the RV for the past two days, it still makes him nervous.

But then, we're *all* a bit nervous. My eyes automatically stray to the rearview mirror, although I don't really expect to spot anyone tailing us. Aaron scanned the RV for tracking devices before we left Baltimore, and I don't see how anyone could possibly have followed our winding, purposeless path over the past few days. Our orders were simple: get out of the area, keep to back roads, await further instructions.

Which is exactly what we've done. Yesterday was rural Indiana. Today, we watched rural Ohio flicker past the RV's windows like a perpetual video feed from The Farm Channel. And it will probably be rural Tennessee or whatever tomorrow, since no one has gotten back to us with the promised "further instructions."

"How long was I asleep?"

"Fifteen minutes, maybe? We're in the outer suburbs of Columbus."

The view outside doesn't really fit my definition of suburbs. In the DC area, builders routinely squeeze three-story starter castles onto lots not much bigger than this RV. What I'm seeing here are mostly modest-sized houses, even a few mobile homes, surrounded by large swaths of land.

This stray thought is all it takes to stir Daniel from his corner in my head.

Land's cheaper here than it is in DC. That's why you see more single-story houses and fewer townhomes or condos.

Mmhmm.

I leave it at that, hoping he'll take the hint. It's getting really hard to mask my annoyance at Daniel's interruptions. Part of me wants to pop a permanent wall around him. He seems unable to restrain himself from commenting on every thought that enters my head, no matter how inconsequential. Maybe he's only making conversation, but it would be nice to just stare out the window and let my thoughts wander without Daniel constantly bringing my train of consciousness to a screeching halt.

For as long as I can remember, my head has been subject to double occupancy. Sometimes, like now, it's triple, although most of the ghosts I've picked up have been a little more respectful of boundaries. These mental hitchhikers, for lack of a better term, all have something left unfinished, something tethering them to this world and keeping them from moving on to the next. I help when I can, because tying up their loose ends is the quickest path to getting my head back to myself, and it's usually a fairly simple, if somewhat time-consuming, matter to send them on their way. This one guy, Abner, just needed to see that his sudden death hadn't also resulted in the starvation of his dog. Another hitcher, Josephine, couldn't let go until she knew her little girl would be okay without her.

Some cases, however, aren't so easy. My decision to help Molly Porter's ghost deliver a message to her grandfather is the reason that I'm in this mess. The reason my foster brother, Deo, is involved. The reason he's sick.

Now Jaden is mumbling at the back of my head as well, although I can't really fault him, since he's trying to rein Daniel in.

> Man, you know she hates that, right? Hates. It. Why can't you just chill until she asks you somethin'? Give the poor girl time to think. To just be.

Jaden doesn't always follow that advice himself, but he generally avoids chiming in unless he has knowledge that's actually relevant. With Daniel, it can be about anything. What looks good on a fast-food menu. Whether it's chilly enough to wear my wool socks.

To be fair, I don't think Daniel *can* hang back and do nothing quite as easily. Jaden doesn't have a body to go back to. Graham Cregg made sure of that when he had him killed, simply to see if I'd be able to pick up both Jaden's spirit and his psychic ability.

Given that Jaden is dead, he'll soon be moving on to whatever comes after this life. Daniel's future, on the other hand, is far less certain.

> I was only trying to help. How am I supposed to know what Anna already knows?

But Jaden is having none of it.

> Have you taken a good look around in here? You see those file cabinets with names? Abner, Emily, and so on? Those are full freakin' lifetimes of experience that Anna can access anytime. So, unless you know somethin' that's not in one of those files, somethin' she actually needs to know, why not give her a little peace?

Daniel doesn't respond at first, but I can feel him stalking around like a caged animal. That sounds stupid for someone without a body, but I don't have another descriptor for the constant, restless movement of his consciousness inside my head.

> Yeah, well, I have to do something or I'm going to end up insane. Not everyone can be all Zen Buddha like you.

The *Zen Buddha* comment starts Jaden wondering if it was an insult to his race or his religion. Or maybe it was a compliment? And Daniel's pacing is making me crazy.

Be still! Be quiet! Both of you, okay?

I shake my head to clear it, then lean back into the seat and rub my temples.

"Another headache?" Aaron asks. "Is Jaden—"

"Jaden's not the problem." I'd love to tell Aaron that the real issue is his older brother, but Daniel is determined to keep his family oblivious to the fact that he's joined the circus in my head. "I'm just tired, I guess."

Aaron smiles. He can definitely commiserate on that point. Neither of us has gotten more than a few hours of uninterrupted sleep in the past few nights.

"Find a campground," he says. "It'll be dark in another hour anyway. Might as well stop now. It's not like we actually have any place to *be*."

❖　❖　❖

Taylor pulls the edge of the curtain back a fraction of an inch and peers through the tiny gap.

"Two." Her whisper is so low I have to strain to hear. "A man and a woman . . . staring at the door. So I guess three, since I can't see the one who knocked."

That knock startled the hell out of us—well, except for Deo, who's propped up against the wall, pretty much out of it. I persuaded him to come to the table, but he's barely touched his bowl of Campbell's Chicken & Stars, the only thing he's been willing to eat for the past day. His fever keeps going up, despite the Tylenol, and the arm where he was injected is so swollen that it strains against the fabric of his shirt.

Aaron peeks outside. "Whoever they are, they're not armed. Not planning any sort of violence. Otherwise, I'd be picking up that vibe."

Yeah, well, your premonitions aren't foolproof.

"You've been wrong before." Taylor couldn't have heard Daniel's comment in my head, so the fact that Aaron's premonitions are sometimes wrong must be common knowledge in the Quinn family.

"False *positives*. Never a false negative." But Aaron reaches into the windbreaker slung over the back of his chair and pulls out his gun as he speaks, so maybe he's not entirely convinced either.

Knock, knock.

The pounding is more insistent this time, so loud that even Deo startles.

Only for a second, though, and then he slumps back against the wall. Seeing him like this, lacking the energy to even hold up his head, stirs a wave of anger so powerful that I suddenly *hope* it's one of Cregg's people—or better yet, Graham Cregg himself—on the other side of that door. Any qualms I might have had about killing him a few days ago are long gone.

"This is stupid," I hiss, moving toward the door. "It's probably the woman from the campsite office."

Aaron hesitates for a moment and then nods. "I'll cover you."

I bite back a nervous laugh. This entire situation is beyond absurd. How did I land in a reality where anyone has to say he'll *cover* me?

The door opens to reveal pint-sized versions of Iron Man and Buzz Lightyear side by side on the bottom step. Just beyond them is a tiny girl in green makeup, with green hair, red gloves, and a red antennae headband.

The laugh I was holding in explodes out of me. I press my hand over my mouth and back away from the door. All three kids chant, almost in unison, "Trick or treat!"

"Holy crap," Taylor says from behind me. "It's Halloween?"

"Whoa." Aaron turns away, surreptitiously tucking the gun back into his jacket. "Hang on, kids. Let me see what we've got."

There's no candy, so Aaron sends the kids off with a large bag of Doritos to split between the three of them. They look pretty happy as they make their way back to Mom and Dad, who wave at us a little apologetically.

The one good thing about the interruption is that it seems to have given Deo a bit of energy. He raises the edge of the blind to peek at the kids. Deo loves Halloween. Admittedly, you'd be hard-pressed to find a foster kid who *doesn't*. Halloween is one of the few times we get a shot at a whole bunch of candy we can (usually) keep for ourselves. Back when Deo was seven, he was placed in a foster home run by a fervently fundamentalist couple who didn't celebrate Halloween. He swears that played no role in his decision to run away, but I don't think it's entirely a coincidence that he hit the road on the morning of October 31st.

We've both been too old to work the trick-or-treat circuit for several years now, but Deo still dresses up, and he usually cajoles me into joining him. I think he likes the fact that there's one night a year when a guy can wear makeup and outlandish clothes without anyone giving him grief.

"What was the little girl supposed to be?" Aaron asks as he closes the door. "An alien? Or a grasshopper?"

"Mantis," Deo says. "From the Guardians of the Galaxy series."

Taylor sniffs. "You mean Gamora. I actually *saw* that movie."

Deo pushes away from the table and puts his bowl in the sink. "No, Taylor. Didn't you see her antennae? Second film. *Mantis*." There's an edge to his voice, but on the positive side, this is more energy than he's displayed in the last twenty-four hours or so.

He's given Taylor a wide berth since we left Maryland—well, as wide as possible when four people share an RV. But she's crossing the line when she questions Deo's knowledge of the Marvel Universe.

Aaron swears that Taylor doesn't really blame Deo for shooting Daniel. She's just upset—understandably—that her oldest brother is lying in a coma three hundred miles east of here. She knows it's not really Deo's fault and that most of the blame lies with Graham Cregg, and Ashley, one of the many people Cregg has under his thumb.

Long story short, Cregg forced Ashley to sneak into Daniel's room at the trauma center and unplug the equipment that was keeping him alive. I screamed for a doctor, but it was pretty clear that they considered me suspect number one. The doctors managed to resuscitate him, but Daniel's soul, his psyche, whatever it is that makes him *Daniel*, had already joined the ever-shifting cast of no-longer-living characters inside my head. We were outside the building, trying to avoid hospital security, when the news reached us that Daniel was still, technically speaking, alive.

That hasn't changed. He's alive, but there's very little brain activity.

Well, at least inside his *own* head. He's been exceptionally active inside mine.

I add my dishes to the others in the sink and follow Deo back to the little room at the rear of the trailer where he's been sleeping. He's already stretched out on one of the pull-down bunks, and he gives me a slightly annoyed look when I rest my hand against his neck.

"How high is it, D?"

"A hundred and one."

He's much too hot for me to believe that number, and even if he wasn't, I've known him long enough to tell when he's fibbing. He's subtracted a degree. Maybe two.

"Did you take more Tylenol?"

"Mmhmm. I'm okay, Anna. Prob'ly just a bad cold."

Which is another lie, because he doesn't want me to worry. And I don't call him on the lie, because I don't want *him* to worry. But neither of us believes this is a cold. I mean, it's not like Deo never catches a case of the sniffles, and he even had a nasty bout with bronchitis last year, just before our therapist, Dr. Kelsey, finally managed to get him a spot at Bartholomew House, the group home where we were both living when this insanity began. But what are the odds that he would start feeling like crap from purely natural causes less than forty-eight hours after Cregg's medic jabbed him with a syringe full of who-knows-what?

If he's not better tomorrow, I'll have to force the issue. Get him to the doctor and . . .

And what? What will you do then?

I have no idea what I'll do then, but I'm not going to admit that to Daniel.

They could run tests. Maybe give him something stronger than Tylenol.

They'll ask for IDs. Insurance. Probably report you to the authorities, too, since I'm sure the State of Maryland has listed you as runaways.

Yeah, well, if Deo doesn't get better soon, I won't have a choice. What did they give him? You were there for months, Daniel. Months.

Sorry, Anna. I was working on getting data, tracking down information on which kids they had in the—

But you were working with Ashley, who was with their med unit. She had to have known something about what drugs they were using.

Ashley's job was to take vital signs. Keep records. She wasn't in the loop.

There's a long pause, and then he adds:

> Or at least if she was in the loop, she didn't tell me any-
> thing beyond rumors and speculation. I do know that
> there were a few kids who had . . . reactions . . . to the
> various serums they were testing. But most of the re-
> actions weren't life-threatening. I can't see Ashley will-
> ingly hurting any of those kids.

That seems like an odd thing for Daniel to say, given that Ashley's the one who pulled his life support. But then she's also the one who stepped in to save me from Lucas, so I kind of get what he's saying.

> He'll be okay, Anna. You're overreacting. Deo's a tough
> kid, and it would be really stupid to risk—

Daniel stops abruptly, probably because he can tell that he's pissing me off, and slides back into the corners of my consciousness. I'm not going to argue with him, because in the end, nothing he's said is relevant. If Deo doesn't get better soon, I'll be taking him to a doctor, consequences be damned.

❖　❖　❖

The light burns, even with my eyes squeezed tight.

The man knows this.

He likes this. Likes that it causes me to cower against the back wall with Daciana. Likes that it keeps both of us off guard, unable to see any-thing as he descends the narrow stairway into this damp, dark, and frigid hole.

"Hello, ladies."

After so many hours—or is it days?—in the pitch black, the beam is a white, glaring sun. He keeps it trained on our faces as he speaks.

"I'm taking volunteers tonight. Which one of you would like to come upstairs first?" He pauses, waiting, as though he really believes either of us would volunteer to follow him. *"I brought food, if that provides extra incentive. And while I believe there's enough for both of you, I'm never very good at judging these things. It could be that only the person who volunteers will have dinner."*

My stomach, long past the point of simply growling, howls at the mention of food. We finished the last two granola bars yesterday and split the last of the moldy Pop-Tarts this morning. But the gnawing sensation in my stomach hasn't quite reached the point where it can compete with the pain from my hand, which is now short one finger.

Neither of us moves.

Cregg gives a long-suffering sigh, and a moment of complete silence follows. Then Daciana staggers forward.

"And hunger will enforce them to be more eager." Cregg laughs softly, although I don't think it's hunger pulling Daciana toward him. He's doing it, doing that thing with his mind again.

"Help. Please help." Daciana looks back at me, clutching her hands—her still completely intact hands. And then her head jerks back forward, and she screams something at him in her native language.

Cregg winces at the noise in the small space. Daciana falls silent mid-shriek, giving me one last imploring look over her shoulder as she starts up the stairs.

I've only seen Cregg do his mind-control trick when he was seated and focused, and he's standing now. But he's standing perfectly still, staring intently at Daciana as she climbs the narrow stairs that lead up from the basement. Will breaking his concentration also break his control over her?

This may be the best chance I'll get. Maybe the only chance.

Pa's voice fills my head. You ever need to get away from a guy, don't hesitate for a minute, Molly. Kick him hard as you can in the nuts and run.

I wasn't able to do that with Lucas. I tried, but he was too strong. Too fast.

Cregg is older and slower. His eyes are squinted, nearly closed, and he's only ten feet away.

Do it!

The buzzing starts before I cover half the distance. It fills my ears, and my feet become lead weights, pinning me to the ground.

His narrowed eyes shift between me and Daciana now. My legs crumple beneath me, and I feel my left arm fly above my head. It hovers there, completely out of my control.

Cregg backs slowly up the stairs, keeping that hateful floodlight shining directly into my eyes until he nears the top. When he moves the light away, however, his face has changed. It's not Graham Cregg anymore.

It's Myron.

And then it's Cregg again, and the buzzing peaks, rising to a constant whirr. He invades my mind like a physical force as he pulls my arm down again and again, smashing my injured hand into the concrete floor on the exact—

"Anna! Come on, babe. It's Aaron. Snap out of it. You're hurting yourself."

I open my eyes the tiniest sliver, certain that the blinding light will hit my eyes again, that I'll see Cregg, that I'll see Dacia's face staring down at me from the basement stairs. But the room is nearly dark. The only light streams in from the window—a tiny crescent of moon peeking through the pines.

I'm not in a cold basement cell. I'm still on the floor, but the surface beneath my hand is carpeted. Aaron's face is directly in front of me. His grip on my left arm loosens as he sees me gradually working my way back to reality. I pull my hand into my lap, remembering the pain from the dream, but it begins to fade as I flex and realize I still have five fingers, not four.

"Where are we? Where's Deo?"

"We're somewhere in Ohio," Aaron says, stifling a yawn. "Deo's still asleep."

"Although I can't imagine how." Taylor's voice comes from behind me, and I turn to see her huddled on the other side of the bed that I apparently abandoned in the heat of my nightmare. Her knees are tucked under her chin, and her short auburn hair sticks up in messy tufts on one side. She looks as tired as Aaron. She also looks kind of pissed.

"I'm sorry I woke you." I don't add the word *again*, and neither does Taylor, but it hangs in the air, unspoken.

She snags her pillow from the bed. "I know I said I'd do this, Aaron, but I'm moving to the pullout sofa. You and Deo can fight over who gets to deal with her because I am *done*."

Aaron looks embarrassed. "Wow, Taylor. Kinda cold, don't you think?"

"Cold? It was *cold* of you to ask me in the first place!" Taylor takes a deep breath, and then her voice softens a little. I can't see her eyes in the dim light, but it sounds like she's close to tears. "Anna, I'm really, really sorry you're going through this, okay? But I'm even more sorry that Molly is dead. I tried, but I just can't lie here and listen to her being tortured every night while you process her memories or whatever."

It's a valid point. None of us were especially eager to go to sleep tonight. We've already experienced two nights of interrupted sleep thanks to my dreams. After I woke up screaming around two a.m. that first night, I just stayed up, blearily combing through conspiracy theory sites on my battered laptop—partly because I was barely coherent and the articles don't require many brain cells, but also because those sites have been our most reliable source of information so far. Which is kind of scary when you think about it.

"I didn't ask you to stay in here with me, Taylor. In fact, I specifically said to let me work through the dreams on my own. *I'll be fine.*"

"Maybe," Taylor says. "But you don't sound fine, and none of us can sleep while you're *working through it*. I can't even sleep afterward, because your nightmares give *me* nightmares."

Jaden's nervous laugh echoes inside my head.

> Tell Taylor she has it easy. She's only getting the audio feed. In here, it's all five senses. Like being in the middle of *Saw* or one of those Freddy Krueger movies.

Daniel begins to shift toward the front, and I know he's going to defend Taylor before he even begins. But it doesn't need to be said. Taylor's not the most tactful person on the planet, but she's absolutely right. It could take me another week, maybe longer, to work through the memories that Molly left in my head when her spirit moved on.

I ignore Daniel, pushing both voices to the back of my head as I begin to stack the mental bricks that give me a modicum of privacy inside my own mind. Neither of them like it behind the wall. I guess it feels crowded, and I'm sure it's harder for them to follow what's happening out here in the real world. But it's impossible for me to process two conversations at once, even if one is my own internal chatter.

To be fair, though, the nightmares are new to Daniel and Jaden. I, on the other hand, have been through this at least nine times. Maybe more, since there are scattered fragments that don't belong in any of the cabinets lined up at the back of my mind. On the plus side, a hitcher leaving means I get my head back to myself. But when they go, my mind begins unpacking their memories, sorting them away for future use. And while some of the memories are useful, my hitchers don't always pass away peacefully in their sleep.

The dreams are part of the process. Nightmares where it feels like there's a huge weight on my chest. Where I'm drowning in my own vomit. Where a semitruck is headed straight toward my car and there's no way to avoid it. And as bad as the others were, I'd go back and work through the departure dreams of every single previous inhabitant in my head—twice, three times even—if it allowed me to avoid another replay of the last few days of Molly Porter's life.

Especially now that my mind is adding in bits and pieces of my own history. That always happens, but usually it's a good thing. It means the dreams are coming to a close, that I'm almost finished assimilating the memories. In the past, though, it's been things about my day or something I've been reading that drifts into the dreamscape. Not my own personal nightmare with Myron.

I quickly check my mental walls, especially the far corner. Back there, the walls are always up, and so heavily fortified that I rarely think about them. Rarely think about *him*.

Back when I was six, Kelsey and I designed my . . . well, not mind *palace*, since it's nowhere near as elaborate as Sherlock's. More of a mind *office*. But anyway, we labeled and organized everything. That was an important step, not just so that I could find information when I wanted but also to keep their memories from overwhelming me or intruding in my day-to-day life. It was important to label Myron, too, so that I'd have a visual reminder that he can no longer hurt me or anyone else. His memories aren't simply in a file cabinet. We locked that cabinet and wrapped it in duct tape, which Kelsey says was my contribution, so my six-year-old self must have believed duct tape to be impervious. Then, we walled that entire cabinet up behind multiple layers of brick and mortar and stashed it in the most remote corner of my mind, as far away as possible from the rest of my thoughts and memories.

The Myron corner is still intact. Every brick is in its proper place. Not a single chink in the mortar. Despite the cameo appearance from Myron, this was just another Molly dream.

Taylor is still talking when I tune back in, saying I handle the dreams better with Aaron in the room, anyway. "Or Deo can come in here," she says, "if you and Aaron insist on being total prudes. But me? I'm going to put on my headphones and crank up the music, because I will not listen to that again. I can't."

"It's okay, Taylor. I understand."

And I do. Taylor and Molly were best friends, like sisters, really. Just because I can't opt out of the horror show in my head doesn't mean it has to be inflicted on anyone else. Well, anyone *outside* of my head.

Taylor nods and gives me a little mouth twitch that might be a smile as she squeezes past Aaron and into the main cabin of the RV. There was a bit of guilt in that look but a tremendous dose of relief, too.

"I'm sorry," Aaron begins, but I shake my head.

"Just . . . go back to bed, okay? I won't be able to sleep for a while anyway. Maybe I'll sit outside for a bit. Or take a walk around the lake."

I close the bathroom door behind me, splash some cold water on my face, and run my fingers through my hair so that it doesn't look quite so much like a haystack.

By the time I'm dressed, everyone else seems to have settled back down. Taylor is sprawled out on one side of the foldout couch, so I guess Aaron has joined Deo in the back on the other cot. I'm a little annoyed to see that when Taylor said she was putting on her headphones, she really meant Deo's extra pair that I loaned her back at Kelsey's beach house. I know it's unbelievably petty of me under our current circumstances, but if she's going to be a jerk toward Deo, she should damn well give those back.

The breeze that greets me when I step outside is much chillier than I expected. I turn back, planning to grab my hoodie, but then I hear a voice behind me.

"Looking for this? It was in the truck."

I startle, bumping my shoulder against the edge of the trailer.

"Oh, God. I'm sorry. Are you okay?" Aaron stands a few feet away holding my hoodie and a plastic grocery bag.

"Yeah, I'm fine. But . . . Aaron, you should go back to sleep. You know you'll get stuck with most of the driving again."

Taylor has taken a few shifts in the driver's seat, but she's more than a little nervous about towing an RV. Deo's not old enough to drive, and I'm something of a liability behind the wheel right now. Even if I wasn't punch-drunk from lack of sleep, I never know when one of Jaden's visions will hit.

"Oh," I say as that last thought sinks in. "The visions. *That's* why you came out here."

Aaron gives me a blank look—a perfectly reasonable reaction, since he wasn't privy to the twists and turns of my internal monologue.

"I meant that you're here because you're worried I'll have another flash-forward and tumble off a cliff or something. Or that one of Cregg's people is—"

"They generally avoid placing RV parks on the edge of cliffs," he says with a teasing grin. "The worst you're likely to find nearby are a few gently rolling hills. And I agree with what you said earlier. I don't think anyone is still following us, if they ever were. But I'm still not going to let you wander around out here alone."

"We can go back inside, then."

"I'm wide awake." That brings a wave of guilt, since I'm the reason he's wide awake, but then he adds, "And I thought it might be nice to have a few minutes alone with you when I'm not stressed out about keeping this giant tin can in the proper lane. I even brought us a midnight snack."

His voice rises at the end, hopeful.

"Sure," I say. "Sounds like fun."

He holds my hoodie open, and I slip my arms into the sleeves. We walk along in silence for a few minutes. Aaron seems a little tense. I glance around at the motor homes lining either side of the path. Is he picking up bad vibes from one of them?

But then Aaron reaches over and takes my hand in his, smiling the tiniest bit when I don't pull away. Was he just trying to work up the nerve? Maybe Taylor was right when she said that neither of us is very good at this romance stuff.

His palm is warm against mine. Comfortable and right. By the time we reach the edge of the RV park, the muscles in my shoulders begin to loosen, and for the first time in days, I feel relaxed.

Two wooden picnic tables and a small playground frame a narrow trail sloping upward through the trees. "I was over this way earlier," Aaron says as he leads me toward the path, "trying to find the dumping station."

"Blech." I've learned much more than I ever wanted to know about RV dumping stations, gray water tanks, and black water tanks over the past few days.

He laughs. "Don't worry. The station is in the other direction. But . . ." He pauses as we hike the last few steps to the top of the trail. "I *did* find this."

He motions with his arm to indicate the panorama that has just come into view. The hill overlooks a shining strip of water that reflects the stars and the tiny sliver of moon hanging above.

I *remember* this. I saw this river, from almost this same angle, when I was half asleep in Porter's truck three days ago.

Aaron tugs me onto a grassy patch at the crest of the hill. For a moment, the moonlight on the river reminds me of the view from the windows at Memorial Hall, when Deo and I were trying to escape from Cregg. I push that thought firmly out of my mind and lean back against Aaron's chest, unable to shake the sensation that I'm doing this for the second time.

"It's nice," I say. "Are you sure this is still Ohio?"

The line didn't make a lot of sense when I remembered it from the vision, but now we've both experienced Taylor bitching about driving for hours through farm country.

He pulls me closer and laughs. "Hey, it's not all cows and corn. And to be honest, I think that bit"—he points across the river—"that might be West Virginia."

The kiss that follows those words is every bit as wonderful as I remember from the vision. The only change is that there's an extra track playing in the background now as I remember what Jaden said about the visions. They aren't always bad. Sometimes, they let you experience the good things twice.

> For you, maybe. I didn't like kissing my brother the first time, and that was just a vision, so—

I shove Daniel back, hard and fast, but not quickly enough to keep Aaron from noticing that I've tensed up.

"Something wrong?" Aaron asks, pulling away to get a better look at my face.

"No. It's just . . . this kissing thing is new territory for me. I'm going to have to work on ways to keep my walls operational."

"Oh. Not cool, Jaden. We finally get away from Taylor and Deo, and . . ."

"It wasn't exactly Jaden's fault."

I'm so, so tempted to keep going. To just tell him that it's *Daniel* causing trouble. I still think it would be easier on everyone if they knew that Daniel was still here—fully alive, fully himself. If they could speak to him, even though he's not in his own body. But Daniel insists that it's his call to make, although he's been a little contradictory on the reasons why we can't tell them. First, he said it would upset them, and then he said he didn't want to get their hopes up.

> Both, okay? It's *both*.

I scramble to come up with some explanation that doesn't break my stupid, forced promise but also keeps Aaron from thinking Jaden is a total creeper.

"I . . . um . . . I had a vision the other day, and I saw this. The view of the river . . . us . . . here. To be honest, I wasn't sure if it was a vision or a dream, since I was half asleep, and Jaden . . ." I trail off, keeping myself from having to tell him a lie. Everything I've said so far is true, even if it's not the real reason I turned into an ice cube right in the middle of kissing him.

"You're sure that's all?" His voice is doubtful. Worried.

"Mmhmm."

Aaron sighs and gives me his one-sided smile, the one I feel I've known forever, even though we only met a few days ago. And yeah, it's been an intense couple of days, but the real reason he seems so familiar, so comfortable, is that I have all of Molly's memories, too. Memories that were accumulated over years, not mere days. That smile was one of Molly's favorite things about Aaron, one of the things that had her more than a little bit in love with him when she died.

Aaron's smile broadens, and I realize how very easy it would be to follow Molly down that path. "Well, damn," he says. "Here I thought I was being so original, surprising you with a romantic view, and . . ."

Okay, maybe it's just *me* who's not good at this. Between that smile and the teasing look in Aaron's eyes, I'm almost able to forget that we're not really alone here and pick right back up with that kiss.

Almost.

I shift gears, glancing over at the grocery bag. "The snack wasn't in my vision. So that part's still original. Whatcha got in the bag?"

He takes out a partial package of Oreos, along with two red Solo cups and a thermos of milk. We munch contentedly for a few minutes, staring out at the river.

Aaron pulls out the last cookie and offers it to me. I shake my head, but he insists on sharing it.

"Thought there were more left," he says. "Taylor must have gotten into them."

Which, of course, reminds me that none of us, Taylor included, would have gotten a crack at these Oreos if Deo wasn't sick. For the past year, he's been a gastronomic black hole, sucking in every scrap of food in his orbit. But he's barely eaten anything today, and that thought definitely harshes the tiny bit of mellow I've found here in the moonlight with Aaron.

"We should get back. Keeping that huge tin can in the proper lane is going to be a lot harder if you're exhausted."

Aaron is quiet for a moment. "I'm thinking we should just hang here tomorrow. There's . . ." He seems to be looking for the right words. "There's a major hospital two hours in either direction. Maybe someone should take a look at Deo. I'm not buying the nasty cold excuse. Are you?"

I've been thinking the same thing for the past day and a half, but hearing him say it out loud makes it seem even more real.

"No," I say finally as I shake the last few drops of milk from our cups and toss them into the bag. "I don't think it's a cold. Neither does Deo. But we both know that getting him medical care would complicate things. And . . . if it's from that injection, then . . ."

I stop, realizing that I'm repeating everything that Daniel said earlier. The practical arguments.

"I know that," Aaron says. "But it doesn't matter. If Deo isn't better soon, we're finding him a doctor."

That comment pretty much sums up the difference between the Brothers Quinn. Aaron puts others first. Tears sting my eyes, and I turn away to hide them as I gather up the trash from our midnight picnic.

I wasn't being selfish, Anna. Like you said before, those are practical arguments. And I damn sure didn't mean we'd let Deo die or anything. It's just—you do know there are more lives at risk right now, don't you? I'm trying to balance—

I shove Daniel back again, wishing he'd stay the hell *put*, so that I can focus on what Aaron's saying. I've already missed the first part.

". . . earlier to pick up Sam's message, I let them know Deo's sick. And that we need to talk sooner than planned."

Sam is not only Aaron's grandfather but also his business partner at Quinn Investigative, a small private detective agency. Everyone calls him Sam, including his grandkids, although Taylor has been known to call him Popsy when she's angling to get her way.

"I'm going to call back in the morning," he adds. "Hopefully Sam and Mom will be able to get Magda in on the conversation, too."

Magda Bell is the woman who's bankrolling this expedition. We haven't gotten explicit orders from her yet, but we'll be searching for more adepts—kids (and possibly a few adults) with special abilities due to their parents' participation in a government experiment called the Delphi Project. Magda originally planned for Daniel to head up the operation, since he'd been undercover with Delphi for several months, but after he was shot, she decided that the four of us were an acceptable substitute. In addition to Aaron's experience as a private investigator, he and Taylor both have skills that could help in the search. Magda seems to think my ability to block some forms of psychic manipulation could be useful, too. Daniel and his knowledge of the Delphi program are also temporarily housed in my head, even if it's not something I'm at liberty to share.

"I don't know about you," Aaron says, "but I'm ready to find out exactly what Magda wants us to do so that we can get started. The less time we give Cregg's people to regroup, the better."

I shiver, less from the cold than from the memory of that night. Graham Cregg writhing on the floor in the testing room at The Warren, flames engulfing his jacket. The final look Dacia gave me as she was kneeling over Lucas's body. Cregg's last text message—another Shakespearean barb about death and revenge. Steering clear of Cregg and his people is one point on which all of us, even the voices in my head, can agree.

CHAPTER TWO

Marietta, Ohio
November 1, 2019, 6:11 a.m.

Sleep is a lost cause after the second dream jolts me awake around dawn. On the plus side, I didn't rouse the entire household by screaming this time, probably because Aaron was sprawled out on the other side of the king-sized bed.

Taylor's right—Aaron has a calming effect on me. The bed is warm and comfy, and I don't want to wake anyone else by moving around the camper. So I stay put for a while, browsing on my phone. There's nothing new online about the fire at The Warren . . . or I guess I should say nothing new and substantive, since there seem to be plenty of conspiracy theories about what happened. No one has blamed it on aliens yet, but that's pretty much the only stone left unturned. This would have comforted my former hitcher Bruno. He always liked to think the aliens were above that sort of interference. They might come down and check us out from time to time, maybe even do a few experiments. But Bruno didn't believe aliens would risk official first contact until they knew that all of us here on earth could treat each other humanely. So . . . definitely not anytime soon.

With Bruno on my mind, I wander over to his favorite website. It's oddly quiet. No new videos or links on the Zeta Reticulans. Not even an Elvis sighting. In fact, the only section of *AllGlobalConspiracies* that has posted anything new in the past eighteen months or so is *Paranormal and Parapsychology*. That section is actually hopping—a bunch of first-person audio interviews have been added, some with transcripts, and many of them have comments.

I plug in my earphones and click on a random interview.

A woman's voice, husky with just a hint of Southern accent, says "Telephone interview with JP, age eleven. Telepathy, with Tourette's-like outbursts. All names redacted."

There's a pause, and then she continues. "It's been awhile, <beep>. Hope you and your mom are doing okay?"

"Mmhmm." The kid's voice is hesitant, barely audible.

"You ready to talk about your AMAZING PSYCHIC POWER?" The interviewer sounds a little like a voice-over on those late-night infomercials for the latest totally miraculous cleaning product that will revolutionize your life.

The kid laughs, more at ease now. "Yeah. Sure."

"Okay, so . . . when did you decide to begin reading people's thoughts?"

"What? Ummm . . . never. I didn't . . . I mean, it just happens. For as long as I can remember."

"So, you're saying you didn't choose this. This is just how you are, like me having brown eyes or being left-handed."

"Right."

"Can you turn it off?"

"No . . . not exactly. I can't always connect the thought to the thinker, but when I'm around people, it's always there. I block it most of the time, using some of the tricks you taught me—like how you filter out a TV show playing in the background. And sometimes it's better in a large group, because it's like dozens of TVs playing softly. That's why school was okay most of the time. With so many voices, I could ignore them."

"Just most of the time, though?"

"Yeah. If everyone was focused on the same thing, or if a kid was really angry or hurt, then I couldn't block their thoughts or keep those thoughts to myself. It's like the pressure built up, and I'd blurt it out. But I couldn't help it, I swear."

The boy seems upset, and the woman says, "Take your time. No rush."

"They said I was doing it to get attention, but I don't *want* everyone looking at me. It just happens. Some people think too loud, just like some people talk too loud, plus the kids . . . the mean ones . . ."

"They learned how to push your buttons?" The woman reminds me a bit of Kelsey—not so much her voice but more her way of coaxing the boy to open up.

"Yeah. And once a couple of kids learned that they could make everyone laugh and get me in trouble at the same time just by thinking something like *fart* really loud . . . well, I couldn't be in a regular class anymore."

"So then you were taken to the *special school*." She emphasizes the last two words.

"Yeah, but they didn't do much teaching really. They just wanted me to show them what I could do. To hone it. They kept trying to talk my mom into signing papers that would have me as an overnighter . . . Most of the kids there don't leave except for trips. But she wouldn't, and after a while, we got spooked. Packed up and moved."

I tap to pause the audio.

Daniel, Jaden—do you think he was at The Warren?

They both say no, and then Jaden adds:

You didn't get options at The Warren. There weren't any day-trippers. No one had contact with their families. Anyone who left didn't come back, but like I've said before, most of the wabbits that Cregg's people "disappeared" weren't kids.

Daniel agrees.

I wasn't there long, but I didn't get the sense that any of the parents signed papers. About half of the older kids there were trafficked in from Eastern Europe. A decent number of the little kids, too—less red tape than here and refugee kids disappear all the time. The others were taken from psychiatric hospitals, like Jaden. Cregg generally didn't snatch kids in the US, although—

Aaron's arm curves under the pillow, circling my waist. I put the phone and earbuds on the shelf behind me and slide under the covers again.

"Another dream?" he asks groggily.

"Mmhmm. Not too bad, though."

"You should try . . . to get . . . some more . . . sleep." The last word is barely audible.

I know he's right. I'm still in serious sleep deficit. I snuggle up with my head on his chest.

Warm. Comfortable. Safe . . .

And, of course, that reminds me that Deo's in the other room, feverish, sick, and certainly not safe until we figure out what Cregg did to him.

I stay still until Aaron's breathing is regular again, then slip out from under his arm and go into the kitchen. If last night's soup didn't tempt Deo, maybe I need to pull out the big guns. The boy has *never* turned down bacon.

While the camper isn't exactly large, it's more modern than many houses I've lived in. Big-screen TV. Fireplace. Dishwasher, a decent-sized fridge, even granite countertops. I pull a skillet out of the drawer beneath the stove and start layering the slices in the pan. Thanks to a year of working the morning shift at Carver's Deli, I can manage bacon and eggs. Eggs are easy, and all bacon requires is a certain tolerance for pain. As usual, the bacon pops, and I end up muttering a few choice words that make the ghost of Emily MacAllister, the most puritan of my former hitchers, clutch her metaphoric pearls. But a few spatter burns are a small price to pay, if I can coax Deo into eating.

By the time I've finished scrambling the eggs, Aaron and Taylor have joined me in the kitchen. But still no Deo. I snag some bacon, grab a slice of the toast that Aaron is buttering, and add a dab of grape jelly. If Deo won't come to the bacon, the bacon will come to him.

He's lying on his back when I push the door open. That bothers me. In the seven years since we met, I've never seen Deo do that. He's a die-hard belly sleeper.

"D?" No response. I repeat his name. This time, his eyelids flutter, and the fist clutching my heart loosens a tiny bit.

I put the tray on the ledge near the bed and brush my hand against Deo's forehead. It's hot, hotter than last night, and dry. And the room doesn't smell . . . right. I mean, rooms usually smell off when someone is sick, but this isn't the same kind of *off*. I know this from group homes I've been in—a virus can sweep through a group home like a germ-fueled tornado. But several sets of parental memories in my hitchers' files confirm that this isn't a normal sick smell. The odor in the room is distinctive, but it's more like . . . I don't know. Ozone, maybe? Kind of like the Metro station, minus the reek of food, sweat, and perfume.

The room *feels* wrong, too. Charged, almost as though there's static electricity in the air.

Jaden stirs inside my head, like he wants to say something, but then slides back. I'm tempted to nudge him, to ask what he was going to say, but I've been shushing Daniel so much that it hardly seems fair to encourage Jaden to speak up.

I brush a stray bit of hair out of Deo's face and try again to rouse him. "I brought you some breakfast. Do you think you can sit up? At least drink some orange juice?"

Deo's eyes are still closed, but he sniffs, and then gives me a ghost of a smile.

"That's right. Bacon. Toast. You have to eat something, kiddo."

I spend the next few minutes trying to coax him into eating, even waving a slice of bacon under his nose. His nostrils seem to flare a little, like he's breathing it in. But it was such a tiny change in expression that I could have imagined it.

Aaron is in the doorway now. "Maybe we should try to prop him up? See if we can get some liquid into him, if nothing else?"

I nod and grab Deo's upper arm, trying to avoid the swollen area on his bicep. Aaron grabs his other arm, and we lift. We've managed to halfway prop him up when Aaron jerks back abruptly, banging his head on the top bunk.

"Ow!" Aaron rubs his head as Deo slumps back down onto his pillow. "What the hell?" He takes another step backward, into the main cabin. His windbreaker, with the gun in the pocket, is slung over one of the kitchen chairs, and he grabs it.

I follow him back into the main room. "What's wrong?"

"Vibes." He opens the blind partway, looking out at the campground. "Something's *wrong*. The thought I picked up . . . well, *one* of the thoughts . . . was about slamming a guy into the side of a school bus."

He nods toward the window. The RV life seems to attract a lot of folks who hit the road at the crack of dawn. It's not even seven thirty, and most of the slots near us are already empty. No school bus, though.

"Maybe it was another camper and not a school bus that you saw?"

He shakes his head. "No. It was a high school student. He was even thinking how the guy's head would look as he bashed it against the words on the side of the bus . . . *Marietta City Schools.*"

Aaron pulls out his brand-new burner phone. He and Taylor reluctantly tossed their phones into the trash outside the Walmart where Porter handed over the RV. I'd chunked mine and Deo's out the window before we even got there, spooked by that last text from Cregg. Porter didn't even grumble (much) about buying four replacements. I guess living with Molly taught him that teens are more willing to share a toothbrush than a phone. The phones aren't the latest model, but they're still better than the refurbished one-step-up-from-flip-phones that Deo and I had.

Aaron turns the screen toward me. "Look at the map. The school is nearly *eight miles* away."

"What's your usual range?"

He huffs anxiously. "A city block. Maybe two, depending on how angry the person is."

"You're sure it was *at* the school? Maybe the guy was waiting for the bus somewhere closer."

He sinks into one of the recliners near the door. "I don't think so. And . . . that's not even the weirdest part, Anna. Like I said, that was just *one* of the vibes. There were four, maybe five, others that came rushing in all at once. A bit of road rage from someone on the I-77. An office worker who wants to bash her boss with a coffee maker."

"Does this happen a lot?"

"No. This happens *never.*" He leans over and looks out the window again. "I mean, yeah, sometimes, when I'm in a crowded place, I'll get multiple signals. That's only if there are a lot of people really close by, though. A mall, a theater, an amusement park. And . . . the vibes I picked up just now are miles away from here. It doesn't make sense! I don't have that kind of range. If I did, I'd have gone totally crazy long ago."

He's seriously freaked out. I've only seen Aaron this way once before, at the jail after our little run-in with Dacia. His pupils are dilated, and his knuckles are stark white against the deep green of the jacket he's clutching.

A jacket that I've just remembered has a gun in the pocket.

Aaron follows my eyes down to the windbreaker and then laughs nervously, handing it to me. "Yeah, maybe you ought to take this." He looks a little embarrassed as I carefully drape the jacket back over the chair. "On the good news front, none of the premonitions were Cregg or Lucas."

I sit down next to him and take his hand. After a few minutes, he begins to relax.

The camper is oddly quiet, however, and after a moment, I realize why. "Where's Taylor?"

"Said she was going over to the bathhouse to grab a shower."

After the experience of emptying the various tanks yesterday, the four of us reached a mutual agreement to use the campground facilities whenever possible. We'd also agreed to follow the buddy system, however.

"I told her to wait until you could go with her, but . . ." Aaron shrugs, knowing he doesn't need to finish the sentence. It's Taylor. *Of course* she didn't listen.

When I get to the bathhouse a few minutes later, I see Taylor's bright-blue toenails peeking out from under the shower door closest to the exit. I toss my backpack onto the floor, pull out my shower bag, and enter the second stall. I wait a few minutes, hoping the water will heat up, then simply sigh and step under the tepid spray.

Taylor's shower falls silent. "That you, Anna?" Her voice is slightly muffled, so she must be toweling off.

"Mmhmm."

"Did you sleep okay? I mean . . . after . . ." There's a hint of guilt dimming her usual chirpy tone.

"Yeah. Not too bad."

"See?" Her voice is back to full chirp now. "You're better off with Aaron in there, just like I said."

I ignore her and rinse the soap from my hair as quickly as possible. I mean, she's right, but I'm still annoyed at the way she's been treating Deo, so I'm not inclined to concede any point that will make her feel vindicated.

Even though I half expect Taylor to ignore the buddy system again and leave without me, she's sitting on the bench when I step out of the shower, absorbed in something on her phone. As I'm brushing my teeth, she says, "Breaking news. The government is officially pinning responsibility on a group with ties to West Coast separatists."

It takes a second for me to realize she's talking about the fire at the Delphi facility in Port Deposit where Deo and I were being held. The Warren, as it was called by the kids they were experimenting on.

"Really?" I ask around a mouthful of toothpaste. "That seems . . . convenient. Any mention of Cregg or the others?"

"No mention of *Graham* Cregg, although Cregg Sr. is still spouting off on Twitter about how this is just one more indication of lax port security, yada yada. And how it shows the Western separatists aren't as peaceful as they claim. Twelve bodies were found in the wreckage. No mention of that Dacia person, but . . . Lucas died shortly after he was taken into custody."

"Good." The word surprises me even as I speak it, and I feel a wave of guilt for being glad that anyone, even a monster like Lucas, is dead. But then I remember that he killed Molly's mother and turned Molly over to Cregg. That he was one of the people who kidnapped Deo. That he raped Molly and would have done the same to me if Ashley hadn't intervened.

The wave of guilt is barely a trickle now.

I begin shoving things back into my bag, and then Taylor grabs my arm. "I *know*, okay? You aren't exactly quiet when you dream, and . . . I know. Aaron does, too."

"You know . . . what?"

"What Lucas did to Molly. Why didn't she . . . ?" Her voice trails off. "Why didn't *you* tell us?"

I'm pretty sure she knows the answer, but I give it anyway. "Because Molly asked me not to. I think it was the one bit of dignity she felt she could hold on to. And really, Taylor, what difference would it have made?"

"I'd rather have found out some other way than hearing her screaming in your dream. Besides, it wasn't Molly's fault."

Taylor, who has apparently decided she's tired of this conversation, stalks out of the bathhouse. I follow after her.

"I know it wasn't her fault, okay? I'm sorry you found out like that. But it was Molly's decision. Not mine."

She gives me a curt nod, and continues toward the camper, but not before I see the tears in her eyes.

Which sucks, because Molly also wanted to spare Taylor and the others any additional pain. And I blew it.

As soon as that thought is formed, I hear Jaden sigh.

Girl, you need to stop beatin' yourself up. Molly's moved on. She's not worried about whether you kept her secrets. And you don't need to feel guilty about Lucas bein' dead, either. There's a dozen or more girls in The Warren who would tell you that him being dead is a very good thing, and some of them weren't even as old as Molly. Personally, my only regret is that Cregg's still alive.

He laughs and then continues.

Oh, damn. Now you're gonna feel guilty about that, too.
Girl, you need help.

Jaden's right—Lucas was a monster, and I don't regret that it was my hands that dealt the deathblow, even if I wasn't fully in control of them at the time. But I'm pretty sure the bigger monster is Graham Cregg. He's still out there, and that's on me.

The world would be a better place without Graham Cregg in it, even though I'm certain Lucas would have abused more of the girls in The Warren if Cregg hadn't made it clear that he disapproved. Cregg clearly saw himself as superior to Lucas. And yet Cregg didn't seem to have the slightest qualm about violating the *minds* of those girls, making them harm themselves and each other. Making them kill.

But shooting someone who was writhing in pain on the floor wouldn't have been self-defense. And even though I wasn't thinking about it at the time, right now, I'm kind of glad I didn't kill him. I'm pretty sure he knows more about my origins, how I'm connected to the Delphi Project, and whether I still have family who are alive. Even more important, however, is the fact that he knows what drug they used on Deo.

A thin wisp of something brushes against my forehead, and I wipe it with my sleeve instinctively, thinking at first that I've collided with a spiderweb. That seems unlikely, however. I'm in the middle of the dirt road that runs through the RV park, so it would either be one hell of a spider or else a fragment of web picked up by the wind.

I can't really pin down why the sensation unnerves me, but it has me on edge to the point that I startle when my phone vibrates, signaling an incoming text. It's not a number I recognize. The area code is 240, however, one of the two that serve the Maryland suburbs around DC. Probably Kelsey's new phone, although I'm not sure how she got this number. Either way, I wish she'd called instead. It would be nice to hear her voice.

When I open the text, I read:

Conscience is but a word that cowards use, devised at first to keep the strong in awe.

I very nearly drop the phone. I don't even have to comb through Emily's memory banks to identify this quote as Shakespeare. *Richard III.* It's quite possible that Deo and I would have watched that, even if I'd never picked up Emily, even without her memories of a repertory group she acted with back in the early 1950s. In the version we watched last year, Richard was played by Benedict Cumberbatch, who I like on general principle, and who Deo likes because he also plays Doctor Strange.

Graham Cregg peppered me with Shakespeare quotations, mixed with the occasional pithy biblical quote, when they were holding Deo and again when we were leaving Maryland, so I have no doubt that the text is from him. His texts are the reason we tossed our old phones. The reason that we all have burner phones that Cregg *should not* be able to locate.

While I don't know how Cregg got the number, the fact that he clearly *does* have it is not good news. I run the rest of the way to the trailer. Aaron is in the main cabin, right where I left him, still scanning the local newspaper. He looks tense, and I suspect he's trying to see if anyone acted on the barrage of angry thoughts he picked up earlier. As much as I hate to add any additional worries, I don't have much choice.

I drop the phone into his lap. "Text message from Richard III."

"Hmm," he says, after reading it. "No misspellings, so I'm guessing it's Cregg, not Dacia?"

"It's Shakespeare. So, yeah, definitely Cregg. How could he have gotten the number? I haven't called anyone. Porter, Kelsey—none of them have my number. I didn't even use it to answer e-mail. The only time I've used it other than browsing was day before yesterday when you and Taylor went on a food run and she called to see what I wanted. Should I respond?"

"Uh, *no*," Taylor says from behind me. "Why would you do that? Responding would enable him to pin down our location. Right, Aaron?"

"Probably," he says, then all three of us jump as the phone buzzes again.

Full fathom five thy mother lies, of her bones are coral made.

I'm pretty sure that's a misquote, but I ignore it for now, continuing with my line of thought.

"This time yesterday, I wouldn't have even thought of texting him back. But Deo is *burning up*, Aaron! I don't believe for a moment that it's not connected to that injection. We can't just roll into an urgent care and expect them to have any idea what's going on with him. Cregg is the only person I can think of who knows what was in the needle they used and how to reverse those effects, so yes—I want to keep that line of communication open . . ."

Jaden's voice cuts into my thoughts.

It's connected. Like I told you before, we were their lab rabbits. They shot us up with all kinds of crap to see if they could get a little more bang for their buck, you know? Ramp the psychic stuff up a bit. Never saw a reaction like Deo's with my own eyes, but there were enough stories at The Warren that I'm sure he ain't got the flu or whatever. And . . . that smell you noticed in his room earlier? I didn't want to say nothin' then, didn't want to worry you. I picked up that scent all the time in The Warren. I'm guessin' Daniel did too.

I don't hear anything from Daniel, but he must nod, because Jaden pauses briefly and then continues:

> That's what I figured. Always the new ones, right, just after they got there? Anyway, Anna, the thing you need to remember is that whatever you grabbed out of that fridge is just one of . . . hell, I don't even *know* how many magic potions that they cooked up in that place. Will said they kept spreadsheets comparin' the different formulas and side effects, so there must have been a bunch of them. Most of them got better in a few days.

> *But some of them didn't?*

> Yeah. But I don't have any numbers, any statistics. Mostly just rumors that spread around The Warren. Maybe it's on that thumb drive Daniel sneaked out of the place.

I'm tempted to push for Daniel's input on the issue, but getting information out of him is torturous at the best of times unless it's some pointless little factoid. I feel Aaron and Taylor watching me, waiting for me to continue what I was saying. So I set aside my questions for Daniel until later.

"Jaden says he's seen Deo's symptoms before," I say. "It's definitely a side effect of what they gave him. And some of the kids didn't get better, so I may have no choice but to respond to Cregg. I don't want to put the two of you at risk, though. Just . . . help me get a weapon. A gun, or even a knife. Leave me and Deo at—" I scratch my forehead again in response to that weird tickling sensation and then continue. "Just leave us at a hotel and keep going. If all goes well, we'll meet up later."

Daniel and Jaden are both struggling to be heard, but I ignore them, stacking the bricks up to keep them out of this discussion. Aaron's expression tells me that he's about to argue my point, and I can't hold down two fronts at once.

"No way," Aaron says. "We're *not* splitting up. I get that we need to keep our options open, but can't we just hold off a little longer? Unless you think we need to get Deo to a doctor right now . . ."

Another buzz from my phone interrupts Aaron. Even knowing that it's my only line of communication with Cregg, I'm sorely tempted to grab the phone and hurl it against the wall.

Is this a dagger which I see before me, the handle toward my hand?

"Hey, wow. I recognize that one," Taylor says, reading over Aaron's shoulder. "We just finished reading *Macbeth*, and that's the scene where he imagines he sees a knife pointing toward King Duncan's—" She looks up suddenly. "Wait, didn't you just mention a knife?"

"Yeah," Aaron says, casting a suspicious eye around the RV. "You did. What about the other quotes?"

He hands me the phone and then goes back into the bedroom. I try to remember what was happening when the first text came in. *Conscience is but a word that cowards use . . .*

"I was thinking about what Taylor told me. That Lucas is dead."

Aaron is back now, with a small device that looks like a walkie-talkie. He walks around the room scanning as I speak.

"And also feeling bad that I didn't shoot Cregg when I had the chance, but I didn't want to have that on my . . . *conscience*."

"Ah-ha," Taylor says. "So what about the other one? *Full fathom five*, blah, blah."

"It's from *The Tempest*, but it's a misquote. It should be *father*, not *mother*. And I wasn't . . ."

I stop, remembering the other reason I was glad I hadn't shot him. "Wait. I was thinking that he might have information about my parents. Whether they're still alive. What they did at Delphi."

Aaron starts to take the scanner back into the room where Deo is sleeping, but I stop him. "There's no bug here, Aaron. The other two texts came while I was outside. I was walking from the bathhouse, out in the open."

He takes a step toward me with the scanner.

"No. I didn't say any of it aloud. Those were thoughts. Just thoughts. So unless that scanner can pick up a *psychic* bug, I don't think it's going to help us."

Another buzz, but this time, my phone is dark.

"Not mine," I say. "Seems to be coming from over there."

Aaron's windbreaker is draped over one of the chairs. He pulls his phone from the pocket. "Give every man thy ear, but few thy voice."

"Obviously Shakespeare," Taylor says, "judging from the *thys*. And it's a very appropriate quote for the person who was just scanning for listening devices."

"Did you feel anything weird a moment ago?" I ask Aaron. "Like something brushing against your forehead. Almost like a feather."

"Yeah," he says. "When I went back to get the scanner. I just thought it was my hair. Is that what you felt when Dacia read your mind?"

"No. I don't think it's Dacia. That was different. More like Pop Rocks on your skin. This was much more . . . delicate, I guess. And fleeting. Both times it was gone almost before I noticed it. Plus, Dacia has a tough time getting inside your head without touching you."

Taylor turns off her phone. "You guys should do the same. This is too freakin' creepy."

Aaron shakes his head. "I . . . don't think that matters, Tay. It's not like they're haunted or something. They're just phones. Just tools that he's using."

I wince, remembering how one of my temporary hitchers used Cregg's phone as a tool to get her revenge. After bursting into flames, the cell phone had partially melted and adhered to Cregg's chest. And now he's using our phones to taunt us.

"Don't care," Taylor says as she slides her phone to the other end of the kitchen counter. "I'm leaving mine off. If Graham Cregg is poking around in my head, I do not want to know."

CHAPTER THREE

Somewhere in Kentucky
November 1, 2019, 2:14 p.m.

Deo seems a tiny bit cooler now, but that could be wishful thinking. I finally managed to take his temperature a few hours ago—it was 104 degrees—and after a five-minute struggle, I got him to swallow a few sips of orange juice to wash down another dose of Tylenol. I'm tempted to stick the thermometer in his mouth again, but he's already a little restless, and I don't want to wake him. I tuck the covers back around him and let the motion of the road under our wheels rock him to sleep.

We'll need to be stationary with a decent internet hookup for the meeting with Magda this afternoon, but none of us could stay put after we got the texts from Cregg. It felt like we were being watched, so hanging out the rest of the day at that RV park wasn't an option, even though it's entirely possible that the watcher is moving right along with us. Two more messages arrived for Aaron while we were packing up the trailer to leave. Each time he had that itchy feeling just above his eyebrows.

Now, all three of us are hypersensitive, feeling that weird tickling sensation even when we don't get a text. It reminds me of this time when a girl at my foster home had lice. Every single kid in the house, and most of the adults, went around scratching their heads for days, even though we were all checked and came up clean. Just the *idea* of something crawling around on our heads was enough to make us itchy.

Aaron picked a highway at random, one we hadn't already been on, and started driving. We debated tossing the phones and getting new ones. Taylor was 100 percent behind that idea, even though she had to admit it doesn't make much difference. The problem isn't that Cregg has our phone numbers, even though I'm still not sure how he got them. The problem is that he can get into our heads. Unless there's a way to stop that intrusion, new phones would be pointless.

Deo's phone has been in silent mode, but when I checked it a few minutes ago, there were three messages waiting from earlier this morning. I'm guessing they're all from The Bard, but I didn't read them. Deo's asleep, not to mention half delirious with fever. Looking at the texts would be too much like peeking at his dreams.

The bacon and toast I made this morning, long past cold, are on a ledge on the other side of his bunk. I lean across him to retrieve the plate, but just as I grab it, a strange noise—a high-pitched, almost electrical whine—fills my head.

nnnnnNNNNNN

"*—seen those hummingbird feeders, right? The ones that look like they have flowers around the bottom?*"

"*Sure.*"

Aaron pauses, gauging traffic so that we can merge onto US 280 before continuing. "Well, this feeder had a nail straight through one of those flowers. Looked like somebody pounded it in with a hammer, but Peck swears it flew straight out of that tree house and lodged in the feeder. And the house itself—there's an indentation in the siding shaped exactly like a two-by-four. Assuming the old guy's telling the truth, it's a miracle no one was killed."

I glance down at the oddly shaped scrap of green notepaper in the center of my palm and feel a wave of relief. "At least we can find them now. Let the parents—the little girl, too—know they're not alone. Doreen said that wasn't the only time she'd done something like that. And the dad . . . like Peck said, he's not stable. They could be in serious—"

NNNNNNNnnnnn

When I snap out of the vision, the first thing that hits my senses is that weird metallic scent I noticed earlier. It's joined by the fainter aroma of the bacon, which is now scattered, along with the triangles of toast, all over the bed and the carpet.

I sit there for a moment, thankful that I slumped to the floor this time rather than pitching straight forward. There's still a bruise on my forehead from where I whacked it on the sink at that rest stop the last time one of Jaden's visions occurred. Another fall like that, and I'd have to seriously consider walking around in a helmet.

The jolt seems to have knocked down the wall around Daniel and Jaden, too, because Jaden says:

> Yeah. I got so I could feel them comin' on, too. Not *much* notice, but enough to keep me from crackin' my head open.

> *You mean the noise? That whining sound, like the emergency broadcast signal?*

> Nah. I'd just feel kind of woozy for a second. But, hey, this is your brain. Everyone's wired differently. Maybe that noise is your cue to stop and drop before you roll.

The flashes that hit when I'm fully awake are much clearer, much easier to hold on to, but the details still skitter away like a dream if I don't pin them down. So I focus on the vision, trying to mentally catalog everything I can remember. The paper in my hand . . . pale green, folded, but with irregular edges. It had contact information on it for one of the second-generation Delphi kids—someone like me, who inherited the ability from a parent who was in the program. I remember feeling happy we'd managed to get the information but also worried about something the woman—Doreen Peck—had told me.

Aaron and I were in the truck, but I don't think we were pulling the trailer. The intersection is clear in my mind. A gas station on the right as we turn onto US 280. That rings a bell, but it's faint enough that I'm pretty sure it's not one of my own memories. More like some memory left behind by one of my hitchers. Josephine seems most likely. Her first husband was a long-haul driver, and she preferred riding with him to staying in the tiny apartment they shared in Opelika. They spent many hours on US 280, which runs between Birmingham and Savannah, before the marriage went belly up.

I'm used to digging around in my hitcher files, but I'm not used to being watched while I do it. Daniel's presence feels almost physical, like he's reading over my shoulder.

Are there Army posts along the route?

Umm . . . yeah. Fort Benning.

Then that's where you should start. The adepts they've been tracking are almost always within thirty miles of a post.

Why?

A lot of their parents are still in the military. Some might have retired, but even then, they usually stick close for the medical benefits, cheaper groceries at the commissary, stuff like that.

Jaden is saying something now, but it's like he's in a tunnel. The space inside my head isn't massive enough for him to be that far away, although I've begun to think it's a lot like *Doctor Who*'s TARDIS—bigger on the inside. Or maybe my head just hasn't figured out how to process these internal conversations. I've never had two hitchers in my head at the same time who actually spoke to each other. The only other time I had double occupancy, one was on her way out, and the other was still trying to figure out where the hell his body was.

I guess Jaden was asking Daniel for the floor, because I feel them switch places in the queue.

> I've been thinkin' about those texts and wanted to mention this kid at The Warren. One of the second-gen adepts. Thirteen, maybe fourteen, years old. Most everyone called him Snoop Dogg, which was funny 'cause he was as white as they come. I didn't know him that well, but he was really upset one day, and my roommate, Will, talked to him—

Jaden laughs.

> Although I guess you couldn't call what they did talkin' since they never said a word. Just mental chitchat. Anyway, Will said the boy was really good with telepathy close-up—in fact, he had a tough time controlling it, kind of like Will did. But Cregg's people were also trainin' him to pick up short bursts of thought long-distance.

How long-distance?

> *Really* long-distance. Across state lines, maybe even cross-country. He'd given them financial information

from some dude on Wall Street. Stuff from a few politicians, too. I didn't get the sense that distance was a limitation so much as stability and stamina. He could only hold the connection a second or two at a time, so he had to grab as much as he could. Kind of like with my visions . . . he couldn't control it. They kept pushing him to try harder, but when he pushed too hard, it would be weeks before he could do it again. Only—

Only what?

I could have sworn Will said he was relocated. That he wasn't at The Warren anymore. Will was upset about it, worried that maybe the kid snapped or something, from how hard they'd been pushing him. But yeah, they could be using Snoop to pluck phone numbers out of your head. And he could be relayin' those little snippets of thought to Cregg. If you're close by, he can just grab the thoughts out of thin air, the same way Will did. But for people at a distance, he needs something that belonged to you—kind of like Taylor when she locates people.

But . . . I didn't leave anything behind. Well, except for the clothes I wore when they brought me in. I think that was true for Deo, too. Would they even have had time to collect those with The Warren burning down around them? And either way, it doesn't really explain Aaron.

I don't add Taylor, even though I'm pretty sure that if we turn on her phone, we're going to find several messages in iambic pentameter.

Jaden responds with a mental shrug. Then he swaps places with Daniel again.

Damn it. Could you guys stop trading places so quickly? You're making me queasy.

Sorry. Doesn't matter whether they grabbed your clothes or not. Ashley and the other techs had already packed up the blood samples and other items from the med lab when the Delphi crew was told that we might have to relocate on short notice. I can't imagine anything being better for tracking you than your own blood.

Still doesn't explain how they could track Aaron . . .

I scoop Deo's uneaten breakfast back onto the plate and carry it into the kitchen. There's a video intercom on one wall near the kitchen that connects to the truck. I tap the call button, and the interior of the truck pops up a second later on the small screen.

"What's up?" Aaron says.

I start to speak, but then I notice Taylor's head. Most of her auburn hair is covered by a shiny silver hat. "Is that . . . aluminum foil?"

She colors slightly. "Yes. So what? We already know that at least some of the conspiracy theories are true. Maybe a tinfoil hat actually affords some sort of protection. I'm perfectly willing to look stupid if there's a chance it will keep a homicidal maniac from combing through my brain for information. I'll get a stocking cap later and line it with foil so it's not as obvious, but this will have to do for now."

What truly scares me is that Taylor's comment almost makes sense. If I thought Taylor's solution would keep Cregg and his mental bloodhound out of my head, I might be willing to give it a try, but even Bruno didn't believe foil hats provided any sort of protection.

As worked up as Taylor is about this, I'm almost hesitant to stay on the topic. But they need to know what Jaden told me about Cregg's psychic spy, and maybe it will make them feel better to know that it's not actually Cregg in our heads. One of his lackeys, yes—but not Cregg.

"It might not even be this kid," I add, once I've brought them up to speed, "since Cregg shouldn't have anything personal of yours to track you with. But if it *is* him, Jaden says he can't keep it up for long. Just short bursts, and then he's tapped out for days, maybe even weeks. Have you gotten any more texts?"

"One," Aaron says, "just before I started driving. But nothing for the past hour or so. What I don't get is *why* Cregg would do this. He's got a tactical advantage now, if he can occasionally snag information from our minds. Why not keep that secret? Now that we know, we'll be more cautious, more careful about what we think."

"It doesn't work that way, though, at least not long term. I wish it did. There are many times that I'd be overjoyed to keep my thoughts shielded from my hitchers. I can manage it for a while with my walls. But I have to sleep, and even when I'm awake, my mind strays, usually to the very thing I'm trying to block out. Here's an example—for the next few minutes, don't think about pink elephants."

There's a long silence, and then Aaron says, "Yeah, I see what you mean."

"So telling us is actually to Cregg's advantage," Taylor says. "He can still find out what we're thinking, and he can scare us at the same time. Maybe scare us enough that we give up and go home. And, to be honest, that sounds like an exceptionally good idea to me. I'm tired of driving around in freakin' circles waiting on Magda's instructions."

Aaron sighs. "As you've said at least a dozen times today. Give it a rest."

"I would probably agree with you, Taylor. But . . . we actually have a destination now." They both give me an expectant stare, and I continue. "Fort Benning, Georgia. And we need to run a search for a woman named Doreen Peck, to see if we can locate her exact address."

Taylor looks confused, but then recognition dawns on her face, and she heaves an exasperated sigh. "Great. Another coming-attractions trailer. Does anyone get shot this time?"

❖   ❖   ❖

Near Louisville, Kentucky
November 1, 2019, 4:32 p.m.

When the video call from Sam comes through, I'm surprised to see he's not alone. Michele—Aaron, Taylor, and Daniel's mom—is also in the room.

And so is Daniel. Or, at least, his body is there, hooked up to a variety of tubes and wires. I don't think it's the same hospital room—this one is still small, but it's larger than the little nook they had him parked in before. The biggest change, however, is that the monitor shows steady blips, up and down. While I don't have a clue what those blips mean, I'm positive it's better than the flat line I saw the last time I was in the same room with Daniel.

"We were going to do this at the office," Sam says, "but your mom wanted to see you, and we try not to leave Daniel by himself, so I said we'd set up here. Porter said to tell all of you hello, by the way. He wanted to be here, too, but as you can see, this room is a tad small, and your mom seeing you takes priority. Hang on and let me see if I can get Magda in on the call."

While we wait, Aaron pushes a button to send the video to the large television screen over the electric fireplace. I get my first clear glimpse of Michele's face a few moments later when Sam pivots the computer around. The circles under her eyes look almost like bruises. She doesn't look like she's slept or showered since we left Baltimore. The secrecy feels even crueler to me now that I see the toll that the past few days have taken on her, and I send a mental grumble Daniel's way. He doesn't fire off a snarky comment in return, so either he's not following things too well from behind the wall or his resolve is weakening about keeping his mother in the dark.

Aaron also decided to keep them in the dark about Cregg contacting us, at least for the time being. Taylor disagreed initially, although that may have been, in part, because she wanted to leave her tinfoil hat on. Aaron eventually convinced her that there was no point in worrying them unnecessarily. I didn't weigh in, figuring they know their family better than I do. But I definitely don't want to inform Magda until we have a better sense of who she is and exactly what her goals are.

"Okay," Sam says. "I think I've got it."

The screen goes blank for a moment, then splits into two frames: the hospital room on the left and a middle-aged, slightly overweight woman on the right. I'm surprised to see the night sky through the windows behind her, but then I guess London is five or six hours ahead of us. She's not at all what I'd imagined the wife of the celebrity psychic host of *Breaking the Veil with Erik Bell* would be. True, it's been a few years since the show was on air, but Bruno never missed an episode, and Erik Bell's ruggedly handsome face is vivid in my memory.

The room behind Magda looks like something out of *Architectural Digest*, with a vaulted ceiling and lavish furniture in varying shades of white and gray. Despite the stylish background, however, she's wearing what appear to be workout clothes. Her graying hair is parted in the middle and pulled back into a severe knot that doesn't exactly flatter her features. She looks almost as tired as Michele.

"Magda," Michele says, "I'm glad you could join us. I know your schedule can be . . . unpredictable."

I assume she's referring to Magda's twin daughters. They were affected by the Delphi drug given to Erik Bell, although no one has bothered to explain exactly *how* they were affected. All I know is what

Aaron told me—that the girls are so intensely "gifted" they can barely function.

"We have about half an hour. The nanny can handle them alone at bath time. Usually." Magda sits up a little straighter, putting on a *let's-get-down-to-business* face. Her tone is formal, and I can't really pin down the accent beyond European. There's British in the mix but also a hint of something else I can't place.

Sam picks up her cue, and a quick round of introductions follows.

"Before we begin," Magda says, "I want to be very clear about one thing. I could hire a far more qualified and . . . mature . . . team if I simply wanted someone to go in and ask questions. In fact, I was already planning to do that for the first individual you'll be interviewing since his situation is a little precarious. You're being tasked with this partly out of respect for Daniel's previous efforts but also because you have talents that I think may be more useful in the field than actual investigative experience. At a bare minimum, they'll allow you to connect with these kids and their parents, because you understand what it means to be an adept. Well, the three of you, at least." She squints at the camera. "Where is the other boy? Is he still unwell?"

"Deo's sleeping," I tell her. "He still has a dangerously high fever. We need to find out what was in the vial I turned over to Sam."

"We overnighted it to London two days ago," Michele says. "Did you receive it, Magda?"

"I did. It arrived yesterday. But I haven't yet been able to reach the . . . acquaintance . . . I mentioned. She travels frequently for work. It could easily be weeks before I hear back."

Aaron shoots me a worried look and then asks, "Isn't there anyone else you could contact?"

"No one I would trust to understand the research"—Magda glances between our faces—"or to keep this issue confidential. I'm sure you're worried about your friend, but it's entirely possible that he's simply contracted a normal illness. Temperatures can spike rather dramatically in children."

"He's . . . *fifteen*," I object. "Well past the age for typical childhood diseases. And the injection site is hot and swollen. Jaden, one of the hitchers Cregg had me pick up in his test, says it's definitely the serum. He saw similar reactions from others who were being held by Delphi. And Will, one of the other patients they killed—"

I stop, considering exactly what I want to say. If I tell Magda they were testing multiple formulas, will that be more or less likely to light a fire under her to get this specific vial tested? I'm guessing less.

"Will saw the same thing. So we need to get someone to analyze the contents as soon as possible. Maybe you could get her cell number from her employer, or"—I shrug—"something? We can't just sit here and watch him get sicker."

"Did anyone die from these injections?" Magda asks.

"Dozens of people died in their custody. We don't have specifics on the cause of death for most of them, but I think it's safe to surmise that whatever they gave Deo *could* be fatal."

"If he's not better in two days," Magda says, "we'll revisit the issue."

It's pretty much what Aaron and I had already decided, barring a significant turn for the worse. But Magda's tone is harsh and business-like, and I can't help but bristle at her cavalier dismissal of Deo's health.

She continues, either unaware of or unconcerned by my reaction. "I'm wondering, however . . . Perhaps we *do* have that information. Surely something like fatalities, cause of death, and so forth might be on the portable drive that Daniel smuggled out of the Delphi facility?"

Personally, I think it's highly unlikely that Cregg's people would keep a spreadsheet with entries like *executed by gunshot* or *death by experimental injection*, but Sam is nodding.

"It's possible," he says. "Michele and I discussed that earlier. But the file is encrypted. We're still working on the password."

An uncomfortable look flits across Michele's face, and then I hear banging at the back of my head. Reluctantly, I tug out a brick to let Daniel speak.

What is it, Daniel?

CAQ07122003MAQ.

At first, it seems like gibberish, but then I realize it's the password.

Ohhh-kay. But exactly how am I supposed to pass along that information without letting them know that you're here with me instead of there, hooked up to all of those tubes?

Umm . . . yeah. I guess that's a problem.

Daniel is always so damned sure of himself, so positive that he has all the answers. It's kind of refreshing to hear him at a loss for a change.

A note. I'll just tell them you slipped me a note when we were leaving The Warren, and maybe it's the password.

You think they'll believe that?

Maybe, maybe not. Do you have a better idea?

When I tune back in to the conversation, Michele is telling Magda that she plans to go back to the house and search Daniel's room again.

"I don't think it's there," Sam says. "I don't think it was ever there. We searched the house pretty thoroughly before the break-in . . ."

"The *what*?" Aaron asks. "When did that happen?"

Michele gives Sam a reproachful look, so I suspect this was something they'd agreed not to tell Aaron and Taylor. It makes me feel a little better that we're not the only ones keeping secrets.

"Sorry," Sam says and then proceeds to explain that the Quinns' home was broken into the day after we left town. "Nothing stolen that we could tell. Just tossed the place pretty thoroughly. I'm guessing they were looking for your dad's papers, but we moved all of Cole's research to a safe-deposit box last year."

"Well, that's one mystery solved," Taylor says softly. I'm not sure what she means, then I realize they could have easily taken things that would enable Cregg's psychic bloodhound to track her and Aaron's thoughts. A missing sock or two wouldn't be noticed in the chaos.

Aaron is worried now about his mom's safety and asks whether they've got police watching the hospital and the house.

Magda clears her throat. "Maybe this conversation could continue later? Once I'm off the call? I think the best course of action might be for me to hire someone who can crack the password—

"Wait," I say. "That may not be necessary. Daniel gave me something. It's in my backpack. In the bedroom."

Aaron and Taylor quirk their brows almost in unison. Taylor, being Taylor, looks suspicious. Aaron just looks a little confused as he moves aside to let me squeeze through.

I pull the bedroom door partially shut, wishing I could close it. But that would seem like I'm trying to hide something, so I just grab my backpack and sit against the wall as I rummage around for a pen and a scrap of paper. Daniel repeats the password, but the pen keeps skipping on the too-smooth paper of an old ATM receipt as I write.

I'm on the last digit when Taylor appears in the doorway, startling me. "What are you doing?"

"This one digit was unclear, so I darkened it. Pretty sure it's a three, not an eight. This stupid ATM paper smudges." I realize as I'm saying it that it was a colossally bad choice, since it's my bank, my account number, my almost nonexistent balance on the front of the receipt.

I don't wait for Taylor to ask more questions, just push past her into the main cabin where Aaron is telling them about the vision I had earlier.

"But you don't know exactly where it was happening?" Magda asks.

"Actually, we do," Aaron says. "We pulled up the intersections near Fort Benning on Street View, and Anna was able to pinpoint what she saw in the vision. Only one family named Peck in that town, and they live less than half a mile from that intersection, so . . ." He trails off, realizing that I'm back and everyone is now looking at me.

Clutching the slip of paper, I slide onto the bench next to him. "Daniel gave me this when we were leaving The Warren. That's what the kids at the Delphi facility call the place." I read the numbers off, feeling Taylor's eyes on me the entire time. "At least, I'm pretty sure that's a three before the last three letters. Could also be an eight . . . it's a little smudged."

"You've had this note all along?" Taylor asks. "And you didn't say anything?"

"Sorry." I paste on an apologetic smile. "With everything going on, it kind of slipped my mind. And this was the first time anyone told me you were looking for a password."

The last bit is at least half true—no one discussed it with me directly, although I vaguely remember Taylor and Aaron talking about it in passing.

"Easy to see how that could happen, under the circumstances," Sam says. There are general nods of understanding all around, except, of course, for Taylor, who still has one auburn eyebrow cocked in a dead-on imitation of Spock.

"That's it. I'm in." Michele flashes us a relieved smile before turning back to her laptop. She scrolls through for a moment while the rest of us wait. "Whoa. There's a lot here, Magda. I think I should to turn this over to Sam and let him figure out the best way to get the information to you. Then we can reconvene and—"

"No," Magda says, her tone very much that of someone who is paying the bills. "I mean, yes, do that, but obviously that will take time, and we can't afford to wait. Can you look now and see if there's a map? Daniel said there were several epicenters with sightings of second-generation adepts, but I believe the largest one is in North Carolina."

We wait in silence. Finally, Michele nods. "Found it." She slides her chair toward the camera and turns her computer screen toward us. The image is just a black-and-white outline of the states, with red dots scattered across, and *Incident Report* at the top of the page. The resolution isn't great, and I can't say how many dots there are in all, but they tend to cluster. Two are on the East Coast—the smaller one near Washington, DC, and the other much larger grouping near the border between North and South Carolina.

"Each of the red dots is someone Cregg's people think may be connected to Delphi," Sam says. "Either an original participant they've tracked down or a kid who inherited the altered gene. That big red splotch is Fort Bragg and the surrounding area. Daniel was stationed there for about six months. His dad, too. It's the PSYOP headquarters for the Army, although they've got a new acronym now—MISO."

"Because it makes so much more sense to name the psychological operations HQ after soup," Taylor mutters. "At least PSYOP made sense."

Her grandfather ignores the interruption. "I'm not surprised you'd have a cluster of adepts there, since most of the people in the Delphi program probably cycled through Bragg at some point. And when the project at Fort Meade closed down, some of them may have re-upped."

I hold up my hand in a *stop* motion.

"Maybe it's because I'm late to the team, but Delphi didn't have any reservations about kidnapping the kids they held at The Warren, and I didn't get the sense they were understaffed or underfunded. If there are adepts wandering around in plain sight, if they have all of these incident reports and so forth, why weren't Cregg's people grabbing those kids already?"

Magda begins to answer, but I can barely hear her over the banging at the back of my head. I suspect Daniel's information is based on actual firsthand evidence, so I opt for once to focus on the internal chatter instead.

> They *were*. Cregg had two field teams in North Carolina up until about a month ago. Ashley said they'd brought in three, maybe four, kids before they called the last team back to The Warren.

> *Why did they call them back?*

> No clue. Maybe they were worried about getting caught if there were too many disappearances at once. Or maybe they were worried about having to move additional kids, since that was also about the same time we started hearing rumors that we'd be relocating most of the people at Delphi.

I remember Jaden's sarcastic use of that word when I picked up his ghost in Cregg's lab.

> *So do you mean relocated as in physically moved to another location or relocated as a euphemism for permanently removed?*

> That was above my pay grade, but I'd guess mostly the former.

Jaden chimes in, agreeing.

Depends on their age. Like I said before, Cregg's got this weird thing about not killin' kids. Okay . . . that came out wrong. What I mean is he's totally down with killin' an adult when it suits his purposes. Kids get a free pass, though. No matter how dangerous. The Fudds weren't even supposed to use corporal punishment on them, aside from the taser if some kid got out of control and they couldn't sedate him. Two Fudds died in the line of duty while I was there, both times due to a kid, so . . .

As Jaden's voice fades away, Magda's fades in. ". . . so, obviously, we need to investigate the cases at Fort Bragg immediately."

"What about the lead in Georgia?" I ask. "I sensed that kid is in danger, and we had her location on the note I was holding. I'm certain of it."

"That's just *one* child, though. There are at least a dozen adepts in the Fort Bragg area. And we don't know for certain that it's too late for the six who were abducted."

"Abducted?"

The look Magda gives me—actually the look that *everyone* gives me—makes it clear that I missed something while I was focused on Daniel and Jaden.

"Magda just told us that six kids have vanished in the past week," Sam says. "I saw something on the news this morning, but the headline just said North Carolina, so I didn't make the connection. Usually I pay more attention to the news, but we've been a little preoccupied with Daniel's condition."

"Also," Magda says, clearly annoyed that she's having to repeat herself, "I have a local source who claims the disappearances are tied to the military program in question. Several of the children who are missing—maybe even all of them—had parents who were given the Delphi drug when they were in the military, before the program was turned over to the CIA in 1995."

"But if these kids have been abducted and it's related to Delphi," I argue, "that means Cregg already has them, right? Unless you think there are others he might be going after in that area right now, wouldn't it make more sense to first check out the case in Georgia where we have a child who is currently in danger? Then we can focus on finding the new Delphi location and rescuing those kids? I mean, not just the four of us, obviously, but . . ."

"Whoa, whoa, whoa," Michele says. "We need to back up a bit. Our agreement was that Aaron, Taylor, and the others would be questioning the families, trying to get information on kids who were affected by these experiments. No one said anything about them going into an area where there's an active, ongoing investigation of kidnappings. I've got one son lying here in a hospital bed. I'm not about to let my other two children—"

Taylor starts to protest, but Aaron gives her a look that, for once, silences her.

"Mom," Aaron says, gently but firmly. "We've been over this before. Taylor and I aren't safe until the entire program and everyone involved in it is exposed. Even if North Carolina is crawling with Cregg's people, we're not in any more danger there than we would be at home."

"But right now, no one even knows where you *are*, Aaron. You could just wait there until . . ." She trails off, and I think even she recognizes the weak spot in her argument. Wait here until they've rounded up all the Delphi kids they can find? Wait here until they find us, too?

Sam squeezes Michele's arm. "There was a time when I would have agreed with you on this. You know that. I'd have said to step back, turn over our information to the government, and let them investigate. But I don't trust the current administration any more than I do Ron Cregg's group. They would exploit these kids in a heartbeat. Aaron knows what he's doing, and he'll know if they're in any danger. He always does. And he'll get them out of there."

Magda sighs loudly. "I have no intention of putting anyone in danger. We've created a very logical cover story, accompanied by identification to support it. I think the parents will be eager to talk to them, since I'm offering an eventual safe haven for their children and economic assistance to the family in the interim. Money, as they say, talks. But I can hire a security firm to do this instead, if you—"

"No." Aaron shakes his head emphatically. "We're on this. We want answers, too."

"Very well. Your first interview is scheduled for tomorrow afternoon. I'll confirm that and contact you with details once you arrive." Magda's eyes turn toward me. "And as for the child in Georgia, Aaron said that these visions from your . . . hitcher . . . always come true. Is that correct?"

"Yes. The events happen exactly as I see them."

"Then it doesn't matter when you go to Georgia, does it?" She gives me a tight little smile. "You'll get that information regardless, so why should we deviate from the plan?"

Her question is clearly rhetorical. She doesn't wait for an answer but turns her focus to the group as a whole.

"Aside from getting whatever information you can find on the missing children," she says, "our goal for now is to locate these other adepts, offer financial assistance if needed, and tell them that someone will be in touch shortly. Blood samples would be very helpful—I'm going to need those from the four of you, as well. And I expect you to press for any information you can find on twins. Obviously, that is my top priority, and Daniel mentioned there might be a set of twins in North Carolina."

Even through the wall, I can sense Daniel's annoyance. So I pull out the brick again.

What now?

> Sorry. I'll be quieter. It's just that this is one reason I was
> reluctant to work with her. Everything else will come
> second to her personal agenda.

"Transfer the data to me as soon as possible," Magda says, "so my assistant and I can develop an action plan and cross-reference with the information that we've been accumulating for the past year. Oh, and you might want to start looking at options for a safe house. It will need to be large enough for at least fifty people, maybe more."

"Okay," Michele says. "Do you have a location in mind? And what is the approximate budget?"

"I'm less concerned with the budget than I am with finding a place that's therapeutic. These children need sunshine. Fresh air. But it also needs to be somewhat isolated, since the adepts have a variety of talents that could be difficult to hide in an urban setting."

Michele and Sam assure her that they'll forward the data and begin searching for a suitable location.

"Thank you. Get an early start," Magda says, glancing at Aaron. Then she reaches forward, and her side of the screen vanishes.

Taylor gives the computer a half-assed salute. "Yes, ma'am."

On the surface, I can't argue with Magda's decision to wait on the kid in Georgia. At least not on logical grounds, to the extent that any of this can even be *considered* on logical grounds. But the entire thing just feels wrong, like we're twisting fate or whatever. And that's doubly true when I know there's a very real possibility that Graham Cregg's little brain thief plucked the information from that vision right out of my mind. They could be headed toward Georgia already.

You're the resident expert, Jaden. What do you think?

Jaden considers the question briefly, and I can tell even before he answers that he's bothered by the whole thing, too.

> Based on my experience with the visions, they're
> right. What you saw happen *will* happen, so . . . wait-
> ing shouldn't matter. Logically. But I'm with you. Feels
> wrong.

"It just feels wrong," Aaron says.

I chuckle at his unknowing echo, and he gives me a puzzled look.

"I agree," I tell him. "But Magda's bankrolling this expedition. The person with the money calls the shots."

"Yeah," Taylor says. "Did you see her house? TV psychics must make a butt-load of money."

"Don't start planning your future career," Michele says. "Magda had money when they married. Her great-grandfather founded one of the largest engineering companies in Europe. And speaking of your future, Taylor, I'm in the process of registering you for an online school. You'll have to start the semester over"—Taylor's groan is loud and protracted, but her mom doesn't even pause—"but at least you won't be getting up at six in the morning or dealing with Mrs. Wembly every day."

"Nor will I be graduating with my friends or going to prom or doing any of the things that make school *bearable*."

Michele's expression softens a bit. "It is what it is, Taylor. None of us asked for this."

Then Michele turns to arrangements for me and Deo. My situation is relatively simple, since my eighteenth birthday is just over four weeks away. After that I'm a free agent, and I'm certain the State of Maryland will be relieved that it is no longer required to keep tabs on me. I'm perfectly okay with going the GED route for my few remaining high school credits, and that means I'll just need to catch up in my online college classes—classes that I haven't even thought about since Cregg's people started taking potshots at us.

Deo, however, has several years remaining in the system. Michele tells me that they're working to get Dr. Kelsey instated as his guardian, at least on a temporary basis. Baker—that's Daniel's former partner with the DC police—is backing up her claim that Deo and I are still in danger and shouldn't return to Bartholomew House for the time being.

"But . . . won't that cause problems for Kelsey? A conflict of interest, or whatever?" I have a vivid memory of a session with Kelsey when I was six, just after we managed to evict Myron. Kelsey scooped me into her arms that day to comfort me and then spent the first few minutes at our next appointment apologizing for what would be considered an ethical lapse by others in her profession. If hugging a distraught six-year-old is a lapse, I'm pretty sure they don't allow psychiatrists to become a patient's guardian.

Michele sighs. "Kelsey decided to retire. There were . . . questions . . . about her role in your departure from Bartholomew House, and rather than deal with the hassle, she's transferring her patients to another therapist. She told us she was planning to retire soon, anyway."

That's an exaggeration. She was planning to stop taking *new* patients and work part-time for the next few years. I feel horrible that she's been dragged so completely into this mess that she was forced to quit early. And it really bothers me that I'm hearing this from Michele, rather than from Kelsey herself. I haven't gone this long without talking to Kelsey in years.

"Does she have a new number yet? If so, could you get her to call me? I don't want her to quit her job, and I'm sure Deo—"

Sam chuckles. "Kelsey told us you'd say that. She also told us to remind you this is *her* decision, that it's already made, and that she'll call you soon."

A guy in a lab coat rolls a gurney into the picture while Sam is talking. I can't follow exactly what he's saying to Michele, but as we wrap up the conversation, they begin moving Daniel onto the gurney to transport him for some sort of test or a therapy session.

Watching them roll Daniel's inert body out of the room is difficult for me, so I can only imagine how it's affecting Daniel. What sort of tests are they running? What will the results mean for his long-term health? It's hard to shake the feeling that we should be returning to that hospital immediately, before going to North Carolina or to Georgia.

"Has your mom or Sam told you whether the authorities still think I had anything to do with the attempt on Daniel's life?" I ask Aaron. "I was going to ask, but things wrapped up kind of quickly."

"Well, I'm sure Baker doesn't think that. He knew Daniel was undercover with Delphi. I'm not even positive Daniel is still at the same hospital, so it may not—" Aaron sighs as Taylor interrupts him.

"Different room, same hospital."

Aaron raises an eyebrow. "And you know this how?"

"Pink scrubs on the guy who came in with the gurney. Those aren't typical. Plus, why would they move Daniel from the shock trauma unit? He's still in a frickin' coma. But yeah, Magda was so busy giving marching orders for tracking down these so-called adepts that we didn't get a chance to ask several questions, including the most important one of all."

She pauses for dramatic effect. Aaron sighs again and waits several beats before giving her the cue she wants. "And exactly what question is that?"

"These kids she has us searching for can read minds," Taylor says. "Even at a distance, given Cregg's little trick with our phones. Or they can blow things up. Or see the future. And God only knows what else. So the most important question of all is this—if we find them, what the hell are we supposed to do with them?"

CHAPTER FOUR

Near Louisville, Kentucky
November 1, 2019, 8:12 p.m.

After dinner, I heat up a slice of pepperoni pizza—something else that Deo usually scarfs down in seconds—and put it on the tray along with more Tylenol and a bottle of Gatorade. He's still not awake, still not interested in the food, but he's now in his normal sleeping position, on his belly with the covers tugged over his head, and it looks more like he's sleeping and less like he's dying. That's a good sign, right?

I hold on to that thought and try to ignore the fact that the sharp burnt-air smell seems stronger than ever. Pulling down the covers a tiny bit, I press my hand against his neck. Still much too—

nnnnNNNNNNN

"*—seen those hummingbird feeders, right? The ones that look like they have flowers around the bottom?*"

"*Sure.*"

Aaron pauses, looking both ways before merging onto US 280, then continues. "Well, this feeder had a nail straight through one of those flowers. Looked like somebo—"

NNNNNNnnnn

I back away, leaning against the cabinets on the opposite wall as a knot of panic forms in my chest. Back at The Warren, Jaden said he never got the same vision twice, except for his very last vision, the one where Lucas shot him. That vision repeated over and over, and it's how Jaden knew he wouldn't get out of that testing room alive.

Before I can even form the question, Jaden is front and center.

> Yeah, but . . . that vision ended with me taking a bullet. And it was a repeat of the full vision, every single time, not just a short clip. Like I said before, though, it's your head, and your mileage may vary. It's already varying—I mean, I got a vision almost every day, sometimes *more* than one a day, and it's been a lot longer than that for you. I really don't think seein' that tiny flash means you're gonna—

Daniel's voice cuts in.

> Touch him again.

What?

> Deo. Touch him again.

I'm not following Daniel's line of thought, but I go back over to the bed. As soon as my hand brushes against Deo's skin, I hear the high-pitched whine. Then, I see the inside of the truck and once again hear Aaron talking about a hummingbird feeder with a nail through one of the flowers.

I jump away from Deo this time, banging my elbow sharply against the closet.

I'll be damned. He's an amp.

Clenching my teeth, I rub my elbow. "What in God's name is an amp, Daniel?"

It's not until I see Aaron and Taylor in the doorway that I realize I've spoken aloud.

"Okay," says Taylor. "I'll bite. What *is* an amp? And while you're at it, maybe you can explain why you're talking to Daniel?"

I could lie. Tell them I meant to say *Deo*. Or . . . something.

That's exactly what Daniel wants me to do, but I push both him and Jaden to the very back of my head and wall them off again. Not telling anyone that Daniel has taken up residence in my head was a lie of omission, but now we're heading straight toward a lie of commission and . . . nope. Sorry. Not going there. Maybe if it was just Taylor. But I don't like the hint of suspicion I'm seeing in Aaron's eyes right now. This is as far as I can go with Daniel's little charade, because I will *not* flat-out lie to Aaron.

I motion toward the kitchen. "Let's go in the other room, okay? Deo needs his rest."

"Daniel is in your head, isn't he?" The question rushes out of Taylor's mouth before I can even close the door. "You've been lying to us the entire—"

I take a deep breath and sit down at the table. Aaron and Taylor follow suit.

But Taylor is too angry to listen. "I don't believe it. You're lying! Daniel's not dead, so there's no way you could have picked up his . . . soul or whatever."

She's clearly upset, so I ignore the fact that she's completely reversed her argument in the span of less than ten seconds, first calling me a liar for hiding the fact that I've picked up Daniel and then calling me a liar for claiming that I did. Although I never actually made it to the claiming-I-did part. Taylor just filled in the blanks for herself.

I rub my eyes with my palms and direct my comments toward Aaron, who seems willing to give me the benefit of the doubt. At least for now.

"It wasn't intentional, believe me. I picked Daniel up by accident when security was pushing me out of the room. I assumed he was dead. Hell, Daniel himself assumed he was dead. I didn't have *time* to say anything when we were at the hospital, since we were trying to get out before security caught up with me. And when we found out they'd managed to bring him back . . . well, you'd have to ask him why he didn't want to tell anyone then. I've never entirely understood . . ."

I trail off, aware that I've opened the door for what Taylor's about to ask, and I really didn't want to do that. Daniel hates being in the back seat, and I don't fully trust him to back off when time is up.

"Fine, then," Taylor says. "Let me ask him. If he's really in there, that is. And don't tell me he won't come out, because I'm not buying it. Daniel would talk to me. He wouldn't let me worry like this."

A wheedling tone creeps into her voice, and I realize Taylor is just being contrary. She has absolutely no doubt that her brother is in here—in fact, that last remark was aimed straight at him. Taylor has her oldest brother wrapped around her pinky every bit as much as she does her grandfather.

I'm now realizing there was a very real silver lining to keeping Daniel a secret. He's already proven himself incapable of keeping quiet inside my head, popping up with a comment any time it suits him. Now, however, any inclination he might have had to keep his presence hidden has vanished. I'm pretty sure he'll be asking me to pass information along every few minutes. Even worse, he'll want to cut out the middleman and join in the conversation himself, or more likely, *lead* the conversation.

A loud thump echoes at the back of my head, but I ignore it, because I can feel Aaron watching me. I'm afraid to meet his eyes, afraid to face his anger, his disappointment. But when I force myself to look up, I find neither. He just looks concerned.

"Come on, Tay," he says to his sister. "Anna's too smart to let you manipulate her. Personally, I think she's telling the truth."

"You *would*."

"But," Aaron continues, "if you need proof, I think we can get it without forcing Anna to let Daniel . . ." He trails off.

"I usually describe it as moving to the front. It's a bit like the difference between driving a car and riding in the back."

Of course, Daniel and Jaden aren't exactly in the back seat right now, but I don't go into that. I'm pretty sure that when I put a hitcher behind the wall, it's more like riding in the trunk, and I don't really want to set Taylor off again by making her think her brother is being abused.

Aaron glances at Taylor, hesitating before asking his next question. "Does this mean Daniel is dead?"

I shrug. "No clue. *He* seems to think it might mean that, but . . . he doesn't know either. I wanted to go back in, to see if we could . . . make a transfer, I guess. But there was no time. And I'm not even sure it's possible. All of my other hitchers left of their own accord. Like Molly."

Except for Myron. But I'm not going to discuss Myron right now, so I shift back to Daniel.

"None of my other hitchers had a body to move back into. So, even if we go back to the hospital—"

"Is that how you knew the password to the flash drive?" Aaron asks.

I open my mouth to respond, but Taylor beats me to it. "Of course it is. I even caught her with the pen, but she gave me some bullshit about the number being smudged."

"I'm sorry, Taylor. This wasn't my decision to make."

"Oh, gee, where have I heard that excuse before? First about Molly and now Daniel. But I have a news flash for you, Anna. It's your head, your mouth, and you decide what comes out of it. Maybe Aaron doesn't mind you lying to him, but you don't get a free pass from me."

Taylor slams the door so hard when she leaves that the entire camper shakes.

"Should we go after her?" I ask.

Aaron slumps down in his chair and closes his eyes. "Let her blow off some steam. She's just upset about Daniel, and Taylor always needs someone to blame when she's hurting. I keep hoping she'll grow out of it, but I'm beginning to wonder. So . . . what did Daniel mean when he said Deo was an amp?"

I'd almost forgotten the comment that started this whole drama. I want the answer to that question, too, but my face must show how reluctant I am to deal with Daniel right now.

"Is he causing trouble?" Aaron asks. "Not that I have any idea what I'd do if he is, but . . . hey, it was difficult enough when I had to share a *bedroom* with Daniel. I can't even imagine having him share my head."

"I don't think he's trying to cause problems. He's just . . . bored. Restless. He keeps talking when I'm trying to think or . . ."

"*Ohhhh.* That was Daniel interrupting us last night, not Jaden." He rolls his eyes when I nod. "Figures."

I pull out a few bricks in the wall, and Daniel is, of course, right behind it.

You should have let me talk to Taylor. It would make things easier for her.

Maybe it would have been easier if we'd just told her from the beginning.

If I'd known you were going to let it slip like that, maybe I would have.

Just tell me what you meant, okay? So that I can get this damn wall back up, just in case Cregg's snoop is poking around. What is an amp?

Exactly what it sounds like. An amplifier. A signal booster. Must be the same formula they used on that Eastern
European girl a few months before I arrived.

Jaden asks Daniel something that I miss. I really don't like when
they do that. It's similar to the sensation you get when there's something
you can't quite remember, then it vanishes. I'm tempted to ask Jaden to
repeat what he said, but Daniel barrels ahead.

Yeah, that's why they sealed off the north wing. Ashley
heard that they'd planned to test another kid with that
same serum, but they decided to wait until they could
find some way to keep her out of range of the other
adepts. But then the girl died, and it was back to the—

What? You said the reactions weren't fatal.

I said *usually* not fatal. Anna, I didn't have any idea that
they were testing the amplify serum again.

What was her name? The girl who died?

I don't know. It was before I was assigned to The Warren. I was only undercover with them for a few months,
and there was a lot that I didn't have access to.

Daniel's voice fades away as Jaden moves to the front.

Sonia. Her name was Sonia. No clue on the last name.
She came maybe six, seven, months after I did, and she
was a blank. That means she didn't have any psychic
tricks goin' on. Just plain folks, you know? But then the

Fudds juiced her up with somethin', and the other girls roomin' near her said it was like they were on speed. Sonia walks in the room, and suddenly Maria's pickin' up thoughts from people way outside The Warren, even when she's not tryin'. It's like she can't turn it off. And one of the Zippos . . . those are the kids who start fires? She nearly torched the place, even though she could barely toast a marshmallow before that. I never went near Sonia, but I heard some wild stories about that a week or so after they amped her up.

I send Jaden a silent thank-you for the info and turn to Aaron. "Call your mom. See if she can find any information on Daniel's flash drive about a girl named Sonia. Or anything about an amplifying serum."

Feeling helpless, I go into Deo's room and sit on the floor, watching him. The front door opens, and I hear Aaron and Taylor talking, but whatever they're saying washes over me, unprocessed.

Five minutes or so later, Aaron sits next to me and pushes his phone into my hands. "Mom texted what she could find, but . . . there's not much, Anna."

What he really means is there's not much that's likely to help us. Sonia was fifteen years old when she was brought into The Warren on February 23, 2018. She's listed as "average intelligence; good health; asymptomatic." Three weeks later, she's listed as dead.

In the period between admission and death, there are a few medical notes dealing with the week after injection with something called CA3. She suffered from fever and delirium for five days and then showed a sudden improvement. Four additional entries, terse and to the point, detail incidents with other patients, a few of them violent, after she was released from the infirmary. On one occasion, half the kids in the cafeteria began tossing food, plates, and cutlery at her for no apparent reason. Later that same week, the room adjacent to Sonia's caught fire in the middle of the night, injuring both residents. Two other wabbits in The Warren complained that her presence was making them crazy, including the one Jaden mentioned, Maria. I actually remember her—she was one of the girls who spied on me while I was there.

The final medical entry notes a relapse, twenty-two days after admission, with her fever spiking at 105.6. An MRI revealed cerebral edema. Sonia died two days later.

Aaron reads my face and immediately launches into all the reasons I shouldn't freak out. "There was no label on the vial that we sent to Magda. We don't know if it's even the same serum. It could be a new-and-improved formula, less risky."

Taylor is leaning against the doorway now, her outburst from earlier apparently forgotten or at least set aside for now. "And even if it's the same, Deo might respond to it better than this Sonia girl did."

As much as I appreciate their efforts, I'm still freaking out. Everything they just said could be true, but it's equally likely that the new-and-improved formula is *more* of a risk, not less. Or Deo could be *more* sensitive to the serum than Sonia was. When you're dealing with mad scientists who felt it was perfectly okay to test my psychic skills by murdering three people in cold blood, I don't think you can assume they're all that worried about safety protocols.

I resist the urge to check Deo's temperature again. It probably hasn't changed, and I don't want to risk another flash from our eventual trip to Georgia. But it's a punch in the gut to think that touching Deo is somehow toxic now—at least for me. And for Aaron, too, I guess.

"I think we can safely assume it's the same—or at least a similar—serum," I say. "That's why you had the multiple flashes earlier today, why your range was extended. You touched Deo when we were trying to get some fluids into him."

A sheepish look crosses Aaron's face. "I wasn't going to mention it, but yeah, that occurred to me, too. I can try again, but . . ."

I can't blame him for sounding reluctant. All I got when I touched Deo was a snippet from a vision. The violent thoughts Aaron picks up with his "spidey sense" aren't pleasant, even when they come in one at a time. He was seriously freaked out this morning by the sudden onrush.

"No. I tested it twice. The vision kicked in both times. I don't think we need additional data points."

Taylor leans over Deo's bunk. She presses her hand against his neck and holds it there for several seconds. "He's really hot. But . . . I'm not getting anything aside from that. Whatever this amp stuff is, it doesn't seem to affect me."

"Maybe it would have an effect if you were doing a reading?" Aaron asks.

"Maybe. No way to test that right now, though."

Taylor's "readings" are kind of like GPS signals she picks up from objects that allow her to track the object's owner. But Taylor's little gift from Delphi isn't something that just hits her out of the blue like Aaron's early-warning system or Jaden's future flashes.

Aaron hands Taylor one of the wearable thermometers I asked him to pick up when he drove into town earlier, and Taylor attaches it to Deo's forehead.

"Thanks, Taylor."

She doesn't respond until the three of us are back in the main cabin, and as she turns toward me, I can see instantly that we're going to be finishing our little chat about Daniel. "I've decided to take you on your word, Anna. You don't have to prove to me that Daniel is hitching a ride, hopefully temporary, with you right now. But if we're going to work together, I expect the truth—and I mean the *full* truth—from here on out. You seem to think that your primary obligation is to your hitchers, but it's not. If the four of us are going to be cooped up in this tiny tin can, if we're going to be living and working together pretty much 24/7, complete honesty is mandatory."

I'm tempted to argue the point, in part because Taylor sounds like a sanctimonious little brat right now. And the very fact that I'm thinking that about her illustrates the problem with what she's just said. Would telling Taylor my honest opinion of her right this minute be at all helpful to our living and working together? In my experience—for that matter, in the experience of every single hitcher I've housed—complete and total honesty is overrated. Society would collapse if everyone told the pure, unadulterated truth.

But for the sake of harmony, I simply nod, acknowledging Taylor's comment without making any stupid promises. Hoping she'll just move on.

And she does. Sort of.

"With that in mind, I want some answers. If you don't want to let Daniel come forward to give them, that's fine—you can just relay the information yourself."

Aaron gives me a questioning look. "If that's not a problem for you, I have a few questions as well. Actually, that's not true. I have a *lot* of questions, but I'll try to keep it to a few."

"It's not a problem."

"Good," Taylor says. "I have two questions up front for security purposes. First, what was Dad's favorite movie?"

Aaron's eyebrows shoot up. "What happened to taking Anna on her word?"

"As Mom used to say when demanding our computer passwords—trust but verify."

I resist the urge to tell her to kiss off and instead start unstacking my mental bricks. Might as well get this over with. But to my surprise, Daniel doesn't exactly rush forward.

Come on, Daniel. You know she's not going to drop this.

There's a long silence, and I'm about to nudge again when I feel him shift toward the front.

I'm going to answer Taylor's questions, but before I do, you and I need to get something straight. I'll admit I don't like being cooped up in here. I'm bored and . . . maybe this shouldn't feel like a tight space. It's not like Jaden and I take up any room, physically. But it *does* feel that way, and I'm more than a little claustrophobic by nature, so this is kind of like being in a prison cell.

All the more reason we need to get you back to Baltimore and into your own body.

Would you let me finish, please? My point was that I don't like being in here, but you need to give me a little credit. I'm not a damn body thief. You don't know much about my time in the military or with the police, but I worked on finding and stopping human traffickers. Most of their victims were girls who never had any choice in the matter. So, the only way I will ever take control of your body is with your explicit consent. *Shawshank Redemption.*

It takes a second for me to realize the last bit is Daniel's answer to Taylor's question. I relay his response to her, but my mind is still back on his comment.

I'm sorry.

You don't have to apologize. I get it. I'm not an invited guest. Just . . . let's find a way to get through this, okay?

It would be a lot easier if I didn't constantly feel like he was hiding things. I felt that way occasionally with Molly, too, but the things she was hiding were always about Lucas. Always about something she didn't want to face herself. It feels more purposeful on Daniel's part, and I'm not really used to my hitchers keeping secrets. They all realize pretty quickly that I'm their archivist. All of their memories will be stored away in my files when they move on, so what's the point of hiding the bad stuff?

Except, again, for Myron. I instinctively shove the thought of Myron away, like I always do. Like Kelsey taught me to do. But maybe that's part of my issue with Daniel. The only other hitcher who was secretive, who could block me out of his thoughts almost completely, didn't exactly have my best interests at heart.

I've missed Taylor's next security question, so I ask her to repeat it.

"What is your secret that I'm never supposed to tell?"

When Taylor's question registers, Daniel retreats so quickly that it's like there's a vacuum in my head, sucking him backward. Claustrophobic or not, it's clear that he'd love to find a way to stack up my mental bricks and hide behind them right now.

Jaden laughs, but it's a nervous laugh.

> Whoa, dude. I get the feelin' your baby sister just sucker punched you.

Taylor's expression is a teensy bit smug. There was only one security question. She just wanted to hit Daniel with this particular question before his guard was up. "I was serious about what I said before, Daniel. We're way past the point of secrets. You have information that we need to know. And I'm tired of you expecting me to keep Aaron in the dark. It's not fair. If you don't want to tell him, then fine. I will."

I already know the answer to Taylor's question. She's talking about Daniel's ability to sway the minds of others—sort of like a Jedi mind trick and an Imperius Curse rolled into one. Daniel used it on Lucas, back at The Warren when we were trying to escape. He tried to use it on me, but the mental walls I keep up in public to help protect me from new hitchers kept him out. His psychic ability is the same as Graham Cregg's, although I get the feeling Daniel is stronger. Cregg has to stop, has to really focus, in order to control someone. Then again, it's probably easier to convince someone that he gave the wrong order—especially someone like Lucas who wasn't exactly the sharpest knife in the drawer—than forcing someone to snip off one of her fingers.

Still no response from Daniel. Aaron is staring at Taylor now, mouth open, clearly pissed that he's been kept in the dark about something, even if he doesn't know what it is.

> *Is it because you've pushed Aaron? Or both of them? Is that why you didn't want him to know?*

> No. There may have been some . . . I mean, yeah, I did nudge them when I was a little kid. There's this one time I'm pretty sure Aaron remembers. But I don't use it on family anymore. Not since I learned to control it.

I get that sense that he's holding something back again.

> Okay, fine, Anna. I made two exceptions over the course of . . . what? Eighteen years, total. But I don't use it on *anyone* without a damn good reason. And before you go all what-about-me, I was trying to protect you and Deo or I'd never have attempted to nudge you, either.

> *How did you manage to hide an ability like that as a kid?*

> Pretty easy when you can make people forget, Anna. When you can make them do the things you want. Sam figured it out when I was about seven. Made me see

why it was wrong. Helped me learn to control it. And to his credit, he never told anyone else. Said he'd keep my secret as long as I kept my promise not to coerce people, especially not family. For the most part, I did keep that promise . . . only Taylor was in a bad place after Dad was killed and then Molly, too. I didn't like that dark hole she was slipping into. She's got scars on the underside of her arm. Tiny, symmetrical cuts. When I found out . . . it just . . . it hit me hard, okay? I tried to take the easy way out, the fast fix, because I couldn't let her keep hurting herself. But eventually Taylor figured things out.

So . . . what do I tell her?

Whatever you want. She's going to spill to Aaron any-way . . . and maybe she's right. I'd still rather keep Mom out of this, but . . . that may not even be my call any-more. Taylor needs to tell him everything, though. *All* of it, including how she found out. If I don't get to have secrets, neither does she.

I expect both Aaron and Taylor to be staring at me when I tune back in to the outside world, but for once there are no expectant eyes awaiting me. Aaron is staring at Taylor, and Taylor is looking down at the table, clearly much less enthusiastic about this whole question-and-answer session now that it's actually under way.

"Daniel says go ahead and tell him. He says maybe you're right about keeping too many secrets. Just make sure you tell him *everything*."

I cast a pointed glance at her arms. Taylor colors slightly, but nods.

"I was going to anyway. I meant what I said about no more secrets. Aaron already knows that I was cutting. He and Mom just didn't have the same tools to try and help me that Daniel had. His heart was in the right place, but . . . you can't make someone stop hurting. I lost Dad and Molly in a matter of months, and I needed to work through my pain, just like Anna has to work through the Molly dreams."

"Back up," Aaron says. "What do you mean, Mom and I didn't have the same tools? What was Daniel doing to try and make you forget? He can erase memories?"

"Not exactly. But he's pretty good at planting happy thoughts to replace them. Making people think maybe they did something they didn't do . . . or vice versa. It worked on me for a while. But then cognitive dissonance—and *yes*, Aaron, I know what it means—kicked in. Plus, there was this little part of me that started connecting Daniel's happy thoughts with the cutting. That was an illusion, and it was definitely not what Daniel was trying to achieve, so he backed off. What finally helped me was being able to *do* something. Finding Molly's body wasn't easy. But being able to put my ability to use, being able to do something *constructive*—that's what pulled me out."

Aaron's jaw tightens as she speaks. Then he turns to look at me next to him on the bench, and for the first time, there's suspicion in his eyes. Anger, even. Is the anger directed at me or at Daniel? Either way, it's disturbing. I slide a little closer to the wall, increasing the distance between us. A flicker of hurt, or maybe it's guilt, crosses his face, and then he looks back to Taylor.

"So," he says. "All of that time he was scoffing at us—no, let's be honest, at me. Scoffing at *me*. He never really gave you any crap about it. But all that time, he was doing the same damn thing."

Except no one *knew*. Tell him that, Anna. He's an open book. Anyone could tell when Aaron was getting premonitions. It's different with me. Different with Taylor, too, because she has to turn it on. His ability was a *liability* in terms of keeping the family under the radar. That's why—

Aaron is calling my name, so I push Daniel back.

"He used it on me, or at least attempted to. Didn't he? When Mom was trying to talk me and Taylor out of poking into Molly's death."

"I don't know, Aaron. And please, don't ask me to get in the middle of what's clearly a protracted family squabble. When you're yelling at each other, you're also yelling at me. Can we just focus on questions about Daniel's work at Python and what he knows about the Delphi Project and save the personal stuff until we get him back into his own body? Please?"

I can tell he's reluctant to let it go, but eventually his expression softens and he nods. "Sure. They've kept me in the dark this long. A little longer won't make much difference. And . . . sorry if you were caught in the cross fire."

> *That goes for you, too, Daniel. I'm not passing notes back and forth. You can tell them anything you want once we get you back to Baltimore.*

Daniel doesn't respond, possibly because Taylor is speaking and he wants to listen.

"You're making a big assumption there, Anna. Daniel might actually be dead, for all you know, and this might be our only chance to tell him good-bye. To get closure."

There's a slight hint of manipulation in her voice, and I feel it working on Daniel. Jaden, who has been hanging well out of the way until now, laughs.

> Man, she is good. I bet you gave her *all* your cookies when you were little kids, and did her chores, too. Don't let them bully you, Anna. No offense to ol' Dan here, but it doesn't matter if he's dead. If he can't return to his body, you can scoop him back up and let him say his good-byes.

That is an excellent point, Jaden. Thank you.

"Not going to work," I tell Taylor. "Get to your actual questions, okay?"

Her lips tighten. "Fine. My first *actual* question is why aren't we currently en route to Baltimore? Mom looks like death on toast because she's worried sick about Daniel. And yeah, I get that the authorities might think you had something to do with his current condition, but he could clear you when he wakes up."

> As she just noted, *if* I wake up. *If.* No guarantees I'm coming out of this, and there's more at stake right now than just me.

I sigh. This is really the same damn line of questioning as before. But I pass his words along to Taylor, since it's clear we're not going to get anything of substance done until she's vented.

"Screw Delphi. Screw Magda," Taylor counters. "We need to head home. And you agree with me, don't you, Aaron? I can tell you do."

"Yeah," he says. "I mean . . . I don't know."

For the next couple of minutes, I relay their personal messages back and forth, even after saying I wouldn't. In the end, though, I'm glad. Daniel has his own walls, maybe not as substantive as mine, but there are things he's hiding. And as he tries to think of the best way to convince Taylor that we need to stay the current course, his guard drops a bit, and I pick up more than just words. I'm getting his thoughts now, as well, random emotions and ideas peeking through like bright flashes of color and light.

At the front is his fear, vibrant, amorphous flashes of red-orange. Fear that he really is dead. Fear that he might not like his afterlife accommodations so much. I also get a glimpse of the huge twisted knot of guilt at his core, the color of a day-old bruise. The guilt spins out in five directions. Five . . . people. I don't see them as images, it's more the feelings he attaches to them. The first three are easy to recognize—Aaron, Taylor, and his mom. Daniel feels responsible for them, partly because his dad is gone now, but it goes deeper, especially toward Aaron and Taylor. Almost like he's the reason they're in danger and he must fix it.

The fourth person is a woman. Again, I don't get a name or an image, it's more his feelings that come through, and they're complicated. Love, anger. I don't think it's Ashley, but I could be wrong.

And I'm certain that the last one is a kid. There's that same sense of responsibility that Daniel felt toward his family, mixed with love and . . . fear, but it's a different kind of fear. Daniel's feelings about the kid . . . and I'm pretty sure it's a boy . . . are shot through with the same red-orange as his fear about death. The color of fire seen through the windows of the lab at The Warren as Deo and I ran . . .

Bwee-om. Run, Anna.

The kid in Room 81?

My focus is pulled in two directions at once—as Daniel realizes he's inadvertently let something slip, and as Taylor realizes I haven't exactly been paying attention.

"Sorry, Taylor. Kind of drifted off, I guess. Could you repeat?"

"Who. Is. Ashley? I want to know what Daniel did to piss her off so badly that she snuck into the hospital to kill him."

I already know this part from when Daniel first came on board.

"Daniel said she didn't have a choice. You guys saw her at the hospital—she was an emotional wreck. Ashley had to video the whole thing so that they could see that Daniel was actually dead. Otherwise, they were going to kill her . . . sister."

As I say the last word, it hits me.

That's the woman I sensed, isn't it? Ashley's sister?

That was private, Anna. You had no right.

It's hard not to laugh out loud at the irony—no, the outright hypocrisy—of that statement.

You're in my head. You pick up on my thoughts, my feelings, interrupt me at every turn. And now you're claiming a right to privacy?

There's a very long pause, and when he finally answers my question—which admittedly was kind of rhetorical—he's clearly annoyed.

Fine. Yes. I was thinking about Ashley's sister. But it's *none* of your business. So unless you want me poking around back there in the corner marked *Myron*—

Stay away from that corner, Daniel Quinn. You have no idea what you're messing with. This matter isn't open for discussion or debate. Keep the hell away.

Just in case Daniel didn't get the point that he needs to steer clear, I do a little mental redecoration. Myron's corner is no longer drab gray brick with a simple label. It's now draped in barbed wire and emblazoned with a biohazard warning sign, along with, a skull-and-crossbones. *Danger, Keep Out, No Trespassing,* and *STOP* in red neon letters.

Okay, okay. I get the point. But, you need to get mine, too. What you saw a few minutes ago is none of your business. And it's definitely not Aaron and Taylor's business. Just as everything I now know about *you*—your stray thoughts, your occasional fantasies—is none of their business. If I ever get out of here, I'll keep your secrets, Anna, but only if you keep mine.

"Are you okay?" Aaron asks. "You look upset."

"I'm fine," I say, although I would give anything to have Daniel Quinn fully corporeal and outside of my head long enough for me to punch him. What he just said is nothing short of blackmail. It's not as though I've thought anything all that horrible, at least not that I can recall, but no—I wouldn't want to have my private thoughts laid bare in front of Aaron and Taylor.

Fine, Daniel. You win.

But then Aaron asks the logical follow-up question to the information I just gave them about Ashley.

"Why was her sister there? Was she one of the girls they brought in? One of their guinea pigs?"

Yes. Ashley joined Python and got herself assigned to the Delphi Project to try and get her sister out of there.

I pass along Daniel's response, even though I can tell that's not the full story. It's partly his tone, but there's also the fact that I didn't sense a girl. This was a woman. An adult. Midtwenties. Daniel's age, maybe a bit older.

"Do you think Cregg kept his deal with Ashley?" Taylor asks. "Do you think he let her sister go?"

I don't know.

Despite his best efforts, Daniel can't mask the flood of emotions behind those three words. He may not *know*, but he definitely *fears*.

And what he fears is that they're both dead. Ashley and . . . Sariah. Her name is Sariah.

But he's pretty sure that the kid from Room 81 isn't dead. No name comes through. Daniel just thinks of him as *The Kid*. And he's not sure if it's a good or a bad thing that The Kid is alive.

What?

Daniel ignores my question.

That's why we can't go back to Baltimore. Tell them that, okay? Cregg must know by now that I'm in a coma, not dead. If he didn't know it before, he's got that Snoop kid poking around, so he'll probably pick it up. If I'm alive, that means Ashley failed, and I can't imagine him letting that slide . . . although I guess there's some chance he might let her and Sariah live if he believes I never handed over the password. But if I suddenly wake up, how long do you think it will be before he gets one of his people into the hospital to have another go at me? Or at Mom? Taylor? Aaron?

Ashley knew you were awake, though. Couldn't you have already given the password to your mom?

Could, but didn't. Ashley straight-up asked. It was one of the first things she said when she came through the door, and thinking back, I'm pretty sure she already had Cregg on the line. I was still so out of it from surgery, I didn't think anything of the question—I just said no, there hadn't been time. But . . . you see what I mean, right? As much as I would love to get out of here, we're all safer if I stay put for now.

I can't argue with his logic. And when I explain things to Taylor and Aaron, neither can they.

The conversation shifts to more practical matters—what Daniel learned during his months at Delphi and then logistics about the investigation we'll need to launch once we arrive in North Carolina. I dutifully ferry Daniel's answers to Aaron and Taylor, but my mind keeps going back to a scrap of sentiment I picked up from Daniel that bothers the hell out of me.

How could it possibly be better for that kid in Room 81—or *any* kid for that matter—to be dead rather than alive?

CHAPTER FIVE

Somewhere in North Carolina
November 2, 2019, 1:22 p.m.

Aaron was up at the crack of dawn. I don't think he slept well. He came to bed long after I did, and he tossed fitfully, either trying to get comfortable enough to sleep or wrestling with the same thoughts I was. Part of me wanted to snuggle up next to him, but that felt awkward enough even before he learned that his brother is inside my head. So I just hugged my pillow and pretended to be asleep.

On the plus side, the magic pills Kelsey prescribed did a decent job of keeping the Molly dreams at bay for once. I had only one dream that I can remember, and it didn't end with the sight of Dacia Badea swinging a baseball bat toward my head. It definitely *started* in the basement with Dacia, but Deo wandered into the dream about halfway through, and then Dacia morphed into one of his Marvel characters. She-Hulk, I think. And then Deo and I were running toward the deli where I used to work, with Dacia Hulk hot on our heels. We'd almost made it—I could see the front door and even smell Joe's cheddar-jalapeño bagels—when I jolted awake.

Dacia is creepy as hell, but to the best of my knowledge, she doesn't swell to twice her normal size and turn bright green when she's angry. If she could do that, I'm pretty sure she'd have flipped into Hulk mode when she saw Lucas lying in a pool of blood on the floor of the lab.

So even though my heart was pounding when I woke up from the dream, I wasn't screaming in terror, and it was much easier for me to fall back asleep afterward. Partly because Aaron was sleeping on the other side of the bed. But it's also because Molly's final moments are beginning to merge with my usual dreamscape. I know from experience that this means that the dreams will start tapering off. And if the dreamscapes merge, I'm much happier seeing a Dacia/She-Hulk mash-up than Cregg morphing into Myron and back.

Thinking of Cregg immediately starts the tickling sensation on my forehead. I'm almost certain it's my imagination, but that doesn't make it any less real. And the fact that I was thinking about Myron just now makes me even more paranoid. I don't want Cregg anywhere near those thoughts, so I push them away.

But they don't *stay* away.

A text comes in on Aaron's phone when we're maybe twenty miles northwest of Fayetteville, but there's no name attached. I tense up automatically, but Aaron shakes his head.

"Not him," he says after glancing at the screen. "Too many digits for a US number. Must be Magda."

I press the button, and a computer voice reads, "Pin drop your location to meet courier at two p.m. EST."

"It's 1:27," Aaron says. "Find someplace we can reach before two. Ideally, someplace with decent food. I'm tired of burgers and pizza."

After a brief search, I send Magda the coordinates for an Asian place. Daniel, who spent the better part of a year in the area during his military training back in 2014, swears the food is good.

The road leading into Fort Bragg is pretty much nonstop strip malls, with the occasional fast-food restaurant and hotel to break things up a bit. The restaurant Daniel recommended has the same slightly run-down industrial vibe as everything around us.

"You sure about this place?" Aaron asks as he pulls the RV toward the back of the lot.

"Not in the slightest. Like I said, it's Daniel's recommendation."

He grimaces, probably not happy with having to take advice from his brother. But the aroma wafting out of the restaurant when we step outside supports Daniel's thumbs-up rating.

"I'm going to check on Deo real quick, and then I'll be right in."

"Sure," he says. "I'll step in and test the atmosphere. We might need to eat outside."

I'd assumed he was worried about the quality of the food, but I realize now that he's probably equally concerned about the size—and maybe the mood—of the crowd inside. It's just after the lunch rush, but the place still has about a dozen cars in the lot. "I have no problem with dining alfresco," I tell him.

Aaron glances around and laughs. "Not sure that term really applies to this parking lot, but okay." The smile he gives me as he enters the restaurant is still not as open and trusting as it was this time yesterday, but it's infinitely better than the look in his eyes last night when he first learned about Daniel.

Taylor is already bounding down the steps of the RV when I reach the door. I'm very glad to see that she's abandoned the foil cap.

"Deo's asleep," she says. "I looked in maybe five minutes ago. Gave him some of the Gatorade and more Tylenol around noon. He sat up to drink this time. Even got out of bed to pee, although he was kind of shaky. But the room still smells like a lightning storm just hit, so it's probably best for you and Aaron to both steer clear. I left a note for him, in case he wakes up."

"Thanks." I follow Taylor into the restaurant, feeling oddly deflated. I *am* thankful for Taylor's help, but I also feel like she's doing my job.

Deo is my family, my responsibility, and the idea that he's somehow poisonous to me, at least for the time being, twists my gut.

That doesn't keep me from eating, however. Daniel may be a pain in the ass, but he's got good taste in Thai food. Aaron even seems relaxed once we've eaten, possibly because the crowd has thinned out a bit.

A young woman enters while we're waiting for the check and the large take-out container of soup that I ordered just in case Deo's appetite returns. After a quick glance down at the clipboard in her hands, she peers around the room. The business suit she wears looks oddly formal here—aside from the servers and the three of us in our jeans, almost everyone else is wearing some variant of camouflage.

> It's called an ACU. Used to be BDUs, but they changed the name and fabric a while back.

Jaden sighs.

> Now see, man? That's exactly the kind of trivia that did not merit an interruption. I swear, you need to get a filter in the worst kind of way.

I push Daniel and Jaden to the back, with a silent reminder that they need to stop the rapid switch-offs if they don't want me to hurl.

"Aaron Quinn?" the woman asks as she approaches.

"Yes . . ."

"Delivery. I'm gonna need to see ID."

The girl smacks her gum as she scrutinizes both sides of his license, stares at his face, then back at the card. Apparently convinced, she tosses a box onto the table along with Aaron's ID and then shoves the clipboard into his hands.

"Signature at the bottom to indicate acceptance, please."

Once she's gone, Aaron opens the box, and we peek inside. There are a bunch of documents, along with a stack of twenty-dollar bills, an envelope marked *Skolnick*, three credit cards, a plastic bag containing about a dozen clear sample collection tubes and packets of needles, a car key, a fake driver's license for Aaron, and two identification badges on black lanyards. *Bingley, Darcy, and Wickham, Attorneys-at-Law* is emblazoned across the bottom. The one with Aaron's face reads, *William Collins, Associate*. On the other one, below the photo taken last year for my student ID, is *Elizabeth Bennet, Intern*.

"Well, I guess we know Magda's favorite book." I'm surprised that Aaron and Taylor both give me blank looks. "What? You never read *Pride and Prejudice*?"

"I watched the zombie version," Aaron says. "Does that count?"

"No. It does not. Anyway, she made you the bad guy."

"Which character am I?" Taylor asks. "And why bother with a car? We have the truck."

"I don't know. And I don't see any other—" Aaron's phone dings with an incoming text. We all tense up, but it's Magda again.

Courier confirmed delivery of packet. Car is rented for a fortnight but can be extended if necessary. Truck far too conspicuous for our purposes.

Taylor drops her jaw dramatically and turns to look out at the parking lot. There are three pickups among the seven or eight vehicles parked outside, including one in an adjoining lot that's pretty much an exact duplicate of Porter's F-150. "Magda really doesn't have a clue about where we are, does she?"

A second ping, and then:

Working on documents for the children, but these should suffice in the interim.

It takes a second for me to realize that by *children*, Magda doesn't mean the kids we're trying to locate. She means Taylor and Deo.

Taylor got that too, and she looks like she's going to blow a fuse. "Anna and I are the *same age*."

I feel kind of bad for her, because she's right—technically, we're both seventeen. I'll be eighteen in a few weeks, and Taylor has eight months to go, but it still doesn't seem fair. "I'd be happy to trade places, but it's my face on the ID, so I don't think we have a choice."

The phone pings again.

Documents in packet combine my files with those your brother collected. Link follows to submit recording. First interview with Skolnick on enclosed printout is scheduled 11/2 @4PM. Compare the photos; if they match, give him the envelope.

A location pin pops up for a coffee shop in downtown Fayetteville, followed by the promised link.

Taylor is still stuck on Magda's second text. "What does she expect me to do, just sit in the camper all day? Watch YouTube and babysit Deo?"

Okay, I don't feel so bad for her anymore. "Deo doesn't need babysitting . . . at least not when he's well."

"Really? That's hard to believe, given the way you hover over him." The words are barely out before she says, "I'm sorry, okay? I'm just pissed. You wouldn't like it either if they benched you. And who the hell does she think is going to use those needles?"

Arguing with Taylor is about as productive as kicking a wasp's nest, so I ignore her. But as I look at the next item Aaron pulls out, I'm tempted to tell her that I'd be more than happy to hang in the camper with Deo. The document is a spreadsheet, with the name and photo of each "adept" we're seeking, along with the addresses, telephone numbers, and pictures of people we're supposed to question in regard to that adept. I'm surprised to see that about half of them are teachers, but I guess teachers are more likely to witness odd behavior by kids than anyone aside from parents.

In addition to the spreadsheet, there's also a list of the questions she wants us to ask, the specific protocol we need to follow for making contact, and a deadline for submitting reports from each interview. There's even a handy little column at the far left where we can check off each item as completed. All in all, it's an excruciatingly detailed exercise in micromanagement, and I'm very tempted to make a reference to Lady Catherine de Bourgh. But since I don't know if that character was even in the zombie version of *Pride and Prejudice*, I keep the observation to myself.

Aaron taps the top item on the list and then looks back at Magda's text. "Okay, it would have been nice if Magda had given us a little more notice. In less than two hours, you and I are expected to"—he glances around, and even though we're down to just us and the restaurant staff now, he lowers his voice—"impersonate attorneys."

I grin. "Nope. Just you. I'm only required to impersonate an intern. But I doubt they'll even believe that when I'm dressed like this." I flick my hand at my jeans and sweater.

"Yeah. I don't have anything either." He curses under his breath and then peels a couple of bills off the stack in the envelope, handing them to Taylor along with a credit card and the keys to the truck. "I hate to dump this on you, but I don't think the restaurant is going to appreciate us leaving the RV here and blocking a quarter of their parking lot."

Taylor's eyes narrow, but she takes the keys and sighs. "Sure. I'm a team player. I'll pay our tab, find a campground, park that hulking monstrosity, and babysit. Because, you know, that's what *children* do."

❖   ❖   ❖

Fayetteville, North Carolina
November 2, 2019, 3:56 p.m.

We find a parking spot a few blocks away and head toward the café with a couple of minutes to spare. I wish we could have parked closer, because I feel like we're conspicuous. There was no time to make it to a shopping mall, so we had to settle for Walmart. Aaron looks reasonably professional from the waist up, but his pants are nearly an inch too short. My shoes pinch like hell, and they're hideous. One consolation is that I will never have to worry about Deo stretching them out by trying to squeeze them onto his feet. He'd be far more likely to toss them into the nearest dumpster.

"Don't be nervous," Aaron says. "If all goes well, the only thing you'll have to do is press the button on my phone to start recording. And take notes."

"That doesn't seem redundant to you? Because I'm thinking *you* could push the button, and I could take notes later. That way, I could just wait in the car."

Aaron ignores my hopeful smile. "Nice try, but no. You're with me. Like I said, I'm pretty sure you'll just need to play the role of assistant, but the café might be crowded, given that this is pumpkin-spice-everything season. If it's a happy, peaceful crowd, I'll be fine, but . . ." He shrugs it off. "Anyway, a successful attorney can't be seen jotting down his own notes, can he? I need my assistant for that." He straightens his tie and shoots me an over-the-top smug look.

"If you can convince anyone that you're a successful attorney in those pants, you should quit this detective gig and take up acting."

"Hey, no dissing the suit. There wasn't a lot to choose from." He gives me a head-to-toe appraisal and says, "You did okay, though. That looks really nice on you."

"Thanks." It's the first time he's seen me in a skirt—actually, the first time I've worn one in years. It's one of those sweater skirts that likes to travel north, requiring me to tug it down every couple of steps. I'm pretty sure Aaron's compliment is aimed less at the outfit and more at the legs it keeps revealing, but I'm perfectly okay with that.

The guy we're meeting, Dean Skolnick, is Magda's "local source" on ties between the missing kids and Delphi. He's forty-one, white, a former reporter with the local paper who now does freelance jobs and teaches occasional classes in journalism at a nearby community college. His photo reveals a resigned smile, dark glasses, and a receding hairline. Divorced two years, no kids. Originally from Pittsburgh. MA in journalism from University of North Carolina. A 680 credit score. Libertarian. An arrest eight years ago for possession of less than one ounce of marijuana. DIRECTV customer. Owns a Camry. And that was just what I gleaned from the first of the three pages of info Magda gave us.

The café is a funky, brightly colored little shop that sits next to a small theater. I spot Skolnick through the window as we approach, pouring a stream of coffee into the trash bin to make room in his cup. I'd have said that Magda's background check left no stone unturned, no skeleton unearthed, but I now know something that was *not* in his dossier. Skolnick drinks his coffee extra light.

Aaron pauses in the doorway, taking the mental temperature of the place. The interior is narrow, cramped, and, just as Aaron feared, it's packed.

"Everything okay?"

"Yeah, it's cool. Well, except for the toddler." He nods toward the back. I can't actually see the kid, but sure enough, a loud wail pierces the air, followed by the crash of a plate onto the floor. "He needs a nap. Hopefully, they get him out of here soon. Otherwise I might lapse into a temper tantrum in the middle of our interview."

"Ha. Funny." He doesn't respond, so I add. "You *are* joking. Right?"

Aaron tries to keep a straight face, but his mouth twitches and then erupts into a grin. I give him a sharp nudge with my elbow.

"Yes. I'm joking. Come on, let's do this."

Skolnick is dressed in jeans and a flannel shirt. A computer case is slung over one shoulder, and he's taken his milky brew to the only empty table, a two-seater near the front window. A green accordion file folder sits next to his cup.

"Dean Skolnick?" Aaron extends his hand, flashes the ID badge, and prepares to launch into the cover story that Magda or someone in her employ cooked up. Our firm is investigating clients for a potential class action suit against a pharmaceutical company that may have caused personality disorders in children whose parents took the drug. "I'm Will Collins, with Binkley, Dar—"

"Save your acting skills. I already know who you're working for and why. Bell contacted me last year based on a couple of articles I wrote, but I didn't have anything concrete. Now, though . . ." He glances around us and then lowers his voice. "The only reason I agreed to talk at all is because she's paying me enough to get out of town. Fresh start and all that. So pull up a chair and let's get this over with."

I exchange a look with Aaron. Magda gives us a metric ton of information on this guy but leaves out the part where he's a *paid* informant. We could have worn our jeans. Lovely. Just freakin' lovely.

Since there are only two chairs and since the toddler seems to be winding up for another shriek, I suggest that we take the discussion outside.

"Good idea," Aaron says with a note of relief.

Skolnick is less enthusiastic, but he gathers his things, and we retreat to a patio squeezed between the buildings. It's an alcove, really, with brick walls on three sides. The area is mostly empty thanks to an overcast sky and wind gusts that send leaves skipping down the sidewalk and whirling beneath the tables.

Once Skolnick finally picks a table, he parks himself in the chair that faces the street, and we take the other two. I push the record button on Aaron's phone, and Skolnick begins.

"You already know I was a reporter. I covered military *life*, not policy issues, but things that had an impact on the community. Good and bad. PTSD, the Military Ball, effect of deployment on the kiddos, that kind of stuff. They've got one person covering all of it now. Pretty much every local newspaper has cut a third to a half of their staff in the past decade, so I wasn't exactly shocked when I got the pink slip a few months back . . . especially since I'd been butting heads with my editor about this story."

Skolnick chews a bit of dry skin off his lower lip and looks around nervously before continuing.

"The whole thing really started a while back, just a few years after I began work at the paper. We had a bunch of murders here in town—not exactly unusual, but more than the typical number that year. Many of them were chalked up to PTSD after Afghanistan. The four soldiers who killed their wives—those even got national press. There was some speculation about it being caused by a malaria drug they took, and that may have been a factor, I don't know. But on top of the murders, we had a whole slew of violent episodes . . . again, a lot of people coming back from war, so that's to be expected, but I noticed a pattern. There were far more episodes in a specific unit within the PSYOPS battalion, or whatever the hell they're calling it now. Significantly more . . . like by a factor of ten.

"But here's the kicker. When I start looking back through the crime files, I find out it's been that way for nearly a decade. So I dig around, and am promptly told to *stop* digging around—not just by the paper but by the military. Nothing to see here, move along. And so I did. I was a new reporter, and I wanted to keep my job. Also the incidents seemed to be tapering off. But even though I dropped it, the thing always sat at the back of my mind, you know?"

Aaron and I both nod, and Skolnick goes on. "So, flash-forward to earlier this year, late April, maybe early May. Like I said, I'm the one who covered all of the slice-of-life military stories, so if some kid from

Bragg won a science fair or whatever, that was my beat. Well, this time it was a quiz bowl instead of a science fair . . . you know, kind of like *Nerd Jeopardy?*"

The *nerd* qualifier seems unnecessary, but I simply nod again.

"Anyway, one of the girls who was just abducted was on the show, and she was smoking everyone else. Expert in every topic. Real whiz kid. Four rounds of competition, and she didn't get a single question wrong. So, of course, I'm assigned to do a write-up. I didn't bother with an interview—just watched a clip of the show and typed up a few paragraphs about the local Einstein, along with a picture of her holding a trophy, proud parents in the background. The story's done, and I've moved on to the next assignment, but I happen to click back on the article for some reason a few weeks later, and I notice the comments. Usually, I'd get one or two for a story like that. They're linked to Facebook, so you'll see, 'Grandma is so proud of you, sweetie!' And maybe a crude comment or two, or a bit of spam, if interns aren't moderating the section close enough."

He chugs a bit of his coffee-flavored milk and then continues. "This time we had three or four dozen. Not a single atta-girl in the bunch. Couple of them are calling her Scary Clary—her name's Nicki Clary—and the overall consensus among commenters is that she's a dirty rotten cheat. I would've just written it off as teens being assholes, but there's a few parents in the mix, too. Apparently, when Clary was in eighth grade, one of her teachers had a glitch in the multiple-choice test program she was using. It spat out the wrong grading key. The teacher is grading away, and Clary gets her usual A-plus-plus. But her other top students are going down in flames, so the teacher checks, and it's the *wrong* key. Of course, the kid says she didn't cheat, and the teacher doesn't see how she *could* have cheated, how she could have gotten access to the key, unless maybe she's hacked into the teacher's home computer system or whatever. So she purposefully rigs it the next time. Prints out a key, but Clary's version of the test has the questions in a different order. And sure enough, Clary hands in a test with all the right answers, except they're attached to the wrong questions."

Skolnick goes on. His eyes still dart around at the slightest noise, but he also seems to like the sound of his own voice and opts for many words when a few would get him out of here faster. The short version is that the teacher filed an academic dishonesty report. Clary's parents filed a lawsuit. School backed down, because even the teacher had to admit she had no idea how the girl could have gotten the test key. The incident would most likely have been forgotten by the students if not for the fact that the teacher shifted to essay exams whenever possible for the rest of the year. That pissed the students off enough to cry foul when they heard about Nicki Clary's quiz bowl win.

"To be honest, I'd still have ignored the story if I hadn't scrolled back up to look at the picture and something clicked. The last name *Clary* isn't all that common, and the dad's face looked familiar. So I check back, and sure enough, he's one of the guys who lost his cool back in 2002 or 2003. Supposedly a nice guy, but someone bumped his shoulder in the line at Wendy's, and he went mental, started banging the other guy's head against the counter, then pulled out a knife. If it hadn't been for a couple of Rangers in line who subdued him, that would've been another murder on the books that year, and—"

"So, how old is the daughter?" Aaron asks. "Nicki?"

Skolnick shakes his head, clearly annoyed at the interruption. "I don't know. She was a sophomore last year. Sixteen, maybe? She was born a few months after her dad's court-martial, so you do the math."

I don't have to do the math. I just flip to the second page of Magda's spreadsheet. Nicola Clary is listed about halfway down. Fifteen, actually, since she skipped a grade—which is no surprise, given her ability. Her school photo reminds me a little of an adolescent Amy Schumer. Blonde and curvy but with a more guarded smile. I slide the page over to Aaron.

"Yeah, that's her," Skolnick says, glancing at the picture.

"Was her dad given a dishonorable discharge, or what?" Aaron asks.

Skolnick shakes his head. "Actually, I suspect the fact that his wife was pregnant—and maybe the rumors about the malaria drug—convinced them to go easy and just slap him with an Article 15."

I have only a vague idea what that means, and the question in my head lures Daniel to the front.

It's sort of an administrative punishm—

Don't care, Daniel. Busy right now. If I want to know, I'll google it later. Or I'll check Abner's file. He was in the Navy. So if I need to know military lingo or Morse code, I'll comb through his memories.

I'm. Trying. To. Help.

Daniel slinks back, and I return to the outside world, already in progress, where Skolnick is giving me an odd look.

"Sorry . . ." I debate which of my standard excuses to use. Oncoming migraine? Didn't sleep well? But the point is moot, since Skolnick's already back to his story.

"So, yeah, anyway, the comments on that story aren't just talking about the Clary kid. They go off on a tangent and start talking about this Lentz kid, who sent three pencils flying toward a teacher at once, without even touching the pencils. Some say that the pencil story is bullshit, but the others are swearing on a stack of Pokémon cards or whatever that they're telling the truth. And then someone says, do y'all remember Jeremy Bieler's brother, that little kid who ripped off the arcade last summer? Of course, I hadn't heard of either of those kids, but the last names seemed familiar—and when I went back and checked, both had a parent who lost their shit back in 2002. So I decided to dig a little deeper, even though I was pretty sure my editor—"

Brakes squeal on the street in front of us, and Skolnick jumps so hard that coffee splashes onto his shirt. But it's just a mom in a mini-van, angry at a delivery truck that stopped suddenly on the other side of the road.

Skolnick curses, then goes inside. To get napkins, I guess.

"Why do you think he's so jumpy?"

"Don't know. I'm not picking up any threats, aside from that driver being really pissed and . . . the baby in there who needs a nap. But Skolnick's reaction does have me wondering why he's leaving town in search of a fresh start." He takes my hand across the table. "What was going on with you a minute ago? When you tuned out?"

"It was nothing." I'd really rather leave it at that, but Aaron's eye-brow quirks upward, and even though it really *was* nothing, I don't want him to think I'm keeping secrets again. "Daniel was just trying to be helpful, fill in some info."

When I mention Daniel, Aaron's face closes a bit. It's a subtle change, like a wisp of cloud passing across the sun, but I wish I'd kept quiet. Especially when he lets go of my hand.

But dropping my hand could partly be due to the fact that Skolnick's back, dabbing at his shirt with a paper towel. "Where the hell was I?"

"Some kid was ripping off a fun center," Aaron says.

"Yeah, Hunter Bieler. Five years old at the time. He was at one of those summer day camps because his mom works and his dad's not in the picture anymore."

I scan the list that Magda gave us. Hunter Bieler is wearing one of those cheesy smiles that kids paste on for their school photos. He's a little older than five here, missing a couple of teeth, and his curly reddish-blond hair is unruly. Cute kid. Dillon Lentz is also on the page, only a bit younger than the Clary girl.

"These day camps take the kids on field trips a few times a week," Skolnick says. "Like this miniature golf and arcade place over on Skibo Road, where each kid plays a round of golf and gets a handful of tokens to play the video games, foosball, whack-a-mole, whatever. Only one of the high school kids working behind the counter notices that the kids from this one camp are having an amazing streak of luck. Well, as much as you can at one of those places. He realizes he's paying out way more of those cheap-ass prizes than usual on Fridays. So he starts watching a little closer and sees all the kids keep circling back to this one little guy, Hunter, who's extraordinarily lucky. Every time Hunter touches a machine, it's like he's flipped a switch—the thing starts spitting out tickets. And he's the generous type, because he shares the tickets with all of his buddies."

"Did they figure out how . . . or if . . . he was doing it?" Aaron asks.

"Nope. Even after management gets involved, they can't prove anything. I mean, was it the kid's fault if their machines were malfunctioning? The owner even grabbed Hunter's arm and pressed it against the machine. And, of course, nothing happened . . . well, nothing aside from the camp taking Happy Town arcade off their weekly rotation and the kid's mom threatening a lawsuit 'cause the owner manhandled her baby boy."

Skolnick finishes off the last of his coffee.

"Same thing with flying-pencil boy. He was in a classroom for kids with behavior issues, and they had a camera set up in the back as a monitoring device. It did indeed show three pencils flying toward the teacher. But both of Lentz's hands were in the frame, so the video evidence cleared him. In fact, it cleared the entire class."

"So," Aaron says, "who did they think threw the pencils?"

"Good question. And also one of the many questions swept under the rug, not just in this case, but every time something weird happens in this town. Maybe it's . . . what do they call it? Cognitive . . . something . . ."

"Dissonance?"

He points a finger at me and nods. "Yeah. That. Three teachers lost their jobs in Cumberland County, but Tamara Blake, this school counselor, who was one of my sources before she got herself killed, said there's a lot of that dissonance stuff going on. I can't get any info out of the teachers at the DoD schools inside Fort Bragg, but I'm guessing it's the same there. Nobody wants to be called crazy for saying they've got kids in their classrooms who can read minds or make the blinds dance up and down just by looking at them. Or turn the computers on and off without going near them. The teachers who say that kind of stuff go on administrative leave and then end up working at Hardee's. Or land in a mental hospital. So they just say nothing. Grit their teeth and hope they get a freak-free class next year."

Skolnick's comment makes me grit *my* teeth, because I truly want to smack him. Yeah, it sounds like some of the kids were using their so-called gifts in ways that weren't exactly ethical, but having been in a similar situation, I can't help but think about the hell they've been going through trying to pass as normal. Did this Nicki Clary go look-ing for the answers, or do they just pop into her head? Did the Lentz boy launch those pencils on purpose, or does he struggle like Aaron did just to keep from going crazy in a school setting? And yeah, the Bieler kid crossed a line at the arcade, but at least he shared the plastic-spider rings, miniature footballs, and cheap candy. He didn't hoard the loot for himself, and it's not like those places aren't already ripping kids off.

Maybe my expression telegraphs my thoughts to Skolnick, because he backs off a bit. "Not saying it's the kids' fault, of course. This is obviously connected to something that happened with their parents. I don't know exactly what, but I'm pretty sure it has something to do with that program they claim to have shut down back in 1995 where they were trying to create these psychic supersoldiers who could spy remotely, walk through walls. Clooney even did a movie about it a few years back."

Skolnick goes on to say that when he submitted his story to his boss in late August, he hit a brick wall. "The e-mail came back so fast I thought I'd accidentally sent the damn thing to myself. But no, he got it. Just didn't bother reading past the first sentence or two. Said we were running a newspaper, not a science-fiction magazine. Two weeks later, I'm the victim of 'budget cuts.' Three weeks after that, the Bieler kid disappears. The count is now up to six. Well, seven, if you count the Bieler kid's sister, but that happened last year, back before his little arcade heist, and police are pretty sure it was a custody thing."

He chews at his lip again. "I decided to visit some friends up in Maine a few weeks after I got fired. Old college buddy and his wife. We went camping. Hit some sporting events. She posted half a dozen pictures on Facebook during the ten days I was there. Good thing, too, because as soon as the Bieler kid went missing, my editor called to tell me he was handing my research over to the police. If I hadn't had an ironclad alibi, I'd probably be awaiting trial right now. So, as much as I hate what happened, and as much as I know their parents are worried, I can't be the one to submit this to the police. Especially not after what happened to Tamara."

It takes me a moment to place the name. "The school counselor you mentioned? What happened?"

He snorts. "Robbery gone wrong, they're saying. Yesterday up near Charlottesville, where she moved earlier this year. Last time we spoke, the psychic kid who was her main source on all this had disappeared, too. Wouldn't be surprised if she's dead, along with her mom. I was an idiot to go check this out for her, but like I told her, and like I told your boss, my involvement ends here." Skolnick shoves the file folder toward us. "The pictures are in there. It's the Clary girl, I'm positive. Just give me my money and let me get the hell out of here. I don't want to be responsible for any more bodies, and I sure as hell don't want to become one."

My hand shakes as I remove the contents of the folder. Magda didn't say anything about having to look at pictures of dead kids, and I suck in a sharp breath when I see the first one.

"It's her," Skolnick repeats. "She's even wearing the same clothes as when she was reported missing. I've got a printout of the AMBER Alert."

The other pictures are more graphic. I can't make it beyond the first two. It's definitely the Clary girl. Even close up, it's hard to tell the cause of death. Her clothes are ripped, and most of the flesh is missing from one of her arms.

"Animals," Skolnick says, and I nod before I even realize that he means *actual* animals, not the two-legged kind. "The place has been abandoned for a few decades. Coyotes get in. Raccoons. Stray dogs, too—there are a lot of them around here. People get transferred overseas, can't afford to take them, too lazy to find them a new home." I shiver. It's partly from revulsion at the idea of someone's former pet mauling this poor girl's body and partly from the slow drizzle that's starting to fall.

Aaron shields the photos from the rain with the file folder as he looks through them. "Where were these taken?"

"A few miles north, just off Highway 24. There's a bunch of federal land up that way, donated by the Rockefeller family. Used to be some sort of resort—golf course, horse stables, and so on. Now it's all rotted and falling apart. People go up to Overhills Lake to hunt and fish these days, and there've always been a few who would ignore the posted warnings and go exploring in the ruins. Teenage kids looking for a place to drink or screw. I'm surprised someone hasn't stumbled on her body before now, although it was in one of the smaller cabins. And trespassing on federal lands has gotten a bit riskier under the current administration, so maybe they're steering clear. I wasn't exactly happy about scaling that fence, myself, but Tamara was freaking out about this kid's visions and . . . Anyway, I'm *out*. Wish I'd told Tamara no the first time. Might be better for the Clarys just to keep hoping than to know their kid ended up like that."

Aaron finishes with the photos and gives me a nod. I tuck them, along with the rest of Skolnick's papers, into the folder and then give Skolnick the envelope with his name on it.

He thumbs through the bills inside, then stands, stuffing the envelope into the pocket of his jeans. For a couple of seconds, he just looks at us. "This wasn't part of the bargain, but . . . I got something else Tamara Blake sent me. The last interview she did, just before they found her. Give me your number, and once I'm out of town, I'll send it to you."

Skolnick enters Aaron's number into his phone. "One more thing, and I'm telling you this as a favor. You two look like you're maybe a year out of high school. This Magda Bell person needs her ass kicked for sending you into the middle of this. I don't know how things work over in Great Britain, but if she thinks your fake business creds will get you into any schools in the US of A, she's crazy. They'll want a government-issued ID. The parents of the kids on that list you keep glancing down at? They're scared, and they have reason to be. They're not going to talk to you, because they want to stay alive. They want their freaky kids to stay alive, too."

Skolnick turns back just before he reaches the sidewalk. "The smartest thing you could do is get back into your car and get the hell out of here. A person who lines little kids up and executes them gangland style is someone *you do not* want to cross."

CHAPTER SIX

Fayetteville, North Carolina
November 2, 2019, 4:33 p.m.

Aaron and I exchange a confused look. The Clary girl's body was grue-some, but there's nothing to suggest a gangland-style execution. I didn't even see a bullet wound.

"Should I go after him?" Aaron asks as Skolnick jogs down the sidewalk.

"Do you think he actually knows anything else?"

"Probably not. I'm guessing that last comment was based on the information from Blake that he promised to send later."

Back at the car, I text Magda, promising to send the contents of Skolnick's thumb drive when we get back to the main computer. Her reply is almost instantaneous.

Next interview is B. Pruitt. Offer $3K reward for info about missing kids. Also inquire re: twins.

"Have you checked the list for twins?" Aaron asks.

"I skimmed through. No duplicate last names on the list. Do you know what exactly Magda's twins . . . do?"

"Nope. Mom doesn't know either. She told me she tried to politely steer the conversation in that direction when she and Magda were discussing my abilities and Taylor's, but—"

Aaron cuts himself off abruptly, and I can tell from the set of his jaw that he's angry. Which I've learned almost certainly means he's thinking about Daniel. And since I don't want to talk about Daniel, I pretend to be absorbed in the list.

He drives in silence for several minutes, and I can feel the tension, like he's trying really hard not to go there. But eventually he blurts out, "Does my mom know? About Daniel, I mean? That he can alter people's thoughts. Memories."

I feel Daniel stirring in the background, but I already know the answer. "No. He never told her."

"But how does a kid *hide* something like that? You'd think she'd have caught on at some point." When I don't respond, he says, "I know you said you didn't want to get in the middle of this, but—"

I cut him off with a bitter laugh. "Oh, I'm already in the middle, Aaron. I don't have any choice. But I *do not* want to argue with you. Even indirectly. You Quinns seem to be all about arguing. You squabble one minute, and then you're fine the next. But I'm not good with conflict. It ties my stomach in a knot. Same with Deo. When you grow up in foster care, arguments frequently end with someone getting hurt. And all too often, that someone is you."

He doesn't speak again until we pull up next to the RV. Taylor's parking skills leave much to be desired—at least a foot of camper hangs out onto the drive.

I start to get out of the car, but Aaron pulls me back.

"I'm sorry, okay? I don't want you in the middle of this either. And I'm not angry at you. It's just . . . really, *really* awkward talking to you, knowing he can hear everything I say. This is the brother who would rat me out for the slightest infraction of house rules, the one who always ruined everything. Who gave me endless grief about using my abilities—abilities I can't exactly turn off—and here I find out he's been a hypocrite all along."

I was trying to keep him and Taylor safe. Why can't he get that?

I don't answer Daniel. I just push him back behind the wall. Bullheadedness seems to be as much a Quinn family trait as arguing.

"But worst of all," Aaron says, "I finally find a girl that I really care about, and Daniel is closer to her than I am. That's so messed up."

I blink and stare at him. He's jealous? That's what this is all about? A tiny part of me is flattered, but mostly I'm just pissed.

"Daniel and I are not *close*! He's just . . . I'm *stuck* with him, so don't—" I take a deep breath to calm myself. "You know what? I'm not doing this. You and me . . . we do not discuss Daniel. We do not discuss your feelings about Daniel, your history with Daniel, or the many reasons you want to smack Daniel. I'm not going to facilitate your stupid sibling rivalry."

I slam the door for emphasis and head for the camper. But Aaron hurries around the front of the car to head me off.

"Anna, wait." His eyes are pleading. Sad hazel puppy-dog eyes. My anger melts away quickly, so maybe the whole flattered vs. pissed thing was a closer call than I thought.

"You're right. I just keep making things worse. I don't mean to, it's just . . . I'm sorry." He wraps his arms around me, and even though I feel like I should resist, I can't. The tension floats away as I breathe him in. He always smells a bit like a pine forest to me. Or maybe a pine candle is a better description, since it's like I'm wrapped in this warm, safe glow that kindles a tiny flame at my core.

"I'll try harder. Promise." He tips my face up to meet his eyes. "Are we good?"

"We're good."

He stares into my eyes for a long time. I'm certain he's going to kiss me, so I reinforce my walls to make sure Daniel doesn't disrupt us. I close my eyes, open my mouth slightly . . . and then I feel his lips against my forehead.

I stand there, feeling stupid, as he pulls down the stairs for the RV. Yes, I know *why* he didn't kiss me. I even kind of get it. We both know we're not really alone. But it still feels a lot like I've just been friend-zoned.

The ozone smell hits my nose as soon as Taylor opens the camper door, before I even see Deo. He's leaning against the wall, like he doesn't entirely trust his legs to support him, as he rummages through the RV's tiny pantry. Even though he looks weak, relief floods through me. Deo is up. He's dressed. He's on the prowl in search of food.

And for the first time since we left The Warren, his clothes match. He ditched the ratty sweatpants and T-shirt and is now wearing his green ensemble. It's not his favorite, and the dark-green pants are slightly wrinkled from being stashed in his duffel, but even his socks match. He looks like he might have run a comb through his black hair as well.

I know that this could be only a temporary reprieve, based on what Jaden and Daniel told me about the drug. But, hey, I'll take what I can get.

Aaron is right behind me on the steps. He goes rigid and then backs up, his expression strained and nervous.

"I'm . . . um . . . I'm going to check on some . . . things. Out in the truck."

I'm torn between wanting to follow him and wanting to talk to Deo.

"Taylor? Maybe you could go help Aaron?"

Deo heads toward the table with the box of Cheerios. Taylor grabs an elbow to steady him. He gives her an odd look but doesn't pull away.

"Yeah. Sure," Taylor says. "Just let me get Deo settled first. And grab some shoes." Once Deo is at the table, she heads back to where she stores her things, adding over her shoulder, "He already ate the soup. And your leftovers. Bottomless freakin' pit."

I carry a bowl, a spoon, and the milk over to where Deo is sitting, being careful to keep my distance.

"So you're feeling better?"

"Yeah."

"You had me worried there, turning down pizza. And *bacon*."

"You're making that up. I'd never turn down bacon."

"How's your arm?"

"Better," he says around a mouthful of cereal. "Still sore, but it's not throbbing like it was last night."

"Um . . . you probably mean night before last. You sort of skipped last night. What about the fever?"

"Down about three degrees, so . . . about where I *told* you it was last time you asked me." He gives a weak version of his usual grin.

Taylor comes back in, now wearing shoes and a sweater. "I'll stay close. In case you need me."

Deo's eyebrow quirks up, and once she's gone he asks, "So . . . what did I miss? Last thing I remember, Taylor was giving me dagger eyes. When I wake up, you're nowhere to be found, and she's dishing out the fever meds and . . ." He colors slightly, more noticeable now that his brown skin is so pale, and then shakes it off. "Helping me to the bathroom. What made her go all Night Nurse?"

"Well, for one thing, she knows about Daniel."

"How?"

"She and Aaron sort of overheard me talking. Yes," I continue, in response to his look, "out loud. To Daniel. Something surprised me, and . . . anyway, Taylor seems to be handling her brother being in my head better than him being in a coma."

"Okay." Deo gives me a little *gimme-more* gesture with his free hand. "That explains Taylor, but it doesn't explain you. You don't just *ask* about my fever . . . you do that mom thing where you put the inside of your wrist against my forehead or my neck. Plus, right now, you're looking at me like I might break. What do you know that I don't?"

No sense putting it off. Deo is way beyond tenacious when it comes to ferreting out secrets. "It's the injection," I begin, and then kind of stall out.

"Yes. I kind of figured that part out by myself."

I sigh. "There's this weird side effect, D." I explain what Daniel and Jaden told me about the amplifying serum, how he seems to be operating as a signal booster for me and Aaron. But when I get to the part about Sonia, the girl who died, I stop. Jaden picks up on my hesitation.

Deo needs to know, Anna. His body, his mind.

It will scare him.

Jaden gives a mental shrug and then continues.

Fifteen ain't a little kid. Would you have wanted to know?

And yes, of course I would have, so I take a deep breath and spill the rest.

117

He shovels in more Cheerios as I talk, clearly going for nonchalant. But his hand shakes slightly on the third bite, and then he puts the spoon down.

"It's going to be okay, though. Magda Bell has the vial I took from Cregg's lab. She knows someone who is going to examine it. We'll find a cure . . . an antidote. I promise."

Deo huffs something between a sigh and a chuckle. We both know I'm making promises I have no real power to keep.

"So, Daniel and Jaden only know of that one other . . . amp?"

"Yes. And this might not even be the same formula. That was months ago."

"And you just get a bit of one of those visions when you touch me? That's it—no other ill effects?"

I nod. "Just the vision."

He reaches across the table, his hand hovering a few inches over my arm. "Not that I don't believe you. I just want to see if I feel anything when it happens. You okay with that?"

"Yeah." I lean back against the padded bench so I don't smack my head on the table. "Go for it."

The high-pitched hum begins before Deo's hand even connects. I make it to the part of the vision where I realize I'm holding a piece of paper in my palm, and then I'm once again looking at Deo, who is yanking his hand back to his side of the table so fast it's like he received a static shock.

"You okay, D?"

"Yeah. I felt . . . kind of a tingle. And, do you smell anything odd? It's almost like . . ." He sniffs the air, then makes a face, trying to pin down the odor.

"Like the Metro, right?"

"A little. Although, in some ways, it's more of a feeling than a smell. You know the way the inside of your nose feels when you come inside after being out in the cold?"

"We've all noticed it. I think it's a little stronger now, actually. Whatever it is, it's coming from you. Deo and Jaden said it's a side effect of the injections."

He sniffs the skin on his forearm and then wrinkles his nose. "Would a shower help?"

I grin. "It couldn't hurt. But I don't think you're quite up to that yet."

"Later, then. Where were you guys?"

I catch him up on the other events of the past few days, including our interview with Skolnick and the creepy texts from Cregg.

"Yeah, Taylor told me about the messages. I read the ones he sent me, but they didn't make any sense. So, what's next? Did Aaron call the police to report the girl's body?"

"No. Magda wants us to locate the other missing kids before we pull in the police. We're supposed to talk to some teacher tomorrow. Offer her a reward. I'm . . . not exactly sure we should do that, though."

"Why not?"

"Well, she's a teacher. Some of these kids were her students, and all we're doing is asking her to help us find them. What if she's a person of conscience?"

"Even people of conscience can use a little extra cash."

"True. But—think of it this way. How would Kelsey have felt if someone had offered her money for any of the extra things she did for us?"

He gives me a little shrug of admission. "She'd be insulted."

"Exactly."

"Have you heard from her? Dr. K, I mean."

"Not directly. But Aaron's mom says Kelsey is petitioning the state to give her legal guardianship over you."

"Whoa. Can she *do* that? And, hey . . . what about you?"

I smile at the indignant note in his voice. "I'll be eighteen before the paperwork could even be filed, kiddo. And yeah, apparently she *can*, since she's closing her practice. Do you think Carla will give up her parental rights, though?"

"Don't know," he says. "Depends on whether she's currently letting Patrick use her as a punching bag."

Carla is Deo's mom, although I use that term very loosely, since she tends to side with Patrick, Deo's abusive stepfather, rather than her own child. Even though Deo doesn't remember, I'm pretty sure the burn scars on his arm are from Patrick, and anyone who would stay with a man who did that to her child doesn't deserve parental rights. About once a year, Carla gets fed up with Patrick abusing her and waltzes back into Deo's life, because she's lonely now and he's her only kid. And every single time, she goes back to Patrick and tries to coerce Deo into coming, too—which would mean pretending to be someone he's not, because Patrick is a homophobic jerk who insists that Deo "act like a real boy" as long as he's under his roof.

The last time this parental charade played itself out was a few weeks before I picked up Molly. One of Deo's former foster parents took it upon herself to share with Carla the fact that Deo seemed to have a crush on a girl for a change. Not exactly breaking news, since Deo is bisexual and has always been attracted to people based on personality regardless of how their private parts are configured. But Carla seized on it, thinking that all it would take was some persistent discipline, something that Patrick excels at dishing out, and her boy would be "normal" and they could be a "real family" again.

Deo's old enough to recognize the pattern with his mom but not so old that it doesn't hurt. Not so old that he doesn't still harbor a tiny bit of hope that maybe this time his mom will choose him instead of Patrick.

I reach over and very nearly squeeze his hand before I remember that's now verboten.

"I'm okay." He gives me a tired smile as he pushes his mostly empty bowl of Cheerios to the side. "Carla's games don't bother me anymore. Living with Kelsey would be awesome. Assuming we ever get back to Maryland . . ."

He retreats to his bunk, still a little wobbly. I'm glad he grabs our old laptop and his earbuds to take with him, rather than simply collapsing into the bed.

It's progress. And even if it's only temporary, I'll take it.

CHAPTER SEVEN

Fayetteville, North Carolina
November 3, 2019, 11:36 a.m.

My nose comes to life before the rest of me. Some wonderful person has made coffee. Aaron and Taylor are talking softly, too softly for me to follow anything other than the rise-and-fall rhythm of their voices, and I drift off again for a minute or two. It doesn't last, though, since my brain is harping on our assigned task for the day.

Bernadette Pruitt, our designated interviewee, is a fifth-grade teacher at Baker Elementary, the school that one of the kids on our list attends. More importantly, Pruitt taught at one of the four Department of Defense elementary schools in the area until last year when budget cuts forced her to take a lower-paying position at Baker. Magda's theory is that she'll have information about what's going on inside Bragg, and the salary cut might mean she's disgruntled enough to talk, especially if we wave the promise of a reward.

After talking to Skolnick, however, I'm less convinced of that. He was definitely correct about Magda's cover story having gigantic holes. Maybe in the UK it would be possible for us to stroll into the school offices, wave bogus badges from a law firm, and state that we were investigating for a potential class action suit against a pharmaceutical company. Or maybe Magda's kids have never actually attended a school, and she's woefully out of touch.

We toyed with the idea of snagging a discarded badge—there are always a few tossed into the trash outside of a school. In my experience, the photographs are so awful that we'd probably skate right past security. But the names wouldn't match the credentials Magda provided.

So we're subverting Magda's plan and doing a stakeout near the school this afternoon. We'll follow Pruitt and ask our questions outside of school property. The address and phone number we have for Pruitt are a bit dated, but we do have her photo, the make and model of the car she bought last month, and the tag number, thanks to Sam. I'm still not excited about the prospect of interviewing her, even off school property, but it beats the hell out of getting arrested for trespassing in a place surrounded by security cameras and guards.

When I finally drag myself out of bed, Taylor is the only one in the main cabin. She's stretched out in one of the recliners with a tablet in her lap, Deo's purple earbuds in her ears, and glasses with dark-green frames perched on her nose. I've never seen her in glasses. Her drawing pad sits on the table next to her chair, and at first I think she's trying to do a remote viewing. But the pad is covered with handwriting, small and neat, not sketches.

Taylor finishes whatever she's jotting down and pushes the glasses on top of her head. "Good morning, Anna. Good morning, Daniel. Although, if we're aiming for accuracy, it's nearly afternoon."

I sigh. "Good morning, Taylor. And you should add Jaden if we're going to do a full roll call every morning."

She shrugs dismissively. "Jaden's dead. And I never met him when he was alive, so I doubt he's too upset at my lack of greeting."

Jaden laughs.

Nah, man, she's way wrong. Tell her I'm wounded. *Mortally* wounded.

I tsk. "Never knew you were such a bigot against the dead, Taylor."

Her eyebrows shoot up. "Oh, wow. I didn't even think of it, but this means Daniel is *un*dead. So . . . is he more vampire or zombie?"

"Hmm. Good question. I'll go with vampire. He's a royal pain—"

Taylor cuts me off with a groan. "Pain in the neck? That's worse than the puns Aaron comes up with."

I squeeze past Taylor's outstretched feet to go check on Deo.

"He's still asleep, and he's *fine*. I checked on him a few minutes ago. He was up in the middle of the night raiding the pantry, so I guess being sick threw his clock out of whack. And before you ask, Aaron's off getting fishing gear."

"Fishing gear? You're kidding, right?"

"Nope. It was his idea. I was online scouting out the area where Skolnick says he saw the body, and, while it *is* on military property, that section is open for hunting and fishing. So Aaron went on post and registered for a permit to fish at Overhills Lake. We can hike over to the abandoned resort buildings from there. The area is open 24/7 most days, but they've got some sort of military exercise scheduled beginning tomorrow. So we'll either have to go after you get back from talking to the Pruitt woman or wait until next week."

"No," I say. The idea of leaving Nicki Clary's body out there that long is appalling. "Sooner is definitely better."

I snag a breakfast bar from the pantry and pour the last of the coffee into a mug.

"Make more if you emptied the pot," Taylor says. "I have work to do."

"Diving right into your school assignments?"

"Ha. No. I sent Mom a text and told her not to bother. If I can't finish with my friends, I'll take the GED. School isn't exactly high on my list of priorities right now."

"Then what are you doing?" I ask as I reload the coffee maker.

"Research." There's a very explicit, unspoken *duh* at the end. "And now that you're finally awake, I can shift the interview to the big screen. It's always easier to spot the lies when their faces are big."

"Interview?"

"Yeah." She clicks the link to send the content on the tablet to the display over the fireplace. "With Cregg. It aired last night."

I look up, expecting to see the face that's visited so many of my nightmares during the past week. But it's not Graham Cregg. It's his father. That's better, although there's still something about the man's expression—his fixed, ingratiating smile—that unnerves me.

Senator Ronald Cregg is in his late sixties, about fifty pounds heavier than his son, with a fringe of silver hair and rimless glasses. He might have been handsome when he was younger, but he looks like an elderly accountant now, the kind who would know all of the tax loopholes.

Right now, Cregg—no, I can't think of him as just Cregg. That name is too firmly connected in my head with his nightmare of a son. Right now, *the Senator* is parked in the middle third of the screen. The younger man to his left is introduced as a spokesperson for the FBI Joint Terrorism Task Force. To his right is a woman in her early fifties, identified as Juanita Breyer.

"She looks . . . familiar."

Taylor raises one eyebrow and clicks pause. "She should. Governor of Texas? Switched over to Unify America just after the 2018 elections? Breyer is Cregg's main opponent for the UA nomination. You don't pay much attention to politics, do you?"

"Not the minor parties. I mean, obviously, I've *heard* of Unify America. I'm just not familiar with Breyer."

I'm tempted to add, in my defense, that I know far more than Taylor does about politics in the 1950s and 1960s, when my hitcher Emily MacAllister campaigned for Adlai Stevenson and later for Kennedy. I could also give Taylor a lengthy lecture on the political factions of post–World War I Germany and the rise of McCarthyism in the United States. And I'm very familiar with the politics of the Rwandan Civil War, thanks to another hitcher, Didier. He was lucky enough to immigrate in the late 1980s but could do nothing to help his family members who were still in his native country when the genocide began.

"Well, I would certainly *hope* you've heard of Unify America," she says, settling back into the recliner. "You could have had your head in a bucket of sand for the past two years and still have heard of UA."

She has a point. After the tumultuous 2016 election and its aftermath, Senator Cregg and a handful of others in Congress and at the state level saw an opportunity to spin off their own brand of politics, pitching it as "a reasonable alternative for reasonable people." Several dozen legislators and a lot of state officials formally switched their party affiliation, hoping to pull in disaffected voters from both main parties. They made some progress during midterm elections, thanks largely to being extremely well funded. While they're still nowhere near as strong as the two major parties, it was the best showing for a third party in decades.

Taylor clicks play again, and once the introductions conclude, an inset window pops up with a familiar video of a large building blazing against the night sky. It's Memorial Hall, the building that Deo and I found ourselves in when we escaped from The Warren, and this is the same clip that we watched while waiting on Daniel to come out of surgery. The newscaster repeats the mostly bogus story we heard before about a domestic terrorist group funding its operations through profits from a human trafficking ring.

"Senator Cregg, I'd like to start with you, since many of the questions that investigators have center on the involvement of your son, Graham, who was injured in the attack. Can you give us an update on his condition and how he came to be at the facility when the fire broke out?"

"I'd be happy to, Joseph. First, Graham is doing much better. He sustained serious burns on his hands and torso. While he's currently in stable condition, it was touch-and-go earlier this week, and recovery will likely take longer than usual due to some unrelated health issues that he's facing. As to your other question, as you may know, Graham is on the board of Decathlon Services. He's also CEO of Python Diagnostic, a security logistics firm that operates out of Aberdeen."

"And he's a psychotic murderer," I mumble. "Don't forget that one."

"Earlier this year," the Senator says, "he grew concerned about some suspicious port activity in the area, and he had some people keeping an eye on the situation, including one who managed to gain a foothold in the group that was occupying the underground bunker. Last week, that young man—who is currently in a coma due to injuries he received in the attack—notified Graham that the group, which he referred to as a terrorist cell, appeared to be splitting into two factions and that violence was brewing. He was worried about the safety of several dozen young women and children who were being held, presumably against their will."

"You lying son of a bitch." Taylor wads up a sheet of paper and hurls it at Senator Cregg's face on the TV screen. "Daniel was *not* working for you."

Daniel has a similar reaction.

That takes some nerve. He has a real talent for spin.

What does he gain by pulling you into the story?

I don't know. Extra sympathy points, maybe? Or a tiny bit of truth in his sea of lies that reporters could confirm— at least the hospitalization part—if they go looking?

On the screen, the FBI guy is clearly annoyed. "If I may interject, Senator, the responsible thing would have been to contact the authorities. Perhaps then your son and the young man you mentioned—"

The Senator's opponent is nodding her platinum head in agreement. "That's exactly the point I've been making. This sort of vigilante attitude toward our security—"

"Excuse me, Governor Breyer," the Senator interjects. "I was answering a question concerning the status of my son, and I'd like to finish. As I've already noted, I passed information along to the Department of Homeland Security earlier this year. After months went by with *no official action*, Graham was concerned not just about the national security implications but also about the immediate safety of these young women—concerned enough to personally fly one of Python's helicopters to the location and even enter a burning building to rescue the last few from the fire. So it's a bit of a slap in the face to wake up and see that your heroic actions that saved the lives of nineteen people, most under the age of eighteen, are being used as political fodder not just by the Washington elite, which doesn't surprise me, quite frankly, but also by members of my own party."

All three of them begin talking over each other now, and Taylor lowers the volume. When the news anchor finally gets control of the conversation again, he gives the other two guests a few minutes to basically repeat their talking points and then returns to Senator Cregg. There are a couple of questions about his connections to Decathlon Services Group, the parent company of Python, which the Senator dodges with the practiced grace of a seasoned politician, noting that he has long since terminated any ties to the company and it's only his son who has an ongoing relationship with Decathlon.

The next question, however, seems to take him by surprise.

"Senator Cregg, have you seen the article in today's *Guardian*?"

"No, I'm afraid I haven't."

"Okay, I'll summarize quickly. The story links Decathlon Services Group to a covert government program that was ostensibly closed in the mid-1990s. Something that originated with a military project called Stargate."

The Senator shakes his head. "If you do your research, you'll see that links between DSG and that program were minor. They handled some logistical arrangements for the Delphi Project, much as they have for hundreds—no, thousands—of other government initiatives."

"Okay, but to be clear, this wasn't just your average government initiative. The article claims that the program was attempting to create psychic superspies—maybe even supersoldiers. And the recent terrorist attack and your son's involvement have spotlighted Port Deposit and the surrounding area. The residents have some . . . interesting stories that give weight to the claims about the Delphi Project. Spontaneous fires, objects that move on their own—"

Breyer shakes her head incredulously. "Are we really going to talk conspiracy theories? There are so many other things that we need to be discussing—civil liberties, the national debt, foreign relations. This is a waste of time."

The Senator ignores her. "The DSG allegations are spurious, but I will note that the other issues you just mentioned are under investigation. It's quite possible that some . . . military technology . . . was acquired by the terrorist group that was occupying the Port Deposit facility. This is something I warned the current administration about several months ago after there were rumors of lax security surrounding the two military bases where the original research was conducted. The situation is under investigation, but that's really all I can say at this time."

"By *military technology*, do you mean something that could cause the type of activity they've been repor—"

"That's all I can say at this time."

Breyer rolls her eyes. "This is far from the first instance Senator Cregg has teased the media with ludicrous allegations in order to draw attention to his campaign. Tell me, Senator, do you also have information connecting the government to the Illuminati? Or maybe you've uncovered new information about the aliens at Area 51?"

The Senator's eyes flash, but he covers quickly with his usual smile. "If I *did* have information on any of those things, it would be classified, and not something that I could share outside of committee. You'll just have to keep an eye on the news like everyone else so that you'll know when I have more information."

"Ooh, burn," Taylor says as she switches off the TV. *"You're just a measly governor. I have access to information you could never even dream of."*

"He's bluffing, though. Right? I mean, why would he reveal anything about the Delphi program. If they dig too deep, won't that just point toward his son? And eventually toward him?"

"Maybe," she says. "He's a slimy devil, though, and he's very good at misdirection. Most of what he just said was false, but . . . he drops in little bits of fact, too. For example, if I didn't know he was lying through his perfectly capped teeth about Daniel working for Cregg, I'd probably believe him."

❖   ❖   ❖

Fayetteville, North Carolina
November 3, 2019, 3:40 p.m.

Aaron casts a wary eye toward the building. "Yeah, I know it's an elementary school, but it's still a *school*. You think fifth-graders in detention don't have anger-management issues?"

I laugh, even though I can tell he's only half teasing. "I don't think detention is even a thing in elementary school. And the kids have already gone home."

"Not all of them . . ." He looks glumly off to the right where a few dozen kids in the after-school program are playing kickball and climbing on the playground equipment. They seem fairly carefree, but judging from Aaron's expression, one of those little tykes has a mean streak.

I glance back down at the information sheet on Pruitt, even though I've pretty much committed the details and her photo to memory. She's forty-three, African American, married. Her husband has been deployed to the Mexican border for the past few months. One kid is in high school and the other is enrolled at a local community college. She's been teaching for nearly twenty years at various schools around the country.

Aaron glances over at the picture. "She looks like there are many, many places she'd rather be."

He's right. Pruitt's expression is only a notch above a scowl, and my hope that we'd be interviewing a teacher who had only her students' best interests at heart fades a bit.

"Maybe she has bad teeth and doesn't smile for pictures?" I suggest.

Once again, I raise the cheap binoculars we picked up earlier today, and watch. A few minutes later, the side door to the school opens, and another cluster of teachers straggles out. This is the third wave of employees, and at first I think we're going to be waiting a bit longer. But Pruitt catches the door with her shoulder just before it closes, holding it open for another teacher. They chat for a moment. Pruitt grins and throws her head back, laughing at something the other woman says. So much for my theory about bad teeth.

Aaron starts the car, and we follow when she pulls her black SUV out onto the street. It's clear that he's tailed a car more than once. He stays back, never close enough to spook Pruitt, although it doesn't look like she's paying much attention, anyway. She keeps gesturing with her hands, so she must be talking to someone on her car phone.

About three miles from the school, Pruitt pulls into a shopping center. We park a few spaces away and approach her as she closes the hatchback of her car.

"Are you recording?" Aaron asks.

"Not yet." I click the voice memo and then tuck the phone back into my skirt pocket, reminding myself that this really *is* legal in North Carolina, even if recording someone without her consent feels wrong to me.

"Ms. Pruitt?" Aaron says.

"Yes?"

He does the introductions, following Magda's script. Bernadette Pruitt's eyes were guarded from the moment she saw us, but the gates come all the way down as soon as Aaron says the word *students*.

"I told you people last year, I'm not sharing information about my pupils or their families. If the government wants that information, they'll have to get a warrant. If my supervisor tells me to talk to you, I will."

"We're not with the government, Ms. Pruitt."

She gives us both a head-to-toe assessment. "That might be the first true thing you've said. But if so, what I told you goes double. You need to get back in your car and leave me alone."

"We're prepared to offer a three-thousand-dollar reward if you have . . . useful infor . . . mation."

Aaron trails off as Pruitt's eyes narrow to thin, dark slits, just before she turns on her heel and marches off toward Food Lion.

"We're trying to get some help for these kids and their parents," I say, hurrying to catch up with her. "Aren't you worried that more children will disappear?"

I really hope that the question will tap at Pruitt's conscience. But when she turns back to face us, it's clear that it had the opposite effect. She glances down at the badges around our necks and snatches her phone from her purse.

Fortunately, we're ready. Magda has a recording enabled on the other end, and a live person who will confirm our cover if anyone clicks through the automated options. So Aaron just smiles and holds his badge closer so that she can see the phone number at the bottom.

"I don't blame you at all," he says. "You *should* verify our story."

"Sugar, I don't give a damn about verifying your story. That's not my job. You're harassing me when I told you under no uncertain terms to leave me alone. On top of that, you just tried to bribe me. So I think I'll let the police verify your story."

A woman who's loading her toddler into one of those fire-truck grocery carts casts a nervous glance in our direction. She's too far away to hear what we're saying, but Pruitt's body language is conveying her anger loud and clear.

"And," Pruitt says, "given that we had six kids up and vanish in the past week, I think they'll be very interested in what you have to say."

I take an involuntary step backward as Bernadette Pruitt presses the button on her phone.

CHAPTER EIGHT

Fayetteville, North Carolina
November 3, 2019, 4:18 p.m.

"Let's go," Aaron says softly. I start to follow him, even though I'm certain that Pruitt will complete the call either way. She'll tell the police what we look like. The car we're driving. I certainly would if I were in her position.

Daniel zooms to the front of my head so fast that I nearly trip over my feet.

Let me nudge her.

I want to tell him no. I don't like his ability on general principle, and I definitely don't like the idea of giving him control. And we haven't tested this. Yes, I picked up Jaden's visions when I picked up Jaden. I also had the abilities of Oksana and the Furies back in the lab, until they jumped ship. But that doesn't necessarily mean Daniel will be able to work through my body to "nudge" this woman. All of the others were dead. Daniel is not.

On the other hand, Pruitt is calling the police right this minute. I'm not sure we have another choice. And since I'm certain that Aaron wouldn't be cool with his brother walking off with my body, I slide back. Although, to be honest, it feels more like I'm sucked back by the sheer force of Daniel rushing forward.

"Hang up." The voice is still mine but somehow deeper. More commanding. "You made a mistake."

A muscle twitches in Pruitt's face, and her thumb clicks the screen to stop the call. "I made a . . . mistake." Her voice is flat.

"We're trying to help. You'll come with us and tell us what you know."

She nods. "You're trying to help. I'll . . ." The twitch hits her face again, and I can tell she's fighting it.

"You'll *come with us*." Daniel stresses the words this time.

"I'll come with you." No twitch, but her voice rises slightly at the end, like she wonders why in hell she's agreeing to this.

And I understand how she feels, completely and totally, because Daniel's words echo in my mind, and I find myself thinking, *I'll come with you.*

Ha. As if I have a choice. I try to shake my head to clear it, but nothing actually moves since Daniel is now in control of my motor functions.

Daniel takes the woman's arm and leads her toward our rental car. His gait is almost as unsteady as hers, however. I feel a bit like I'm walking in stilettos, something I've done exactly twice and never for more than a few minutes.

Aaron just stands in the middle of the parking lot, mouth open.

"Are you coming?" Daniel asks, glancing back at him. "I mean, I'd be happy to handle the questioning myself, but you have the car keys. So either hand them over or get moving before we attract even more attention."

There's no *push* this time, no coercion when he speaks to Aaron, but his—*my? our?*—tone makes it clear that Daniel is losing patience.

Aaron follows, still with that look of shock. And even though I can't help thinking, *Way to screw up my love life, Daniel*, I also know that's really not the most important thing right this minute.

My reflection in the car window ripples as we approach. One second it's me holding on to Pruitt's arm, and the next it's Daniel. He's wearing his uniform from The Warren—his Fudd uniform, as Jaden would say.

This isn't new. I saw Molly this way on several occasions when she was strongly present. When she was angry, or upset, or just close to the front of my mind. I also remember vividly the shock of seeing my nine-year-old face morph into that of a woman in her eighties when I saw Emily in the mirror once. There were random glimpses of a few of my other hitchers, too. And I saw Myron in the mirror more times than I care to remember.

Pruitt slides into the back seat without any sign of resistance, and I catch one more glimpse of Daniel's face in the window—dark-blond hair, his square jaw clenched.

How long can you do this? Control her, I mean.

Not nearly as long as I could in my own body. Stop distracting me.

Oh, that is rich, coming from the guy I'm currently allowing to borrow my body. But I retreat a bit further, back toward the mental cabinets that house the memories of former tenants.

Jaden is back in the cobwebby corners, too. It's the first time I've been inside my own head when I was carrying more than one hitcher, and for some reason, I imagined I'd just hear him and kind of sense his movements, the way I do when I'm in control. But I actually *see* him.

It's weird. He looks the same as he did when I first saw his body in the lab—same blood-drenched clothes, same bullet wound on the side of his head. The only difference is that his eyes are open now and his face is no longer slack and expressionless.

> Hey, if it's weird, that's on you. Your head, your rules. Maybe you're one of those visual learners. Need to see a picture.

> *I am, actually. But I think we both could do without seeing you like this.*

> Made my peace with it already, Anna. And it's kinda like drivin' an ugly car, anyway—it's mostly everyone else stuck lookin' at it. My question is why you don't see Daniel in a hospital gown, or all bloody from getting shot.

The question takes me aback, because I'm not sure *why* that's the case. But I can't stop to puzzle things out right now. The waves of annoyance flowing from Daniel suggest that our conversation is distracting him, and while I kind of like having him discover exactly how annoying that sort of distraction can be, I know his focus needs to be on getting answers from Pruitt.

Aaron pulls the car over to the far end of the parking lot, away from potentially prying eyes.

Daniel stares intently at Pruitt. "You're going to answer my questions, okay? Because you want to help."

Her eyes narrow slightly, but there's no twitch this time. She just nods.

"*Our* questions," Aaron says. "I've got a whole list of things that I'm supposed to ask."

I feel my eyes roll, and then Daniel says, "Fine, Aaron. But I don't know how many times I can . . . *convince* her. So I'm telling her to spill what she knows. If there's anything she misses, and if we have time, then you can jump in."

Aaron agrees, although he doesn't seem especially pleased with the arrangement.

Daniel turns back to the woman. "So, Mrs. Pruitt, I need to know about some of the children you've taught. Specifically, the ones who can do things they *shouldn't* be able to. Everything you can remember, from the beginning. When you first noticed what they could do, whether the school administrators and military leadership are aware of what these kids can do. And this conversation is entirely private. No one will ever know you've spoken with us."

There are a few beats of silence, and then Pruitt begins talking at a rapid clip, as if she wants to spill everything as quickly as possible so that this will end sooner. I'm perfectly okay with that, since I'd rather not prolong the experience either. As was the case when Molly took over, it's like I'm watching everything and listening to everything through a sheet of plastic. Only, it seems worse this time. Whenever Daniel sends another mental nudge Pruitt's way every few minutes, to redirect her or keep her on track, I feel it. Blocking Daniel's mental manipulation with my walls was fairly easy when I was on the outside and he was in his own body. Now that we're squished together in a single package, however, not so much.

You feel that, Jaden? Or is it just me?

Yeah. I feel it all right. Don't especially like it, either. You okay?

I nod and fall silent, trying to follow the conversation on the out-side. While I know that I can always listen to the recording later, I want to stay aware of my surroundings. I trust Daniel—okay, I *mostly* trust Daniel—to give my body back. But I really, really hate not being in control.

Pruitt gives a rapid-fire overview of her time with the Department of Defense schools at Fort Bragg. The first year she was at Fort Bragg seemed pretty routine, except for a few odd stories she heard among the teachers. The second year, however, she had a kid named Javier Perez in her class.

"Nice enough kid," she says, "but he had what they call impulsivity issues. He'd blurt things out, disrupt the class. Only after a while, I realize he's not just blurting random stuff. He's blurting out what other kids are thinking. Sometimes, it's things *I'm* thinking, like this one time my bra hurts, and I want to take the damn thing off and shove it in the trash, and he broadcasts that to the whole class. You know how long it takes to restore order when someone says *bra* in a fifth-grade classroom? When I asked him about it, he said he couldn't help it. Said I was just thinking too *loud*."

I definitely sympathize with this Javier kid. I know exactly how hard it can be to shut off someone else's too-loud thoughts inside your own head.

"Did you report it?" Aaron asks.

"No. I wanted to *keep* my job. I just tried to steer clear of him when I could. Tried to get a song running through my head any time thoughts of a personal nature popped up. The kids talked about him, though, about what he could do. Then a month or so later, someone I don't know—someone from the military—stops by and starts asking questions about the kid's so-called impulsivity. And the next thing I hear, Javier is being homeschooled. Which I thought was a good idea, only . . . we started hearing that excuse a lot."

My phone vibrates to signal an incoming call. I guess Daniel forgot it was in my skirt pocket, because he startles.

Pruitt gives him an odd look before continuing. "The next year, I got a firebug. Vanda Carter set her own sleeve on fire while taking an end-of-year exam—worst case of test anxiety I've ever seen."

"Vanda . . ." Aaron glances back down at our list. "That's one of the kids who's missing, isn't it?"

"Exactly," Pruitt says. "Of course, the principal claimed publicly that the girl used a match or a lighter, but she didn't. I was watching her. One minute she's chewing on the end of her eraser, and the next minute she's on fire. A week later, we hear that her parents have decided to . . . you guessed it, homeschool. Got so bad we used that as a code word for kids who had one of these psychic talents . . . we called them *homeschool candidates*. Only there were rumors that the kids weren't being homeschooled at all. That the authorities were keeping those kids in a separate school somewhere on Bragg where they couldn't hurt anyone or attract media attention."

After she was laid off from the school on Fort Bragg, Pruitt thought maybe that would be the end of it. She tried to look on the bright side—wouldn't having a classroom full of normal kids be worth the salary reduction? Only she soon realized that the problem wasn't confined to Fort Bragg. There weren't as many of the bizarrely gifted at Baker Elementary, and most of the teachers simply laughed the stories off as urban legends if anyone asked—since they knew that everyone unwise enough to pursue the issue in the past no longer worked at Baker Elementary.

"One thing was different at the public school. Two years back, a whole slew of investigators swooped in and started asking really detailed questions about classroom behavior. Claimed they were from a foundation that provided financial assistance for families of children on the autistic spectrum. But the actual autistic kids never seemed to qualify for that program, only the kids on the *psychic* spectrum. Even then, interest faded if it was low level—a boy who would occasionally turn in an assignment that hadn't even been assigned yet, or a basketball that seemed to veer off course just enough to swish through the net almost every time this one girl attempted a shot. That kind of stuff. Anything that ended up in the papers, though, like that Bieler kid—"

"Hunter Bieler?" Aaron asks.

Daniel gives his brother a cautionary look for interrupting. Aaron glares in response, and even though it's not really *me* that he's giving the evil eye, I still feel a twinge of hurt.

"That's right," Pruitt says. "Hunter. A friend of mine who teaches first grade had him as a student last year. Had to assign him a seat in the middle of the classroom. Otherwise, he'd tap the wall and make the lights go out, crap like that. The boy was watching out the window one day when the weather was nice, and next thing my friend knows, the little jerk is over by the wall sharpening his pencil. He taps near the outlet, and a split second later, the fire alarm goes off. We've got an unplanned fire drill on our hands, and the Bieler kid—along with everyone else—is out on the lawn in the sunshine. Running around with his buddies rather than working on fractions."

When it's clear that Pruitt is reaching the limit of things she remembers, Daniel and Aaron start to ask more pointed questions. Aaron mentions the school counselor, Tamara Blake, and Pruitt says she didn't know her but definitely knew of her. Blake was apparently one of several cautionary tales that convinced the other teachers and administrators that their heads should be kept in the sand at all times. And that was just because she lost her job. Imagine if they knew she was murdered because she spoke out.

The last question that Daniel asks is the one at the top of Magda's list. "What about twins? Have you heard of any twins who are gifted?"

"Gifted." Pruitt gives a bitter laugh. "*Gifted?* Clearly you've never been around these kids. I have to deal with them as part of my job, but those kids shouldn't be allowed in a classroom. Shouldn't even be allowed to exist. They are a curse from God, not a gift. His judgment for our sins as a nation and—"

YOU WANT TO HELP US.

This time, Daniel's push is more of a shove. It echoes inside my head. Jaden's too, apparently.

Man, he needs to learn to use his indoor voice.

Pruitt's cheek does that weird twitch, and she repeats the words. "I want to help you. What was the question?"

I'm glad to see that Aaron is glaring at Pruitt now, instead of me. Sure, we've both said that these powers are more curse than blessing, but that doesn't mean everyone else can chime in. And there's a difference between being cursed *by* God and being a curse *on others sent by* God. That last claim bothers me a whole lot more.

"Twins," Aaron says. "We asked about twins."

"The only ones I know of are the Bieler kids. That poor woman has lost both of them now. Last year, the girl vanishes. Apparently, it was a custody issue. Their dad is a nutcase hermit out in Wyoming. And now Hunter's gone."

I really want control of my body right now so that I can check the list for Hunter Bieler's sister. I'm almost certain she's not on there.

"Maybe the dad grabbed him, too," Pruitt says. "But with five others disappearing at the same time, that seems unlikely. At least she's still got her older boy, and he's normal, thank God. Maybe it's a blessing in disguise."

If I were in control of my hands, it would be really hard not to whack Pruitt with the clipboard I'm holding. I seriously doubt their mother thinks the disappearance of two of her three kids is a blessing, disguised or otherwise.

Daniel blasts her again, nearly as loud as the last time. "This conversation *never happened*. You passed out in the parking lot. We're going to drive you home."

As Pruitt sits there absorbing this, Daniel slides back—although it really feels more like he stumbles back. He probably won't admit it, but this clearly drained him.

"Thank you for driving me home," Pruitt says in a small, uncertain voice. "I've got a splitting headache."

She's not the only one. It feels like there's a metal band squeezing my skull. I grab a couple of Advil from my bag and dry swallow them, then offer the bottle to Pruitt.

"I can't take those things," Pruitt says. "They eat my stomach up. Do you know if I hit my head? Or do you think I might've had a stroke? Maybe I should go to the hospital instead."

Daniel moves back toward the front, ready to give her another push. But I'm not giving over control again unless it's absolutely necessary.

"No, ma'am," I tell her. "You said earlier that you forgot to eat lunch. Don't you remember?"

She looks confused, and I feel kind of bad about gaslighting her. But then she gives me a hesitant smile and says, "That's right. I remember now." The address Pruitt gives us, which is not the one we have in our files, is nearly thirty miles in the opposite direction from the RV park. Great, just great.

My phone vibrates again as Aaron is pulling out of the parking lot. A text this time.

"Is that you, Anna?" Aaron whispers.

At first, I think he's just asking whether it's *my* phone making the noise, but then I glance over at him and realize the question has a double meaning.

"Yeah, it's me."

"You okay?"

"Really bad headache," I say, slumping down in my seat. "And it's making me queasy."

"Maybe it's a flu going round," Pruitt says from the back seat. "That could be why I wasn't hungry at lunch. I'm always hungry at lunch."

Is this story going to stick with her, Daniel? Or is she going to figure out she's been tricked ten minutes after we drop her at home?

It will stick.

Daniel doesn't sound completely sure, however.

Okay. Fine. *In the past*, it has always stuck. But we're in uncharted waters here, Anna. I've always been in my own body. Persuading people has never given me a headache. So, no, I can't guarantee a damn thing, but . . . the woman would've called the cops fifteen minutes ago if I hadn't jumped in.

We drop Pruitt at her house. Her older daughter thanks us and walks her mom, who still looks shaken, into the house.

For a moment, I feel bad for putting Pruitt through this. Then I remember her nasty comment about Delphi kids—kids she taught, kids she owed at least a little bit of understanding. Maybe she needed shaking up.

I curl up in the car seat and close my eyes, taking deep breaths to curb the nausea and the pain that shoots through my temples each time we hit the slightest bump. It's a good half hour before the Advil I took starts to kick in enough that I can think about anything, and that's when I remember the messages that came in while Daniel was captain of the Good Ship Anna.

My first thought is that it might be Cregg, but Daniel doesn't remember feeling the tickling sensation. When I check, it's two different numbers. The first is a voice mail from Kelsey—her new number and a message to call when I get a free minute or two. I'm sure it's due in part to my throbbing head, but hearing her voice brings tears to my eyes.

The second is a text from Dean Skolnick. No message, just an audio file.

I start to push play, but Aaron asks me to forward the file to Taylor first so that she and Deo are up to speed by the time we get there. "We've only got about an hour until dark, and I'd like to get to the lake before the other fishermen clear out. We'll be less noticeable that way."

So I forward the file to Taylor and then click play.

There's no introduction, just a girl's voice. "It's a bumpy road. Not like potholes, though." She has a faint lisp, which blurs the last two words together. "Uneven. More like a dirt road. Later, when they opened the trunk, I saw a bunch of tall pine trees. But . . . I think they learned something from Nicki running like she did. The boy I was in this time . . . his hands and feet were bound. Although he couldn't move much anyway, because he was piled in the trunk with the other four kids."

A woman asks, "Do you know which *one* of the boys you were . . . seeing through?" The voice is deeper than the girl's, and it seems vaguely familiar, with its hint of a Southern accent.

"I'm pretty sure it was Hunter," the girl replies, the lisp worsening, "because later when they had the other kids in the building, I could see the two girls really good. One of them was right near these animals— like drawings from a children's book—that were painted on the walls in the room. I never got a close-up look at the two boys at the far end, but I saw their feet once I was inside, and they were bigger. So it had to have been Hunter. And he was a sweet little kid. He . . . he didn't deserve this. No way."

The girl is crying now, and another woman's voice, fainter, tells her they can stop if she's too upset.

"No. I want to, Mom. Like you said, maybe she can get the cops there to listen. Maybe they can find the guys who did this . . . or at least find the kids' bodies."

"Take your time," the first woman says. "No rush."

I hit the pause button and replay the last few words. A strange sense of déjà vu hits me. I remember listening to this voice, saying these same words, huddled under the blankets in the bed while Aaron slept. And again, talking to someone different, yesterday on the drive to Fort Bragg.

"What's wrong?" Aaron asks.

"I think I know her. Not personally, but . . . I've listened to several of these interviews. Tamara Blake writes for—or rather, she *wrote* for—*AllGlobalConspiracies*."

I click play again, and we listen to the rest of the interview. The girl describes being inside Hunter's mind as two guys hauled him out of the trunk and carried him inside an abandoned building. The other four children were still knocked out, and Hunter pretended to be unconscious, as well, hoping for a chance to get away. The men lined the kids against the wall and shot them as they slept.

Except for Hunter, who wasn't asleep. When the first shots rang out, he began screaming.

"After Hunter screamed," the girl says, "the man who was bragging about his sex life before starts cursing and saying the kids were all supposed to be asleep. That he didn't sign on for this. So the third person, the woman, shoves the guy out of the way."

The woman? A chill runs through me, and for a moment, I'm certain she means Dacia Badea.

I take a deep breath and rein in my overactive imagination. *Woman with a gun* doesn't necessarily equal Dacia. I've never seen her with a gun. I don't even know if she can shoot. Daniel said Cregg had at least a dozen field agents. It's a little paranoid—not to mention sexist—to assume that Dacia is the only woman doing his dirty work.

The girl continues. "She points the gun straight at Hunter's face. I only saw her briefly, but she didn't look angry like I expected. More sad, really. She said, 'I'll make it quick for you.'"

CHAPTER NINE

Fayetteville, North Carolina
November 3, 2019, 5:37 p.m.

I run the tape back a few seconds and listen again.

"It's Dacia," I tell Aaron. "She's the one who shot Hunter."

"You're sure?"

"Yes. Back at The Warren, she told me she made it quick for Molly. Quicker than she would for me."

We're pulling into the campground now, and it looks . . . wrong, although it takes me a moment to pin down why. The trailer is right where we left it. The truck, however, is gone, and when we get inside, we find that the RV is empty.

That wouldn't unnerve me nearly as much if we hadn't just learned that Dacia was in the area recently. I guess that's not entirely logical, since we know people were here killing adepts—killing kids—but I'm certain Dacia blames me for Lucas's death. And I'm also certain she'd be happy to return the favor by killing Deo.

Aaron calls Taylor, but she doesn't answer. So I try Deo, and after a couple of rings, he picks up.

"Where are you guys?" I ask, trying to tamp down the panic in my voice.

"Um . . . Taylor had to go . . . get something."

I don't think it's a complete lie, but there's definitely something he's leaving out. "Okayyyy. How long do you think you'll be?"

"Don't know. Took maybe fifteen minutes to get here, and . . ." He pauses for a moment. "It looks like she's almost done."

"So . . . I take it you're feeling better, then?"

"Better? Yeah, absolutely, especially now that I'm out of that damned RV and breathing some fresh air. My temperature is normal again. Arm feels fine, too."

"That's . . . great!" I try to sound enthusiastic, but then I remember that the girl at The Warren was better too. Until she wasn't.

Deo, as usual, knows exactly what I'm thinking. "Anna, you're worrying based on a sample size of one. Just a single very unlucky girl. And we don't even know if they gave me the same formula. What's that saying Emily had about borrowing trouble? *Sufficient until the day . . . ?*"

"*Sufficient unto the day is the evil thereof.* And dear God, if you're quoting Emilyisms, the fever must have fried your brain."

While we wait for Taylor and Deo, I go back to the bedroom so I can return Kelsey's call. My plan is to keep the conversation light. Kelsey just lost her job, which means the State of Maryland isn't paying her to be my twice-weekly lifeline anymore. But I'm weak, and it feels so damn good just to talk to her again that I end up spilling everything—well, except for the fact that Deo's recovery might just be temporary. That can wait.

"Are you sure this is a good idea, Anna? Six people—six children—have been killed! Maybe you should just call the police? Give them an anonymous tip?"

"Magda wants blood samples. I doubt the police will let us stroll into the morgue and get those. And there's no reason to assume Dacia is still in the area. They don't know we're . . ."

I hesitate, realizing that there's actually one other thing that I haven't told Kelsey because I didn't want to worry her. Now that Cregg has his mind spy, he could very *easily* know we're here.

The feather-brush sensation moves across my brow.

"Anna?" Kelsey prompts. "Are you still there?"

"Um, yes," I say. "We'll be careful. Aaron should be able to tell if there's any—"

The phone vibrates with an incoming text from an unknown number. I tell Kelsey there's another call coming in and that I'll let her know as soon as we're back from Overhills. And then I reluctantly open the message, wondering which bit of wisdom from The Bard will pop up on my screen.

But it's not a quote this time.

I don't tell him everything. I won't help them kill my own kind. And I have nothing to do with Dacia.

I text back, asking who this is, but there's no response. A second try, this time asking explicitly if he's Snoop. Nothing.

The front door slams, followed by Aaron and Taylor's raised voices. And as much as I don't want to go into the middle of that, I need to let Aaron know about the text.

"Yeah, well, I'm tired of doing nothing!" Taylor's chin is jutted out toward her brother. She's clutching a kid's sneaker in each hand—one navy blue and the other rainbow colored. "And we both know I can pinpoint the location a lot faster with his sneaker and my drawing pad than you can by poking around a bunch of empty buildings on a military base."

"I get that, Taylor. But do you really think it's smart to go around letting people know what you can do?"

Usually, Daniel would chime in at this point, noting the sweet, sweet irony of Aaron saying those words. But Daniel remains at the back of my head, silent, and it's Jaden who steps in with an explanation.

He's asleep.

A pause, and then:

Okay, he says not asleep, just resting his eyes. Either way, it's kinda weird. I haven't felt sleepy since you picked me up. I usually meditate when you're sleeping. Daniel, on the other hand, paces around like a damn tiger in a cage. You need to stash some Xanax or something in the file cabinets you got back there.

Yeah, I wish.

Taylor rolls her eyes, apparently at something Aaron said. "And anyway, Hunter Bieler made machines do freaky stuff just by touching them. Apparently, his sister had some sort of talent too, or they wouldn't have grabbed her. So their mom wasn't exactly a skeptic when I said I was a psychic who might be able to track them down."

She snatches the take-out bag we grabbed on our way back and heads for the front of the trailer. Aaron follows. Even though he must know Taylor has a valid point, he doesn't seem ready to admit it yet, and I feel a little sorry for her. I suspect at least half of what he's unleashing on her stems from his frustration with the whole Daniel situation. He gives me a brief apologetic smile and then closes the door behind them, I suppose as a small concession to my comment yesterday about how much Deo and I hate arguments.

Deo is at the table, doctoring a trio of tacos with hot sauce. He's in his purple ensemble today, and for the first time since Cregg abducted him, his hair is swept back in its usual quiff. He's even wearing eyeliner. There are still dark circles under his eyes, though, and he's paler than I've ever seen him. I smile, even as I feel the sting of tears—happy, relieved, worried, all at the same time.

I sit down across from him, deciding to wait until we're all in the same room to discuss the text. For now, I'm just going to sit here with Deo and enjoy the fact that he's better.

"You look good," I say.

Deo grins, and it's almost like the past few days never happened. "I *feel* good. And I smell good, too. Well, at least *better*."

He's right. The singed smell is still there, but it's much fainter. Barely noticeable under his cologne.

"You, on the other hand . . ." His mouth twists.

"I don't smell."

"Noooo . . . but you *look* worse than that time you had the stomach flu."

"Hosting Daniel while he's tampering with someone's mind is rougher than you might think."

Deo's eyebrows shoot up. "You went Professor X on someone and I missed it?"

"Yes. And with any luck, there will *not* be a sequel."

Overhills, North Carolina
November 3, 2019, 9:10 p.m.

I don't know yet how much of the girl's vision that we listened to was accurate, but she definitely got the tall trees part right. Her comments about the bumpy road were dead on, as well. The first quarter mile or so is in reasonably good shape, but by the time we reach the fork where the main road branches off to curve around the abandoned homes in the area, the impact of the recent rains becomes apparent. Each time Aaron tries to maneuver around a rut or massive puddle, he hits another. It's like navigating a minefield, although in retrospect, that's an unsettling analogy when you're driving on roads used for military training.

Despite Aaron's desire to get out here earlier, it was nearly nine when the four of us piled into the truck and headed north. The problem wasn't Taylor's remote viewing. That took far less time—and far less food—than usual. Maybe it was having the sneakers or knowing a description of the area—or maybe Deo's amp ability gave her a boost—but Taylor managed to pin down the specific building in barely an hour, fortified by only two burritos.

Our discussion of the text message I received was pretty straightforward, as well. We all agreed that it was almost certainly from the kid they call Snoop, although I have no idea how he got hold of a phone without Cregg around. Jaden agreed that the comment about Dacia definitely sounded like Snoop—it was well known at The Warren that there was absolutely no love lost between the two of them, partly due to Dacia being jealous of Snoop's ability. Even though she can comb a person's mind for much more detailed information than the stray bits and pieces Snoop picks up, Dacia requires physical contact, or at the very least, close proximity in order to read someone. But Jaden also heard through the grapevine—which was exceptionally accurate in a facility full of psychics—that Dacia was pissed about something that Snoop plucked from her own head. Apparently, it's perfectly okay for her to invade *other* people's privacy, but she didn't like the tables being turned.

In fact, we'd have been on the road well before nightfall if not for strong differences of opinion as to exactly which of us would be going. Aaron initially planned to go by himself, but Taylor gleefully reminded him of his buddy-system rule.

I was actually okay with the idea of Deo and me sitting this one out. I still have a low-grade headache, and while Deo's feeling better, he's been too sick to go tramping around the woods at night in November. Also, if the girl's vision was correct, we'll be walking into a house where five children were recently murdered. The four who were still drugged may have moved on. People who die in their sleep often do. But Hunter Bieler was awake and screaming. I could very easily end up with another hitcher, and that seems like a bad idea when my mental hotel is already overcrowded.

Unfortunately, Daniel's ability to nudge someone's mind in a different direction is the strongest tool in our collective psychic arsenal. Aaron's vibes can warn if trouble is coming, but they're not very helpful in terms of getting *out* of trouble. So I need to be here. I'll just have to work extra hard to keep my walls intact.

I tried to talk Taylor into staying at the campground with Deo since she'd already done her part with the remote viewing, but both of them balked at that. Deo clearly has cabin fever after being cooped up in the RV for so long. And even though being around Deo still seems to make Aaron jumpy, having an emergency boost for his spidey sense might not be a bad thing.

By the time we reach the lake, the clouds obliterate whatever moon there is in the sky. Aaron has just navigated through an especially deep puddle, so deep the standing water touched the rims, when he slams on the brakes. Two deer, a large doe and a smaller one, freeze on the shoulder of the road, their eyes bright yellow-green in the glare from the headlights.

They eventually move on, and so do we. It's too dark to actually see the lake, but I catch a whiff of it on the breeze after Aaron pulls off the main road—and yes, I'm using that term very loosely. Taylor and Aaron both have flashlights, so we pair off and make our way down the road toward a wooded path just south of the lake.

"You feeling better?" Aaron asks.

"Mmhmm. Advil to the rescue."

He picks up the pace a bit. Once we're a little farther away from Deo and Taylor, he takes my hand and says in a low voice, "Should I apologize for being an asshat today? Or are you sick of hearing it?"

"You weren't an asshat. Or at least, not a *total* asshat. And given the stress we're all under, a little asshattery is probably to be expected."

Aaron laces his fingers through mine and rubs his thumb along my palm. "I really am trying to keep things separate in my mind, Anna. But that was weird today. One minute it was you, and the next I'm seeing Daniel's expressions on your face . . ." He huffs in annoyance. "I know he didn't have a choice. *You* didn't have a choice. But it still pisses me off that he ended up hurting you by taking control."

Remind my sanctimonious baby brother that I'm new to this, too. I had no idea how nudging Pruitt would affect either of us.

I sigh, and Daniel adds:

Fine. I'll go to my corner. I'm tired, anyway.

"I'm okay now, Aaron. Really." I'm tempted to tell him that Daniel is feeling the impact, too. But then I recall the chaste little forehead kiss I received last night. Frequent reminders that I'm tethered to Daniel probably won't improve that situation.

The path from Overhills Lake to the area that locals once called The Hill is barely visible on Taylor's GPS app, and even though this is the more direct route, it's soon apparent that it won't be the quickest. A fallen tree blocks the path. Most of its roots have been yanked from the earth, and several of them point upward. Dozens of smaller obstacles block our progress, and on several occasions we have to veer off the path into the woods in order to move forward. And there's mud, lots and lots of mud, including one patch so viscous that it nearly sucks off my sneaker.

About five minutes in, Aaron's flashlight picks up the battered ruin of a building. A barn, or maybe a stable. Something startles and skitters off into the woods.

"What the hell was that?" Taylor says from behind us.

"Raccoon, probably." Aaron's words are followed by a series of howls off in the distance that don't sound even faintly raccoonish.

I shudder, thinking back to the image of Nikki Clary's body. "We should have waited to interview the Pruitt woman and come out here earlier. I hate the idea of those kids' bodies being mauled by the various creatures of the night, but I also don't like the idea of those creatures mauling us."

Aaron nods. "Yeah. Those noises are making me reconsider our leave-the-gun-at-home decision."

"Nope," Taylor says. "That was still a good call."

The one thing that all of us—even Aaron—agreed on was that the gun had to remain at the camper. You need a special permit to bring a gun on post. If we encounter the military police, the fishing gear and permit in the truck will back up our excuse—well, at least for Aaron. The rest of us can say we came along to goof around and watch him fish.

I pull my pepper spray out of my pocket. "I have this if we need it."

Deo pats the front pocket of the backpack he's carrying over one shoulder. "I'm armed, too." I snort, knowing that he's referring to the kneesock full of pennies he carries in his bag. Although, to be fair, it came to my rescue one night when we were on the streets, and I'm pretty sure it could take out—or at least seriously discourage—whatever that was that took off through the woods.

Taylor waves her tiny pink flashlight, which is about the size of a lipstick, in a wide arc in front of her. "Don't tell the Howling Raccoons, but this little beauty doubles as a stun gun. Popsy gave it to me the first time I went out on a date. So, you don't need your pistol, Aaron. We'll protect you."

She snickers as she says it, and Aaron tells her exactly where she can shove her teeny-tiny stun gun.

"Fine, then. If something leaps out of the bushes, you'll have to make do with Anna's pathetic pepper spray." She drops back a few paces to chat with Deo, and I hear him laugh a moment later.

"Well, they certainly seem to be getting along better."

"True." Aaron lowers his voice to a whisper. "I'll deny it if you ever tell Taylor I said this, but she's actually got a good heart. Daniel's accident hit her hard, and . . . she tends to lash out when she's hurting. She usually regrets it later, but . . ."

Personally, I think that Aaron should tell Taylor every single word of what he just said to me. Maybe she'd learn to avoid ripping into the people around her anytime she's in pain. But Taylor is his sister, so I keep that opinion to myself.

The trees thin out ahead, and we see a narrow road that winds around several houses. Even though the moon is barely visible, the clearing appears almost eerily bright after our trek through the forest primeval. We stick to the tree line rather than taking the shorter path along the clearing—and my eyes dart around, constantly looking for movement.

Apparently, it's just me, though. Aaron, our personal First Alert system, is relaxed. I don't know if it's the fresh air or the exercise, but he actually seems more at ease than he's been in the past few days. Maybe it's just my overactive imagination, combined with how much this place reminds me of the abandoned campus Deo and I ran through to escape from The Warren. Like the Tome campus, the buildings clustered around this circle are in various states of disrepair. One is little more than a burned-out husk. A brick chimney stands out against the night sky like a defiant middle finger, but the rest of the house is now mostly obscured by bushes and vines.

Taylor kicks a chunk of brick off the path and snaps a quick photo of the building in front of us. "Hard to believe this place used to be a vacation resort."

It *is* a bit hard to believe, given the current state of disrepair, but members of the Rockefeller family and various government leaders once vacationed at Overhills. During its heyday, according to the article Taylor found online, the complex stretched over forty thousand acres. In the 1910s and 1920s, wealthy Northeastern families traveled to Overhills to hunt, to play polo, tennis, and golf, and to swim in the lake and indoor pool. A railroad line was built to transport people and goods to the area. Some built houses here, and others stayed at the country club. But then the Great Depression hit. Even the elite had to cut corners, and the club was closed. After that, the place remained a family vacation retreat for the Rockefellers and a few of their friends until they sold it to the government in the early 1990s.

"Well, at least people are still getting some enjoyment out of the golf course." Deo nods to the open area off to the right. "Did you notice the circles on the map?"

Taylor shows us the map, and sure enough, there are dozens of overlapping circles on the green. "What are they? Crop circles?" Taylor asks, and I can't help thinking that between this and the foil hat, she and Bruno would have gotten along quite well.

"No," Deo says with a laugh. "People use the area for mudding. You mean, your mom owns a Jeep and you've never gone mudding?"

Aaron and I both snort at the mental image of Michele Quinn's lavender Jeep spinning out in the mud.

"Mom would freak," Taylor says. "But honestly, a mud bath might improve the aesthetic."

Taylor's phone beeps softly, indicating that we're approaching Croatan Cottage. The glass is missing from most of the windows on the top two floors, and the ones on the bottom floor have been boarded up, though the door has been *unboarded*. Several plywood sheets and planks are scattered among the pinecones on the front lawn.

Aaron shines his flashlight through the doorway into a large open room. It's empty, and the four of us slip inside. The beam glints off broken glass, either from the windows or from beer bottles. On the far side of the room, someone has placed part of a foam mattress in front of the fireplace.

"Still not my idea of romantic," Deo whispers. "But it's actually an improvement over the make-out room at the Tome School."

"Not sure this is a make-out pit so much as a site for military field exercises." Aaron nods down at several discarded brown plastic packets, shining his light on the label: *MEAL Ready-to-Eat Individual Chili with Macaroni.*

"Yum," I say. "So . . . do we make noise to scare away any potential critters or keep quiet in case the authorities are patrolling the area?"

"Stealth mode. I'm not sensing anything human, but no need to take chances. And if a bobcat jumps us, Taylor can zap it with her Hello Kitty stun gun." Aaron pulls Taylor's sketch of the building from his pocket and unfolds it.

"Staircase is that way," Taylor says, pointing down a narrow hallway. "Third floor."

"Of course," Aaron says with a sigh. "Three-story house, so naturally the room we're looking for is all the way at the damned top. And we need to check every room on the first two floors before we go up those stairs. I have no intention of getting trapped up there."

"I thought you weren't picking up any vibes," Deo says.

"I'm not. But we've just found out you're an amp. How do we know the Delphi people haven't created someone who acts as a suppressor?"

That thought hadn't occurred to me at all, and judging from the look on the others' faces, it hadn't occurred to them either. So we don't argue the point. We just work our way past the piles of assorted debris and start searching the house, with Aaron taking the lead and Taylor and Deo bringing up the rear.

The first floor is clear of everything aside from trash and a thriving ecosystem of insect life. We also discover a truly horrifying rat's nest in one of the closets on the second floor. The tiny ratlings squeal, and when two of them scurry across Deo's boot, it's all I can do not to shriek.

I'm still keeping a wary eye out for the rats as we climb the final flight of stairs. There are fewer rooms up here, since it's the attic level. Two of the doors are wide open. A third door hangs at an odd angle, and has been pulled to, but not quite shut.

"My money's on that one," Aaron says. He gives the other rooms a cursory check, then shoves the final door with his foot. It doesn't resist at all, but the rusty hinges screech like banshees in the silence.

And sure enough, the flashlight picks up paintings on the wall. Two dogs playing on a sandy hill. A chained pup howling up at the hook that holds him captive. The most surreal is the giant face of an English bulldog surveying the room from its triangular nook near the roof.

The light also picks up a hastily scrawled message on the wall, near the open door to the children's bath on the far side of the room.

WE DO IT *FOR* YOU

"Looks like it's written in blood," Taylor says, her nose wrinkled in disgust. "Leave the bodies in a creepy place—check. Scrawl a crazy message in blood—check. Someone clearly studied his copy of *Serial Killing for Dummies*."

"Yeah," Deo says. "What do you think the message means?"

"I don't know," Aaron replies. "But I think it's pretty clear we've found the right place."

Taylor reaches into her pocket and pulls out the specimen tubes, handing several of them to Aaron. "At least we won't need the needles to get Magda's samples."

Even though she's trying really hard to sound tough, I notice the little catch in her voice. They move forward into the bedroom, and I follow at first but stop just inside the doorway, sensing . . . something. A presence. That sounds hokey, like something that Erik Bell would say on *Breaking the Veil*, but it's the best description I have. It's a fainter version of what I felt when I picked up Jaden's spirit in the testing room at The Warren, a sense of something—some*one*—nearby. In pain. And I shouldn't be sensing anything at all. My walls are up, fully fortified. I'm pumping every bit of effort I can muster into keeping them intact.

Aaron's flashlight reflects off a chunk of porcelain on the floor and then illuminates several small bodies slumped against each other, their backs against what's left of the bathtub. Only three of them are visible at all from this angle, and the shadows obscure their faces. But I'm pretty sure the kid closest to the door is Hunter Bieler.

The feeling we're not alone grows as I step inside. I avert my eyes to avoid seeing the blood and the bodies inside the bathroom, but it doesn't help.

I have to get out of this room.

Moving back, I accidentally brush against Deo. The *NNNN* sound that I keep getting just before one of Jaden's visions begins, along with what sounds like someone crying. I jump away, nearly tripping over the threshold, but as soon as Deo and I are no longer touching, the humming noise ends. The cries end too, after a moment.

"You okay?" Deo asks.

"Yeah. I just . . . Move a little closer, okay? Not touching, just closer. I need to check something."

He inches a bit closer to me, and sure enough, I hear the voice again. And yeah, it's definitely someone crying. Pretty sure it's a kid, and it's almost certainly Hunter, since he's the only one who didn't die in his sleep.

When I back away from Deo, the sound fades away. But not before I hear the kid calling for his mom.

Damn it, damn it, damn it.

"What's wrong?" Deo asks.

"I need to stay back. Go with them. Or wait on the stairway. I think your amp is messing with my mental walls. Either that, or this kid is really strong."

Or maybe you don't really want to keep your walls up? The voice asking that question is my own, not one of my hitchers, but there's a hint of Kelsey in there as well.

Deo gives me a hesitant look but then joins Aaron and Taylor on the other side of the room.

I lean back against the doorframe and breathe deep, focusing on every trick Kelsey taught me to keep hitchers at bay. The Hotel Anna is currently overbooked, and there really isn't room for another guest. The Molly dreams are finally tapering off now. Do I really want to pull in another kid who was murdered when I'm only just now beginning to get some sleep?

All good arguments for leaving him here. Only . . . I can still hear him. It's so faint that I'm not sure if it's real or an echo of my conscience. I already left one kid behind. Daniel said there was no way we could help the kid in Room 81 back at The Warren, but—

I was right, Anna. Jaden said the same thing. There's no way we could handle that kid.

You also said that Cregg wouldn't hurt him, didn't you? That Cregg doesn't kill freakin' kids. Well, there are five dead kids in that bathroom who beg to differ, Daniel!

Yes. Obviously, I was wrong! But, Anna, Hunter's already dead.

No kidding! And I'm sure you're thinking maybe that's for the best, right? Just like the kid back at The Warren?

What? No! First, that's not—that situation is complicated, okay? And second, my point was that we can't *fix* the fact that Hunter is dead.

Maybe not. But I can help him find some peace. Either way—

Between arguing with Daniel and trying to keep my walls in place, I don't even hear Aaron until I feel his hand on my arm.

"We have to go! Right now!" He pulls me toward the hallway.

"What happened? Where's Deo?"

"Deo and Taylor are already headed downstairs. I got a vibe. Someone's coming. I think we've got a couple of minutes, but . . ." Aaron gives me a puzzled look. "What's the matter?"

"I can *hear* him, Aaron."

"Hear who?"

"Hunter Bieler. He's crying . . . God, he's terrified, he's crying for his mom, and I can't just . . ." I shake my head.

Taylor's voice echoes up from the lower floor. "Aaron! What's wrong?"

"We're coming," he yells back and then turns to me. "Are you sure you can handle taking him on?"

"No. But I'm positive I can't handle leaving him here."

Aaron is still talking, but I barely hear him as I run back toward the bathroom, nearly tripping over one of the pipes in the floor. I yank bricks out of my mental wall as I go, praying that there is only one spirit in this room.

The shadows hide Hunter, for the most part. Only one shoulder and part of his face are fully visible. His eyes are open, wide and glassy, fixed on the shoe of the girl next to him. The white tiles behind the tub are sprayed with something dark, and I am glad beyond belief that the room is too dim for me to see clearly. Seeing five dead kids right now would push me over the edge, and since I'm about to pick up the spirit of a kid who was murdered only a few days ago, I need to hang on to as much calm as I possibly can.

I lean down to touch Hunter's arm. Before my fingers even make contact, loud, hiccupping sobs rush into my head. I stumble back, and probably would have landed on my ass, but Aaron's arms reach out to steady me. The flashlight briefly illuminates Hunter's right side, which is spattered with blood. I squeeze my eyes shut and turn away, knowing I'm too late, knowing that Hunter Bieler has already gotten a clear look at his own dead body.

Mom? Bree?

Hunter—

The woman! She's got a gun she's got a gun she's got a gun—

It's going to be okay, Hunter.

That makes him freak out even more. I'm about to try again, but Jaden stops me.

Anna, you're almost as wound up as the kid is right now, and when you're like that, your voice comes over like I AM THE GREAT AND POWERFUL OZ to those of us here on the inside. Maybe just focus on what's goin' on out there? We got this.

I'm a bit taken aback by that. I'd never really thought about how I might sound to the hitchers. But Jaden's right. I don't have time for explanations right now, so I quickly stack my bricks back into place and focus on getting us out of here.

My body isn't exactly down with that plan, however. I lean back against Aaron, fighting a wave of dizziness. He hooks an arm around my waist, and we go. Taylor and Deo are on the second floor waiting. As soon as we reach the landing, Aaron reaches out to grab Deo's shoulder.

"What the—" Deo begins, but we all catch on when Aaron winces and pulls his hand back. He braces himself against the wall and grips his forehead in his hands for a moment. It almost looks like he's trying to squeeze something out of his head.

"Their Jeep is on the dirt road now." He continues down the stairs, holding the rail tightly. "If they take a right at the fork, I think we'll be okay. But if they circle around by the lake . . . they'll probably see the truck."

I try to remember how long it took us to get from the highway to the lake. It was slow going, given the condition of the road, but I think it was still less time than we spent walking from the truck to here. And that's assuming they've only just now turned onto the dirt road.

"So we stick to the story, right?" I ask, following Aaron. "We tell the MPs we were fishing and wandered off exploring."

"What?" He shoots an incredulous look over his shoulder as we head out into the night. "No! It's not the military police. It's Dacia. She's got two men with her."

"So much for that Snoop kid not telling them everything," Taylor says.

We don't bother sticking to the tree line this time, hoping to shave off a few minutes by running across the golf course. Even though I'm scared, it feels good to run. Running is one thing that always quiets the chaos in my head.

Right now, however, the endorphins merely reduce it to a dull roar. Jaden and Daniel are both trying to calm our new guest, but they aren't having much success. Daniel doesn't seem to be good with kids, and while Jaden *does* appear to have the knack, Jaden's clothes are blood drenched, and he's wearing a wound that's pretty much identical to the one that Hunter just saw on his own head. That would have your average adult in hysterics, let alone a six-year-old boy.

Molly, at age fourteen, is the youngest hitcher I've hosted, and she'd had the better part of three years to adjust to the fact that she was dead. Hunter's had less than a week, based on the information in Tamara Blake's interview, which has been spot-on so far, right down to the dog paintings on the bathroom walls. That doesn't make Hunter the freshest hitcher—Jaden had only been dead about ten minutes. But thanks to Jaden's visions, he'd known what was coming for weeks. He'd accepted his death as inevitable.

I'm not sure a six-year-old can grapple with that concept at all, but if he can, it's going to take time for him to adjust. As soon as we reach the truck, I'll see if I can help calm him down. Right now, though, I need to focus on putting one foot in front of the other.

"Why do you think those bodies are here?" Aaron asks. "Why go to all this trouble to leave them in this exact location? On a military base? I don't think it was just to set a trap for us. They could have done that somewhere else . . . and I don't get the sense they knew we'd be here."

"Then . . . why?"

We stop a few yards into the path through the woods to let Taylor and Deo catch up. Aaron leans back against a tree, catching his breath. "I think . . . I think they expected the military to find those bodies. We know that two of them were kids who hadn't had much success hiding their abilities. Maybe the others were, too? And maybe . . . they're here as a message to the unit that was tasked with keeping these Delphi kids undercover."

I nod. It makes more sense than any other explanation, only . . . "I just don't get what changed their view on killing children? Cregg seemed appalled at the idea, and that's not just based on my conversation with him but also on Jaden's experience, and . . ."

"And Daniel's," Aaron finishes when I hesitate, giving me a weak smile. "It's okay. I'm adjusting. You don't have to censor yourself."

Deo and Taylor catch up, both panting. I don't care how good he was feeling earlier, you don't bounce back that quickly from a high fever and several days where you could barely eat.

"You okay, D?"

"Yeah," he says, still keeping his distance. "But I need to stay back so this amp thing doesn't cause trouble for you two. And . . . buddy system. Taylor's even shorter than you are."

I expect Taylor to give him a dirty look, but she nods, clutching her side. "I do yoga. I do *not* run."

"Well, you won't have any trouble keeping up with us on this damn path," Aaron says. "Run through here, and you're likely to break an ankle. Just walk as fast and as carefully as you can."

When we reach the abandoned stable, Aaron stops and motions to Deo. "Need to see if I can pick her up again. Which I hate, because I get other stuff, too—bar fights, domestic disputes. So if I look like I want to punch someone, it's because I do. But it's not aimed at any of you, so don't take it personally."

Aaron's body tenses as he braces himself for another onslaught. It must be agonizing to sense so much violence at once and have no way of stopping any of it.

"Aaron . . . maybe just move a little closer to him without touching? It might boost you enough to pick up Dacia but not the rest."

It does help . . . He still gets a flash from a jerk who's about to kick his girlfriend's cat across the room, but otherwise the only info he picks up is that Dacia and company have just pulled up to Croatan Cottage.

"It won't take her long to figure out we're gone," he says, pulling me back toward the trail. "And given the mud, they'll know exactly which *way* we've gone. But we should be able to reach the truck before they can circle back around on the road."

"You can move faster than us," I tell him. "Go on ahead and bring the truck closer."

"Yes," Taylor says. "Go!"

As much as Aaron doesn't like it, he knows we're right. I might be able to keep up with him, but Taylor and Deo can't. And he'll need to start up the truck and get it from where we're parked to the path.

"Take this," I say, shoving the pepper spray into his hand. He squeezes my arm, and then he's gone.

Shortly after I drop back to keep pace with Taylor and Deo, another definitely-not-a-raccoon howls, seemingly in the direction we're running. My hand, which had been clutching the pepper spray, suddenly feels very empty. Deo's apparently thinking the same thing, because he pulls out our trusty sock full of pennies and keeps it ready to swing.

Peering off to the left, I scan for headlights on the road that loops around The Hill. Even though the brush is dense, I catch glimpses of the sky between the trunks of the tall pines. No headlights, though, and when I turn back, I run smack into a branch that juts out into the path. It digs a nasty groove in my cheek.

Behind the walls in my head, there's a steady murmur of consoling words, faint but rhythmic—*it's okay, it's okay, it's gonna be okay.* I can't tell if it's Jaden or Daniel, but it seems to be calming Hunter down. Or maybe he's just silent because he's gone into shock.

The sound of an engine revving in the distance silences the background chatter in my brain. A squeal of brakes, then another roar.

"Son of a bitch," Deo says, looking stunned.

Dacia's crew didn't take the road to the lake.

They've got a Jeep and a footpath.

Who needs a road?

CHAPTER TEN

Overhills, North Carolina
November 3, 2019, 9:55 p.m.

We have maybe a quarter mile head start, but I have no idea how long that will last. Deo grabs Taylor's arm, half dragging her as we try to pick up the pace. We smash our way down the path, oblivious to the bushes and vines clutching at us as we pass.

The sound of the Jeep grows louder as we near the fallen tree. It's not exactly a huge hurdle—only a few feet in diameter. But maybe the roots, jutting up like wooden talons, will slow them down a bit.

I don't even see Aaron until I'm over the tree. His shoe is wedged beneath one of the roots and he's clutching his ankle, clearly in pain. When he sees us, he reaches into his pocket and pulls out the keys, tossing them to me. "Go. I'll hide in the woods. Come back when you can."

"Yeah, right. Like we'd leave you here alone." I toss the keys to Taylor and help Aaron up. "If you have time, circle back and see if we've made it to the trailhead. But if you see the lights of that Jeep, get out of here. Call the MPs. Tell them we were out here fishing, we found bodies, and someone in a Jeep tried to run us down."

The engine revs again in the distance. Taylor and Deo look confused, but they don't argue.

"Be careful!" Deo says, and then they're gone.

I snag Aaron's shoe from beneath the tree, and he hands me the pepper spray I gave him earlier so that he can put the shoe back on. He tests the ankle, then clenches his fist, although I can't tell if it's to handle the pain or out of anger. "Should have been more careful. Damn it."

"Come on. We need to get off the trail."

Aaron puts some of his weight on me, and we work our way into the brush as quickly as we can without breaking too many branches—an almost impossible task when we're trying to move together.

"No," Aaron says. "We need to go flat." I'm not clear what he means until he drops to the ground and begins to belly-crawl through the mud and bramble. I catch a flash of headlights through the trees as I lower myself to the ground, followed by the unmistakable sound of wheels spinning in the mud.

"Oh, dear God, please let them be stuck." I tug the sleeves of my hoodie down to protect my hands and follow Aaron.

My prayer goes unanswered, because I've barely hit the ground when I hear the Jeep break free of the mud. Instantly, that same mud, cold and damp, begins seeping through my clothes, and I wish I'd worn more layers. As soon as I'm a few feet in, I turn back and kick hard, spraying leaves and branches back onto the muddy surface of the road behind me, hoping to cover our tracks and disguise the tunnel of broken branches and briars we're creating as we burrow through. Then I resume my commando crawl deeper into the woods, trying to keep my mind off the spiders, snakes, rats, and God only knows what else that could be in here.

As I crawl, a song begins running through my head—no words that I can make out, just a low melodic and familiar hum. It's infuriating, because I can't quite place it. But the music is also kind of soothing, taking some of the edge off my panic.

Our progress is excruciatingly slow, and the roar of the Jeep grows louder by the second. When they hit the mud near the fallen tree, the wheels spin noisily. I look back over my shoulder and see patches of headlights through the branches.

The road seems farther away than I'd thought—maybe a hundred yards. As I watch, headlights arc upward and then back down, the engine roaring as they try and fail to get over the tree.

A moment later, a door slams, barely audible over the idling of the engine. Aaron is moving into the muddier but slightly less densely forested area just ahead of us. I grab the leg of his jeans to halt him. If someone has gotten out of the car, they might hear the rustling. Might see through the leaves I kicked back for what they really are—a half-assed attempt to cover our footprints in the mud.

The Jeep revs again and then backs up to have another go at it. The lights shoot up a bit higher and stay there for several seconds, illuminating the lower branches of some of the shorter pine trees, before falling. A man yells for the driver to go farther back this time. When they approach for a third pass, it sounds like the driver has the accelerator smashed all the way to the floor.

This time, the lights arc up and over. Someone—a woman—gives a loud whoop that trails off as the taillights recede into the night.

My breath whooshes out in relief as the taillights fade out of sight. That relief is short-lived, however, since I know it would have been much better if it had taken them a few more tries. The tree slowed them down, but was it enough time for Taylor and Deo to make it to the truck?

The song in my head shifts. I know this one—"Such Great Heights"— and the disconnect between body and brain is very disconcerting. My heart pounds like an off-balance washing machine, but my head echoes with the musical equivalent of Ambien.

I crawl a few feet forward until I'm level with Aaron. "So," I whisper, "do we hold here until it's safe to call Deo and Taylor, or work our way back out to the—"

But Aaron is still holding his breath. In fact, his entire body is tensed, ready to spring. He holds one finger to my lips. After a moment, I hear someone stomping into the thicket behind us. I press my face into Aaron's shoulder, muttering a silent curse. It didn't even occur to me that the man who was shouting out directions to the driver never got back into the Jeep. They must have noticed the broken branches, or maybe the fact that only two sets of footprints continued on after the tree. A second later, a beam of light begins moving in a wide arc through the woods.

Option A: we can start moving again, trying to stay ahead of the guy who has both a heavy-duty flashlight and, I'm quite certain, a gun. Option B: we can freeze like the deer in our headlights earlier tonight and pray he doesn't see us.

Neither plan is good, but I'm leaning toward the second one. Our bodies are both so covered in mud that there's a slight chance we could avoid detection until the man is close enough for me to use the pepper spray clutched in my palm.

The melody in my head shifts again, and it's off-key now. "Somewhere Over the Rainbow," I think. Then Daniel's voice breaks through my thoughts.

> Go with Option B. When the man gets close enough, I'll convince him to go back to the road. To tell them no one's here. Or . . . something.

Aaron has pulled one leg under him, ready to push forward. I curl my free hand in the fabric of his jacket and pull him toward me.

"You sure?" Aaron whispers, his mouth so close that I can feel his lips moving against my cheek.

I nod, even though I can't tell if he's asking whether I'm sure about us holding this position or if he's figured out what Daniel's planning.

As we inch slowly back toward the tangle of bushes and pine needles behind me, I shift slightly so that my head is on Aaron's shoulder. Now we can both see, at least partially, through the tangle of leaves and branches.

This is the closest Aaron and I have been physically in days, aside from the interrupted kiss the other night and the occasional hug. And there's a man with a freaking gun walking toward us, which scares the hell out of me, so you'd think that my body would be too busy worrying about self-preservation to think about anything else. But that just seems to fan the flame. Every inch of me is pressed against him, and I feel a warm tingle deep inside, a sharp contrast to the wicked cold of the mud caked on my body. His arm tightens around me, and he presses his face into my hair, breathing deeply.

I hear Daniel's exasperated sigh, but I ignore him for a second more, pressing my lips against Aaron's neck.

Not the time for this, Anna.

If this doesn't work, it will be the only time. Are you sure you can nudge this guy fast enough to keep him from shooting?

I'm not certain of anything. But do you have a better plan?

He knows I don't. I pull away from Aaron ever so slightly and prepare to give Daniel control.

Take over with Hunter, okay? Jaden's trying, but I think he's tone deaf.

What?

Daniel doesn't respond, but I understand what he means—and also why the odd songs were running through my head—as soon as we switch places.

Hunter lies curled up in a ball on his side, arms wrapped around his knees, silent. Unlike Jaden, he's not bloody, maybe because the shadows hid that from me when I first saw him. I can't even see the gunshot wound. His eyes are open, though, with the same blank stare I noticed back at the cottage. Is he still seeing the shoes of the dead girl next to him? Or does he see Dacia's face as she promises to make it quick for him, the way she claimed she made it quick for Molly?

Jaden is hunched down in the far corner, keeping his distance from Hunter. And Daniel's right. He *is* trying, but the poor guy couldn't carry a tune in a paper sack. He's reached the part of the song where trouble is melting like lemon drops. At least a quarter of the notes are off-key.

As I take over the song, Jaden gives me a grateful look.

He chilled out a little when Daniel started singing. Might be okay to stop now, but . . .

I shake my head, unwilling to risk it, and sit down near Hunter with my back against the newest cabinet in the room, the one labeled *Molly*. The other cabinets are all the same dull gray-green as the file cabinet in Kelsey's office, the one that I stared at for hours during the weeks when Kelsey was helping me organize the chaos in my head. But for some reason, Molly's cabinet is painted a deep purple, covered with an explosion of brightly colored musical notes.

Without even thinking about it, I segue into Beethoven's "Für Elise," one of the songs Molly could play by heart. There are no words to this song that I know of, so maybe it will be less distracting to Daniel. Right now, anything that distracts him could be fatal to all of us.

Keeping my thoughts quiet and my panic level low would probably help Daniel as well. But I can't *not* look, can't help peering through my lashes as the beam of light slices through the woods, moving closer to our hiding spot every second. The light reminds me of Molly's dreams, of Cregg blinding her and Dacia with his flashlight each time he entered the basement. But the man definitely isn't Graham Cregg. This guy is taller. Larger, and vaguely familiar.

When the light passes beneath his face again, I recognize him. He's one of the guards from The Warren. I saw him in the cafeteria once, talking to the guy who accompanied Dacia to the police department the night she interrogated me. He was armed when I saw him at The Warren, but only with a taser. Now, there's a rifle slung over one shoulder.

Daniel seems to notice it at the same moment I do. The string of curse words echoing in my mind makes it clear that he does not believe this is a good thing.

Jaden's nodding.

> Yeah, that's him. Name's Grady. I don't think he was around Dacia as long as Whistler, but still long enough he might have built up some resistance. I'm guessin' you're gonna need to shout.

He's clearly talking to Daniel, so I save any questions for later, even though my mind lingers on the idea that he might have become resistant. I didn't even know that was possible.

I slide closer to Hunter and hum louder. The last time Daniel had to "shout," it was like someone had turned my internal volume to eleven, and who knows how that kind of noise might affect the kid. He's still curled up chin to knees, and aside from the vacant stare, he looks almost exactly like the picture in the file that Magda put together, the picture that's been blasted all over the media around here for the past week.

I reach out, wondering if it would help or hurt to touch him. Turns out it's a moot point. His body looks as solid as anything in here, but my hand sinks straight through. I can feel a floor beneath me, I can feel the brightly colored cabinet behind me, I can even feel the mental bricks stacked behind me.

> Yeah, Daniel couldn't touch him either. Maybe . . . I mean . . . everything else here is you. We're not permanent. And—

Whatever else Jaden planned to say is drowned out by Daniel. "THERE'S NO ONE IN THE WOODS. IT'S JUST A DEER."

I don't think Daniel actually *shouts*, because Aaron barely startles. In here, however, the words echo off the bricks as though they were screamed into a megaphone. Hunter flinches once, and then his body slumps again. Jaden and I both wince, our hands flying to shield our ears, even though I strongly doubt it's doing the slightest bit of good. My stomach twists, threatening to expel the burrito I had for dinner.

The man, Grady, also reacts. He turns straight toward us, raising the rifle to his shoulder.

"IT'S A DEER!" Daniel repeats.

I barely hear the shot. My ears are still ringing from Daniel yelling, and things happening on the outside seem fainter when I'm back here. Aaron's body jerks backward, pushing me deeper into the brush—or was that the force of the bullet hitting his body?

For a moment, everything goes in slow motion. My heart stops, and it feels like the air is sucked out of my lungs. Then I realize that the angle of the gun isn't right and Grady isn't looking down at us—he's staring off into the distance a few feet above the bushes where we're hidden.

He watches briefly, then shakes his head, annoyed. Finally, he pulls his phone out and dials.

"Dead end. Nothin' but a deer. Big one, too. Ran off when I shot at it."

He's too far away for the answering voice to be anything other than gibberish, but it sounds like Dacia. And she doesn't sound happy.

"Yeah, I shot at it." His tone is defiant, but he stops and gives a confused look back in the direction he fired the gun. "Been hunting since I was a kid. If I see a deer, and there's a gun in my hand, you bet your ass I shoot."

Another pause, and then he says, "MPs didn't hear shit. I had the silencer on."

Whatever Dacia says next pisses him off. "How the hell was I supposed to know that? No. Definitely *do not* call the Senator. Shoot them. Have Whistler dump them in the lake. I'm on my way."

Grady shoves the phone into his pocket and turns toward the trail. As soon as his back is in sight, my mouth opens, and the words, "That's not a gun you're holding. It's a snake!" tumble out.

The man freezes and casts a nervous glance at the strap on his shoulder. Then he shakes his head, like he's trying to clear it, and takes another step forward.

"NOT A GUN! RATTLESNAKE!"

Does Daniel actually say the words? I don't know. The noise in my head is overwhelming, and this time, Hunter also reacts. In the middle of the chaos, I'd stopped humming, and now the kid's keening almost, but not quite, drowns out the cursing as Grady swats frantically at the strap on his shoulder.

Which is now very clearly a snake. I watch it writhe as Grady's hand wraps around it, as he flings it to the ground.

Aaron lunges forward, but we're farther away than Grady is, and Aaron's sudden motion seems to have triggered a part of Grady's brain that rejects the possibility that his gun could somehow morph into a rattler. Grady's hand lands on the gunstock just as Aaron's lands on the barrel, and Grady, who is standing, has more leverage. It's an uneven tug-of-war, and one that I have no doubt he'll win.

Daniel prepares to send another mental blast, but I scream as loudly as I can, making sure he hears me over Hunter's wails.

Move!

I shove Daniel's consciousness aside. It feels almost as if I'm diving into my body at the same time I'm propelling myself out of the bushes. My right hand flies upward as I flip the safety on the canister with my thumb.

The pepper spray spreads outward, hitting Grady square in the face. He stumbles forward, screaming, hand to his eyes. I lift my thumb, preparing to spray again, but his shoulder catches me in the stomach and slams me to the ground, pinning my left arm beneath him. He's still making strange yelping sounds, wiping at his eyes with one hand as he twists my wrist with the other, forcing me to drop the pepper spray.

I push against the ground, trying to get out from under him, but it's no use. He's too heavy, too strong, and I don't know if he's exhaling the stuff or if it's just blowback, but now I'm starting to feel the effects of the pepper, too. It's not enough to make me cry out like he is, but it sure as hell isn't pleasant.

Then his hand moves to my throat, and I'd be happy to pull in any breath at all, even one laced with chemicals.

Even with my eyes watering, I can still see clearly enough to recognize the barrel of the gun as it advances, stopping mere inches from Grady's temple. The rifle fires once, and Grady collapses, his head falling to my chest. A warm, wet flood begins to wash over my skin.

"Are you okay?" Aaron asks.

I nod, although I can barely hear his words over Hunter's screams in my head. I'd thought the boy was at peak volume before, but the sight of another gun so close seems to have pushed him over the edge.

And while Jaden and Daniel probably wouldn't admit it, based on their recent fatal or nearly fatal encounters with guns, I suspect they're shaken up as well.

As much as I hate to wall Daniel and Jaden inside right now, I don't have a choice. My head is already beginning to throb again, and it's likely to get worse based on my experience this afternoon. So I close my eyes and begin stacking the mental bricks as Aaron lodges one foot under Grady's abdomen and shoves the man's limp body off of me.

Aaron stares down at the body. There's disgust, anger, and something I can't identify in his expression. And then music blares from the man's jacket—an upbeat song called "Happy" that played incessantly a few years back. I don't know if it's the shock of the past few minutes or the total incongruity of the music, but I laugh nervously.

He grabs Grady's phone and checks the screen, then stashes it in his pocket as it falls silent.

"Probably Dacia calling back. We need to get going."

I nod, trying to sit up. That movement, combined with the vertigo that comes with moving back and forth inside my head and the sight of Grady's blood on my shirt—*please please please let it be just his blood and not his brains*—is the final straw for my stomach.

Aaron steps aside, and I'm grateful to him for giving me that modicum of privacy. When I finish retching, he helps me up. From the look on his face, he's pretty close to hurling, himself.

"I've carried a gun for two years now," he says gruffly, retrieving the pepper spray and Grady's flashlight from the bushes where they rolled during the struggle. "First time I've ever used one on somebody, though."

Aaron's still favoring his injured left ankle, but he's able to put a bit of weight on it. Our ability to move as a team is apparently cursed, however, because now my eyes burn so badly that I can barely keep them open. When we're a few feet away from both Grady's remains and the remains of my dinner, I run smack into a bottlebrush pine about a foot shorter than I am.

"You sure you're all right?"

"I will be. Give me a sec." It might help if I could wipe my face, but when I look down, every inch of my clothing is either muddy, bloody, or possibly contaminated from the spray. I unzip my hoodie and toss it on the ground, but even my T-shirt is drenched.

Aaron puts the gun down and removes his windbreaker.

"Here. Put this on."

I add my drenched tee to the pile on the ground and slip my arms into Aaron's jacket. It's not exactly clean, but the inside is dry and still warm from his body.

He uses the hem of his sweatshirt to quickly wipe the area around my eyes. It helps—a little—and I start moving back toward the trail.

"Wait," Aaron says, crouching down to turn my ruined hoodie inside out.

"Don't bother. It's old. We need to go. You heard him. He said *shoot them.*"

"Can't leave it. Evidence. DNA." He quickly rolls the hoodie up, then ties the sleeves together, forming a loose ball. "And maybe Dacia wasn't talking about Taylor and Deo. Maybe . . ."

But he doesn't have another logical interpretation for what Grady said, and neither do I. Maybe they brought more kids out here to kill and dump? As much as I want Deo and Taylor to be safe, I can't bring myself to hope for that option either.

I pull my phone from the back pocket of my jeans. My touchscreen is now covered in a spiderweb of cracks, but the phone still works. I tap one of the icons, and a map opens. "Find Deo," I say as we begin pushing our way back to the trail.

Aaron gives me a questioning look over his shoulder.

"A tracker app. Taylor installed it right after Porter bought these phones. She put it on your phone, too. Might not help if one of us gets nabbed again, but we'd be dumb not to at least try. There could be one on Grady's phone too. You should turn it off."

"That's his name?"

"Yeah. Daniel and Jaden both recognized him. A guard at The Warren, mostly worked with Dacia."

Aaron huffs. "I don't want to sound ungrateful for Daniel pulling our asses out of the fire, but why bother making the man see a deer? Why not just say that about the snake to begin with?"

"I don't know. But this is hard on Daniel, at least when he has to work through me. It's a lot easier to make someone believe there's a deer in the woods than to convince him his gun has morphed into a rattlesnake."

The location app is taking longer than usual, maybe because of the cloudy night, or maybe the phone really is screwed up. I'm about to get Aaron to pull it up on his phone instead when the voice finally says, "Locating Deo."

I keep one stinging, watery eye on the uneven ground below me and the other on the screen, almost too scared to look, terrified that the location pin will show that Deo is now in Overhills Lake. But when the pin eventually appears, it shows he's about a quarter mile south of us, near the house where we found the bodies. A wave of relief rushes through me, and I flip the screen around to show Aaron.

"Thank God," he says. "But why would Taylor go back there? They were supposed to get the hell out of . . . here."

I can tell from Aaron's expression that the thought hits him at the same instant it hits me. Maybe Dacia just decided it would be easier to go back to the house and leave Deo and Taylor's bodies with the others, rather than dumping them into the lake.

As soon as our feet are on the other side of the fallen tree, we start running. I hold back, torn between keeping pace with Aaron, since he's the one with the gun and the flashlight, and knowing that I could move faster.

Aaron clearly realizes it, too. He grabs my arm and pushes the gun toward me.

"Go. You can shoot, right?"

I give him an incredulous look. "Aaron, my eyes are streaming like Niagara Falls. Even if I did know how to use a gun, which I don't, I'd be more likely to kill them accidentally than save them!"

"Okay, then. Back to plan A." He takes the rifle from me and keeps going, even though he looks like he's going to keel over every time he lands on the sore ankle.

When we're a few yards away from the dilapidated stable, the roar of an engine coming from the road ahead stops us cold.

"Holy mother of God," Aaron says. "How did they make it back around so fast?"

My phone begins to vibrate, signaling an incoming text. Under the circumstances, any sane person would ignore it, especially when it could be another quote from Cregg. But something—either habit or instinct—makes me pull the phone from my pocket.

Deo's name flashes on the screen. The text is short:

can u make it to stable?

Aaron and I exchange a look as the noise of tires spinning in mud reaches us.

It might be Deo. But it might also be Dacia with Deo's phone.

"I could ask him something I don't think she'd know, but . . ."

He understands as well as I do how pointless that would be. Dacia has pulled information from Deo's mind at least twice. I have no idea what she knows and what she doesn't.

"Text back yes. If it's Dacia, she may not expect us to have the rifle."

I send the message and then catch up with Aaron, who is now shining Grady's flashlight into the abandoned building. Turning back to look at the trail, I see a faint glow to the south, with fragments of brighter light filtering through the brush.

We duck into the building, and something scurries along the wall into the corner. I manage to stifle a shriek, but it's a close call. With everything that has happened today, my nerves are frayed down to a few thin strings.

The two of us crouch low, Aaron in front so that he can keep watch around the doorframe and shoot if necessary. I rest my hand on his back and feel his muscles twitching beneath the fabric of his shirt, like they were earlier when he was reading Grady's thoughts.

Now that I've stopped moving, the clatter in my brain returns. It's muffled by the wall but still there. Hunter has calmed down a bit. Someone—I think it's Jaden—is humming again.

I get a quick glimpse of a no-longer-white truck through the trees as it approaches the stable. A wave of relief comes over me before I remember that this means nothing. Dacia could have shot Taylor and snatched the truck keys from her hand.

And then Aaron's shoulders suddenly relax. "It's them. Let's go."

"Are you sure? It . . . it felt like you were getting a vibe just now."

"I was. From Taylor. She was thinking she wished it was Dacia that she'd hit with the truck." His brow furrows. "And something else, but it doesn't make sense."

Deo steps out of the truck the instant Taylor pulls into the clearing. I'm so relieved to see him that I rush forward to hug him, remembering only at the very last second that I need to hold back.

Aaron tosses my hoodie into the back of the truck. Then he wipes the rifle down with the sleeve of his sweatshirt and throws it into the bushes. I crawl into the cramped back seat with Deo, sliding as far to the right as possible to give him some room for his longer legs, and reach into the middle console for the Advil we bought earlier, dry swallowing three of them.

"You were supposed to get out of here," Aaron says to Taylor. "Get back to the main road and call the military police."

"When you tossed me the keys, you put me in charge, and Anna said to use my judgment. I made an executive decision not to leave your ungrateful self behind." Taylor turns the truck back to the south, away from the lake. "And as it turns out, the MPs came to us. They were parked on the other side of the path when we came out of the woods. Two guys in uniform, talking to some people in a truck, over by the lake. Fishermen, maybe?"

She twists the wheel to avoid a puddle.

"The MPs started driving toward us when they saw us run out of the woods," Deo says. "But then that Jeep comes ripping through like a bat out of hell, and we were yesterday's news."

Deo has one hand inside his jacket, like he's holding something against his side. I'm about to ask him about it, but Taylor starts speaking again.

"Dacia's driver nearly broadsided the MPs' vehicle, and boy were they pissed. We ran to the truck and got out while we could."

"Do you think the police got a good look at the truck?"

"I don't think they could have made out the tags, but they'll know the color. Maybe the make." Taylor glances into the rearview mirror. "It's your turn now. Where did you get the gun you tossed into the woods? And why is there blood in Anna's hair?"

Deo gives me a startled look. "I thought it was mud."

"It's not her blood," Aaron says. "One of Dacia's guys stayed behind. I finally managed to get the gun away from him."

He doesn't finish his explanation. The blood I'm wearing does that for him.

Taylor floors the accelerator as soon as we reach the clearing. Even though the bumps were larger on the trail, at least she was taking them at a reasonable speed then. I lean my head against the seat and close my eyes, praying I don't get sick again.

When we're just beyond Croatan Cottage, Taylor spins the wheel to the left and brakes abruptly. "Deo noticed this when we circled back around."

She's talking to Aaron, but I open my eyes anyway. The headlights are shining on a battered wire fence. The part that was supposed to block off the road has been flattened, probably by the people who use the area for mudding. But the section to the left is still standing, and there's a large orange-and-black sign tacked to it, reading, *Off Limits to Unauthorized Personnel.* There's a space at the bottom for additional information, and someone has written in with a marker: *Overhills area closed 11/4/19–11/14/19 for live fire training.*

We barely have time to read it before she reverses, spins back out onto the driveway, and we're moving again. "So, what do you think?"

"I told you that on the phone this morning," Aaron says. "The guy I bought the permit from said—"

"You saw the meal packets in there," Taylor says. "The soldiers use that place when they train. So they'll find the bodies, right? Maybe not the Clary girl, but once they find these . . ."

"Yeah. They'll widen the search." A sick look crosses his face. "And I'm pretty sure they'll also be looking for anyone who had a fishing pass today."

"But," Deo says, "won't they realize the bodies aren't fresh? I mean, they usually do that whole time-of-death thing on the cop shows."

I shrug. "The kids weren't killed recently. But I'm pretty sure they're going to be equally interested in the two MPs. Grady told Dacia to shoot them and dump them in the lake—or maybe he was talking about the fishermen you mentioned. We were afraid they meant you."

"I didn't hear any shots as we were leaving," Taylor says.

"Silencers," Aaron says. "At least on Grady's gun."

A high-pitched whimper causes Aaron to look back questioningly at Deo.

"Um . . . Deo? What the hell is that?"

Deo's jacket is moving. He gives me an apologetic smile and is about to answer, but Taylor beats him to it.

"He was outside the fence, right below that off-limits sign, shivering. There's no way we could just leave him there. He's starving!"

Deo pulls a tiny pup out of his jacket. Taylor is right—he's nothing but skin and bones, and he's frantically trying to nurse on the side of Deo's thumb. "I tried to get him to eat some of this cheese cracker I had in my backpack. He won't take it."

"But what about the mother?" Aaron says. "She'll be looking for him."

"Probably not," I say, taking the pup from Deo. "I don't think he'd be this thin if there was a mother in the picture. His eyes aren't even open yet. I'm surprised he's still alive."

Aside from a few months at one of my first foster homes, I've never had a dog. But my hitcher Abner owned dogs from the time he was a kid. There's this one childhood memory of his that I kind of wish was my own. He's lying on the grass, laughing, as a half-dozen puppies crawl over him, tugging at his shirt, licking his face. They always had puppies at his family's farm, and there were a few times they had to intervene to save a runt who wasn't thriving.

"See?" Taylor says. "The mom is dead. We *had* to bring him with us."

"Yeah," I say. "Either dead or she abandoned him. Sometimes the mothering instinct just doesn't kick in. It would be better if we had some milk. And an eyedropper. But . . ."

I grab a small piece of cracker from Deo's hand and chew it until it forms a thin gruel in my mouth. The puppy balks at first when I try to get him to take it from my pinky, but by the time we're back on Highway 24, he's eaten a little of it.

"There's no way we can keep a puppy in the RV, but I guess we can find a shelter," Aaron says. "One of those no-kill places."

Taylor sniffs. "Ooh, the Almighty Aaron has spoken. News flash: you are not the boss. We'll put it to a vote tomorrow."

The arguing doesn't stop, but I ignore them and continue coaxing the little guy to eat. It gives me something to focus on aside from my aching head and worries about my new hitcher. I don't regret picking Hunter up, but I have no clue how I'm going to deal with him. Maybe Kelsey will have some ideas.

Every few minutes, Aaron looks in the side mirror. As do I. We're headed in the most obvious direction, back toward Fayetteville, and they know what we're driving. I keep expecting to see Dacia's black Jeep zoom up behind us.

But we make it across town without any sign of her. Taylor pulls into a Walmart, over Aaron's objections, and she and Deo go in search of puppy formula while I keep the little guy warm inside Aaron's jacket. After we pull around to the dumpster in the back and ditch my hoodie, Aaron finds a parking spot near the entrance and pushes the phone button on the dash. "Call Sam."

"Don't tell him about Hunter," I say as the phone connects. "I mean, you can tell Sam if you really want, but I don't want Magda to know yet. I think she'd want me to pressure him for answers to her twin questions, and—"

"Hey, Aaron," Sam says. "I'm on my way back from the hospital. Needed to give your mom a break. She's running herself ragged. We don't like to leave him alone. Too many studies showing that coma patients really do know if you're there."

Aaron shoots a frustrated look over his shoulder, aimed more at Daniel than at me. I just give him a helpless shrug. Personally, I'm fine with him telling Sam and Michele that Daniel is not actually in that body, but it's not my call.

"So," Sam continues, "what's up?"

There's a long pause after Aaron fills him in on the evening's events, and then Sam says, "Hitch up the camper and hit the road tonight. I'll let Magda know what's up. Sounds to me like you've stumbled into the middle of a rather lethal pissing contest between Cregg's people and some of the personnel at Bragg. Both Cregg and the military will have the same information you do, same list of contacts, so they'll be watching for you to pop up."

"That's pretty much what we thought," Aaron says. "I'm going to head to Fort Benning and see if we can track down the lead Anna got through her vision."

As Aaron is talking, it occurs to me that Snoop could have extracted that from my head, too. Cregg's people could already be in Georgia, interrogating the Pecks. Could already have tracked down the adept.

I'm pretty sure that's not the case, though, based on the vision. I remember feeling relieved to have that asymmetrical scrap of green paper in my hand. We'd just talked to the Pecks and we'd gotten the info we needed.

That's another positive side about the visions that Jaden didn't mention, and something I'd kind of forgotten over the past few hours. No matter how dangerous it seemed at Overhills, I *know* that we make it to Georgia. And even though I can't help constantly checking each time I see headlights, I know that Dacia's people aren't going to track us down here in the parking lot and shoot us. I wish I'd remembered that when my heart was pounding out of my chest as we ran through the woods, or when Aaron and I were crawling through the mud to get away from Grady.

"What was it they scrawled at the site again?" Sam asks.

"*We do it* for *you*," Aaron says. "We didn't take a sample from the wall, but I'm pretty sure it was written in blood. There was certainly enough of it around."

"Weird," Sam says. "Almost as though they were trying to make it appear that the murders were . . . dedicated to someone."

"Like that Hinckley guy who shot Reagan back in the eighties?" Aaron sounds doubtful.

"No," I say. "One of the words was underlined, remember? *We do it FOR you.* I . . . I think Dacia wrote it. I mean, it sounds like her phrasing. Think back to what Pruitt told us. The people at Fort Bragg had been trying to keep this hushed up, to keep the Delphi kids under wraps. We know that at least two—no, three—of the ones killed were cases where the military failed. Hunter, the Clary girl, and . . . the other one . . . the one Pruitt said was a firebug. So maybe the message was that since you couldn't handle these kids, couldn't keep them from using their abilities, from letting people know that they were adepts . . ."

Aaron nods. "You couldn't control them, so we did it *for* you."

CHAPTER ELEVEN

Cusseta, Georgia
November 4, 2019, 3:14 p.m.

The day is unseasonably warm and humid, with barely a hint of breeze reaching the screened porch. I'd much rather be in a T-shirt and jeans—anything would be preferable to this wool skirt and jacket. But even though Carl and Doreen Peck seem to be very casual people, I don't think informal clothes would help sell my cover as Elizabeth Bennet, legal intern.

I stifle a yawn, partly because Carl Peck is off on another tangent, but mostly because I'm sleepy. After we finished telling Sam about what we'd found at Overhills, we headed back to the RV and were on the road to Georgia by midnight. Aaron drove until around four in the morning and then pulled off so that we could catch some sleep in a parking lot.

A few hours after we stopped, Magda called. Apparently she couldn't wait until after sunrise our time to let us know that she'd talked to Sam and she wasn't happy that we'd left without contacting all of the names on our list or that we'd had to abandon the rental car with the keys under the seat.

Not that Magda had any viable alternatives to suggest. Given everything we'd just witnessed at Overhills, staying in the area would have been beyond stupid. But I think what had her most upset was learning that one of the twins she was seeking is now dead. And Hunter and his sister were the only set of Delphi-affected twins that Daniel knew of aside from Magda's daughters.

I'm really glad I told Aaron to hold off on letting anyone know that I picked up Hunter's spirit. The kid has a major case of PTSD—although is that the correct diagnosis when the traumatic event actually kills you? Maybe PTDD—post-traumatic death disorder—is a better descriptor. At any rate, Hunter isn't stable enough to answer Magda's questions, and since Magda doesn't seem to enjoy taking no for an answer, it's up to me to protect him.

The gentle back-and-forth motion of the porch swing that Aaron and I are currently sharing isn't helping me stay alert. Carl Peck is holding court in one of the two rockers that were once white, judging from the bits of paint that cling to the wicker backs. I sit with my legal pad in my lap, wishing the old geezer would just give us the information that we know they have. But he doesn't seem inclined to make things easy, possibly because he likes having an audience.

"When that tree house blew," he says, "chunks of wood went flying ever'where, some pieces with the nails still attached. Fifteen, maybe twenty, people were watching, but I don't think more'n a couple saw what caused it. *Who* caused it."

Peck stops and takes a long, slow swig from his beer. The pause is clearly timed for maximum effect. I get the sense that he's told this story dozens of times, over many cans of beer, while sitting around the table with his poker buddies.

Carl Peck is not especially handsome, even for a man in his seventies. His belly strains at the buttons of his chambray shirt, and he has more hair on his face than on his head. He is, however, picturesque. The colors of the Coors Light can are an almost perfect match for the streaks of silver-white in his beard, the blue of his shirt, and the red of the baseball cap, now hanging from one rail of his rocking chair. He looks like something that Norman Rockwell might have painted if he woke up in a really pissy mood.

"And here's *why* no one saw who caused it," Peck continues. "Most of them was lookin' at the boy. What was his name, Doreen?"

Doreen, nine years younger than Peck, according to info Sam sent us, leans against the frame of the open porch door. A bead of condensation hovers at the bottom edge of her glass, where only a few thin brown lines of tea now rest between the melting crescents of ice. She's been staring dully into the backyard while her husband talked, her eyes fixed on the dilapidated jungle gym. Doreen Peck is either bored with this story or bored with her husband. Maybe both.

"His name was Tomás," she says, eyes never moving from the jungle gym. "After Miranda's dad. But they usually called him TJ."

"That's right, that's right. Anyway, it was the birthday boy's big day, and the grandmas and uncles and so forth all had their cameras pointed to'rd him as he made his way up into that new tree fort. Too bad no one was takin' a video. That would have gone viral damn fast."

Peck leans toward us at this point, blue eyes twinkling. "Me, though? I was lookin' at Peyton, his little sister. She's a cute little bug when she gets mad, and she was sure as hell mad right then, 'cause her daddy had just told her she was too little to go up in that tree house. Maybe one day, he'd said, when she was bigger. Even a three-year-old knows that means a damn long wait, and Peyton was used to followin' her big brother around like a puppy. Once her daddy walked off to help the boy up the ladder, Miss Peyton parked her tiny butt on the concrete, bottom lip stickin' out and starin' at that tree house with lasers comin' out of her eyes—"

"You mean, like . . ." Aaron hesitates, glancing at me and then back at Peck. "Do you mean beams of actual *light*?"

"No." Peck's tone suggests that he would have added the word *dumbass* to the end if he'd known Aaron better.

I bite back a laugh, but it wouldn't have surprised me if Peck had said yes. A few weeks ago, I'd also have been reluctant to believe that people could stop machinery or set things on fire through the power of their minds. Are laser-beam eyes really that much of a stretch?

"She was just a little girl, not an alien or a demon or what-have-you," Peck says. "What I meant is that she was starin' at the tree house with the *intensity* of a laser. Focused, you know?"

"Yes, sir," Aaron says.

"Anyway, it's while Peyton is starin' at it that the damn tree house explodes, almost like a tornado hit it. The boy—Thomas, TJ, whatever—fell out. Broke his arm. Lucky it wasn't worse. Like I said when you first showed up, I told his daddy that thing was too high up for a kid his age. But he was one of those types always thinks he knows better. That's the tree right over there." He jerks one thumb toward a tall oak in the yard next door. "The lowest branch is ten feet up, and that ain't a safe height for no eight-year-old's tree fort. Shoulda picked one of the other trees."

Aaron nods agreeably, then asks, "Did anyone else notice the girl?"

"Someone sure did," Peck says. "Miranda—that's the kids' mama? She definitely noticed, and she swooped the kid up and ran inside. I'm sure most people thought it was to get the little girl out of harm's way, but I was close enough to hear what she said."

He pauses, waiting for his cue.

"What did she say?" Aaron finally asks.

"She said, 'No, Peyton! *Bad, bad* girl!'"

I've kept quiet for most of the interview, partly because Peck seems like the type who sees women as peripheral. But I'm not sure Aaron will ask, and I want to know.

"How did the girl react when she found out her brother was hurt?"

Peck gives me a little smile, which makes me think this is another cue he was waiting to hear. "That's a good question, young lady. Because you'd think she'd have just been sad, right? Like I said, she was crazy about her big brother. No matter how mad she was about him gettin' that tree house, she wouldn't wish him no harm. And she *was* sad, just like you'd expect. She was bawlin' her head off when they carried the boy out to the carport to take him over to the hospital. But she was *also* tellin' her mama and daddy that she was sorry. That she wouldn't do it again."

He raises his eyebrows in a *what-do-you-think-of-that* expression. Then he relaxes back into the rocker, resting his folded hands on his stomach.

Aaron shuffles through the papers in his lap. "Did you talk much with Mr. Hawkins about his time in the military?"

"Occasionally. We'd shoot the breeze from time to time, usually about our tours in Iraq. We served in different wars, but it's always the same . . ." Peck's eyes flit toward me briefly. "Always the same *stuff* goin' on."

"This class action suit is specifically for offspring from one particular military program. Did either of her parents ever mention a program called Delphi?"

Aaron barely has the word out before Daniel comes speeding to the front.

No! Damn it, Aaron. The program wasn't called Delphi when it was at Bragg! That's later. He should know—

Come on, Daniel! Really? If you can't keep quiet, I'll have to put you behind the wall. Understood?

Daniel has been pretty mellow since we left North Carolina last night. I think he wore himself out fighting against Grady. It felt like the inside of my head was bleeding after he shouted that the gun was a snake, and I still had remnants of that headache when I woke up this morning. Plus, he and Jaden have both been occupied with Hunter.

But Daniel's interruption wasn't even necessary. Aaron's already corrected himself by the time I tune back in, noting that it was called the Stargate Project at Bragg.

"He didn't mention any program by *name*, but this one time, Jasper had a few too many, and he starts talkin' about this assignment back in the . . . I think it was the late 1990s. Before he met his wife, before he had kids. Claimed they were doin' some freaky sh—*stuff*. Experiments to predict the future, find lost items, mess with the enemy's head. Said one of the bigwigs over there swore it was possible to walk through walls if you meditated on it long enough. Anyway, Jasper told me he was part of this program. Said they gave him some sort of injections to amp up his *psychic powers*." He does the thing with his eyebrows again to emphasize the last words.

"You didn't believe him?" Aaron asks.

"Well, no. I never saw anything psychic about *him*. He was a bit on the crazy side, you ask me. Nicest guy in the world 'til he got worked up about somethin', and then he had a temper like a bee-stung bear. Pretty sure he hit his wife on occasion. Them kids, too, although never hard enough to warrant us callin' in the cops or anything."

Doreen snorts softly. It's as close as I've heard her come to disagreeing with her husband. She seems to feel me watching her, because she pulls her gaze away from the jungle gym and gives me a long look I can't quite decipher.

"What about the other kid?" Aaron asks Peck. "TJ?"

"Normal eight-year-old boy, far as I ever saw."

"He wasn't Jasper's," Doreen adds. "TJ was Randa's from her first marriage."

I jot this down as Aaron continues questioning Peck. "And you're sure you don't know where they moved to? You said there were grandparents at that party. Maybe you could dredge up a name?"

Peck sighs and gives both of us an annoyed look, which I sort of understand. He stated at the very beginning of the interview, before he launched into the Treehouse of Horror story, that he had no idea where the Hawkins family is currently living.

"Like I told you, we ain't got a clue where they went. Cleared out in the middle of the night back in . . . July. Pretty sure it was July. The house finally went up for sale last month. Maybe you could track down the realtor on the sign out front, see what she knows."

Aaron glances over at me, and I give him a little shrug. It's not like we can tell Peck that I know we'll pull out of his driveway with this information scrawled on a piece of pale-green paper. Explaining that to Peck won't change the outcome. We'll still leave here with the info. The only difference is that Aaron and I will likely have the lead roles in Carl Peck's next story at poker night if I tell him. And I'd really rather avoid that.

Just let me move to the front for a minute, Anna. I'll give him a little nudge, and—

No.

My response is automatic. With Grady it was necessary. Even with Pruitt, since she was a split second from calling the cops on us. But a case like this, where someone just isn't cooperating, is different. It feels wrong to take someone's free will without a damn good reason.

It feels like the kind of thing Graham Cregg does.

"Checking with the realtor is a good idea, sir," Aaron says. "We'll get the number off the sign before we go."

"Let's go now. I'll walk you over," Peck says, giving us a conspiratorial grin as he pushes himself up from the rocker. "While we're at it, we can sneak around back. There's a couple of interestin' little . . . artifacts from that birthday party."

The side of Doreen's mouth twitches downward as she watches Carl slowly descend the porch steps. She gives me another enigmatic look, then retreats into the dark of the house, closing the door behind her.

Doreen knows something. And since I doubt that Carl has a pen and the piece of oddly shaped pale green paper that I saw in my vision tucked into the pocket of his Levis, I need to stick with Doreen.

"Is it okay if I use your restroom? It's a long drive back to Atlanta."

"Sure thing," Peck says. "That iced tea'll run straight through you on a day like this. Don't know where Doreen got off to, but it's the third door down the hall on the right. Can't miss it."

Peck heads off across the lawn. "Hard to believe it's November, ain't it? Not nearly as hot as November 1958, though, when I was in junior high over in Macon. I tell you, it was nearly a hundred degrees in the middle of the month. So don't get started on that global warming crap, 'cause it's just plain ol' nature bein' her usual contrary self, not carbon deposits or whatever."

Aaron shoots me an imploring look as they round the corner of the house, clearly wishing I wasn't abandoning him to the crazy person.

I push the door open and step inside. The cool air is a welcome change, but the hallway is so dark after the midday sun outside that I can barely see.

"Come on into the kitchen." Doreen's voice startles me, even though she's barely speaking above a whisper.

I follow her down the hallway into the kitchen. It's painted a pale yellow, and there's a large butcher-block island in the middle, with deep knife grooves that suggest it's not merely there for aesthetic purposes. The shelves along the back of the island are filled with cookbooks, cooking gadgets, and . . . *frogs*. Lots and lots of frogs. There are at least a hundred of them. A mug shaped like Kermit the Frog sits next to the coffeepot. All of the refrigerator magnets are frogs of one variety or another, and ceramic frogs are scattered about on shelves and counter-tops. Even the salt and pepper shakers are frogs.

"What did you say your name was?"

I pull my gaze away from the amphibian menagerie and take the bogus work badge out of my pocket. "Elizabeth Bennet, with Bingley, Darcy, and—"

Doreen cuts me off with a wave of her hand. "I don't care what company you're with. How old are you?"

I open my mouth, fully prepared to tell the cover story. I'm twenty-two, just finished college. But something about the searching look in her eyes stops me. I think she'll know if I keep lying. And I think she'll stop talking, too.

"Seventeen. I'll be eighteen in two weeks. This is an internship."

Rookie move, Anna. Always stick to the cover story.

Without a word, I push him as hard as I can to the back of my head and stack the mental bricks to block him. It's a quick process, thanks to twelve years of practice, but my speed has probably doubled in the past sixteen days, thanks to Daniel's complete inability to keep his mouth shut.

"You okay?" Doreen asks.

"Yeah. Just . . . a little woozy from the heat, I guess."

"You got any other identification on you?"

"Not on me. But I think my school ID's out in the car." Which will have a different name, so I really hope she doesn't want me to go get it.

Doreen shoots a nervous glance toward the kitchen door. "No. Don't bother. I can tell you're too young to be with the group that came snoopin' around before asking questions. I'm pretty sure they're the same folks who tried to snatch Peyton from her mama when they were at the grocery store, which is why her family had to take off like they did. Miranda thought maybe they were government. I don't wanna believe our government would be behind somethin' like that, although these days . . ." She trails off, shaking her head, and then her eyes sharpen again. "But I'm not stupid. I don't buy your story about a class action suit. Why are you *really* here?"

"You're right," I say, again going with the instinct to be honest with her, and making a mental note to come up with a better cover story next time we talk to Magda. "But we *are* trying to help."

"Why?"

"Because those same people who tried to snatch Peyton snatched me. I got away, but I know what they're up to. I don't want it happening to anyone else."

Technically, that's not true. They snatched Deo. I turned myself over to Graham Cregg of my own accord, even though I was pretty sure he wouldn't honor his agreement to let Deo go. But the underlying sentiment is true. We want to keep Cregg's people from getting their hands on these kids. And that truth must show on my face, because Doreen's eyes soften.

But then she reaches behind her and pulls a cookbook—something by Paul Prudhomme—from one of the shelves and begins thumbing through it, ignoring me. Just as I'm about to try again, to ask her if there's anything at all that she can tell me, she pulls a pale-green piece of paper from the cookbook. It's shaped like a frog, and there's a phone number and address written across its belly.

Doreen clutches the paper tightly, and her words begin to spew out at a rapid clip. "Carl don't know half as much as he thinks he does. He was sleeping like a dead thing when I went over that night to help Miranda pack up. She was scared half to death. No surprise there—someone tried to snatch her baby in the middle of the damn Piggly Wiggly. As soon as they were done with the police, Jasper left town with the kids in one car, and Miranda started throwing food, clothes, whatever she could lay her hands on, into the back of their truck. Jasper told her not to let anyone know where they were heading, but . . . she was worried they might need something they'd left behind. Randa was a lot younger than me, but me and her, we were friends. She'd cried on my shoulder more than once about Jasper's damn temper. I even taped up her finger once when the jackass broke it. She always said it wasn't his fault, but . . . I don't know how much of that was her thinking his temper was due to that Army program and how much was just the typical garbage women say when they're married to a man who likes to beat up on them. I also knew about Peyton long before Carl saw her take apart that tree house. That was the biggest stunt she pulled, but it wasn't the first. Randa had her hands full. Hard enough to control a normal toddler, but one who can do stuff like that?"

Doreen shakes her head. She glances back down at the paper, then folds it in half, still not handing it to me. I'm scared to reach for it, scared she'll change her mind. Which is stupid, since I know she *doesn't* change her mind, but . . .

"Why did they snatch you?" she asks. "Can you move things with your mind like Peyton does—what do they call it? Telekinesis?"

"No. I don't have telekinesis."

This is true, although I can't help flashing back to our escape from the place Jaden and the others called The Warren. One of the hitchers who was briefly in my head, the ones I think of as the Furies, tweaked something in Lucas's body to give him a sneezing fit so violent that his nose was pouring blood. Another was thinking, *Throw him through the glass wall*, and she definitely wasn't planning to use her hands. That wasn't me, and those hitchers are gone now, but it still feels a bit like a selective truth, and I hope Doreen doesn't catch it.

"But I do have some other abilities that they'd like to . . . exploit," I tell her. "We want to prevent that. Our goal is to get these kids to a safe place and, eventually, find a way to reverse or at least control what was done to them."

Doreen looks down at the paper and sighs. "Miranda trusted me with this. I guess now I'm trusting you. If I ever find out you betrayed that trust . . ." Her eyes narrow, and she gives a bitter laugh. "Who am I kidding? There won't be a damned thing I can do except send nasty thoughts your way. You just remember, though, God's watchin' you. And like they say, what goes 'round, comes 'round."

I take the frog-shaped note. "And you think they're still at this address?"

"Yeah. I'm pretty sure it's the fishing cabin that her great-uncle owned. And as of last night, Miranda was there. With TJ. We usually e-mail back and forth . . . but she actually called this time. Sounded scared. Needed to hear a friendly voice, I guess."

"So . . . just Miranda and her son? Where are Peyton and Jasper?"

"That's why Miranda called. Said Peyton had lost control again. This time it was Randa who ended up in the emergency room . . . six stitches and a concussion. She said Jasper has Peyton over on the island, whatever that means, 'cause he couldn't get her to calm down. I'll tell you straight up that the main reason I decided to trust you is that Miranda sounded like she was at her wit's end. She needs help. The whole family needs help."

I feel a rush of annoyance at Magda for making us postpone this trip. If we'd come straight here, the MPs would almost certainly have found the kids during their training. There would be fewer dead bodies at Overhills, although I find it hard to work up much sympathy about Grady. And maybe we could have prevented Miranda Hawkins's trip to the emergency room. I can only imagine how guilty that little girl is feeling, after causing her mom to need stitches.

I'd have one less hitcher in my head too, although my feelings on that are bit more mixed. It would be easier on me, but hopefully Hunter will find peace faster this way.

"Listen," Doreen says, "I'd appreciate it if you kept everything I told you between you and me. Carl certainly don't need to know. That old fool can't keep a secret to save his life. Wish Miranda didn't have to find out I told you, either . . . but I don't see much way around her knowing. Hopefully she'll understand I'm trying to help."

"I'll make sure she does. And we'll do our best to help Peyton. To help her family. I promise."

"You'd *better*." Doreen levels me with a stare as she says the words. It feels like her entire battalion of kitchen frogs is staring me down as well. If I was inclined to break that promise, which I'm not, those frogs would haunt me.

Aaron is waiting by the truck. Peck is still talking, something about bulldogs and a rambling wreck, as Aaron nods, a frozen smile on his face. He perks up, however, when I flash the little piece of notepaper.

"My money's on the dogs," Peck says. "But then I've never much cared for tech—"

"Hey, um . . . we need to be going," Aaron says to Peck. "But we do appreciate your help, sir. And tell your wife thanks for the iced tea."

"Sure thing. Y'all drive safe goin' back to Atlanta, hear?"

"What was he talking about?" I ask Aaron once we're backing out of the driveway.

Aaron shrugs. "Football, I think. I was just trying to nod in the right places by that point. So . . . that's the paper you saw?"

I've been a little cryptic about the specifics of the vision. I can't avoid it, but there's no need for everyone else to have that weird sense of déjà vu.

"Yeah. I knew it was green but didn't realize it was frog shaped. Doreen's kitchen is teeming with frogs. Not real ones," I add, in response to his expression. "But it was still kind of creepy."

"So you don't like mice and you don't like frogs," he says with a little grin. "Not exactly a nature girl, are you?"

"I'm fine with frogs that are actually *in* nature. But frogs staring at you from every square inch of space in a kitchen is freaky. And get this . . . the address she has written here is in North Carolina."

"You've gotta be kidding me."

"Not kidding. But luckily, we won't be going back to Fort Bragg. The place is called Carova. Must be near the coast, or maybe a big lake.

Doreen mentioned an island and said they might be staying in a fishing cabin."

"Okay," Aaron says. "That's better. Hopefully we won't have to go too close to Bragg. The media hasn't mentioned any bodies being discovered. I'm pretty sure it's only a matter of time, though. And I'd rather not be nosing around there until things calm down."

I fill Aaron in on the rest of what Doreen told me, including Peyton's recent rampage. "She's not even four. Kids that age don't have a lot of self-control. Can you imagine knowing that your preschooler might literally tear the house apart if she misses her nap or just has a bad day?"

Aaron sighs. "She sounds like the kid you mentioned back at The Warren."

Daniel is lurking just behind my wall, following the conversation. I get the sense he doesn't agree with Aaron, so I reluctantly pull down the bricks. As nice as it is to have my head mostly to myself, I can't keep him penned up all day.

So . . . you disagree?

Absolutely. Unless this Peyton kid is way more powerful than she sounds, she's minor league compared to The Kid back at The Warren.

Those are the words that Daniel forms into sentences and consciously delivers to me. But Daniel and I have been doing this little mind dance for over a week now, and it's getting much easier for me to pick up the thoughts that hover just below the surface, the undercurrent he's trying to hide from me. These aren't always words. Sometimes, they are colors and images that reflect his emotions, little flashes of fear and anger like the ones that I saw the other day. This time, however, what comes through subconsciously are the words he chose *not* to use. The words he edited out but couldn't entirely block. When he thought *The Kid*, he was picturing the door to Room 81, but he was also thinking, *Sariah's boy.*

It takes me a moment to place Sariah as Ashley's sister. Given our deal about trying to avoid picking at each other's thoughts, I'm not inclined to push the issue, but I can tell that Daniel realizes he's let something slip. If he's going to be annoyed anyway, I might as well get a definitive answer.

So . . . the kid in Room 81 is Sariah's son? Ashley's nephew?

Yes, Anna. Happy now?

I'm tempted to tell him no, because I'd really like the boy's name and maybe a glimpse of a face to add to the voice I still recall in my mind's ear, telling me to run. It feels weird to keep calling him *the kid in Room 81.*

But Daniel has already retreated to the back of my head, sulking about his lack of privacy. Welcome to *my* world, Daniel.

My phone vibrates in my pocket. It's Deo.

Achievement unlocked.

The words are followed by a picture of a tiny brown-and-black puppy. I don't recognize the pink plaid fabric he's resting on, so the pup is either in Taylor's lap or Deo has lost all sense of fashion. At first, I'm not sure what the message means, but then I realize that the puppy's eyes are now open.

It was touch-and-go as to whether the puppy would make it last night. The little guy is tough, but his survival is at least partly due to Deo and Taylor's sheer determination. They came out of Walmart with not only puppy formula, a puppy bottle, and a heating pad, but also a tiny dog bed, training pads, way too many puppy toys, and a bag of treats that the pup won't be able to eat for at least a month or two. Aside from Taylor wrinkling her nose at the instructions for coaxing him to pee and poop, she and Deo have both eagerly taken on the feeding and cleaning tasks. In fact, the heating pad might have been unnecessary. The puppy has been in someone's hands or pocket pretty much nonstop since they found him—although Aaron and I are equally guilty on that front.

Kelsey would probably say we're all trying to compensate in some small fashion for the kids we saw in that room at Overhills, kids who were beyond saving. And she would be right. But it's also just really hard to resist a cute baby pup.

The scenery we're passing has begun to look very familiar. It's not simply that we drove by here on the way to the Pecks' house. It's the angle, and also the number and position of cars on US 280 up ahead, that is ringing my memory bells.

"You've seen those hummingbird feeders, right? The ones that look like they have flowers around the bottom?"

I try to force myself to say something different than what I said in the vision. To say *yes* or *maybe* or anything other than the word *sure*.

"Sure," I say.

The scene from the movie *Groundhog Day* flashes into my mind, the one where Bill Murray's character smashes the clock over and over. But no matter what he does, the thing still flips to six a.m., stuck in an endless loop.

Aaron slows down so that we can merge with the traffic on the highway, and then says, "Well, this feeder had a nail straight through one of those flowers. Looked like somebody pounded it in with a hammer, but Peck swears it flew straight out of that tree house and lodged in the feeder. And the house itself—there's an indentation in the siding shaped exactly like a two-by-four. Assuming the old guy's telling the truth, it's a miracle no one was killed."

I glance down at the scrap of green notepaper in my hand, and the sense of relief I feel isn't diminished at all by the fact that I've experienced all of this before. And while one part of my brain is still trying to experiment, still trying to see if I can change some small element of the way the vision pans out, my mouth just rolls right along with the words I remember saying before.

"At least we can find them now," I say. "Let the parents—the little girl, too—know they're not alone. Doreen said that wasn't the only time she'd done something like that. And the dad . . . like Peck said, he's not stable. They could be in serious trouble right now, and we're—what? At least twelve hours away. Maybe more."

"Yeah. If we leave now, we can be there by tomorrow morning. I just wish I knew what we're supposed to do when we get there. It's not like we have a safe place to take her, or a magic potion we can give her to make her normal. All we can do is turn over the Hawkins's information to Magda, and I'm pretty sure all she can do is throw money at the problem."

"Money's not a bad thing," I say, even though I know he's mostly right. "They probably *need* the money."

He sighs. "Yeah. But they're probably not stupid. Someone dangles money in front of you, there's usually a catch. I think Magda's legitimately interested in helping these kids, but I also don't think that's her only motive. I'm guessing Peyton's parents are going to have quite a few questions. And her dad is former military—not to mention a former Delphi subject—so there's a pretty good chance that he's going to be asking those questions while pointing a gun at us."

CHAPTER TWELVE

Outer Banks, North Carolina
November 5, 2019, 10:14 a.m.

The Outer Banks is a nearly two-hundred-mile archipelago that spans the coast of North Carolina, pretty much from top to bottom. Our destination is at the northernmost tip, where an eleven-mile unpaved stretch of beach suitable only for four-wheel-drive vehicles separates the Atlantic Ocean from Currituck Sound. It ends at the Carolina-Virginia border, thus the name CaroVA Beach.

The last RV park was back in Kitty Hawk, well over an hour from Carova. We dropped the camper in an overpriced and undersized slot there, unhooked the truck, and hit the road again. Deo, Taylor, and the pup are with us, despite Aaron's best efforts to convince them to stay behind. I could probably have done more to back him up, but I'm a little ambivalent on this point. On the one hand, Aaron is correct. Peyton's parents are likely to be armed and dangerous unless we manage to convince them that we're here to help, and I'd rather keep Deo out of that sort of danger. On the other hand, after the trip to Overhills, Deo can justifiably claim he's an asset. It's unlikely that Aaron would have sensed Dacia coming in time for us to get away if not for Deo's amp ability.

My opinion on the matter probably wouldn't have done much to sway the tide anyway. Deo is nearly as stubborn as Taylor.

It doesn't take us long to see why RVs aren't encouraged beyond Kitty Hawk. In some places, like the oddly named town of Duck, the strip of land is barely wide enough for a two-lane road. In others, the road whips and winds in a fashion that would probably have made me carsick if I hadn't insisted on riding shotgun.

The town of Corolla is the last bit of civilization before the road ends, so we scout out a gas station and a pizza place with decent reviews and fuel up. Our waiter is a helpful sort who gives Aaron some tips for driving on the beach, like letting some of the air out of the tires, and says we're lucky it's off-season, because traffic is murder in the summer.

It's still slowgoing. I don't mind the slower pace, though, because the view is absolutely gorgeous.

To our right, the waves are so close they're practically lapping at the tires. On our left, it's sand dunes as far as the eye can see, punctuated by the occasional house. Some of them are gargantuan, more like hotels than homes, with acres of land between them and the nearest neighbor. Almost all of the houses are clearly empty, many with realtor signs out front. This part of the island might be busy when the weather is warm, but right now it reminds me of a town in one of the zombie games I played with Deo a few times. I can almost picture a line of animated corpses shambling down one of the wooden walkways leading to the ocean.

Imaginary zombies aside, it's a relaxing ride. The sound and smell of the ocean chills me out. It seems to have a similar effect on the others, since we all fall silent and just soak up the scenery.

About a half an hour after we first enter the four-wheel-drive area, the navigation app tells us to turn left on one of the dirt trails to reach the address that Doreen gave me. We pull into the driveway of the "fishing cottage" and find that it is indeed a tiny cottage, even smaller than the boathouse at the end of the long pier extending out into the greenish-brown water of Currituck Sound. A white truck that looks very much like the one we're driving is parked outside.

We spent the past fifteen minutes or so of the drive debating who would knock on the door. I eventually drew the short straw, over Aaron's objections, based on Taylor's probably valid argument that I'm the least threatening person in the car. Deo and Aaron both hover around six feet, and while Deo is thin—too thin, after his illness—Aaron is muscular enough to be intimidating, at least at first glance. And although Taylor is shorter than I am, she exudes an energy that reminds me of an angry Chihuahua. The worst those little yappers can do is take a tiny chunk out of your ankle, but you still avoid getting too close. At least she's self-aware enough to realize this.

So Taylor and Deo are hanging in the cab with the pup. Aaron waits behind the truck, on alert, as my apparently nonthreatening self mounts the three concrete steps to the cottage.

My hand is raised in midknock when the door swings open to reveal a tall, very thin woman in jeans and a loose flannel shirt. Beyond her, in the small living room, a boy of around eight is playing a video game. The woman's forehead is marked by a wide bruise. A nasty cut, held together by a neat row of stitches, peeks out from under her dark curls. She looks exhausted.

"You've got the wrong address. This cabin isn't for rent."

"Are you Miranda Hawkins?" I ask.

As soon as she hears the name, her expression hardens, and she yells back over her shoulder. "TJ! Go to your room. Right now!"

The boy doesn't argue. He drops the game controller instantly, giving one quick nervous look toward the door before disappearing into the back of the cabin.

Aaron takes a couple of steps around the front of the truck.

"You need to get back in your truck and go. No one by that name lives here."

That doesn't make any sense. If she didn't recognize the name, why send her son out of the room?

"Mrs. Hawkins, I just want to—"

The door slams in my face.

I knock again. No response.

On the third knock, the door opens, and Miranda Hawkins is back, this time with a gun. I gulp and take a step back, nearly tumbling off the side of the steps. Why didn't Aaron pick up on the threat of violence?

The thought barely has time to register before I catch the fear in Miranda's dark eyes. I glance back at the truck, and sure enough, Aaron's gun is pointed at her.

I feel Hunter's panic rising, so I pull my eyes away from the guns. The last thing Hunter needs to see is another damn gun aimed at him . . . well, at me, but right now, that's pretty much the same thing. Instead, I focus on Miranda's face.

"In case you didn't hear," Miranda says in a shaky voice, "I told you to get off of my property."

"Mrs. Hawkins, we are not here to harm you or your family." I open my hand and show her the frog-shaped note.

There's a very long pause as what I'm holding registers, and then Miranda lets out an exasperated sigh.

"Doreen. Damn it. I should never have let her know where we were going. Jasper's gonna kill me."

"No, no. Listen, please. We're on the same side. The people who tried to snatch your daughter before? They snatched my brother, who's over there in the truck. We were lucky enough to get away, but all four of us are like Peyton. Well . . . not exactly. We have different abilities. But all of them are the result of the same project your husband took part in."

Even though I carefully planned what I would say while I was in the truck, I find myself stumbling over the words. Miranda watches me, not responding. Then again, she also hasn't shot me or shoved me off the steps, so I continue.

"Doreen was very reluctant to give me your information, Mrs. Hawkins. But she's your friend, and she said you sounded desperate, at the end of your rope. We can offer you resources. People who can help Peyton learn to handle her ability. And we're working on a drug to control or reverse the effects."

The only part that is completely true is the bit about resources. We have money that we could give her right this minute. Not enough to start a new life somewhere but maybe enough to pay a few bills. The part about an anti-Delphi drug is a long way from being reality, however. To the best of my knowledge, Magda still hasn't gotten the vial to the researcher she mentioned, and I have no earthly idea how long it would take to create any sort of antidote or even a drug to block or reduce psychic abilities. And though we don't have anyone lined up to help Peyton yet, I realize that could easily be remedied. Kelsey helped me learn to wall off my hitchers. Maybe she can help Peyton and these other kids, too. I'm not sure why I didn't think of it before.

Miranda's gaze jumps nervously between my face and Aaron's pistol. "You come here with a gun and expect me to believe that you want to help us?"

Aaron speaks up for the first time. "We didn't lead with the gun, Mrs. Hawkins. I only pulled it when I thought Anna might be in danger."

As Aaron is talking, I feel Daniel move toward the front of my head. And even though I know Daniel means well, I give him a firm push backward. I'm not entirely sure he *could* nudge Miranda right now. Daniel himself isn't even sure it would work. I can sense that without him saying a word.

But even if we were *both* certain, it's too risky on several levels. She's holding a gun, and who knows how Miranda would react if she sensed someone was trying to influence her actions. Also, if we're going to help Peyton, we'll be in contact with her mom. If Miranda feels like she's been tricked in any way at the outset, it's going to complicate things tremendously.

Finally, I can't shake the sense that Miranda Hawkins really *hates* holding that weapon. Yes, she'd probably shoot me if I tried to jump her, and I'm certain she'd shoot me if she thought her son was in danger. But she's not looking for a fight. If her thoughts had been violent, Aaron would have picked up on them before she pulled the gun.

So back Daniel goes. The fact that he *does* go, without any sort of argument, confirms that this is the right decision, but it also has me more than a little worried about Daniel's state of mind.

I turn my attention back to Miranda. "All we want to do is help, Mrs. Hawkins—"

"Stop calling me that! It's Miranda, just Miranda," she says, her expression unchanging. "Mrs. Hawkins is my mother-in-law."

"Okay. Miranda, then. I'm Anna. The guy over there with the gun—and he's actually a really nice guy—is Aaron. My brother, Deo, Aaron's sister, Taylor, and a still-to-be named puppy are in the truck. If you lower your gun, Aaron will lower his. And after that, if you really want us to, we'll go. But . . ."

I glance up at the bruise on her forehead and lower my voice. This is definitely not something I'm ready to discuss with Aaron. Deo doesn't even know the full story. I even steer clear of talking about Myron with Kelsey. The wounds he left were deep, and I don't pick at that particular scab if I can avoid it.

But those memories could be the key to reaching Peyton's mom, so I pull in a deep breath and go on. "When I was a little older than Peyton, I hurt someone. It wasn't exactly me doing it, and I couldn't control what happened, but it took me a very long time to move past it. And the person I hurt was a *stranger*. Someone I didn't even know. From what your neighbors back in Georgia told us, Peyton loves you. Loves her brother, too. Knowing that she's hurt either of you must be tearing her up inside. She needs help coping with this ability, and with her emotions."

My eyes water as I speak. It seems to be contagious, because a tear sneaks down Miranda's cheek, and her lower lip starts to quiver. I'm a little concerned that this shakiness will spread to her trigger finger, so it's a relief when she moves the gun away from me . . . until I realize she's pointing it at Aaron.

"Here's how it's gonna go," Miranda says. "You toss that gun into your truck. The kids in the back get out. All four of you turn your pockets inside out and whatever else I decide is necessary to prove you're not armed. Then you lock the truck, and I get the key. After that, I will give you a chance to show that you're on the level. That's all I'm gonna promise. And if those terms don't work for you, then crawl back in your truck and get the hell out of here."

Aaron slowly lowers his pistol, and we follow her instructions. When she's satisfied that we're not carrying any other weapons, Miranda motions with her gun toward a picnic table near the dock. "Toss the keys on the grass, then you three head on over there. We'll call you if we need you."

I retrieve the keys and bring them back to Miranda, who's now sitting on the concrete stoop. She nods to the lower step, and I sit down.

"Mama?" The voice is faint and tentative.

"TJ, you need to stay in your room."

"I know, but it's just that I heard her say somethin' about a puppy and I thought maybe—"

"Tomás José, do as you're told."

"I'm goin', I'm goin'."

"He's bored," Miranda says, looking down at her sneakers. "I should have taken him across the Sound for school this morning, but he wanted to stay here with me. This whole thing scared him pretty bad. When he and his dad found me on the kitchen floor, there was blood all over. And Jasper couldn't take me to the emergency room because he had to get Peyton out of here. He grabbed two of our bug-out bags and took the skiff over to the island. Nothing much over there she can destroy, and she was so upset after she realized I was hurt that I half expected her to explode this cabin the same way she did her brother's tree house. So TJ and I waited until the next morning when I was seeing straight to drive into Kitty Hawk to get my head stitched up. Had to tell them I fell, which nobody ever believes, but they'd lock me up in a mental ward if I told them the truth."

She glances over at me and arches an eyebrow. "So what is it *you* can do? Light fires? Toss skillets through the air just by looking at them? Pretty sure you can't read minds, otherwise you'd have . . . known . . ."

She trails off, looking a little embarrassed. I'm tempted to ask exactly what it is I would have known if I was able to read minds. But I don't want to push, so I answer her question instead.

Her mouth twists skeptically when I tell her about my hitchers. "And you can do this because one of your parents was part of that same program that Jasper was in? Back at Bragg?"

"That's my best guess. I was abandoned when I was three, so I don't really know much about my parents. But Taylor and Aaron?" I nod toward the picnic table, where Aaron is keeping a cautious eye on us. Taylor and Deo are sitting on the grass a few feet away from him, watching the puppy toddle around. "Their dad was definitely in the same program as your husband."

"And they're also . . ." Miranda stops and snorts softly. "What do you call a kid who can do the kind of things my Peyton can? Gifted?"

"I think a case could be made for either gifted or cursed, but yes, they both have psychic abilities. A bunch of other kids do too. The people who tried to snatch Peyton earlier this year were just studying them, but . . . something seems to have changed. If you've been following the news this past week, you may have heard about the kids at Fort Bragg who were kidnapped—"

"Killed, you mean?"

My surprise that she knows that already must show on my face, because Miranda looks mildly amused. "Guess I'm following the news a bit more closely than you are. Authorities issued a press release this morning. All six were found on land the Army uses for training. A couple other bodies, too. No leads yet on who did it. So . . . you're telling me those kids were all like Peyton?"

"Three of them for certain. I'm pretty sure the others were as well."

"And you think this group that was collecting the kids before, studying them—you think they're killing them now?"

I shrug, because I'm not really sure what to think on that front. "I'm convinced that at least one of their people was involved. Other than that, it's just conjecture."

She sits there for a moment, thinking. "You're asking me to take what you've said on faith. There aren't any ghosts around here for you to pick up, at least to the best of my knowledge, and even if there were, I wouldn't know what to ask so that you could prove it to me. Though you do seem a little young to be connected to the people who tried to snatch Peyton—they were walking stereotypes, I swear. Dark suits and sunglasses—almost like Will Smith and that other guy in *Men in Black*. That's one reason we got away. Those men stood out like a sore thumb in the Piggly Wiggly parking lot. If they'd been in blue jeans and work boots, I'd probably have been slower to react, and they'd have Peyton. Anyway, like I said, you *look* too young. But . . . maybe they got smarter about that."

Miranda nods toward the picnic table. "What exactly can they do? Can they move stuff around like Peyton?"

"No. But if you want details, I'd rather you asked them directly."

Her eyes narrow slightly. "Fine. What's the girl's name again?"

I tell her, and she calls out to Taylor, who scoops up the puppy and begins walking toward us. When Miranda asks, Taylor gives her a basic overview of her ability and then reaches under her collar and pulls out a chain. At the end is one of those friendship pendants with one half of the heart missing.

"My friend Molly was killed a few years back. I found her body because I had this. She was wearing the other half."

Miranda considers Taylor for a moment and then grabs her gun from the step and goes back into the house. When she returns, the gun is stuck in the waistband of her jeans and she's carrying a plastic snow globe. The curved stand that holds it was once white, but it's now yellowed with age and has a missing chunk near the front.

Taylor gives me the puppy so that she can hold the object in both hands. "Is this Peyton's? If so, I can tell you where she and her dad are hiding."

"No," Miranda says. "That would be too easy. You might have followed Jasper. Maybe you flew over in a helicopter and saw them when they left. I want you to tell me where it came from."

"I can't guarantee anything," Taylor says. "But I need something to draw with."

"TJ?" Miranda calls. "Bring me some paper and a pencil."

The boy brings back a spiral notebook and a stubby pencil. Taylor wrinkles her nose at the lined paper. "Just so you know, this is going to look like crap." Her eyes flit over to TJ, standing behind his mom, and she adds, "I saw you looking out the window. You can hold the puppy, if it's okay with your mom. Just be careful. He's only a few weeks old."

TJ's eyes grow wide. "Can I, Mom?"

Miranda sighs. "Okay, but right here next to the steps. And only for a minute, then you get back inside."

The boy sits on the grass next to the steps, and a huge grin splits his face when I hand him the wriggling puppy.

Miranda shakes her head, and one side of her mouth twitches up slightly. "Score one for your crew. First time TJ has smiled in the past three days. He wants a dog so damn bad, but there's no way we're getting an animal in the middle of this craziness. No telling what Peyton might do if she got scared or if it scratched her."

"Is she able to control it at all?"

Miranda looks a little surprised. "She *controls* it constantly. Peyton just turned four last week, and I don't think you'll find many kids her age who work so hard to keep their cool. If she didn't, I doubt any of us, including Peyton, would still be alive. It scared the hell out of her when she hurt TJ. It was just that one second when she let her guard down. This . . ." She touches the stitches on her head. "She's got an ear infection, okay? Been prone to them since she was a baby, but it took two trips to the doctor for the asshole to finally give her an antibiotic. She'd been feeling miserable for over a week, so her resistance was way down already. And then she was in the cabinet looking for a cookie, and I told her not until after supper. That earned me a foul look, but that would have absolutely been the end of it if Peyton hadn't bumped the shelf. A can of tomatoes landed right square on her toe, and . . . I guess she was still a little mad at me about the cookie, because next thing I know she's screaming and crying and a cast-iron skillet is flyin' toward me."

"Ouch."

"Yeah," Miranda says. "I don't know how long I was out. It was just me and Peyton here when it happened. Jasper had taken the boat across the Sound to pick up TJ from school. They were back when I came to, and there's blood-soaked Cheerios and potato chips all over the floor, feathers from the sofa pillows floating around in the air. Peyton was just rockin' back and forth, saying 'Mama' over and over, so scared that there was no way she could have stopped that thing inside her from lashing out, but she had the control to turn it toward things like feathers and snacks—light stuff, soft stuff—that couldn't hurt me any worse than I already was. That couldn't hurt any of us. So, yeah, my baby can control

216

it, but she's *four*. There are plenty of four-year-olds can't even control their bladders."

She looks over at the picnic table. "How long is this likely to take?"

Taylor is sitting so close to Deo that their shoulders touch. I wonder if she feels that odd tingle when she's using him as an amp.

"Don't know. I'm guessing it will be pretty quick. But . . ." I hesitate and then just decide to say what's on my mind. "This won't really prove anything, you know. I've already told you that there are quite a few people who were affected by the Delphi program. Some of them work for the group that tried to kidnap Peyton. So, even if Taylor comes back with something in her sketch that shows she's clairvoyant, that doesn't prove we're on your side."

"True," she says. "But it will show whether you're telling the truth about *something*. And . . . I don't have any psychic abilities at all. Jasper, on the other hand? You wouldn't want to play poker with him, not unless you like to lose. I don't let him gamble often. You win too much, people start to think you're cheating. Then things get nasty, and I can't really count on Jasper to hold his temper."

She looks confused for a second, like maybe she's trying to find her original train of thought. "Sorry. When I'm tired, I tend to ramble. Anyway, like I was saying, I'm not psychic. But I do have a good sense of people. You listen as much as you talk, and you didn't break eye contact, even when I had the gun in your face. I don't think you'd do that if you were trying to hide something."

Her words make me very, very glad that I ignored Daniel's earlier offer to "persuade" Miranda. Daniel seems really out of it, anyway. At first, I thought he and Jaden might just be overwhelmed dealing with Hunter, but there are no songs on a constant loop in the back of my mind today, so I think the boy's shock is wearing off. I'm starting to actually sense Hunter's presence beyond the ball of pain and fear that was pretty much his entire existence last night. He's aware of what's going on now, and I can feel him paying closer attention each time I look over at TJ, who is laughing while the puppy gnaws on his finger.

We watch them play for only a few minutes before Taylor heads our way with the snow globe in one hand and the paper and pencil in the other.

"Okay," she says, plopping down on the bottom step. "That was kind of a blast. If I'd had Deo around when I was searching for Molly, things would have been so much easier. I've got several sketches for you, actually. There was some interference. I don't think this first sketch is the original owner of your snow globe. In fact, I'm guessing this is where Peyton is, because I can tell it's really close by and it's an island."

The island in the sketch is pointed at one end, almost like an arrowhead. Most of the land is shaded in, aside from a tiny strip on the eastern coast that she's left blank. On that patch of white, Taylor has drawn two circular shapes and one square.

"I don't know what those are," she says, pointing to one of the circles and the square. "But I'm pretty sure the other circle is a tent. A yellow tent, to be precise, but"—she waves the pencil—"my color options are limited to graphite."

Miranda shakes her head. "Like I said before—"

"We could have followed and seen them," Taylor says. "Yeah, I know. But if something is in the printer queue, I have to get it out before I can move on to the next drawing."

She flips the page. There are four small numbered sketches, and she taps the one at the top. "Number one here, as you can see, is also an island, but it's not empty. I think it's New York, but I'm not sure. I've only been there twice. Super crowded, lots of buildings."

The second drawing is like she's zoomed in on a specific part of the island. Narrow strips of land jut out into the water like the teeth of a comb. Streets are laid out in a grid, and she's drawn a star two blocks in and about one third of the way up.

Taylor starts to describe this sketch, but I stop her. "I know this area. You're right. It's definitely New York. Manhattan. Hold on a sec."

I'm used to fading backward into my head to access the memory banks. It's something I've done on a regular basis for much of my life. I ignore the fact that all three hitchers are watching me and head for the file cabinet marked *Didier*.

> You need an upgrade, girl. Who uses file cabinets any-
> more? Wouldn't it be faster to imagine your memory
> banks as something like Siri, and you could just think,
> *Navigate to Didier.*

Jaden isn't the first to note this. Deo laughed when I described my mental storage facility a few years ago, saying that it was like something out of the 1980s.

> *This is a visual Kelsey helped me build when I was a kid. And since it's not broke, I'm not inclined to fix it.*

When I return with the data I need, Miranda is giving me an odd look.

"That's Hell's Kitchen. In Manhattan." I tap the section that looks like a comb. "Those are the West Side piers, and the long strip below is the Lincoln Tunnel. Didier, one of my hitchers, lived in Manhattan when he first arrived from Rwanda in the 1980s, and he worked a delivery job for a pizza place in Hell's Kitchen for a few months. I can't say for certain, but that looks like around Forty-Sixth or Forty-Seventh Street and Tenth Avenue."

Miranda's expression remains guarded, but she's leaning closer to the notebook, so I can tell this has caught her interest. The third drawing is the outside of a four-story townhouse. The door is set into an arched entranceway. Several letter *Z*s are stacked on top of each other above the door and windows on the front of the building. I'm about to ask what they are, and then I realize they're the fire escape.

"The building is brown with a green door." Taylor points to the fourth drawing. "That's the living room. I have no earthly clue what that bean-shaped blob in front of the couch is, but it's painted sort of turquoise. And at some point, this snow globe"—she waves it back and forth and then hands it back to Miranda—"was sitting on it."

"It's a coffee table," Miranda says. "It belonged to my grandmother, and it's now in my cousin's apartment in New York. We drove up there in September to get the keys for this cabin. Her mom rents this place out in the summer, but she hasn't been down here since my great-uncle died. Things were getting tense at Jasper's mom's house, so I asked Aunt Tracy if we could use this place during the off-season. Peyton took a liking to the snow globe when we were there, and my aunt said she could have it."

"She still likes it," Taylor says. "Peyton, I mean. That's why it was in my printer queue. She held it recently . . . only I don't think it made her happy."

Miranda runs her finger over the jagged edge at the bottom. "This was one of the casualties of Peyton's recent . . . outburst. Jasper said she was holding it when they found us."

She stands up and tosses me the keys to our truck. "I have to run TJ over to Knotts Island tomorrow for school. I'll take you to meet Peyton after I drop him. If you and her hit it off, then Jasper and I will discuss this. No promises, and I can warn you he's going to be pissed off. I wish I could call him to give him a heads-up, but his phone died last night, so . . . we'll see. Come on, TJ."

The boy reluctantly gives back the puppy. I thank Miranda for hearing us out, and we're about to get into the truck when she calls back, "There's only room in the boat for four, so two of you will need to stay home. Your gun better stay home, too. We leave at seven a.m., with or without you. And it will be cold as hell, so dress warm."

CHAPTER THIRTEEN

Currituck Sound, North Carolina
November 6, 2019, 6:36 a.m.

"I told you to dress warm," Miranda says, shaking her head, which is snugly covered by the hood of her quilted jacket. Her gloved hand rests on the throttle of the outboard motor as she maneuvers the boat toward the dock.

"This *is* me dressing warm."

That's true. I'm wearing most of the clothes Deo packed for me when we left Maryland, along with Taylor's fur-lined Uggs. My hoodie, the warmest item in my wardrobe, lies in a dumpster somewhere near Fort Bragg, covered with blood and gray matter. Deo's purple denim jacket, which I borrowed as a temporary replacement, was clearly chosen more for aesthetics than warmth.

We opted to stay overnight at a Hampton Inn near Corolla rather than driving all the way back to the RV since we had to be at Miranda's place before seven. The temperature plummeted in the early hours of the morning, dropping nearly thirty degrees, and it's hard to believe that it was warm enough last night that we walked on the beach for about an hour after dinner. Taylor and Deo had even joked about diving in for a swim, although all it took was a single chilly wave hitting their feet to convince them that wasn't such a great idea. Now, a frigid wind mixed with ocean spray whips against my cheeks as the boat skims the brackish green water between Carova and Knotts Island.

TJ is bundled up like Kenny on *South Park*, with just the small patch of caramel skin around his eyes exposed to the elements. Once Miranda has the boat parallel to the dock, Aaron helps TJ heave his bicycle, which bumped against my knee for most of the trip across the Sound, onto the pier. Then the boy climbs on his bike and takes off across the grass toward the dirt road that leads to his school.

Miranda picks up speed as we head back out into open water. We're now moving about twice as fast as we did before, and the temperature shifts rapidly from cold to bloody freezing, even though I'm sitting with Aaron's arms wrapped around me. He offered his coat—twice, in fact—but I know he's only wearing a single layer underneath, and his shoulders would never fit inside Deo's denim jacket.

I'm glad for the warmth, but there's an awkwardness that wasn't there before. I don't need Dacia's ability to read his thoughts to know when something reminds Aaron that he's also—kind of—hugging his brother. His embrace shifts from affectionate to perfunctory and back again several times during the interminably long ride.

By the time I spot the narrow strip of white sand on Long Point Island, my teeth are chattering so hard I'm afraid I'll chomp off a piece of my tongue. The yellow tent is there, just like in Taylor's drawing. Another boat, smaller than this one, lies hull-side up on the grassy area beyond the shore.

Miranda cuts the engine, points the boat toward a little copse of trees, and we begin to drift silently toward the beach. My shivers abate somewhat now that the wind is less fierce.

"Once we're on shore," Miranda says, "I'll go talk to Jasper. After I explain everything to him and see how Peyton is doing, I'll come back and get you. If I just show up with two strangers in tow, it might upset Peyton. Might upset Jasper, too. Most of the time he's easygoing, but he has a bit of a temper on occasion. Pretty sure that was a little gift from this Delphi program, too. Either way, we can't stay long. There's a midweek checkout at one of the event houses we clean, and I'll need to winterize it, with the cold spell coming on. Unless Peyton's doing well enough for Jasper to help, I'll be solo on this one, and it's a beast, so I gotta be there by ten at the latest."

I have no idea what any of the stuff about the house means. Judging from his expression, neither does Aaron. But we both nod.

Miranda is wearing wading boots, so she steps out once we reach shallow water and pulls the boat to the edge of the beach. Once the prow hits dry land, Aaron and I climb across and help her tug the boat up onto the grass beside the smaller craft.

Given the temperature, I'd rather keep moving in order to warm up. This section of the island is covered with low-lying brush rather than sand, however, so there's really not much clear space to walk without landing back in the water. I find a piece of driftwood that's reasonably dry, and Aaron sits next to me, but I can't help noticing that he's returned to maintaining a few inches' distance now that I'm no longer at major risk for hypothermia. It feels like second grade again. *Eww, girl cooties.*

I rub my hands vigorously between my thighs to thaw them out.

"Not exactly beach weather," Aaron says.

"Definitely not. I'd gladly trade with Taylor and Deo, snug and warm in bed right now."

"No kidding." He glances down the beach at Miranda, who is unzipping the tent. "When you talked to Kelsey last night, did she give you any ideas about how to approach Peyton?"

"*Very carefully.* Those were her exact words, actually. I am so hopelessly underqualified for this. Peyton needs a professional. She needs Kelsey, or at least someone with Kelsey's experience."

"Sam's talking to Magda about that today."

"Hmph. Hope he can find a way to make Magda think hiring Kelsey is her own idea. Otherwise, I doubt she'll agree."

When Kelsey and I spoke last night, I was reluctant to even mention the idea of her working with us. After all of the drama over the past two weeks, I thought she might be ready to just head to her beach house and decompress. But Kelsey wasn't just willing. She was eager. Which leads me to suspect that everything she said about being ready to retire was only talk. She just didn't want me or Deo feeling guilty about the impact that all of this has had on her.

"Sam can be very convincing," Aaron says. "And there's no logical reason for Magda to object, anyway."

"Maybe. I only wish Kelsey were here right now instead of me."

"You'll do fine. Miranda said Peyton doesn't like losing control. She'll almost certainly want help, she'll *want* to listen, and she's probably too young to think about whether we have ulterior motives. Her dad, on the other hand . . ."

"Are you picking anything up from him?"

"Not yet." Aaron shrugs, coloring slightly. "But then I had my first ever false negative yesterday. Miranda pulling that gun caught me totally by surprise. If I'd had any idea that she was going to do that, you'd never have been anywhere near that door."

"Um . . . I'm not entirely sure that you got a false negative. What if she wasn't actually planning to use the gun?"

"Did she say that?"

"Not in so many words. It was just something . . . that she almost said. Does that make sense? Don't get me wrong—if we'd threatened TJ in any way, she'd have found the nerve to use it. But I think she was mostly trying to scare us off."

"Maybe. But you're *not* taking any more chances like—" He stops and gives me a sideways grin. "Okay, that's coming out all wrong. As Taylor is so fond of reminding me, I'm not the boss of her or this project. And I'm definitely not the boss of you. Obviously what I *meant* to say is that I'd be much happier if you didn't take any more chances like that, but it is, of course, ultimately your decision."

I smile. "Your mom and Taylor have trained you very well."

"They try. Although, if I'm being totally honest . . ." He trails off, apparently having second thoughts about being totally honest.

A few days ago, I'd probably have just let it lie. But after several consecutive nights of this cold-shoulder stuff, I'm annoyed enough to push it. "What?"

"Nothing. Just ask Daniel to stay . . . on alert, or whatever. In case this Jasper guy goes off his nut."

"I don't know how much help Daniel will be. He seems kind of . . . I don't know. Lethargic."

Now that I think about it, I haven't heard a peep from Daniel since his half-hearted attempt to intervene yesterday when Miranda pulled the gun. I've spent most of the past week wishing that he'd stop pacing around my head, but now that he *is* quiet, I feel like I need to check on him.

Daniel? You're okay, right?

Yes. Just so you know, I *could* have convinced Miranda yesterday, and I absolutely would have if I'd thought she was serious with that gun. What you said to Aaron is right, though. She wasn't going to shoot. I could see it in her eyes. But yes . . . I'll admit I'm tired. Nudging people never drained me in my own body. I mean, like Taylor, I always needed food afterward, but otherwise I actually felt energized. When I do it through your body, it's like getting hit with the flu. But like I said, if you need help, I'm here.

When I open my eyes, Aaron is watching me, eyebrows raised, and I tell him what Daniel said.

"Maybe you need to eat more afterward?"

"But I haven't been hungrier than usual . . ." I trail off as Aaron's eyes flash toward the tent. "What's wrong?"

"Miranda just told him we're here. I think she's trying to reason with him, but . . ." He shakes his head. "Really wishing she hadn't made us leave my gun behind."

"Yeah. Listen, let me take the lead, okay?" Aaron gives me a reluctant look and starts to protest, but I cut him off. "Like Taylor said, I'm less intimidating. If Jasper sees this as a turf war, it could get nasty."

After a moment, he nods. "Fine. Just . . . don't get close to him. He's near the boiling point." His eyes glass over briefly, and then he adds, "Although proximity isn't really going to matter. He's armed."

Miranda emerges from the tent, followed a moment later by her husband, who moves past her at a rapid clip. She calls out to him, but his eyes are fixed on us.

Jasper Hawkins doesn't fit my mental image at all. I'd pictured him as Hispanic like Miranda and TJ, although I probably shouldn't have assumed that. And based on the various comments about his temper and possibly abusive behavior, I'd pegged him as tall and beefy. Again, not necessarily warranted, but I'd imagined him looking like that Alberto Del Rio guy, or maybe The Rock.

But Jasper Hawkins is more like a middle-aged Daniel Radcliffe. Short and wiry, with dark hair, pale skin, and finely chiseled features. His jaw is clenched so tight that the cords stand out on his neck as he storms toward us, his right hand thrust inside his partially unzipped jacket.

I get to my feet slowly, not wanting to set the guy off further.

Jasper is maybe ten feet away from us when he stops cold. He squints at my face for a few seconds, and then his eyes grow large. *"Leah?"*

I instinctively glance behind me, even though I know Aaron is the only person there.

Miranda has caught up with him now. Her eyes narrow, moving back and forth between me and her husband, who is still staring at me, mouth open, arms now hanging loose at his sides like he's in shock.

"You told me Leah was dead," Miranda says. "And even if she wasn't, she'd be what? Forty at least."

Jasper nods, but he still doesn't take his eyes off of me. "Not Leah. But she sure as hell looks like her. Her name is Anna."

Miranda is about to say something else, but she stops, confused. "I don't remember telling you her—"

"Wow." Jasper takes a couple of steps backward, shaking his head. After a moment he gives a stunned, bitter laugh, and adds, "You look just like your mother. Except . . . the nose. That's more like Scott."

Now it's my turn to stand there with my mouth open. I can't find words. I can't even draw a full breath.

I gave up any hope of finding my parents years ago. The State of Maryland did a thorough search when I was abandoned. And Kelsey told me that she did a bit of digging on her own. I don't know if she was hoping for answers as to why I can do what I do, if she thought the trait might run in the family, or what. Regardless of her reasons, the search was a complete and total dead end.

I've met a few other kids who were abandoned, who had no clue about their parents, during my time in the foster system. Most of them said that they didn't care. That they didn't want to know.

I said the same thing.

Of course, I was lying.

I suspect every single one of them was lying, too. Even when you give up hope, you still wonder. No matter how much you protest, you still want to know where you came from. Although I'm luckier than some. I never had to wonder *why* someone abandoned me. The reason was pinned to my dress, along with my name: *This child is possessed.*

Aaron's on his feet now, apparently realizing that the connection between my brain and my body is kind of tenuous. "Are you okay?"

While I definitely appreciate the steadying arm around my waist, him standing up was a bad idea. It's now obvious that Aaron has maybe six inches and forty pounds on Jasper, whose hand moves back inside his jacket.

"Why exactly are you here?" Jasper asks. "Did they let Scott out? Did he send you?"

I finally locate my voice, but it sounds high and reedy when I answer him. "I don't know anyone named Scott."

"We're here to help your daughter," Aaron says. "Or, rather . . . to help *you* help your daughter."

"I don't need your help," Jasper says, glaring at him. "We're doing just fine on our own."

Miranda has been watching all of this in silence, but now she steps forward, tugging off the stocking cap that was covering the stitches above her eyebrow. "You call this *doing just fine*, Jasper? Peyton flinging a frypan at my head without even touching it is *doing just fine*? Having to camp out on this stupid island so she can't hurt anyone else—that's *doing just fine*?"

For a moment, I think Jasper is going to hit her. His hand is clenched nearly as tight as his jaw. Aaron must think so too, because his body goes rigid, and I can tell he's one step from tackling Jasper, even knowing the guy is armed.

But Jasper reins it in. He closes his eyes and takes a deep breath. "Back off, Miranda. Please? Just. *Back. Off.*" His entire body is quivering.

She takes two steps away from him. Her eyes, still blazing, never leave his face. "This is bullshit," she mutters as she pulls the stocking cap back on. "Bullshit. I'm gonna check on Peyton. Try not to kill anybody, okay, *bucho*?"

Jasper leans forward at that last dig, like a dog straining at the leash, but he keeps his feet planted in the sand as Miranda stomps off toward the tent. "Even if you're right," he says, turning back to Aaron, "even if we *do* need help, no way in hell am I taking anything from Scott Pfeifer."

"Who is Scott Pfeifer?" My question is just short of a scream. I remind myself that yelling at the person with the gun is probably a bad idea and lower my voice before continuing. "I already told you I've never met anyone by that name. Have you, Aaron?"

"No," Aaron says, but there's a flicker of doubt in his eyes. "I don't personally know anyone named Scott Pfeifer. But the name does seem familiar. I might have seen it in some of my dad's papers."

"Your dad was with Delphi?" Jasper asks.

Aaron nods. "Cole Quinn. Did you know him?"

"I did," Jasper says. "And the fact that you're his kid isn't exactly helping your case. Quinn left before the program ended, but he worked with Scott and Cregg. Admin stuff. He knew what they were doing and was apparently okay with it. So he's as much to blame for my daughter's condition as they are."

That pisses Aaron off, judging from the set of his jaw, but he keeps his voice level. "My father *died* trying to keep Cregg from starting the program back up. So maybe you didn't know him as well as you thought."

The two men lock stares, neither willing to look away.

Jasper is the first one to break, looking down at the sand and then up again. "Maybe I didn't. But I knew Scott. There wouldn't have even been a Delphi protocol if Scott Pfeifer wasn't there with his test tubes and few dozen enlisted lab rats like me and Leah, helping Cregg play God. And since you're standing there with your arm around his daughter, I think I've got good reason to be concerned."

"Why do you assume she's his daughter?" Aaron asks.

"Because she looks just like her mother! Because I blew up the damn balloons at her first birthday party. Watched Leah write *Happy Birthday, Anna* on the cake. Because I was *this* close to talking Leah into leaving that son of a bitch, just grabbing the baby and getting the hell out of there. With *me*. But no. She decided to give Pfeifer another chance, and he thanked her by blowing her brains out."

I inhale sharply, the words hitting me like a gut punch. When Jasper sees my expression, he shakes his head in wonder or maybe disgust. "You're telling me you didn't know any of this? *Any* of it? Even if your grandparents kept you in their Holy Roller bubble, I figured Rowena would have told you something eventually."

Feeling shaky, I stumble back to the driftwood and sit down, trying to pull myself together. It's beyond stupid to be on the brink of tears over what Jasper just said. Even if this couple he's talking about are my biological parents, they aren't people I know, people I care about. They're total strangers.

"She's been in foster care since she was three," Aaron says. "She doesn't know anything about her family."

"Who is Rowena?" I ask. "And what happened to Scott Pfeifer?"

"Rowena is Leah's sister. She was still living with their parents last I heard, but . . . that would have been, what? Fifteen years ago, maybe. She wasn't as smart as Leah, but she wasn't stupid. Hopefully she's gotten the hell out of there by now. And Scott? He confessed. Got off on an insanity plea, but there was never any doubt that he did it. There was security footage of the whole thing. Fingerprints on the gun. Witnesses who saw him . . ."

He trails off, rubbing his forehead. "Listen, the drug they gave us, it messes with your head. It messed with *my* head, and Scott . . . he was in the program a lot longer than I was. To be honest, he wasn't a bad guy at the beginning. But it's his fault that Peyton can't have a normal life, his fault that Leah died, so you can understand my reaction, right?"

Jasper is clearly feeling bad about dumping all of this on my head at once, and yeah, I do understand his reaction, given what he's told me. But I'm not going to admit that right now, not if I can use that bit of guilt to help Peyton.

"For now," I tell him, "let's put aside everything you've said about these people being my parents. I need to research this on my own. No offense, but it's not something I'm inclined to simply take on faith. But I can promise you this. Regardless of whatever else this Scott Pfeifer may have done, if he was working with Graham Cregg, he and I will never be working together. Cregg kidnapped my brother and damn near killed both of us when I went in to rescue him."

Jasper looks confused. "How do you have a brother? Leah's dead . . ."

"My *foster* brother," I clarify. "But the key point here is keeping Peyton safe, right? Cregg's people may have been experimenting on adults when you were in the program, but as I'm sure you've guessed, they've shifted their focus to the second generation now. When I got Deo out, Cregg had maybe fifty kids in his compound, and he wants to add more. He has money, and he has power. If we tracked Peyton down, you better believe he can, too. And when he does, that gun you're carrying will not be enough to protect her. As noble as it might be to go out guns a-blazin' in defense of your child, you will fail. If you want to keep your family safe, you need support. You need resources. You need a *team*."

I push aside the nagging possibility that the team I'm offering him has been compromised. Snoop could be looking through my eyes, telling Graham Cregg our exact location. But I don't believe that. I keep coming back to the words *I won't help them kill my own kind*. While that could just mean humans, I'm pretty sure he was referring to his fellow adepts.

Jasper is staring down at his feet, silent. But I can tell my words hit their target. Even without the threat of Cregg grabbing his daughter, Jasper Hawkins walked in earlier this week to find his wife unconscious on the floor and his little girl in shock. Next time Peyton loses her temper, someone could end up dead. Jasper knows that. He just doesn't want to admit it.

"The woman we're working with," Aaron says. "Her name is Magda Bell. I don't think she has political connections like Cregg does, but she has money. She also has two daughters who were affected by the Delphi drug, and that gives her a pretty strong incentive to help these kids and try to find a cure."

"So," Jasper says, "that covers what's in it for this Bell woman. What's in it for you?"

"Cregg is the reason my dad is dead, the reason my sister's best friend is dead, the reason my older brother is in a coma. The reason there are six dead kids in Fayetteville. His little science experiments are also the reason I heard every single thought running through your head both when you were storming out of the tent and again a few minutes ago when you were getting ready to slug Miranda."

Jasper puffs up at the comment, his hand moving back toward the holster beneath his jacket.

"Come on, man." Aaron sighs. "You were about to hit her. And you probably wouldn't have stopped at a single punch once you got rolling. But you pulled your shit together at the last second. That took a lot of control, I know it did, because I could feel the rage, the same way I felt my dad's growing up. We kept seven punching bags—the big, heavy-duty kind—in our three-bedroom split-level, so he'd have a place to vent when his blood started boiling."

"So it's revenge." There's no judgment in Jasper's words, just a simple statement.

"Partly," Aaron admits. "But I've got people to protect, too. My family. Anna. I also feel some responsibility toward the kids Cregg's still holding. Assuming he hasn't gone on a full-blown killing spree, I'd like to help them, too."

Jasper asks questions for the next several minutes—questions about Aaron's dad, about this family that I've never met, about the Delphi Project in general. But it's clear that he's just poking our story for holes at this point. Without the anger animating his face, the circles under his eyes are much more apparent, and a lot of the energy has drained out of him. He looks like a windup toy that's down to the last few clicks of the key.

"How is Peyton doing?" I ask when there's a slight pause in his interrogation. Maybe I can shift the conversation back to the reason we're here. "Is she still upset?"

"Comes and goes," he says. "She slept a lot that first day, partly thanks to Ambien. And yes, I checked the dosage online."

Jasper scans my expression, clearly expecting me to judge him. And while part of me is indeed troubled that he drugged a preschooler with prescription sleep meds, Peyton isn't a normal four-year-old. So I just nod and give him a weak smile.

"I thought it was a good sign that she asked about her mama and TJ last night. We did a video call, and Randa joked with her a little. But nights are always the worst. She must've had a nightmare about the whole thing and woke up angry at herself again. Camping gear was floating around the tent when her crying woke me up. I just sat there and rocked her back and forth until she fell asleep. She's still sleep-ing . . . not sure how she'll take it if she wakes up and sees Miranda there, but we're going to have to risk it at some point."

I'm surprised to see tears coursing down Jasper's cheeks. That makes me a little nervous, because I suspect he's not a man who likes people seeing him cry. But he just wipes his face with the sleeve of his jacket.

"They told us to wait six months after we got out of the program before having kids. I waited more than six *years*. Even then I was wor-ried, and if it'd been entirely up to me . . ." He sighs, shaking his head. "But then I met Miranda, and she didn't want TJ to grow up an only child, so I gave in. Don't get me wrong. I love Peyton. I'd do absolutely anything to protect her. But what kind of life is she going to have with that thing in her head? Sometimes I think we'd be better off if we'd all just died."

I assume he means his family, but then he adds, "We thought we dodged the bullet, but I'm thinking now that the ones who went crazy, the ones who removed themselves from the equation before they had others to worry about—they were the lucky ones."

Jasper remains quiet for a very long time. He's clearly weighing his concern about trusting anyone else with his daughter's safety against his hope for her future. It's not an easy silence, and Aaron opens his mouth once, clearly needing to fill it. But I squeeze his arm to stop him. If twelve years of being in psychotherapy have taught me nothing else, it's that the biggest breakthroughs usually follow this type of uncomfortable silence.

Eventually, Jasper huffs out a long breath. His expression is one of disgust, and I'm positive he's going to tell us to keep away from him and his family. But he surprises me.

"If you think you can help Peyton, have at it. But Miranda and I will be there. We'll be watching. I will be watching to be sure that you are in no way connected to either Scott Pfeifer or Graham Cregg. And if I find out you are, you'll both answer to me."

CHAPTER FOURTEEN

Carova Beach, North Carolina
November 6, 2019, 2:34 p.m.

"What game are you playing?"

Peyton Hawkins glances up at my question, but only for a second, and then her eyes drift back to the phone in her hand. "The one wif the flierfries. It's hard."

Carl Peck's assessment of her as *a cute little bug* pretty much sums her up. She has Miranda's dark eyes, but otherwise looks like a slightly darker version of her father, especially now with her brow furrowed in concentration over her game.

"Can I watch you play?" I ask.

She nods, still not looking away. I sit on the love seat next to her and watch as she taps little blips of light dancing through a forest. Okay, she meant *fireflies*. That makes more sense now.

After extended deliberation this morning, Miranda and Jasper decided Peyton was probably ready to leave the island. Jasper said he'd bring her across the bay after she'd had time to wake up a bit, and if she was willing, I could talk to her then.

On the boat ride across the Sound, Miranda kept shooting me angry looks—no, I think *hurt* might be a better word. Based on her husband's first reaction to seeing me, I'm guessing she's had to listen to Jasper talking about this Leah person quite a bit over the years.

So, in an effort to build goodwill, I volunteered to help Miranda with the house they were scheduled to clean, since Jasper wouldn't be around until later. When we pulled up in front of the place, I understood instantly what Miranda meant when she called it a *beast*. It's enormous—more like a hotel, really. There's a wonderfully gaudy sign hanging from the deck that reads, *Isle of View*, with the words painted over a kissing couple wearing old-timey bathing suits. The place itself is shaped like an inverted *Y*, with two wings facing the beach and the third pointing back toward the Sound. Miranda tells me that there are twenty-four bedrooms and an equal number of baths, two elevators, a commercial kitchen, a movie room, and a huge pool. There's a smaller guesthouse at the back, and a storage building. It sits on over ten acres of land, with a large, undeveloped lot to the north and another lot with a vacant house to the south.

Large. Isolated. Sunshine. Fresh Air.

The place fits all of Magda's criteria. And it's for sale.

I sent a text, with a photo of the exterior and the beach, before we even got out of the truck. Magda didn't respond, but she definitely got the message. The property management company called about twenty minutes after Miranda and I started cleaning, telling her not to bother winterizing—and no, I still don't know what that means—because a European family had called to book the estate through the end of the year.

Things move wicked fast when you have money.

Luckily for us, only about a third of the house's bedrooms and baths were used for the last event. Despite that, it still took nearly four hours to clean. Aaron offered to stay and help, but I reminded him that checkout time at the hotel was noon, and someone needed to fetch

Taylor, Deo, and their little fur baby. There was a clear look of relief on his face as he pulled away in the truck. Maybe that was due to this awkwardness that seems to have settled into our relationship when we're between life-threatening crises. Or maybe he just hates housecleaning.

Personally, I was happy for the physical labor. I'm used to scouring the floor at the deli when I'm on night shift, and I've done pretty much every other housekeeping chore imaginable at the various group and foster homes where I've lived. The bed linens weren't as soft in the foster homes, and any view was usually obscured by bars on the windows, but if you've scrubbed one toilet, you've scrubbed them all.

The physical activity also kept me from obsessing over everything Jasper said this morning. Miranda blasted hip-hop and dance music through the house's sound system, and I let the music flow through me and cleaned to the beat. There were a number of chores, like changing the sheets, that were simply a lot easier with two sets of hands. By the time we marked the last item off the cleaning checklist, Miranda seemed much more at ease around me.

Jasper pulled in about five minutes later, conveniently avoiding any work. He stayed just long enough to bark a few orders at Miranda—don't leave me alone with Peyton, keep an eye on us at all times, and be ready to leave by four. Then he took off to pick up TJ from school.

Miranda spent a long time talking with Peyton outside by the pool before introducing us. When they finally joined me in the great room, Miranda cast a nervous glance at the shelves, which are lined with fragile, expensive-looking curios. Several dozen wineglasses are suspended in neat rows from the cabinets above the bar. And then, of course, there are the large plate-glass windows that face the ocean. Peyton seems pretty relaxed right now, but I still hope Magda sprang for renter's insurance.

After Miranda introduced us, we snagged three of the ice-cream bars left behind in the freezer. Then, once Peyton seemed comfortable with me, Miranda stretched out one of the sofas, saying she was going to take a nap. I'm certain she had no intention of sleeping. It was just a way to give me and Peyton the semblance of privacy and still tell Jasper that she didn't leave me alone with their daughter.

Peyton now peeks up from tapping the fireflies and sneaks a look at me. I smile but don't push it. It would be best for her to relax, to get used to me, before I try to talk to her about being an adept. So I alternate between watching her play and sitting silently next to her, looking out at the wide expanse of ocean. The motion of the waves is hypnotic, and between the physical exertion and my lack of sleep, I could almost drift off.

"Whoops," Peyton says as I stifle a yawn. "I always miss that one 'cause he flies so fast."

"You're doing a really good job, though."

"Not as good as TJ," she says. "Do you know TJ?"

"I do. We dropped him off at school this morning."

"He likes school," she says, her lip jutting out petulantly. "But I can't go yet. Mama says maybe one day, but only if I learn to keep my monkey in the box."

"Monkey?"

"Mmhmm. The one in here." She presses four chubby fingers to her right temple and then goes back to the game.

"Ohhhh. *That* monkey. Did your mom tell you I have a monkey, too?"

That finally pulls her attention away from the game. "Does it throw stuff like mine does?"

I laugh. "Not exactly. But it does cause me all sorts of trouble . . . or at least it did before I taught it to behave."

It's hard to decipher the look she gives me, but there seems to be a hint of guilt in there, so I quickly add, "That's not something you can do on your own, though. I had a teacher to show me how. When I was just a little bit older than you, she taught me to build a sort of cage."

She considers that for a moment. "Does your monkey have to stay in the cage all the time? Or can you take him out and play?"

"Well, he comes out sometimes. I just have to be careful. Do you like to play with . . . your monkey?"

A muffled snort comes from the couch. Miranda is definitely awake, and yes, the monkey metaphor is starting to get a little twisted. I'm not the one who came up with it, however.

Peyton nods. "It makes TJ laugh when I float things. He wishes he could do it too."

Ah-ha. Not surprising that a little sister wouldn't want to entirely let go of the one thing she can do that her big brother can't. That raises a question that has been nagging at me every time Magda or one of the others talks about a drug to reverse the effects of the serum. How many kids would want to take it if doing so meant losing something that's part of them? Even if they don't want to take it, will they have a choice? What if their parents want them to take it, but they'd prefer not to?

All of those questions are completely hypothetical until we actually have a cure, however. So I push them aside and focus on reassuring her.

"You need to learn to control it, but keeping it caged all of the time can be tough. The friend who helped me made sure I had a safe space. A place where I could be myself without worrying. But when I was around other people—people who might not understand, people who might . . ."

Who might want to hurt her? Use her? Probably not the best approach when talking to a four-year-old, especially when she's already upset.

While I'm fumbling for the right words, Peyton steps in. "You mean people who might want to steal me because of the monkey? Mama 'splained about that when those men scared us at the piggy store. That's why we had to leave our old house and TJ had to go to a new school. And why we have to share a room and we can't see Nana and Papa like we used to. And it's my fault."

Peyton states all of this in a very matter-of-fact fashion, but her mouth is trembling slightly by the end. She's only a year older than I was when I was abandoned, and I wonder how much she'll remember in a few years. Hopefully she'll have happier memories to overwrite all of this.

"No, Peyton," I tell her firmly. "It's not your fault. But you can make it better by training that monkey in your head. My friend, the lady who helped me build that cage I mentioned, might be coming to visit in a few days. Would you like to talk to her? Her name is Dr. Kelsey—"

Peyton squinches up her nose. "I don't like doctors. Or nurses. They use needles."

"Not this doctor. I'm scared of needles, too. But I've known Kelsey since I was only a little older than you, and she's *never* given me a shot. Never ever. We just talk and sometimes play games to help my brain get stronger. No shots. Pinky promise."

I hold out my pinky. As Peyton curls her finger around mine, I remember the needles in the blood-collection kit that Magda sent. Something in my expression must change, because Peyton frowns.

"*No* needles. My monkey does *not* like needles." She holds my gaze, and it's impossible to miss her implicit warning.

A tiny chill travels up my spine at this glimpse into what Miranda and Jasper Hawkins must face every day. Unlike most preschoolers, who at their worst might pitch a temper tantrum or hurl their broccoli onto the floor, Peyton is a loaded weapon.

"No needles." I hold her gaze until she's satisfied that I mean it.

And I *do* mean it. Mostly because I don't want to lose the girl's trust, but I'd be lying if I didn't admit there's a bit of fear in the mix. If Magda wants a blood sample from Miss Peyton, she'll have to get it herself.

❖ ❖ ❖

I'm watching Jasper's truck retreat down the beach toward their fishing cabin when my phone buzzes with a text from Deo.

> About an hour away. Stopping in Corolla for groceries and Chinese. Veggie lo mein?

I tell him yes, and he tells me I'm too predictable.

While I wait, I'm tempted to go for a run on the beach, but I'm in Taylor's fur-lined boots, which aren't exactly suited for running. Instead, I take a shower, then walk around on the upper deck taking in the fresh air and the view. Afterward, I stretch out on one of the lounge chairs, watching the seagulls swoop along the shoreline. A lone pelican circles above them, dive-bombing the waves every few minutes in search of dinner.

The view and salt air are a nice change of pace after nearly a week cooped up in the RV. Once the sun sets, however, I realize exactly how deserted this section of beach is this time of year. There's only one house with lights on, and it's at least a mile away.

I've never in my entire life been this far from another living, breathing human being.

This sense of absolute solitude is so eerie that I turn inward to check on my hitchers. What better way to remind myself that I'm never *really* alone? Hunter is no longer curled up in an unresponsive heap, but he doesn't seem ready for interaction with me yet. Any time he senses that I'm poking around in the corners of my mind, he retreats behind Molly's cabinet and tries to make himself as tiny, dim, and inconspicuous as possible. That's pretty normal—even with my adult hitchers, it takes a while to adjust to the fact that your body is gone and you've taken up residence in someone else's head. Jaden and Daniel have been unusually quiet today. I guess they didn't have any helpful tips on cleaning a giant beach house.

Jaden snorts softly.

> That's part of it. But personally, I figured there's been enough noise in here today without me adding to it. You got so many thoughts and questions about Jasper's little revelation that it's like bein' in a damn subway station.

But . . . I haven't been thinking about any of that. I've been working.

The front of your head may not have been thinking about it, but back here in the cheap seats? Girl, you've been in full freak-out mode all damn day.

Daniel is clearly in agreement, and before Hunter can chime in to make it unanimous, I promise them I'll call Kelsey tonight.

The breeze coming in off the ocean is too chilly now that the sun is gone, so I retreat into the house and start the fireplace. I turn the music back on as well, because no matter how noisy it may be inside my head, it's way too quiet for my liking on the outside.

A flash of headlights catches my eye a little while later. I go to the window, expecting to see the truck. To my surprise, however, it's Michele Quinn's lavender Jeep. Deo and Taylor exit from the passenger side, and my jaw literally drops when Kelsey slides out from behind the wheel. I guess I won't have to call her after all.

When the elevator door opens, Deo looks around and gives a long appreciative whistle. "I approve the new digs," he says, dropping two grocery bags on the counter.

I take the bags Kelsey is holding and give her a one-armed hug. "I thought it would be at least a few days from what you said on the phone."

She shrugs. "My two remaining clients are adults, and I've worked with them for years. Phone or video sessions will suffice until we find another therapist they like. I don't think that would work so well with a four-year-old, however, and Magda Bell has—temporarily, at least—added me to your team."

"So you just borrowed the Jeep and . . . ?"

"I drove." There's a teasing note in her voice, but also a tiny hint of satisfaction. Kelsey hasn't driven a car since the accident that killed her husband eight years ago.

"Yes, I saw that. Still not sure I believe it, however."

"You got me." Kelsey laughs. "Driving on the beach was fun. No obstacles, just wide-open sand. But I only drove about twenty minutes on the highway. It made me nervous, and Jerome wasn't very patient with me going ten miles below the speed limit."

"Jerome . . . Porter?"

Kelsey met Molly's grandfather when he came to her office to interrogate me and again at the hospital the night Daniel was shot. It's a bit surprising, however, that they're now on a first-name basis.

"Yes," Taylor says. "He and Kelsey called earlier to say they'd meet up with us in Corolla, but we decided to let you be surprised. He rode with Aaron. They'll be here in a few."

It's hard to focus on what Taylor is saying. A furry brown head peeks out of her jacket, accompanied by two paws that are nearly as large as his snout.

Taylor shoves a white plastic bag toward me. "Your lo mein. You'll probably need to reheat it. Thor and I have to run back down and get his stuff from the Jeep."

The name is new, but I doubt it will stick. Deo and Taylor have cycled through five different names for the puppy in the past few days. Yesterday, she was calling him Courage, a cartoon reference that Deo had to explain to me.

"Doesn't your mom need the Jeep for work?" I ask.

"They needed a four-wheel drive, so she loaned it to Porter. He's heading back home tomorrow. Sam needs him to take up some of the slack at Quinn Investigative since Aaron's gone. And it's not like Mom needs the Jeep, anyway, since she's on a leave of absence from work to take care of Daniel."

Her eyebrows lift pointedly when she says her brother's name, and I feel him groan.

You know she's right, Daniel. You need to let your mom and Sam know. It's not fair to make Aaron and Taylor keep lying. More to the point, we need to go to Maryland and try to get you back into your own body.

Which could be permanently brain damaged for all we know. At a bare minimum, I'll be in rehab for weeks. And you need me here. Your body and Aaron's would have been found on Fort Bragg instead of Grady's if I hadn't—

I know.

I also know that his ability is growing weaker, and even though I don't actually think that out loud, Daniel still picks up on it.

I just needed rest, Anna. I'm fine.

Daniel slides back again, clearly indicating that we should table this discussion for another time. On that point, at least, we agree.

Kelsey's hand is on my arm. She's seen me when I'm engaged in inner dialogue enough times to recognize my expression. "Are you okay? Aaron told me there was something you might need to talk to me about."

"I'm okay. This was . . . something different. But we can wait until tomorrow. You've had a long day, and you probably want—"

"Nonsense. As I said, Jerome drove most of the way. Once you're done with your dinner, we'll find a spot where we can talk privately."

244

"Should be easy enough," Deo says. "I think this house is bigger than the hotel. How did you find this place?"

"By helping clean it. Can you help me put those groceries in the kitchen?"

Deo glances pointedly at the plastic bags on the counter across from a fridge and dishwasher, and then raises one dark-blue eyebrow. "Aren't they already in the kitchen?"

I shake my head, pointing toward the double doors on the left. "I guess you'd call this the bar? The kitchen is in there. With a walk-in freezer and three ovens, including one that's big enough to roast an entire cow. And yes, that's an exaggeration, but not by much."

Deo scoops up the rest of the grocery bags and follows me into the kitchen. "I got your texts. Are you okay?" He looks down into my eyes and answers his own question. "No, of course you're not okay. You finally get information about your parents only to find out one of them murdered the other. And I can't even frickin' hug you without triggering one of those stupid visions."

He's right. I don't know if it's because he's upset, but I can hear the faint humming noise when he reaches out to yank open the fridge. The odd smell is stronger, too, although it could just be that he's worked up a sweat lugging boxes out of the truck.

Deo starts slamming groceries into the fridge. I know it's partly because he's worried about me, but I'm pretty sure the news about my mother's death has stirred up a few personal memories for him, too. As a little kid, there were many nights he lay in bed listening as his stepdad beat his mother, worrying that this time Patrick wouldn't stop. Worrying that this time, he might actually kill her.

"I'm okay, D. Really. This is . . . I mean, it's not like I even knew them. I'm not even one hundred percent sure I should believe anything Jasper Hawkins says. He could be making this up as a way to . . ." I stop, unable to think of a reason Jasper would lie. Plus, his expression when he first saw me would have been really hard to fake.

"It's just a lot to take in on top of everything else over the past few days," I say finally. "But I'm fine, really."

Deo slides the last item into the fridge a little more carefully, possibly because he knows eggs don't respond well to anger.

"Sorry," he says. "I'm tired. And . . . you know me. I don't have nightmares. I mean, not often. But every single time I close my eyes the past couple of nights, I see those kids at Overhills. Taylor said it's the same for her, only . . . she didn't have the chance to stop it from happening. If I'd shot Cregg back at The Warren, if I'd found a way to turn that gun back at him, those kids would still be alive."

"We don't know that, D. We *don't*. And even if it's true, even if killing Cregg would have saved those kids, the decision is on me way more than you. *You* were under Cregg's control. I had a chance to pull the trigger and chose not to."

The door creaks behind us. We both turn to look, but whoever it was apparently decided not to intrude.

"I probably couldn't have done it either," Deo says in a lower tone. "Shooting someone—*anyone*, even someone like Cregg—when he's helpless on the floor would have felt like murder. I don't think either of us is exactly wired for that." He gives a bitter laugh. "You know how I always said that a lot of the cops we'd encountered treated innocent people worse than the bad guys do? Maybe there's a reason for that. Maybe you need a little bit of killer in you in order to stop one."

Someone stirs at the back of my head. It's Daniel, and I'm certain that my resident cop is going to defend his brothers in blue. That would be fair, but Deo doesn't need a lecture right now.

Daniel surprises me, however.

He's right, Anna. And that's exactly why you *need me here*.

I push Daniel to the back so that I can focus on Deo.

"You need to talk to Kelsey, too," I tell him. "About the dreams, about the whole amp thing, about everything. And don't be surprised if she gives you a really long hug. From me."

"I just keep hoping I'll wake up and we're back at Bart House. That all of this is the aftereffects of one of Pauline's miserable cooking experiments," he says, rubbing his forehead distractedly. "But yeah, I'll see if Kelsey can work me into her schedule."

I smile and turn toward the door, but he calls me back.

"Anna? Please don't think I'm blaming you for any of this. I'm not. And . . . some parts haven't been so bad. I like spending time with Taylor—although, damn, she can be moody. She's pissed at me about something again, and I have no clue what it is. And Aaron's a good guy. It's just . . . at Bartholomew House, we were doing okay for once."

"Yeah. We were. But . . . things change, D. We've both learned to roll with the punches. We'll get through this. And things *will* be okay again. Better than okay."

I take a deep breath, determined not to say, *I promise*. I've been doing a lot of that lately, plus I'm less certain than ever of my ability to keep any promise I make. So many things are beyond my control right now, and Deo's old enough and smart enough to know when I'm blowing smoke.

And despite knowing all of that, I say the words anyway.

"I promise."

I may not be wired for murder, but apparently I *am* wired for delivering false hope.

Deo's phone buzzes with an incoming text as we're leaving the kitchen. It would be a perfectly normal thing under other circumstances, but anyone who would be texting him, anyone who should have his number, is here in the house.

"Should I check it?" he asks.

"Yeah." My voice sounds shaky.

And sure enough, it's Cregg. Five short words.

Unquiet meals make ill digestions.

We both frown, then Deo remembers his quip about Pauline's cooking.

"We're going to need to tell them about this," he says. "Kelsey and Porter, I mean. And Magda, too, I guess. If that Snoop kid is passing my thoughts along to Cregg, he may already know where we are."

"He said that he doesn't tell Cregg everything."

"Yeah, and then Dacia comes crashing through the woods chasing us down a few hours later. I'm not sure I believe him."

Porter is tugging a suitcase out of the elevator when we return to the living area.

"Anna! It's *so* good to see you." His smile is wide and genuine, and I can't help but think how very different that expression is from the one he greeted me with outside his office when I first brought him Molly's message. It's only been a couple of weeks, but so very much has changed.

I'm glad to see him, too. Part of that is probably Molly's memories of her grandfather, but part of it is just me. Molly was right. Porter is a good man, and I'm glad he's on our side.

The only things I've eaten since our predawn breakfast are two of the ice-cream bars Miranda found in the freezer, so I scrounge around in the take-out bag for a fork and dig in to the lo mein without bothering to reheat it. Porter sits by the fireplace, telling Kelsey and Taylor about the wild horses he and Aaron saw on their drive. "Five of them. Ran right onto the beach just a few miles back and followed along behind the truck for about a half mile. Never seen anything like it."

"Damn!" Taylor says. "Now I *really* wish I'd rode with you guys."

"That waiter at the pizza place yesterday said they run wild on this stretch of the island. About a hundred of them." Deo looks around the room. "What did you do with Loki?"

Taylor rolls her eyes. "Stop trying to make *Loki* happen. It's not going to happen. His name is Thor. And he's asleep, so I put him in his box. *Don't* wake him up."

Deo gives her a confused look and then grabs our backpacks from the corner where he stashed them earlier. "I'll go pick us out a couple of rooms," he tells me as he heads for the stairs. "I'm guessing you want one with an ocean view?"

"Mmhmm." I nod, my mouth too full of noodles for actual words.

Aaron catches my eye and nods toward the kitchen. I leave the take-out container on the counter and follow him.

"I'm sorry it took so long," he says. "How did it go with Peyton?"

"Okay, I guess. She's willing to talk to Kelsey, although I didn't have any idea it would be this soon. Miranda said they'd stop by again tomorrow, but I thought it would just be me talking to Peyton again. And . . . I'm a little worried Jasper will pack them up in the middle of the night and disappear again. You'd think he'd be glad that we're this close to their house, so Peyton can get help without them having to travel. But it just seemed to piss him off."

"I think pissed off may be a permanent feature of his personality." Aaron tips my chin up so that our eyes meet. "Are you okay?"

This is the third time in the past five minutes—the second time while standing in this exact spot—that someone has asked me if I'm okay. I need to find a mirror and make sure I don't have *Walking Wounded* tattooed on my forehead.

"Yes. I'm fine. Really."

Aaron doesn't say anything for a moment, simply continues looking into my eyes. "I called Sam. He e-mailed me what he could find on Scott Pfeifer and the . . . uh . . . shooting . . . in the local papers. You may not want to look at all of it tonight, but I'm pretty sure Jasper was telling the truth, Anna. There's a picture of Leah Pfeifer, and if I hadn't known better, I'd have sworn it was you."

"I want to see it."

A brief hesitation and then he hands me his tablet.

It's not a perfect likeness. Her hair is shorter, and a lighter blonde than my own, although the color could be from a bottle. There's a little dimple at the bottom of her chin that mine is missing, and her nose turns up slightly at the tip. But her eyes, her mouth—they're almost identical. I even have her widow's peak.

Maryland man shoots wife during late-night workplace visit.

I can't focus on the words beyond the headline. My eye moves to a second photo farther down the screen, and I click to enlarge. It's a much grainier image than the first, clearly taken from security footage. The faces are blurred. All I can make out is that it's a man, kneeling on the ground, holding a woman's limp body against his chest. A pistol lies near her feet, and there's a silhouette of two people standing in the doorway behind them.

My stupid eyes are tearing over again, so I hand the tablet back to Aaron. "Can you sum it up?"

"Sure. Pfeifer worked as a research scientist with Decathlon Services Group. The Cregg family made the bulk of their money through DSG, mostly in military contracts. And I'm pretty sure Pfeifer was also with Python, the group that took over the Delphi Project once the CIA dropped it. Sam's going to look back through my dad's research, but . . . I'm almost positive that's where I'd seen his name. I think my dad had this article in his files." He looks at me for a minute. "Sam pulled up some biographical info on your parents. If you're ready—"

"Can you just e-mail it to me?"

He nods, then gives me an odd look and laughs. "Okay, this is proof positive that our relationship has gotten off to a bizarre start. I've woken up next to you for seven consecutive mornings, but I don't know your e-mail address."

I think he expects me to laugh or at least smile. And I do *try* to smile, but his words remind me that for the past few nights he's kept so rigidly to his side of the mattress that it was almost as if I were sleeping

alone. The title of a Death Cab for Cutie song runs through my head—
"Brothers on a Hotel Bed." Aaron's right. It *is* a bizarre start. What worries me more, though, is the feeling that we're moving backward. And relationships that make it generally don't do that.

This really isn't the best time for a relationship chat, however, so I focus on the practical. "Forget e-mail, I haven't checked my messages since we left Maryland. For all I know, Cregg's people have hacked it. I'll just look at what you have later."

Aaron's brow furrows. He can tell he said something that bothers me, but he has no idea what it is.

"Sure," he says. "Let me know."

❖ ❖ ❖

I leave Kelsey's room after talking for nearly two hours, and I feel twenty pounds lighter. Kelsey did what she does best. She sat there, mostly silent, and let me vent until there was nothing left to say. Then she began to work at the tender spots, the ones that I circled around gingerly as we talked.

It hurt. But at the risk of a gross analogy, she knows how to lance a mental boil. Anything that's been festering in my mind has been released. Doesn't mean I won't be dealing with it for some time to come, but at least some of the pressure is off.

Daniel hasn't said anything explicitly, but his grumbles echo back in the peanut gallery. What we tell his mom is his decision. What I tell Kelsey, on the other hand, is mine. Only an idiot lies to her therapist. That's even less productive than lying to yourself. I can count the times I've lied to Kelsey on the fingers of one hand, and most of those times have been in the past few weeks.

I'm almost . . . almost . . . to the point where I think I could look over the rest of the information about my parents. But that would probably be a bad idea, given the late hour. No point in winding myself up when I really need to get some rest.

Taylor is in the kitchen when I stop by to grab a bottle of water. She's digging through the kitchen drawers, frowning, in search of something.

"What's wrong?"

"Stupid headache," she says, rubbing her temples. "You'd think somebody who stayed here would have left behind some Tylenol."

"Check with Deo. He keeps our pharmacopoeia in his backpack."

Her eyes narrow, but her expression seems more hurt than angry. "Never mind. I'll do without."

"I thought you guys were getting along better?"

"We were." She stands there for a moment, clearly weighing her words, then she blurts it out. "Is he gay, or what?"

Her question raises my hackles instantly, because even though I'm pretty sure Taylor isn't a bigot, that's exactly what the two bigots we shared space with at Bart House asked when Deo first moved in. But they had a sneer on their face. Taylor doesn't.

I still answer a little cautiously, even though Deo has been open about his sexuality almost as long as I've known him. "He identifies as bisexual. Why?"

"Nothing. Just needed a little help putting something he said into context."

After she leaves, I take my water back to the bedroom on the middle floor where Deo stashed my bag earlier. It's smaller than some of the rooms—there's barely space for the bed, a dresser, and an armchair. But Deo chose well—it has an exquisite view of the beach.

The light is out, and I'm surprised to see Aaron in the chair near the sliding glass door. Given how early we woke up this morning, I thought he'd have already collapsed. A worn paperback of *Watership Down* is in his lap.

"Yeah," he says, following my gaze. "I found it on one of the bookshelves downstairs, and since I wasn't really following the stuff about warrens and Fivers, I thought I'd give it a try. It's really good for a book about rabbits. But I decided to turn off the light and watch the stars for a while."

It's easy to see why. The moon hangs above the ocean like a giant letter *D*, and the sky is dotted with more stars than I've ever seen. I sit on the arm of the chair and push the curtain back a bit more to get the complete panorama.

"It's like something by Van Gogh."

"I know," he says. "Can't see anything like this in DC. Too much light pollution."

We sit there quietly for a while, but the silence feels heavy and awkward.

"Listen, Anna . . ." He starts in, hesitates, and then says, "I brought my bag in here, but I can move it to another room. I mean, your nightmares have gotten better, and with Porter and Kelsey here, I thought you might feel . . . I don't know . . . weird about me sleeping in here. We're not exactly pressed for space like we were in the RV, so . . ."

"Up to you," I say as I cross over to the corner to retrieve my bag.

I should probably just leave it at that. Leave the ball totally in his court. But I gather up my courage and blurt out what I was thinking earlier. We have to talk about it eventually. Might as well be now.

"Maybe you *should* go. You might sleep better. You've been confining yourself to maybe a quarter of the mattress out of fear that you might accidentally touch the body that's temporarily housing your brother in the middle of the night. If you move any farther away, you're going to fall off the damn bed."

He inhales sharply but doesn't respond. I keep my back to him and start shoving my stuff into the dresser near the door.

I hear the chair creak as Aaron gets up, and then I hear the door-knob turn. But when I look over, he's just standing there, motionless, hand on the doorknob.

And I feel like a total bitch.

"I'm sorry, Aaron."

He turns to look at me, and I continue. "That wasn't fair, and I—"

Aaron's mouth cuts off the rest of my apology. His hand cups the back of my head, pulling me into a kiss. And this kiss is very different from the others we've shared. Those were tentative, almost exploratory. Testing the waters.

This time, it's like diving headlong into the surf. I let the tide take me, curling my fingers into his hair. He presses his face into my neck and whispers my name, then he lifts me up to his height. I wrap my legs around his waist, and he takes a step backward, moving us onto the bed.

He kisses me again, a long, deep kiss, and then moves away, looking down at me. "I think we need to talk."

"No." I pull his mouth to mine again. "I like this better than talking."

"So do I, but . . ."

I run my hands under Aaron's shirt and slide them along the muscles of his back. His breath catches, and for several minutes, talking seems to be the last thing on his mind. Then he pulls away again.

"You don't play fair, Anna."

"This isn't a game," I say. "And we're not opponents."

"No, but we're also not alone. And I don't mean Daniel. Screw Daniel. *And* Jaden. But you've got a little kid in there, too. Are your walls up?"

To be honest, I hadn't even thought about my walls. My entire mind and body were in the moment, here and now. If Daniel and Jaden are perverse enough to spy, then so be it. But yeah . . . Hunter. Just because I was forced to learn absolutely everything about sex when

I unpacked my first set of hitcher memories, that doesn't mean Hunter has to be subjected to it. So the walls go up.

"They're up now," I say, pressing my body against his side. "And, it's not like we'd warp his development or anything. He's a ghost."

"A kid ghost," Aaron counters.

Part of me—probably the bit that was shaped by Emily MacAllister—agrees, but I'm feeling contrary. "Kids wander into the room while their parents are watching R-rated movies all the time. And like I said, the walls are up."

He leans down so that his lips hover just above my neck. "And how sure are you that you can keep those walls up if things get heated?"

This time it's *his* hand sliding beneath *my* shirt, his palm warm against my stomach as his thumb slides along the underside of my breast. My breath hitches in my throat, and my back arches to close the slight space between our bodies.

My walls are still up. But I'd be lying if I didn't admit that we just created several hairline cracks in the plaster.

"Okay, okay. We'll stop." I start to get up, but he pulls me back.

"No. We're not finished. I should have talked to you about this last week—"

"But I only picked up Hunter a few days ago."

"Not . . . Hunter. He's not the only issue, and no, I don't mean Daniel. It's just . . . I've been here every night when you dream. And you don't dream quiet. So . . . I know what Lucas did to Molly. It's bad enough knowing that it happened to Molly, but to hear you reliving it . . ." He shudders. "What I'm saying is that I don't want to make things worse, to stir up any of those memories by moving too fast, especially when . . ."

"When what?" I prod after a few seconds of silence.

He sighs, and there's another long pause before he answers the question. "The night before you escaped from The Warren, Taylor and I were walking the grounds at the Tome School, trying to figure out why we couldn't find any trace of you when she'd clearly tracked you to that location. While we were there, I picked up a vibe. It was brief . . . There was a lot of interference. Maybe because there were so many people in that place or maybe because the compound was underground. But you were part of that vibe. I *saw* you. Heard you scream and saw through the eyes of someone *throwing* you onto a bed. You hit your shoulder against the headboard. It was Lucas, wasn't it?"

When I nod, he says, "I could hear his thoughts, so I know . . . what he was planning. What I don't know and what I haven't been able to get up the nerve to ask you is whether he raped you like he did Molly. Whether those nightmares are hers or yours."

"No." I feel some of the tension drain from his body. "You're right that he would have. I couldn't have fought him off, even with that stupid plastic shiv I made. But Ashley . . . she showed up with some story about needing to take my vitals. And Lucas left."

"It's kind of hard to reconcile Ashley saving you with her killing Daniel," Aaron says. "Or trying to, I guess. Maybe he was right and she really didn't have a choice."

"Maybe." I leave it at that, unwilling to go into the things that I've been piecing together about Daniel and Ashley—or more correctly, Daniel and Ashley's sister—right now. It's partly because of the privacy pact I made with Daniel but also because I want to make a larger point while we're on this subject.

"Two other things. First, I'm not Molly."

"What? I know that," Aaron says. "I'm not—"

"Just hear me out, okay? Molly's memories are just *one* file cabinet in my head. There are nine others. You've just been unlucky enough to be around while Molly's memories were being . . . assimilated, I guess. And please don't make the *Star Trek* joke. Deo beat you to it years ago. What I'm getting at is . . . Molly's memories are more recent, but now that the dreams are wrapping up, they'll soon be like the others. Not things that happened to me, so much as things that I experienced happening to someone else."

Aaron gives a skeptical laugh. "You do know that doesn't make a lot of sense, right? At least not to those of us on the outside of your overcrowded head." He leans down to press a kiss against my temple.

"Maybe think of it like a virtual-reality game? It's very vivid while you're in the game, but once you take off the headset, you don't remember those events as something that happened to you personally. They are Molly's memories, *not mine*. So you don't have to worry about that."

"Okay."

"And second, *you are not Lucas*. When you're touching me, I have never *once* thought about that night. That was about dominance and power. Violence. You know that. If his thoughts weren't violent, you would never have picked them up, right?"

"Right." He traces the curve of my mouth with his forefinger. "I just don't ever want you to feel that I'm taking unfair advantage of this situation. That I'm moving too fast when you're in a shaky emotional state."

"So you're putting me in control of this relationship?"

He laughs. "In control of *this* part of our relationship, yes. For *now*."

I loop my fingers through his, and I flip him over onto his back. Now I'm on top, and I lean down so that my lips graze his.

"Better?"

"Infinitely better."

But neither of us can entirely forget about Hunter. We make it out of PG-13 territory, but just barely, and then stop by unspoken agreement. For a long time, we just lie there, still and silent, and the fire inside me slowly recedes to a flicker. It's not perfect, but it's an improvement. We're on the same side of the bed now, and it feels like we're moving in the right direction.

Then I get a flash of memory from one of my hitchers, Didier, who was the father of twins. For a time when they were toddlers, Didier was certain that he and his wife would never make love again, that they'd never have time alone again. And even though I don't want to screw things up, I have to be certain that Aaron understands one thing.

"Aaron?"

"Mmhmm," he says, sleepily nuzzling the top of my head as it rests on his shoulder.

"You do know that I can't promise we'll *ever* be completely alone, right? Daniel, Jaden, Hunter . . . after they leave, there will be someone else. I've had maybe a year total, out of my entire life, where my head wasn't at least double occupancy."

"I know." He's quiet for a moment, and then says, "And *you* know that any time we walk into a restaurant, there's a risk that I'll go into panic mode because a chef is thinking about whacking his jerk of a manager with a meat cleaver. Is that a deal breaker for you?"

"No, but it's not the same. Unless you're planning to invite that chef home to hang out in the bedroom with us?"

Aaron chuckles. "No. He's not invited." He raises up on one elbow, and even in the moonlight I can see the intensity in his eyes. "But it *is* the same, Anna. My point is that your hitchers are *part* of you. They've shaped who you are inside."

Aaron stops and presses his lips against the hollow of my throat for a long moment. That flickering candle inside me flares back into a campfire, and I take a deep breath to steady myself.

"Don't get me wrong," he says, running his hand along my bare leg. "I *really* like the wrapper. But I want what's inside, too. I want the whole package."

CHAPTER FIFTEEN

Carova Beach, North Carolina
November 7, 2019, 9:27 a.m.

The same sliding glass door that offered a gorgeous view of the beach and the starscape at night has very real drawbacks come morning. I've drifted in and out of sleep since daybreak. Aaron yanked a pillow and blankets over his head at some point, and while that's probably really effective at blocking the sunlight, I don't know how he can possibly breathe under there. He groans when I slide out from under the covers, though, so I guess some oxygen is getting through.

I pull on my jeans and go upstairs to the great room that takes up most of the top floor. As usual, Taylor seems to be the first one up. Despite her headache the night before, she's already seated at the bar finishing up a bowl of Cheerios. The small television behind the bar is on, tuned to one of the morning news shows, where they're currently talking about football. Her tablet is propped up, and she appears to be reading a newsfeed.

t level of multitasking is way beyond my ability before coffee, shuffle into the kitchen to start a pot. When I return with my own wl of cereal, Taylor finally looks up from the tablet.

"Is everyone still asleep?" I ask.

"No," she says. "Porter and Kelsey took the truck into Kitty Hawk to buy Kelsey some office furniture. There isn't a single desk in this entire house, aside from that pathetic little writing desk in the hallway."

"I guess people don't want to think about work when they're on vacation?"

She shrugs. "Maybe. Anyway, Deo went with them to buy clothes because he only has three sets. Kelsey was going to wake you, but Deo said he does your shopping. Is that actually true?"

"Yep. Deo enjoys clothes shopping. I detest it. He knows my size and what I like, so it's a win-win. Believe me, if I picked out my own clothes, my wardrobe would be an even bigger disaster."

Taylor scans my jeans and T-shirt. Her eyes make it abundantly clear that she doesn't think *worse* is possible, but she gives me a weak smile.

"Do you want to wake Aaron or shall I? We have a new situation."

"Another text message from Cregg? Deo got one last night, too."

"He told me. And yeah, I got one. It had a typo . . . *all that glisters is not gold.*"

Before I can tell her that's not actually a typo, she adds, "But Cregg's Shakespeare fetish is an ongoing issue. I said we have a *new* situation."

I strongly suspect that this is another of Taylor's dramatic flourishes, but I trudge back downstairs and wake Aaron. Once we're both at the bar with breakfast and coffee, Taylor takes a deep breath and begins.

"To put it politely," she says, "the excrement hit the fan yesterday afternoon. At least in Fayetteville, but now it's spreading everywhere."

"Yesterday?" Aaron says. "I thought you were monitoring the news."

"So I'm the only one who's supposed to check the news?"

"No," Aaron says. "It's just that you've *been* the one doing it, and we were kind of busy yesterday."

"Yeah, well, we were in the car all day, and you know I hate reading in the car. I already felt lousy due to my headache, so there was no way I was giving myself motion sickness on top of it."

"So ask someone to cover for you next time."

She glares at him, then shoves her tablet toward us and heads for the kitchen, the door swinging to and fro in her wake.

"What the hell is wrong with her?" I mutter as I tap the tablet screen to wake it.

"Something with Deo, I think."

"Again? They were getting along so much . . ." The rest of the sentence dies on my lips as I read the headline: *New Lead in Area Child Killings?*

The picture on the left side of the page, just above that headline, is a shot of the wall at Overhills. *WE DO IT FOR YOU*, scrawled in reddish-brown letters, with two of the bodies just beyond. The others, including Hunter's, are mercifully obscured.

On the right side of the screen, Bernadette Pruitt's angry face stares back at us.

Aaron sighs. "Exact same expression as when she was about to dial the police, just before Daniel nudged her."

Using the word *nudge* for what Daniel does always kind of bugged me. Hearing Aaron say it out loud, however, pushes what was a minor pique into full-fledged annoyance.

"It's not *nudging*. That's Daniel's euphemism, and it's really not accurate. He brainwashed Pruitt. Imperius-ed her, if you want a literary analogy. It may have been necessary, but *nudge* makes it sound like he politely reminded her about an event on her social calendar. So, you can call it whatever you want, but I'm boycotting that word."

Aaron chuckles bleakly. "Point taken. Whatever you want to call it, it's clear that Daniel's effect was only temporary. Otherwise, Pruitt wouldn't be talking to reporters."

I feel Daniel stirring, but I ignore him for now so that Aaron and I can read the rest of the article. Pruitt's account is very close to what actually happened in the parking lot. Her memory of Aaron is a bit vague, but she remembers me well enough to give a fairly accurate description—the type of skirt I was wearing, approximate height and weight, hair and eye color. I'm guessing I stuck in her memory because it was my mouth issuing the commands Daniel gave her.

Pruitt believes we drugged her. She can't remember everything that she told us, but she's adamant that we were asking questions about the missing kids.

"And they asked about the psychic stuff, too. Don't pretend you don't know what I'm talkin' about. Half the people in this town know what I mean, and I can promise you that every single educator and reporter does."

The writer then goes on to note that several of the children whose bodies were discovered at Overhills were rumored to have unusual abilities. The article even links to the earlier pieces on Nicki Clary and Hunter Bieler with Dean Skolnick's byline, and notes that all of the children's parents were, at some point, in the PSYOP unit at Fort Bragg.

"Wonder why they changed their mind?" Aaron says. "Skolnick said they wouldn't touch the story before—"

"Probably the dead bodies," Taylor says, dumping a second teaspoon of sugar substitute into her cup. "Skolnick was only talking about psychic kids cheating on the Quiz Bowl and maybe some dirt on the military. That's not a big enough story to be worth the trouble it could cause for a newspaper in a military town. But now there are dead bodies, and people will demand answers, even ones that sound crazy. Maybe even *especially* the ones that sound crazy. And Skolnick turning up dead was probably the icing on the cake." She glances over at my sharp intake of breath. "Ohhh. Sorry. Guess you hadn't gotten that far. They found him in his car."

Aaron scrolls down. "They're presuming a link between his murder and the others, so I'm guessing it's the same gun, even if they don't say that explicitly."

The article states that the investigation is ongoing and police offered no comment. It ends on a slightly skeptical note, adding that Pruitt's daughter confirmed that two people matching the described abductors dropped her mother off at home after she reportedly fainted in a grocery store parking lot. But she also added that those two people seemed concerned about her—an uncommon trait for a young couple on a killing spree.

"Okay," Aaron says. "So Pruitt gave them our description. It's not like they have names or anything."

Something occurs to me, and even though I kind of dread the answer, I ask him anyway. "What identification did you use to get the fishing permit for us to go out to Overhills that night?"

The color drains from his face. "The one Magda gave me. Which . . . I also used to rent the RV site and the hotel rooms the other night. Damn."

We don't speak for a few minutes, and then I say, "It doesn't mean anyone will trace us here. Lots of people get those permits, right?"

He shrugs. "I guess? Pruitt's description of me could be pretty much anyone, and you weren't there when I got the permit, so . . . they may not connect the dots. Even if they did, forensics will show that the kids died before I got the permit."

"I don't understand why you got that stupid permit to begin with," Taylor says. "I seriously doubt that Dacia's crew bothered with that. So now there's a record of us going onto the property, but not her."

Aaron responds through clenched teeth. "The *point* was to give us a legal cover for being on federal property. In case someone stopped us. Because, yes . . . they *do* check. There are cameras at the gates. And those MPs by the lake? They would have called in our tag as a matter of routine."

"You mean the MPs who are *dead* now? That just proves my point, Aaron. They didn't even have to search to find who was connected to the truck. You just handed them that information on a friggin' platter."

They're gearing up for a Quinn family shouting match, and I'm not in the mood. I slam my hand on the counter. It's marble and doesn't really do much other than hurt, but it's enough to make both of them look in my direction.

"What the hell difference does it make?" I ask. "It takes the police no time at all to track down that kind of information. So . . . enough already."

"Fine," Taylor says, although I can tell she really doesn't want to let it go. "Moving on to what I was *about* to say . . . Two national sites are running some version of Pruitt's story. Not the most reputable ones, but that means the click-bait sites will be all over it. And some of the fringe groups have already picked it up as well—the ones with an agenda."

She ticks off five or six sites, none of which are familiar to me, but then I'm usually an NPR-and-done girl when it comes to the news.

"I don't know about you," Taylor continues, "but the quick spread doesn't feel . . . organic to me."

I'm about to ask her to clarify, but Aaron answers my question for her. "Possibly. But you've got to admit that the story has all the ingredients to take off on its own . . . murder, conspiracy, possible government involvement. Psychic abilities are just the icing on the cake."

"So then it should be on *all* the fringe sites, right, regardless of political leaning? Not just the ones that match Unify America's political views."

Aaron nods reluctantly, and Taylor gives him a grim smile.

"And . . . it's not. As of this morning, only the UA-friendly sites are running the story . . . although I'm pretty sure that's about to change." Taylor reaches over to retrieve the tablet from Aaron and clicks a link to send a video to the monitor behind the bar. It's from the same morning show she was watching when I walked in. "I think you'll find this interesting."

When the picture comes on-screen, Senator Cregg is in midsentence. The Unify America banner hangs behind him, and the chyron across the bottom reads: *WOCAN Terror Group Responsible for NC Child Slayings?*

"I'm getting really tired of that guy's face," Aaron says.

Taylor eyes him caustically. "You only see the curated stuff. I have to wade through *all* of Cregg's garbage. Hold on, though . . . you need to see the first part."

She restarts the video where the dark-haired female anchor recaps the fire at Port Deposit, noting fourteen bodies instead of the twelve that Taylor mentioned a few days ago. I'm not exactly surprised that they're finding more bodies, given the flood of spirits that rushed me in their testing lab. Dozens of people died in The Warren, and I have no idea what they did with their remains. The investigators may well have literally uncovered skeletons in the closets when they dug through the ashes.

"Government officials report that the left-wing separatist group known as WOCAN set the fire to cover their tracks as authorities closed in on a human-trafficking ring the group used to raise funds." The graphic behind her displays the group logo superimposed over a map of the United States with four Western states—Washington, Oregon, California, and Nevada—highlighted. "While their movement has been mostly peaceful, WOCAN has blocked roads in and out of key oil fields in California, and even occupied the Midway-Sunset oil field briefly before the National Guard was called in to remove them. WOCAN has vehemently denied any connection to the events in Port Deposit or to Franco Lucas, who was killed in the fire, but sources close to the investigation say that correspondence found at Lucas's apartment near DC indicate he was a leader in the separatist movement. There are still questions, however, about how the fire began. With more on this, we go to Jason Whelan in Port Deposit, Maryland."

The scene shifts to a male reporter under a dull gray sky standing in front of a sign that reads, *Welcome to Historic Port Deposit. Enjoy Our Terraces and Granite*, which is the most oddly specific welcome sign I've ever seen. A small, round woman who looks to be around eighty is standing next to the reporter, so dwarfed by his height that I thought she was a child at first. She's dressed in a yellow windbreaker, and I get a flash of memory—a teddy bear owned by one of my hitchers, or maybe one of their kids.

"For the past several years," the reporter begins, "residents of this sleepy little port town have experienced odd—some might even say supernatural—events. When asked why, residents without fail point to the Bainbridge Naval Training Center, long presumed abandoned, that sits on the hill overlooking the town . . ."

He turns toward the woman—*Paddington Bear, that's who she looks like*—and says, "With me is Mrs. Edith Parry, who worked as an administrative assistant at the Bainbridge center for nearly two decades. So, Mrs. Parry, when did you realize that something odd was happening in Port Deposit?"

The camera closes in on the woman's face. "Well, I've lived here pretty much all my life. And we all knew—well, at least everyone I worked with in the section that used to be the Tome School knew—that there were secret tunnels running underground, connecting the old section to the newer buildings farther up the hill."

Her voice drops to a conspiratorial whisper, which strikes me as kind of funny since she's talking into a reporter's microphone. "I think there was weapons research going on. Nuclear, or maybe even chemical, and that's why the government hasn't let anyone develop the property. But the place has been vacant for decades, and the weird things didn't begin until a few years back. My cabinet doors started opening and then slamming shut when I was all the way on the other side of the room.

Sometimes, I'd be watching one of my old *CSI* shows, and the TV would flip channels. Every single time it landed on that stupid reality show about that boy band where they barely wear any clothes. If this sort of thing hadn't been happening to other people in town, I'd have thought I was going crazy."

The scene shifts to the riverfront, and a college-aged white guy in a Baltimore Ravens cap replaces the old lady. "Yeah, there's been a lot of insane stuff goin' on around here. This ain't the first fire, you know. There have been weird fires all over town, especially for those of us who live close to Tome School. My bathroom rug caught on fire two years ago. Fire department was clueless. It was like it just spontaneously combusted while I was in the shower."

Ravens Fan morphs into an Asian American couple. The man is carrying a chubby baby in one of those front-pack infant carriers. "Things . . . moved," he says. "All the time. The saltshakers would just slide across the table for no reason."

His wife nods. "A picture that was straight on the wall would tip up a few inches while you were watching. A floor lamp would twitch like it was going to fall over and then right itself. It drove our dog crazy. We even had a structural engineer come out to check the place over, but the problem wasn't the house."

A middle-aged man in a business suit is next, and this time there's a name on the screen beneath his face: Bill Clenney, Port Deposit Town Council. "Yeah, we had one or two people sayin' things, and we laughed it off. There's crazy people in any town, and, hell . . . we got an abandoned school and military base right here. That's gonna get the superstitious types goin', right? So, yeah, at first we'd joke about it at town council meetings, but by this time last year, most of us weren't jokin' anymore. When you see a message write itself on the iced-over window of your car one mornin' like I did? You become a believer real quick."

"Do you remember what the message said?" the reporter asks.

Clenney gives the reporter a withering look. "If words literally drew themselves onto *your* car window, would *you* forget? The message was *Have lovely day!* Not have *a* lovely day . . . just *Have lovely day.*"

"Well, missing word or not, I can't say that message seems very sinister," the reporter says with a laugh.

"But that was pretty much the pattern overall. Aside from the fires a few people reported and some"—Clenney pauses, flushing slightly— "uh . . . violations of privacy, no one reported anything threatening. Sometimes it was even helpful. One woman heard a voice telling her to check on her baby daughter, who she'd just put down for a nap. She was in the shower at the time and ignored it, thinking it was just her bein' overprotective. But then the voice shouted the warning, and Marcie wrapped a towel around herself and ran to the nursery. Sure enough, that little girl had swallowed something she found in the crib. She was turning blue, and if Marcie had waited—if that voice hadn't insisted she go check—her little girl wouldn't be alive today. So . . . weird stuff to be sure, but not your typical Hollywood haunted house scenario with someone comin' after you with an ax or whatever."

"How many of these occurrences have happened, would you say?"

Clenney shrugs. "Two or three reported each week for the past few years, but people kind of got used to it after a bit, and the reports tapered off. But since that underground facility burned down last week? Nothing. Zip. Zilch. Nada."

"Any idea who might have been using the place? Or what they might have been doing over there?"

"None at all," Clenney says. "We all knew there was some activity over that way from time to time because trucks came in. But the property has changed hands a couple times in the past decade, people plannin' to develop it. We sure didn't have any idea there was an active terrorist cell half a mile away. All I can think is they must have developed some sort of chemical that works on your brain." There's a long pause, and it looks to me like he's trying to convince himself.

"So . . . you're thinking this could all have been a sort of mass hallucination caused by a chemical in the air?" the reporter asks. "Or the water?"

Clenney nods, but his face is still conflicted. "That would certainly be the most *logical* answer, even though I have to say it felt very real to me. And . . . I'm not sure how the logical answer explains the baby bein' saved. Or the fires." He laughs. "Maybe the Feds can figure it out. I'm just glad it's over."

As the picture fades back to the studio, the anchorwoman smiles. "Thank you, Jason. While we don't currently have an official answer from 'the Feds' to the Port Deposit puzzle, we do have one member of the federal government with us this morning—Senator Ronald Cregg, who is joining us from his home in Pennsylvania. Thank you for speaking with us, Senator Cregg."

"Always a pleasure, Carissa," the Senator says, smiling broadly. Behind the purple-and-white Unify America logo, a computer background of gently waving red and blue horizontal stripes gradually move toward each other to merge into a solid purple wave, then fan out again.

"So, Senator Cregg, first . . . how is your son?"

"Recovering nicely. I expect he'll be back out here on the campaign trail with me any day now. Graham is . . ." Senator Cregg's smile falters the tiniest bit. Every other time I've seen his face, he's worn one of two expressions—either the too-wide smile of a used-car salesman or the concerned-father look. This new look is more calculating, and for the first time, I see a similarity between the older Cregg and his son.

His mask slips for only a moment, however, and then the politician's smile is back. "He's great at keeping me on track at these events. I tend to wander off and start chatting with people. Need a little more of Graham's focus!"

Having encountered Graham Cregg's *focus* firsthand, I have a pretty good idea what the Senator means. Aaron catches the look on my face and gives my hand a squeeze.

"I'm glad to hear he's doing better, Senator. Moving on now to the events at Port Deposit, we've both just seen the interviews with local residents, and I'd like to pick up on what the town council member said near the end about the possibility of a chemical that affected townspeople. Is that something you can talk about at this stage of the investigation?"

The Senator's face shifts into concerned mode. "I'm not sure that we can count on the administration to give us a straight answer on this, since the existence of a terror cell so close to the nation's capital doesn't reflect well on the president's ability to keep Americans safe. I can assure you based on my own sources that a chemical agent was definitely involved, but there's absolutely no evidence that it was used on the people of Port Deposit. The things they witnessed over the past few years were not figments of their drug-laced imaginations but were instead fallout from an abandoned government project that landed in the hands of the WOCAN terrorists who were occupying that facility and, I'm quite certain, their globalist allies."

"So . . ." The anchor looks confused. "You're saying that something was left behind by the Navy when they abandoned the Bainbridge Center back in the 1990s?"

"No. First, the project in question was not something left behind by the Navy. It was run initially by the Army as part of the Stargate Project, later by the CIA as the Delphi Project, and then finally under government contractors. I won't trace the full course of events—that will be covered in my press conference on Tuesday—but suffice it to say that one of the individuals who was connected to the Delphi Project several years ago was Franco Lucas, who we now know was also working with the WOCAN terrorists prior to his death."

"So then, what exactly was the goal of the research?" the reporter asks, looking a little confused.

"The goal of the Delphi Project was to magnify certain . . . abilities . . . already present in the human brain so that they could be harnessed for national security purposes. Espionage, and so forth. To create superspies. Supersoldiers."

There's a very long pause, and then the woman asks, "What sort of abilities?"

"Telekinesis. Telepathy. Clairvoyance. WOCAN was using that facility for two different purposes, and I don't know if the pranks on the people of Port Deposit were part of the experiments or simply kids acting out. They've been importing young women—and some young men—from Eastern Europe and selling them into sexual slavery. But they were also using that same group of individuals as lab rats to test a serum stolen from the Delphi Project several years ago. WOCAN and their globalist allies have also abducted, and *continue* to abduct, children right here in the United States for these purposes. And now, having gotten the data they need, they're getting rid of the evidence. The fire in Port Deposit and the murder of those six children in North Carolina are just the two most recent examples."

The anchorwoman blinks and then stares at the Senator's image on the screen, owl-eyed, seemingly at a loss for words. "That's . . . that's a very serious allegation. Do you really expect our viewers to believe that WOCAN separatists—who, I must add, have never engaged in any sort of violent activity before—"

Cregg cuts her off yet again. "They've engaged in *plenty* of illegal activity, Carissa."

"I said *violent* activity. Do you have any evidence linking this group—"

"Personally, I consider the takeover of privately owned business a violent action."

She gives him a tight smile. "Fine. But, hopefully you'll acknowledge that the takeover and occupation of a business falls considerably short of murdering children? This sounds more like a Stephen King novel than reality. Do you really expect viewers to believe that there is a drug out there that turns normal—"

"Carissa, I never expect anyone to *believe* anything. The current administration has ensured that people trust absolutely nothing that government officials say, so I *always* provide proof for my claims. What you're about to see is video obtained by a police officer who was working undercover with the WOCAN group. And keep in mind that this is only a select sample . . . We have dozens of additional clips like these."

The Senator steps to one side, and a video pops up where the UA logo was a moment before. I recognize the room the instant it appears. I'm not the only one—Jaden and Daniel come to attention as soon as I see the white cement-block walls, white tiled floors, and rows of white cabinets at the back. If the camera were to pan around, there would be black curtains extending halfway down from the ceiling along two of the walls. The only splashes of color in the scene are the red fire extinguisher near the back and the pink shirt worn by the young girl in the foreground.

I grab the remote from the counter and press pause. "That's the lab at The Warren. I think it's the one Deo and I were in." It's hard to keep my voice steady, because this is also the room where Jaden and three other people were executed to see if I could pick up their psychic abilities as well as their spirits. The room where I watched as Senator Cregg's son hijacked Deo's mind and very nearly killed him. The room where one of my temporary hitchers used my body to somehow explode Graham Cregg's phone and set the lab on fire.

Daniel confirms it.

Definitely Lab 1.

Do either of you recognize the girl?

Jaden answers this time.

Svetlana, although she's younger in this video than when I knew her. One of the Zippos. I remember her 'cause the cafeteria would set out a group birthday cake once a month. And they'd always put a candle on top, but just for show. They didn't light it, but sometimes one of the Zippos would do it if the Fudds weren't watching. Only Svetlana torched the entire top of the cake. Melted the candle, too. We had to pick bits of wax out of the frosting.

I press play again. The girl, who is about fifteen, with reddish-brown hair and pale skin, frowns slightly, concentrating on the pile of paper in front of her. After a few seconds, one of the crumpled balls begins to darken along the edges, and soon the entire pile is in flames.

The girl squeals, but not in fear. There's a happy smile on her face as she looks toward the camera.

"*Ya zrobyv tse!* I did it!"

"Yes, I see," a voice replies off camera. I feel Jaden tense up, but I don't think it's because he actually recognizes the voice. It's just the tone that's familiar—that same flat, almost-bored tone that all of the guards used when dealing with the adepts.

The scene changes to one of the smaller rooms where I spent an entire day being tested for basic psychic ability. A boy of around twelve is seated in one of the wooden chairs, leaning in toward the table. Thin wires of different colors are taped to his scalp. He stares intently at the center of the table where two red plastic cups sit about two inches apart.

I remember this test. We sat there for a very boring three or four minutes staring at unmoving cups. Then we shifted over to staring at unmoving rubber balls, and then to unmoving paper clips. Finally, without comment, the guard jotted something down on her clipboard and removed the wires from my head.

This kid, however, is an entirely different story. They ask if he's ready, and as soon as he says yes, both cups begin to move simultaneously, in opposite directions, as if they're being repelled by a magnetic field. When the cups reach the edge of the table, they tip slightly and dip down about an inch. A tiny bit of water sloshes out of the cup on the right. The boy's eyes narrow in concentration, and the cups slowly rise back up to the level of the table, righting themselves. They hover for a few seconds, oblivious to gravity, until a voice says, "Put them back now." The cups slide into their original positions.

Unlike the girl in the lab, the boy doesn't cheer. He just slumps down in the chair, rubbing his forehead and looking very much like he wants to cry.

The next scene is in the lab again, where a small child is seated in one of the metal chairs, but then the picture cuts back to the anchorwoman. "I'm sorry, Senator Cregg. We have to take a commercial break. Can we pick this up when we return?"

Annoyance at her request causes the Senator's mask to slip for an instant, but then the smile flows back across his face. "By all means, Carissa. Gotta pay the bills."

A commercial comes on, and I watch, not even realizing I'm holding the remote. Aaron gently pries it from my hand and slides it across the bar to Taylor.

"You okay?" he asks me as Taylor fast-forwards through the commercials. "You don't have to watch this if—"

"I'm okay." The words come out a little more sharply than I intended, but Aaron doesn't take offense. He gently squeezes my knee, leaving his hand there when the video starts again.

"Welcome back to *First Light*. I'm Carissa Daly, and for those of you just joining us, we're with Senator Ron Cregg, current presidential candidate and a member of the Senate Intelligence Committee, who has just made some rather startling allegations concerning the separatist group known as WOCAN."

The anchor gives a brief overview, and once Senator Cregg returns to the screen, she says, "Perhaps you could run the first two pieces of . . . evidence . . . again."

His mouth tightens slightly at her hesitation on the word *evidence*, but he says, "By all means."

When the clip of the third test begins, I realize that the child in the chair is much younger than the others. Her feet don't even reach the ground. On the other side of her are maybe a half-dozen electric and electronic devices—a laptop, a lamp, and a cell phone, among others.

A woman's voice asks, "Are you ready *now*?" There's a slightly annoyed emphasis on the last word.

The girl's reply is small and frightened. "Yes, ma'am."

Hunter zooms to the front of my head so fast that I jump, my arm sending the cereal bowl flying off the bar, leftover milk spraying out in an arc behind it. I feel myself being sucked backward, completely taken off guard.

"Bree! That's Bree!"

The voice is mine, just . . . younger sounding, somehow. Hunter has never taken over before, but he's front and center now, so focused that it takes all my effort to push him back and regain control.

Taylor stops the video, and both she and Aaron stare at me, alarmed. I hold one hand up and then return my attention to the chaos inside my head. Hunter is yelling as Daniel and Jaden do their best to calm him down.

Hunter, I'm sorry.

On the other two occasions when I've addressed Hunter directly, he curled up into a fetal ball, once even pulling his thumb into his mouth. He's more frightened of me than he is of Jaden's gory image—or I guess I should say my mind's gory representation of Jaden. This time, Hunter flinches at my voice, but he doesn't move away.

I need you to work with me, not against me, okay? Is that your sister?

Yes. Her name is Sabrina. But we call her Bree. That's her. What is this Warren place you're all thinking about? Why is she there?

Hunter can probably tell that I don't want to answer, that I'm blocking off some of my thoughts. And I really do need to block them, because I have no idea if his sister made it out of The Warren when the fire started. Even if she did make it out, there's still no guarantee Bree or any of the other children are alive.

So I choose my words carefully, trying to keep any stray thoughts from seeping through.

It's a place where they test kids like you and Bree. To see what they can do. What special thing can Bree do, Hunter?

Same thing as me. She can break electrical things when she wants. Not just little things, like me. Big ones, too. But . . . she can do a bunch of other things, too. Like, sometimes she also knows stuff she shouldn't know. I can't do that. And we could always talk without talking.

Judging from the items around her, I'm guessing that the Delphi people are not interested in Sabrina's telepathy skills, although I file that away as something we may be able to use.

But why is she *there*? Mom said my dad stole her. That he took her to Wyoming. Is this testing place in Wyoming?

No. But . . . I'm sure Bree is okay, Hunter. We're going to find her and get her back home.

> Unless. You were thinking *unless*. I could hear it. You
> mean unless she's dead like me, right?

I sigh. Since hiding my thoughts was clearly a bust, I opt for honesty.

> *I don't know, Hunter. None of us know right now. But I*
> *promise I'll try my best to find an answer for you. In order for*
> *me to do that, though, you need to stay calm. To stay back here*
> *with Daniel and Jaden.*

I wait until he gives me a reluctant *okay* and then open my eyes. "The girl is Hunter's sister. Hit play."

Taylor runs the video back a few seconds, and we again hear Bree say she's ready.

The unseen voice tells her to start with the phone, and the camera moves in on the girl. Sabrina Bieler has ivory skin with a light sprinkling of freckles across her cheeks. She's missing the same two teeth that her brother is, and her reddish-blonde curls look like they haven't seen a comb in days. Her lips tighten as she reaches out toward the cell phone. Even before her fingers brush it, I hear a crackling noise. Then the phone's screen goes black.

Hunter really wants control of my hands so that he can reach out for Bree. But he's also a little worried that getting too close to the TV when he's this upset might destroy it.

At the request of the guard, Bree moves on to the lamp, which sputters out when she touches the base. After that, she trashes the computer.

The news anchor cuts in at this point, although the video of Bree continues to run in the background. "Senator Cregg, we're running out of time. But before we go, surely you realize that no one is going to accept a claim like this on the basis of a video? A video, I might add, that could very easily be altered. We have people in the studio who could probably do something like this in a couple of hours."

The Senator's jaw tightens slightly, but then he laughs. "Are you sure you want to admit that, Carissa?"

She doesn't return the laugh, and he continues. "*Of course* I realize that people will need more substantive proof. The video was just . . . shall we say, the teaser for the main event? I'm here this morning to make sure we get the widest possible audience for my press conference on Tuesday. Hopefully, once the media and the American people understand what is at stake, we'll be able to get some action from our government."

"Okay then, Senator." The anchorwoman gives him a puzzled, almost patronizing smile, and then she moves on to entertainment news.

Taylor switches off the TV. "Don't talk about anything important until I get back. I need to pee."

Aaron shakes his head as she leaves the room. "Taylor Quinn, the Queen of TMI."

I'm still staring at the blank screen. "Why are they doing this? Why would the Creggs want to expose the very program that they've taken such pains to hide?"

CHAPTER SIXTEEN

Carova Beach, North Carolina
November 12, 2019, 12:32 p.m.

The puppy, whose name is currently Ein, happily chases the ball that Peyton and TJ are rolling back and forth across the carpet. I don't know *why* the dog's name is Ein. Deo says it's short for Einstein, like in *Back to the Future*. Taylor says no, the name is from some anime show. I don't particularly care, since I suspect the dog will have an entirely new name by this time tomorrow. All I know is that I've become quite attached to the little guy in the past few days. He can't exactly run on the beach with me yet, but he's happy to ride along in my jacket when we go for more leisurely walks.

Since Magda has us in a holding pattern, waiting to see exactly what the Senator reveals in his press conference this afternoon, we've actually had *time* for leisurely walks the past few days. The weather has been pleasant, despite a brisk wind, and it's been wonderful to get some fresh air, and even a little privacy. A place like this is a nice break from the city, and I think Porter was genuinely sorry to leave—although that could have partly been due to the fact that he had to drive Michele's lavender Jeep when he went home.

This afternoon, however, there's no time for walks and no privacy at all, since I'm babysitting. After a tense first session with both parents in the room, Miranda brought Peyton alone to the second appointment, and today, Jasper was supposed to come. But Miranda dropped both kids off this morning, asking if we could watch them for a few hours after Peyton's appointment with Kelsey. Miranda is helping another woman with a cleaning job in Corolla. They need the cash, she says, especially since Jasper has flat-out refused to take any money from Magda.

Despite Jasper's surly mood when he was here on Thursday, I was hoping he'd have chilled out enough to come today. I have a ton of questions about my parents, and Jasper avoided me on his last visit. He's also refused to speak with me on the phone.

But judging from the condition of Miranda's face this morning when she dropped the kids off, her husband is the very opposite of chill. I didn't ask any questions about the bruise on her right cheek, visible even under a thick layer of makeup, but just told her we'd be happy to watch the kids. Miranda was grateful—as she noted, she had nowhere else to leave them—but she also seemed really angry, so I'm guessing that the bruise is from Jasper, not another temper tantrum by Peyton. She seemed angry at me, too. Or maybe she's just angry at my face, which is so much like that of the woman her husband apparently loved and lost.

"Do it now, Pey." TJ bounces the ball and watches as it rises into the air, hovering above the dog's head, just out of reach. Ein yips. I think it's more out of frustration than confusion. This poor pup's understanding of gravity is likely to be seriously skewed by his current playmates.

Peyton isn't even looking at the ball now. Her eyes are on the puppy as he backs away, barking. When she looks at the ball again, it comes down. It bounces a few times and then rolls toward my feet, followed by the puppy.

I scoop the dog into my lap and roll the ball toward Peyton. "How long can you float it in the air?"

"She can hold it a *loooong* time," says TJ. "I got the LEGO TIE Fighter for Christmas, and Peyton made it fly all around the living room. The wing came off when she landed it, but it was easy to pop it back on. That was *so* cool."

Peyton beams. This time, she doesn't bounce the ball to get it started. It just levitates slowly upward from her hand and floats toward me, hanging in midair a few inches in front of my face. Her eyes stay on the ball while it's moving, but then she looks back at Ein next to me. He's standing on the very edge of the love seat, trying to figure out how to get down to the floor where the kids are.

And then Peyton's invisible hands lift Ein from the love seat and plop him on the carpet. He rushes over to the girl, climbing over her legs. I'm worried that he's going to snag her tights, but then she falls backward on the floor, giggling as the puppy tumbles off her belly.

The ball continues to hover in front of my nose, not moving at all. When I pluck it out of the air, Peyton's eyes glance my way for a second, but then Ein takes off, and she follows on all fours, pretending she's a puppy, too. Ein growls playfully when she reaches him, tugging on the edge of her sleeve.

TJ's eyes are still on me, even if his sister's attention has strayed. "She can do it a lot longer than that. Bigger stuff, too." He lowers his voice. "Especially when she's mad. She don't mean to hurt anybody, but . . . little kids get mad real easy."

As I watch his sister with the dog, Miranda's words from the other day come back to me. *No telling what Peyton might do if she got scared or if it scratched her.*

When Peyton is laughing and playing around with TJ and Ein, it's all too easy to forget that she isn't a typical preschooler and that there's a dangerous side to her gift.

I retrieve the puppy—just in case. Deo is out on the deck, so I tap on the patio door to get his attention.

He slides the patio door open. "What's up?"

"I think the puppy might need a little time outside." I shoot a meaningful glance toward Peyton as I hand him the pup.

"I wanna go out, too!" Peyton says.

There's a whiny note in her voice that makes me nervous. But I have several lifetimes of parental memories at my disposal, and I know how to swing a diversion, especially when there are decent bribes at hand.

"How about later? It's snack and movie time! Let's go see if there are any ice cream bars left in the freezer."

Deo's mouth twists as he closes the door, so I'm not entirely surprised to find the freezer bare, despite the fact that there were three full twelve-count boxes when Miranda and I cleaned the house six days ago. I stop and send a text, adding ice cream to the shopping list on Taylor's phone. She's gone into town with Aaron to pick up groceries and meet with a firm Magda contacted to add security features and do some other renovations to the house.

The kids settle for Oreos and milk. Peyton shoves the cookies into her mouth so quickly that I'm scared she's going to choke, and then asks for more, saying she's really, really, *really* hungry. I start to say no but then remember Taylor's appetite after she does a remote viewing. Peyton might actually *be* hungry after her tricks with the ball and the puppy just now.

"I could get you some fruit? Or maybe cereal?" I ask, feeling a little guilty for not scrounging up a healthier snack.

"*More* Oreos." Her lower lip juts out angrily. I'm reminded of the scene where Veruca stomps her foot and sings "I Want It Now!" in the Willy Wonka movie.

I glare back at her but then sigh and put the pack of cookies on the floor. Peyton is not my discipline problem, and there are a lot of fragile things in this house. Better to give the little Wookiee what she wants.

Once I find a movie that satisfies them both, I go into the adjoining dining room with Aaron's iPad. No reason I can't babysit and research at the same time.

I've already combed through the files Sam sent concerning my parents so many times that I could pretty much cite the facts verbatim, but I reflexively click on the link anyway. Leah Elaine Johnson was born in 1978 to the Reverend Thomas Johnson and his wife, Betty Fredericks Johnson, and grew up in a small town near Glen Burnie, Maryland. She had one sister, Rowena Rachel, who was eight years younger. Leah joined the military on her eighteenth birthday, three weeks after graduating from an unaccredited religious school. She was eventually stationed at Fort Bragg, in the PSYOPS unit.

According to newspaper articles written after the shooting, that's where she met Scott Pfeifer, which gels with what Jasper said. Pfeifer was nearly ten years her senior. He began working at Fort Bragg as a civilian consultant during his final year of grad school at Duke, where he earned a PhD in neurobiology. They were married in 1999 but divorced a few years later. My father was found incompetent to stand trial shortly after the shooting and was committed to a hospital for the criminally insane in Jessup, Maryland.

There's no mention of a child in any of the articles. Sam managed to locate a marriage license but no birth certificate. He also found death certificates for Thomas and Betty Johnson, who both died in 2012, but he couldn't find additional information on Leah's sister, Rowena. *My aunt*, although I have a tough time wrapping my head around that concept.

Patient confidentiality kept Sam from getting recent information about Scott Pfeifer, but Kelsey tracked down a friend of a friend who is on staff at the hospital. He's not the actual psychiatrist who works with my dad, but he was able to confirm that Pfeifer is still a patient. The official diagnosis is schizophrenia, and he's relatively stable the vast majority of the time, aside from the rare violent outburst.

Before Kelsey chatted with that guy yesterday, I'd continued to hold out a slight hope that Jasper was wrong about Scott Pfeifer being my father. They were, after all, divorced. Maybe my mom moved away for a while. Met someone new and relatively sane. It requires a bit of mental gymnastics to make this case, but it's far more comforting to imagine a scenario in which my mom was killed not by my father but by her crazy ex-husband who was in no way related to me.

But Kelsey's contact also told her that Pfeifer's more pressing psychological problem is his frequent insistence that he's not Scott Pfeifer at all. He'll refuse to answer to his own name, often taking on an entirely different persona. Usually, he mimics a patient who died at the hospital. So, apparently, I inherited both his nose and his knack for picking up ghosts.

I close the file and open the *AllGlobalConspiracies* website, looking for one of the few Tamara Blake interviews that I haven't listened to yet. When I click the *Paranormal and Parapsychology* link, however, I get a "Page not Found" error. The entire section has been scrubbed.

As I'm checking to see if any other content on the site has vanished, Kelsey appears at the patio door. She motions for me to join her and Deo on the deck.

"We've got a problem," Kelsey says as soon as the door slides shut behind us.

I'm tempted to point out that we've got numerous problems, but her expression suggests that this isn't the time for levity. "What's wrong?"

"I'm guessing you haven't noticed Peyton's leg?"

"No."

"She's wearing tights, so it's not obvious. But she took a bathroom break during our session and got them all tangled." Kelsey pulls her phone from her pocket. "I had to help her get them straight, and . . .

there's a large bruise on her upper thigh. I managed to sneak a photograph while I was helping her with the tights."

Kelsey hands me her cell phone. Her thumb blocks one corner of the photo, but it doesn't obscure the chubby little legs tangled in pumpkin-colored tights or the deep-fuchsia mark on the outside of her right leg, just above the knee.

Wincing, I glance inside at Peyton, stretched out on the floor next to her brother, happily watching *LEGO Batman*. This is far, far from the worst case of abuse I've seen after fifteen years in foster care. Physical abuse is the main reason that many, maybe even *most*, kids are in the system. There was a baby at one house—a kid who couldn't even walk yet—and she had casts on both legs. Sadly, the abuse doesn't end when the kids are taken into state custody. There are plenty of foster parents who abuse the kids in their care—Deo and I met while we were in the custody of one of those sterling examples of humanity. But no matter how many times you see it, the idea that someone could physically harm a small child socks you right in the gut.

"I thought it might have been from last week, when she lost control," Deo says, and I can tell he's struggling to keep a grip on his temper, "but Kelsey says it's more recent."

Kelsey nods. "You can tell from the color. And . . . Peyton more or less confirmed that it happened last night."

I'm reluctant to ask. "What did she say?"

"She said that her daddy had to put her into time-out. That wouldn't explain the bruise, of course, so I suspect *time-out* is just a family euphemism, but I didn't want to push too hard and upset her."

Deo gives a frustrated huff. He looks like he wants to hit something, although I'm pretty sure it's actually someone, and that the specific someone is Jasper. One of the few times I've seen Deo completely lose his temper was when a woman in Walmart smacked her toddler on the arm for grabbing things off the store shelves. The kid began screaming—it wasn't a gentle slap by any means—and Deo's personal history makes him especially sensitive to any hint of child abuse. He was only eight at the time, but he ran toward the front of the store, screaming for security. Our foster mother shushed him and told him to mind his own business. She even apologized to the horrid woman for Deo's conduct.

"Miranda's cheek was also bruised," I tell them. "And the fact that Jasper didn't bring Peyton as scheduled—the fact that he's going back on his statement that she wouldn't be left alone with us? Probably not a very good sign."

Kelsey sighs. "I told him when we met that first day that I'd be happy to work with him, but he and Miranda both said he had his temper under control. That he wasn't abusive. They were defensive about me even bringing it up. I've handled post-traumatic stress disorder patients in the past, though, and he clearly needs help."

"But are Jasper's symptoms really PTSD?" I ask. "Most of the early Delphi subjects had violent episodes. Sometimes delusions."

She shrugs. "It's not *typical* PTSD—and either way, it doesn't excuse anything that Jasper has done. But the violent episodes are almost certainly a by-product of the drug they were given, which seems to affect the amygdala, the section of the brain that triggers the fight-or-flight response. I think you're familiar with that one?"

There's a slight twinkle in her eye as she says it. As Kelsey is well aware, my fight-or-flight response has almost always manifested as flight. I rarely stayed put at the various foster homes where I was assigned. It's a bit of an ongoing joke between the two of us, and she laughs softly before continuing.

"While I doubt that they intended the drug to affect the amygdala, that part of the brain is very close to the fusiform gyrus. Those sections work together sometimes, for instance, on facial recognition. As you may remember from our previous chats, the fusiform gyrus is believed to control things like synesthesia. And"—she gives us a tight little smile—"also psychic abilities, for the few experts willing to admit they're possible."

I went through a phase, around age ten, where I was intensely interested in why my brain was different from others. Kelsey was really the only person I could ask. She did her best, even though I don't think the scientist side of her personality was very comfortable with the answers since they relied heavily on conjecture. I remember sitting on the floor in her office one day with a classroom model of the human brain between the two of us. The model was pretty basic, and didn't have labels for parts like the fusiform gyrus, but Kelsey was able to point out the general location to me as we snapped the larger pieces together.

"But getting back to my original point," Kelsey says, "there are a number of drugs that are effective in treating PTSD. They might be helpful for Jasper's condition as well. Miranda said he's not the 'therapy type,' whatever that means, but I was hoping he might be willing to take an SSRI. Unfortunately, now that I've witnessed that bruise on Peyton, there's an added level of complexity. On the one hand, I'm legally obligated to report this, but on the other hand . . ."

She doesn't complete the sentence, because we all know what she's thinking.

"Yeah," Deo says. "Child Services would be in for a major surprise if they tried to take Peyton against her will."

"And if there's any publicity," I say, "it would be like pointing a big red arrow at Peyton's head."

"Precisely. But even though I'm hesitant to report this, I can't in good conscience allow either of those children to go back to that environment. When do you expect Miranda to return for them?"

"She said no later than three."

"We should make sure Aaron is here by then," Kelsey says. "Hopefully Miranda will be reasonable, but . . . we may need backup."

Ein, who is corralled in a Pack 'n Play we found in one of the bedroom closets, whimpers. I retrieve him, and when I look up, Kelsey and Deo are staring at something to the south of us.

"Maybe that's them?" Deo asks.

It's definitely a moving object, maybe a mile down the beach, but as it gets closer, I see that it's not a single truck. Four—no, make that five—vehicles are headed our way.

Our truck is at the front of the convoy. The four vehicles bringing up the rear are identical dark-gray vans. As soon as they pull into the yard, Aaron hops out of the passenger side. "Did you get my message?" he calls out.

"No." I pat the pockets of my jeans and then remember that I left my phone in the kitchen when I was getting the kids their snack.

The vans are now pulling into the drive, each plastered with the word *Vigilance* on the side. Aaron talks briefly to the driver of the first van and points around to the back of the house. Once the vans begin to file off in that direction, he sprints up the wooden stairs to the deck, and Deo goes downstairs to help Taylor unload the groceries from the truck.

"Those can't be the contractors," I say. "Magda doesn't even own the house yet."

"No. They're from a private security firm."

"Well," Kelsey says, "I guess that solves our backup problem."

"Backup?" Aaron asks.

I nod toward the window, and he notices Peyton and TJ for the first time. His brow wrinkles. "I thought Peyton's appointment was at ten."

"It was. But Miranda needed to work, and she didn't have anyone to watch them."

Kelsey shows Aaron the picture. He curses softly.

"Miranda's face was also bruised," I add. "Hopefully TJ wasn't hurt too, although I wouldn't be surprised."

"We can't let the kids go back into that situation," Kelsey says. "And I'm not sure how their parents, especially Jasper, are going to receive that bit of news. So the security guards may come in handy."

"True," I say as I look down at the last van rounding the corner of the house. "But six security guards seems like overkill. And why do they need four vans to transport six people?"

"Two are for . . . equipment."

I don't know if Kelsey catches on, but it's clear to me that *equipment* actually means *weapons*.

"And the others," he says, "are for the kids. Seven of them."

"What?" Kelsey and I say in unison.

"Yeah. It seems we're no longer the only team Magda has working on this project. All of the kids are from the Bragg area, from our list. Also three nurses and one parent who wouldn't let his kid come alone."

"Couldn't Magda have provided us with a little advance notice?" I ask.

"I *think* that's what our meeting later today was supposed to be about—well, that and the Senator's upcoming press conference. But the lead guy with Vigilance said things came together a little more quickly than anticipated. Given the killings at Bragg, they didn't meet much resistance, and they wanted to get everyone in one easily defendable place."

Kelsey sighs. "It's going to be tough to do intake on seven new patients at the same time. Do you know if they're all stable?"

"I guess?" Aaron shrugs. "They've all been in school, although most were at that school on Fort Bragg. The youngest is seven—that's the boy whose dad came along. The others are mostly teens or tweens." He nods toward the kids. "How long before Miranda comes back to get them?"

"Maybe half an hour."

Kelsey and I exchange a look. We've both been around Peyton enough this week to be a little worried about overstimulating her. And—I run a quick tally in my head—seventeen brand-new people are coming into the house. I'm enough of an introvert that the fact stresses *me* out a little. We should definitely let Peyton adjust gradually.

Aaron and I both go down to the lower level—me to help unload the last of the groceries and Aaron to assist the Vigilance people with getting the new arrivals settled into their rooms. My first thought when I get back upstairs and see the provisions piled up on the kitchen floor and counters is that they've bought enough food to get us through the winter. But given how many people are now in the house, it probably won't last more than a week.

Taylor and Deo come in with another load. She's laughing at something Deo said, so apparently she's worked through whatever her snit was about the other night.

"That's the last of it," Deo says, and we begin the slow process of putting away the groceries. Though we occasionally hear muted voices below us, I'm a little surprised at how quiet the place is, given the number of people here.

I mention this to Aaron when he joins us a few minutes later.

He nods, a frown creasing his forehead. "All of the kids are still sedated. The nurse said they'll probably sleep for another three or four hours. They're all piled into a couple of those bunk bed rooms in the back wing."

"Why sedate them?" I ask. "I thought you said they were stable."

"I asked. The lead guard said the company wouldn't agree to transport the kids otherwise. Worried about *safety*."

"Well, it may be a valid point," Taylor says. "We don't know exactly what these kids can *do*. What if one of them is like Peyton and could send something flying through the windshield? Or what if one of them hijacked the driver's head while he was driving? Sounds like a necessary precaution to me."

Aaron and Deo both look as skeptical as I feel. It probably *was* necessary, but the idea of drugging these kids to transport them feels like a tactic that Cregg and his Delphi crew would have used. A tactic they *did* use, actually, to transport me.

"Maybe," Aaron says. "But I didn't exactly care for the tone that they used when talking about the kids. More like they were cargo or something. Anyway, they won't wake up until dinnertime at the earliest. The guards are taking the ground floor, and the nurses will be in the back wing with the kids, at least for now."

"That reminds me," I say. "Kelsey wants to keep Miranda and her two kids off to themselves so that Peyton can adjust gradually to being around others. So if any of you are in the north wing, you might want to pack up and join the rest of us on the south side."

Taylor and Deo head off to move their things, and the rest of us go into the great room. When Miranda pulls up a few minutes later, I take Kelsey's place with TJ and Peyton. Hopefully her talk with Miranda will be brief, since Senator Cregg's press conference starts in about fifteen minutes. Not that we'd have to watch it live—the man is such a publicity whore that I'm pretty sure he'll have it plastered all over his website and Twitter feed five minutes after it ends. But we're scheduled to meet with Magda soon after, so we'll need to be up to speed.

I have a vague sense of uneasiness about all of this—the press conference, the security guards, the new arrivals—and Hunter's emotions aren't helping the situation. He understood when I told him that we can't really start looking for his sister until we get the go-ahead from Magda, even though I sense he's not happy about a delay. And Magda made it clear that she wouldn't even start thinking about next moves until after we heard the Senator's announcement today.

The biggest source of my discomfort, though, is wondering exactly what Magda's people said to convince all but the parents of the youngest adept to allow their children to come here unaccompanied. I have memories of being a parent, and I can't imagine any of my hitchers letting a child of theirs go off with strangers to a place they've never seen. That has me wondering whether these kids are really here voluntarily, or whether there are some brand-new AMBER Alerts in the Fayetteville area.

The credits roll on *LEGO Batman* before Kelsey returns. They're tired of watching movies and being cooped up in this small room, so as a diversion, I challenge Peyton to see how many of the tattered paperbacks she can "float" off the bookshelf across the room. She makes it to four, and then they all shudder and crash to the ground.

TJ puts them back on the shelf, and she's having another go at it when Kelsey appears at the door. She motions for me to step into the hallway, and I'm happy to see that she's looking far less nervous than before.

"Miranda resisted at first," Kelsey says in a low voice. "But I think she was actually kind of relieved. When Jasper gets like this, she says he tends to go off on his own for a bit to calm down. I asked one of the security guards to drive her over to pick up a few things for her and the kids."

Kelsey frowns at the sight of Peyton, who has three books floating now. "Should we be encouraging her to do that?"

"Oh. I'm sorry. I just—"

"I'm not scolding you, Anna. That was an actual question. I want your opinion."

I stop for a moment and watch Peyton as she concentrates, slowly lifting the fourth book.

"When I talked to Peyton the other day, it was clear that she knows she has to control her ability—or her monkey, as she calls it. She doesn't want to lose it, though. It's part of her, and she's proud of what she can do. I'd really hate for her to become ashamed of it, and I think she already is, to some extent. Except for when she's with TJ. She likes making him laugh."

"You're probably right. I'm just a little concerned about her exercising that muscle too much before she learns to control it."

As I look back over, I see that a fifth book has joined the others. Peyton's face is squinched tight, and then four books fall to the floor. She floats the fifth book over to TJ and lands it gently on his lap. "Read to me, TJ."

I catch a glimpse of the cover, which features a woman's hands splayed across a ripped and tanned male abdomen. I should have checked the contents of the bookshelf before starting this little game.

"Or," I say, plucking the book from his grasp and putting it back on the shelf, "we can go upstairs and play video games?"

"Can we get dinner, too?" Peyton asks. "'Cause I'm really, really, really hungry."

It hasn't been long since she snarfed down half a bag of cookies. My prediction on how long those groceries will last could be optimistic if the other kids use their powers on a regular basis.

Upstairs, I download the "flierfries" game onto our phones, and Kelsey settles the kids on the other side of the great room. Hopefully the game will occupy them enough that she can watch the press conference, too.

One of the kitchen doors swings open, and I see Aaron backing through the door with a tray of sandwiches. He and Taylor are arguing about something, and Deo has joined in. I catch the phrases *cloaking* and *time-displacement tech*, so I'm guessing this is a pop culture squabble, rather than anything substantive.

Taylor carries over a plate of the sandwiches, and Peyton now has a half a sandwich in one hand and is poking at fireflies on my phone resting in her lap. I cringe, imagining the mustard-encrusted fingerprints I'm going to have to clean off of the touchscreen.

We all gather on the three sofas arranged in a circle facing the fireplace. A huge TV is mounted above, and as soon as I catch sight of it, Hunter shifts to the front of my consciousness. He's been incredibly patient and quiet over the past few days. But I know what he's hoping for, and I'm worried that he'll be disappointed.

We may not see your sister today, Hunter. Senator Cregg said he has dozens of examples, and the clips of Bree and the others have aired a lot in the media over the past few days.

That's an understatement, actually. The Senator has been thoroughly lampooned, both by the press and social media. They posted clips of telepathic powers from every B movie and TV show imaginable.

A few creative souls even made their own. The pundits have spent the past few days noting that this stunt has harmed the credibility of Unify America, something that a fledgling third party can ill afford. The Senator's opponent for the party's nomination has taken every opportunity to argue that it shows Senator Cregg isn't a viable candidate and that the party can't be held accountable for the actions of one official.

Hunter has seen the clips along with the rest of us, even though I'm not sure how much he's following. Politics is baffling enough for adults, let alone a six-year-old kid.

> If he doesn't use the clip, can we watch the other video again later?

> *Of course.*

This will make the fourth time I've agreed to watch it again, just so he can see his sister. There's obviously no new information to be gained from the clip, and it was filmed weeks or even months ago, but I *do* get it. If I'd had a video of Deo when he was being held at The Warren, I'm sure I'd have watched it again. Even if I knew it was taped, even if I knew that it didn't guarantee that Deo was still alive, I'd have watched it just to see him. Just to hold on to that tiny bit of hope.

Aaron slides over to make room for me on the center sofa. We're all nervous. Whatever Senator Cregg has on his agenda for today, it doesn't seem likely to be good news.

"I made a few veggie sandwiches too," Aaron says. "So you don't have to pick off the meat and hide it in your napkin." There's a gentle, teasing note to his voice, and my nerves ease the tiniest bit.

"I don't *always* pick off the meat. But thank you." I give him a quick kiss.

❖   ❖   ❖

The lead-in to the press conference is an interview with the other UA candidate, Juanita Breyer. I guess they're giving her equal time or something.

Breyer is complaining about the Senator's "media stunt" when the host, a guy so generically handsome that he could hold a second job as a department store mannequin, cuts her off so that they can switch over to the press conference. Breyer's lips tighten, and she gives an annoyed sniff, then she's gone.

I expect to see a podium inside a conference room, but the Senator is outside. He's standing a few feet away from a mic, whispering something to a middle-aged man in a blue suit, who nods and then walks away. Behind the platform where he's standing is a folding table, and maybe ten yards beyond that, a shooting target—the bull's-eye variety, not the type shaped like a human—is attached to a bale of hay. The setup appears rather incongruous on the lawn of the Capitol Building.

Senator Cregg steps forward, looking around at the reporters and also at the crowd that has gathered nearby. All of the seats are filled except for two in the front row. "I'd like to thank all of you for coming. This is a much better turnout than we Unify America candidates usually get."

He smiles, making it clear that this is a joke, that he knows he'd have the usual cluster of seven or eight journalists and maybe a couple of onlookers in attendance if not for the controversy surrounding his release of the Delphi footage. The reporters respond with a polite chuckle.

"I'm not going to waste your time showing the videos I revealed on Thursday. You've all seen them."

Hunter huffs in disappointment, then slides to the back of my head.

"I knew people would be interested, but I really didn't expect the video to go viral," the Senator says.

"Yeah, right," Aaron mutters, shaking his head at the TV.

"Seven and a half million views last I heard," the Senator continues. "And, of course, it's played repeatedly on your various news outlets. I suspect most of you have had the footage analyzed frame by frame to see if it was altered, as well . . . and if your tech people are competent, you know that it's genuine. So I'm just going to cut to the chase and give you what you've requested. Proof."

The man in the blue suit is back, holding the arm of a gangly boy with a rash of acne across his forehead. The kid looks familiar, but I can't place him. A guard with a rifle follows them onto the stage, and a couple in their late thirties take the two empty chairs in the front row.

"We're going to call this young man John," the Senator says. "As you can see, his parents traveled with him. They understand how dangerous their son and others like him are to the rest of us. They've agreed to this demonstration in the hope that we can find a way to keep both these kids and the nation safe."

The couple nods, the father even giving Cregg an enthusiastic smile. They're clearly on board with this demonstration, but John's expression suggests that he is not. He doesn't seem to be fully on board with his parents, either, judging from the look he just shot in their direction.

The Senator pulls something out of his pocket and holds it up for the reporters to see. It's a rectangular jewelry case, like one you'd use to store a necklace. He flips open the case to reveal three darts atop the velvet lining and then hands the case to a woman in the first row. "Please pass this box around so that you can all see that these are plain, unadulterated darts. I pulled them out of the dartboard in my basement, so they're still a little dusty."

The woman, apparently satisfied, passes the case to the next journalist.

"While you're checking that out," the Senator says, "I'll give you a little background on John, or more specifically, John's father. The man here today is actually John's stepfather. John's biological dad was killed—or more accurately, killed himself—nine years ago, after battling psychosis for over a decade. By all accounts, John's dad was perfectly normal before going into the military, and even for a few years afterward. But he changed once he was assigned to a project at Fort Bragg, known as the Stargate Project. His parents, who didn't see him often since they lived in Indiana, said he became moodier and anger prone. The project ended in 1995, and John's dad left the service a few years later. He married, but bouts of temper and depression followed, and these got worse over time, ending his marriage and, eventually, his life."

Asshat.

I agree wholeheartedly with Daniel's one-word assessment. The poor kid is standing up there looking awkward enough in his too-tight suit, and then Senator Cregg starts talking about how his dad killed himself. Glancing at Aaron and Taylor, I can see that this is one issue on which all three Quinn siblings would concur. It must hit a nerve, given that the official version of their own father's death lists him as a suicide, too. The kid looks miserable. And yes, he still looks . . . familiar.

"Could you pause that?" I ask. "Just for a second."

I hurry down to my room and rummage through my backpack to grab Magda's checklist, then head back upstairs to the great room, flipping the pages as I go.

"It's him, isn't it? Dillon Lentz, the one that Skolnick mentioned."

Aaron stares at the picture for a moment and then nods. "I think so. Not a recent photo, but yeah, looks like the same kid."

When Taylor starts the video again, the last reporter is finishing her examination of the darts. She starts to hand them back to the Senator, but he shakes his head. "No, I don't want anyone claiming I'm some sort of magician, hiding something up my sleeves. Set them over there on the table, case open. And, uh . . . actually stay over there for a moment, so that everyone will know there are no strings or whatever. Just take a few steps to the right."

The reporter wrinkles her nose. She clearly doesn't like the way she's being ordered around, but she follows the Senator's directions.

"Okay, John! You're up." The Senator gives the boy his broad, snake-oil smile.

Dillon, aka John, doesn't return the smile. He simply turns his head toward the table, and one of the darts zips upward, followed in short order by the other two. They hover in midair, parallel to the table, and then fly toward the target so fast that I barely see them move. All three land directly on the bull's-eye, and for a moment, there's a genuine smile on the boy's face.

The female reporter who was standing nearby gasps and takes a step away from the kid, bumping into the stand that holds one side of the huge UA banner that the Senator is using as a backdrop. She manages to pull half of the banner to the ground, revealing a stretch limo parked just beyond the grassy area. The man in the blue suit is leaning against the limo, along with a second man. Two of Cregg's aides hurry over and prop the banner back up.

"That's Whistler," I say. "The one Dacia mentioned when we were at Overhills. He was with her that night at the police station, and I saw him talking to Grady, the guy Aaron—"

I cut myself off, glancing over at the kids. And it's a good thing I do. TJ's game no longer has his attention. He's kneeling so that he can see the television over the back of the couch.

"Look, Pey! That guy can float things like you do!"

Peyton's face appears next to his just as Senator Cregg asks Dillon to collect the darts.

Dillon gives him a curt nod, and then the darts come flying back toward the table, as if he reversed a video.

"Whoa!" TJ says. "Look at that!"

Peyton frowns, clearly jealous of the admiration in her brother's voice. "I could do that!" Then her eyes fall on the rest of us in the room. "I can do *bigger*. I could even float the TV if I wanted to."

I'm pretty sure that the television, which appears to be firmly anchored into the wall, is well beyond Peyton's ability. But it makes me very nervous when the bracket holding the TV starts to vibrate.

"Hoo-boy," Taylor says under her breath.

I start to get up, but Kelsey intervenes, swooping Peyton onto her hip. "I almost forgot! There's ice cream in the freezer for dessert. And if we don't get to it before Deo does, it will be *all gone*. Come on, TJ."

TJ is still staring at the television, but when he catches sight of his sister's face, his eyes widen in understanding. "Ice cream, Peyton! Yum. You love ice cream. Can we eat it on the deck with the puppy?"

I'm impressed at how quickly the boy pivots, but then this is a kid who's had to distract and placate his baby sister many, many times in order to avoid catastrophe.

"Sure," Kelsey says, giving me a *that-was-a-close-one* look as she shepherds the two into the kitchen.

When I look back at the TV, Senator Cregg has just selected a balding African American man from the crowd of waving hands.

"That . . . has to be some sort of illusion," the reporter says. "I don't care whether we inspected the darts or not. No one can do that."

As the man speaks, the pen he's holding jerks itself out of his hand and moves toward Dillon. The boy gives the reporter a tight smile, and raises his eyebrows, as if to ask whether the man is now satisfied that he's not a fraud.

"Come on, John," the Senator chides good-naturedly. "Give Marty back his pen."

Without a word, the pen flies back toward the reporter's hand. He ducks away at first, then plucks the pen out of the air and sits back down, obviously shaken. His companions seem unnerved as well, although a few of them still raise their hands.

The Senator acknowledges a plump woman in red. "Angela, right?"

The woman nods.

"I'll get to your question shortly. But first, can you fetch Angela one of the darts, John? Very, very carefully. Feather side first."

One of the darts rises from the table and slowly moves toward the reporter, her eyes growing wide as it approaches. When it's a few inches from her hand, she reaches out to grab it.

"Now, Angela," Senator Cregg says, "I'd like you to throw that dart as hard as you can toward John."

The reporters gasp in unison.

"No!" the woman says. "Are you crazy?"

"Fine," the Senator says, smiling. "Give it to me."

He steps forward and snatches the dart from her hand, and without the slightest pause sends it hurtling toward the boy. Dillon doesn't flinch but simply halts the dart about six inches from his chest, where it levitates.

Dillon's eyes flash, and he gives Senator Cregg the same thin-lipped, angry smile he wore when looking at his stepfather earlier.

The dart twitches once. Then it reverses course in midair and flies full speed toward the Senator.

CHAPTER SEVENTEEN

Carova Beach, North Carolina
November 12, 2019, 4:43 p.m.

The camera catches a split second of sheer terror in the Senator's expression as he realizes the dart is heading for his face. His arm jerks slightly. I think he was planning to raise it, to ward off the projectile, but before he can actually react, he realizes the dart is no longer moving. It hovers in front of the Senator's face, so close it appears to be touching his glasses.

The guard whips his rifle up, pointing it toward the boy. Someone in the audience screams.

When Senator Cregg steps back, the tiny arrow follows. It continues to point straight at the Senator's right eye, keeping pace like a well-trained dog. He composes himself quickly, though, and reaches up to grab the dart.

"Excellent control, John!" He turns toward the press, smiling as though he'd planned the entire thing, even that bit at the end. "Isn't that incredible?"

I'm amazed to hear a couple of the reporters take the bait. One of them actually starts to *clap*, as though this really were a sideshow and not a press conference. The video switches to a camera showing the reporters, and beyond the rows of chairs, the crowd has grown. Many seem to be passersby, dressed in business suits, headed back to the Metro at the end of the workday. Others appear to have been invited, or maybe they're just staunch followers of the Senator. There are several Unify America signs, and over a dozen purple *Cregg for Our Future* shirts and hats in the crowd.

"Thank you, John." Senator Cregg nods toward the guards, and they lead Dillon off the stage.

Dillon doesn't respond to the Senator or to the reporters, just continues flashing that same seething smile. His mother comes up and places a hand on the boy's shoulder, but he jerks away.

"That is one pissed kid," Deo says.

He's right. But I caught a hint of something else lurking beneath his anger. As with Peyton floating the books earlier, he enjoys letting his monkey out of the cage. He doesn't like hiding it—otherwise, I doubt he'd have hurled pencils at his teacher last year in a full classroom. It's a muscle he wants to flex, to show off.

Before I can make this observation to the others, the Man in Blue returns with another adept. A girl this time, petite, with Asian features. She's dressed less formally than "John" was, but she looks equally uncomfortable.

The Senator introduces her as "Jane." Then he gives the reporters a brief overview of her background, stating that she's twelve years old. He adds that Jane's father, whose whereabouts are unknown, was part of the same unit at Fort Bragg. Subject to the same drug protocol.

Then Senator Cregg gets down on one knee so that he's eye level with the girl. From photos I've seen, this seems to be his standard move when dealing with kids. I guess he thinks it's reassuring. But I've never seen a single kid who looked at ease next to him.

"Okay, sweetie. Could you tell the reporters what you told me earlier this week?"

Jane nods and tries to smile as she looks at the reporters. It's closer to a grimace, actually. Just a quick flash of silver from her braces, and then she breathes in through her nose, like she's trying to calm herself.

"A tornado will land in Alabama about ten minutes from now. Near Tuthcalootha." She frowns, a blush rising to her cheeks.

"Sorry," she says, tapping a forefinger against the silver wires stretched across her teeth. "They're kinda new. Tus-ca-loo-tha." It's better this time, but the sibilant word still causes her to lisp slightly on the final syllable.

"It's the girl," I say to Aaron. "From the interview with Tamara Blake. The one who led us to the bodies at Overhills."

"Shh!" Taylor turns the sound up a notch.

". . . it's a really big one, an EF4, and it comes out of nowhere. A Walmart sign will be ripped out of the ground. They'll find it on the highway, on the other side of the overpath." Jane huffs. "Over . . . *pass*."

"Thank you, Jane." He nods to the Man in Blue again, who takes the girl by the arm.

Taylor's jaw tightens. "*Jane. John.* Why bother with the stupid fake names? Like he gives a damn about their safety."

Senator Cregg tells the reporters that he called local businesses and offered them a cash incentive to close their doors about an hour ago. "I was happy to do this at my own expense. I can't guarantee that everyone will evacuate, but hopefully we can minimize the loss of life."

The camera pans toward the press. Almost every reporter, and a good number of the crowd behind them, has a phone or tablet out, no doubt checking current weather conditions in Tuscaloosa.

Aaron is doing the same thing. A severe weather warning is in effect for the area, but there's no mention of a tornado.

"It will still be a few minutes before you discover that Jane is, as they say, the real deal," the Senator says. "While we wait, I'd like to introduce another young lady. Unlike our first two guests, she doesn't have any special talent, but she was held for over a year by the WOCAN separatists and can give us more information on their operation. Oksana?"

Jaden and Daniel startle at the name, and so do I. Deo, who's on the other sofa with Taylor, shoots me a puzzled look. Oksana was the name of one of the three women whose ghosts I picked up in the Delphi lab—the ones I call the Furies.

The woman who walks on-screen isn't Oksana, obviously. They've just borrowed the name. Compared to the other times I've seen her, she's dressed down considerably, in a demure baby-blue sweater set and navy pants. She wears little to no makeup. Her hair has been lightened to a golden brown, a shade or two darker than my own. It's now shoulder length, with a gentle curl at the ends. The overall effect makes her seem younger, more like a teen than a woman in her early twenties.

But these are minor, superficial changes. The eyes are still the same ice blue. If I were there in person and close enough, I'm certain that a good yank on those curls would reveal short, nearly black hair beneath the wig.

Plus, she's wearing a glove. If I'd harbored any doubts that the woman was Dacia, that fact would have dispelled them. Not the black leather gloves she sported at the police station or the single black glove she wore at The Warren. Just one glove, but it's cream colored. Dainty, like something you'd see on that show *Mad Men*.

Deo is shaking his head. "That's a serious fashion downgrade."

"You've *got* to be kidding me," Taylor says. "She's in photographs on his campaign website, for God's sake! People have seen her at functions . . ." She starts tapping something into her phone as the Senator and Dacia continue their charade. He's telling her that she shouldn't be nervous, that all she has to do is explain what she knows. That this is the first big step to keeping her and the entire country safe.

The weirdest thing is that Dacia actually does seem nervous, flashing her doe eyes at the assembled members of the press as though she's afraid they might bite. When she begins speaking, her voice is timid. Her accent, always thick, lapses further into broken English.

A sick chill hits me. This isn't the voice of the woman who interrogated me at the police station in DC, or the woman we heard in the forest last week. This sounds like the girl in my nightmares, like Dacia when she was Daciana. When the Senator's psycho son was forcing her to climb the stairs from the basement and she was pleading with Molly to help her.

I think it's partly because Dacia's a good actress. She's had to hone those skills over the past few years working with Senator Cregg, shaking hands with donors and colleagues, digging around inside their brains for information that they can use to their advantage.

But the hint of pain in her eyes as she speaks makes me suspect it goes deeper, that she sounds like her younger self because she's tapping into those memories. She spends the first minute or so talking about being hired in her native Romania for a job in the United States. A job watching children. They even gave her a picture of the family, and she exchanged e-mails with them. She was only sixteen, but it was a good opportunity. The company paid her expenses and fudged the documents so that she'd meet the age requirements.

"They bring us in . . ." She pauses, like she's searching for a word. "Against law. Mostly women, but men, too. They bribe the *polițiștii* at the port so we get into country. But there is no family waiting. No job. Instead, they give me *injecție*. Needles. Drugs to . . . change me, to make me do things like you see those children do. But it did not work for me. They test me, and I fail. I want to go home, back to *România*, but they made us to do . . . *diferit* work. They sell us to bad men who hurt us. One of them made me to do *this*."

With that, she takes the glove from her hand and holds it up so that they can all see the missing finger.

The reporters are too busy staring at her hand to notice the look that she gives the Senator. It's nothing short of venomous. Theirs seems to be an uneasy alliance, born more of common interest than trust. The real question is what that common interest may be. I can't piece together the Senator's motives in all of this. Publicity for his campaign? Political cover?

Taylor has apparently found what she was searching for. She pauses the TV, then leans over and tosses her phone into my lap.

"You saw his website before. Look at that third photo. Notice anything different?"

It's the events page from the Senator's election site. An array of photos, arranged in a neat collage, displays Senator Cregg talking to people clearly chosen to span as many races, ages, genders, and occupations in as few images as possible.

The third picture is the same one that Taylor showed me when we were at Kelsey's beach house a few weeks ago. The only difference is that the woman with short black hair has been changed very subtly. Whistler, Dacia's bodyguard or keeper or whatever he is, still lurks in the background. The *Cregg for Our Future* banner is still there, along with all of the Unify America signs.

"They altered it," Taylor says as I hand the phone back. "It's a decent Photoshop job, but I know Dacia was in the picture before. Just wish I'd thought to download it."

"But we should still be able to find it online," says Deo. "We can check the Wayback Machine, or someplace like that, where they archive website content."

I shake my head. "That's not how the conspiracy game works, D. You know that. The Senator's publicity people would just say the *original* picture was the one that was tweaked. And"—I point toward the TV, where Dacia is frozen in the act of revealing her mangled hand—"then they'd say how awful it is that people would call this poor, poor girl a liar, when she has suffered such horrible abuse. Facts are irrelevant to people like that. If they shout it loud enough and repeat it with conviction, they can convince people to believe anything."

They're all looking at me. Deo has heard me rant on more than one occasion about the darker side of conspiracy theories, but I think the others are a little surprised at my ferocity. Sure, the alien stuff is fun. I even enjoy the occasional Elvis or Bigfoot sighting. But having Bruno as a hitcher also made me very aware of how easy it is to get people to believe utter garbage, and the situation has only worsened in the years since his death.

"Well, it's *true*," I say, leaning back into the couch cushions so that they can't see that I'm blushing.

"Of course it's true," Aaron whispers. "And it's also true that you look adorable when you're angry, but I'm not going to say that because it would be very sexist."

My blush deepens, but I can't entirely stifle the laugh. I give him a gentle dig in the ribs with my elbow, and look back up at the screen.

The reporters are in midgasp when Taylor starts the press conference again. Dacia holds her hand up for a moment, making sure everyone gets a good look, before slipping the glove back on.

"Go ahead," the Senator says. "Tell them about the soldiers."

Dacia holds his stare for a moment, her eyebrow twitching slightly. "The two children you see before? They are not the only ones with these powers. This group, the WOCAN? Now they have *soldati* . . . soldiers. Adults who take the drug, but it work for them. At first, it worked better on the girls, but then they fix the drug, so now it works on men, too. I see people light fires with just their minds. People who can know all of what you think. Some can even make you do things you would never do, to hurt yourself or people you love. They put their thoughts into your head so you do not even know what is real and what is a lie."

"How many soldiers?" he prompts.

"Maybe thirty women. Twice that many men. Maybe more. I did not see all—"

Jaden stirs, and I think he's about to say something, but then my attention is jerked back to the television.

"Tornado!" one of men yells out from the back, waving his tablet. "Birmingham news station just reported it touched down outside Tuscaloosa."

One of the mics picks up a muffled f-bomb, which I think is from one of the reporters. A few begin searching on their own devices to confirm the story.

The Senator nods for the Man in Blue to escort Dacia from the stage. When the guard takes her arm, she gives him a withering look and yanks away, walking behind the banner without his assistance.

Once all eyes are again on the Senator, he launches into a spiel about how the tornado couldn't have possibly been faked. Then he starts taking questions from the reporters, telling them a lot of stuff we already know about the origins of the Delphi Project and the initial testing on military. I feel myself tuning him out, and, looking around the room, I see it's not just me. The only one who remains fully immersed, still furiously jotting down notes as Senator Cregg speaks, is Taylor.

When the anchor finally switches to the next topic, Taylor turns off the TV and flings the remote disdainfully across the coffee table. "Pure political theater."

Aaron nods in agreement. "The stuff about the WOCAN group is obviously a lie, and so was a lot of what Dacia said, but the lies were balanced out by a good bit of truth. The big question is one that Anna asked the other day—what could the Senator possibly gain from revealing Delphi like this?"

None of us has an answer, and that question runs around my mind for the next hour while we wait for Magda to call. Kelsey and I use that time to get Miranda and the kids set up in one of the suites in the remaining empty wing on the second floor. After seeing her reaction during Cregg's conference, I'm convinced that keeping Peyton at least somewhat separate seems like a smart move. She's a stick of dynamite on her own, and we have no idea what kind of psychic skills the kids who arrived earlier today possess.

The lead guard from Vigilance joins us as we're setting up for the meeting with Magda. Aaron introduces him as Miller. He looks to be in his forties, although that could just be due to his receding hairline. What hair remains on his head is blond and cut close. His tan uniform is a shade or two lighter than the one the Delphi guards that Jaden calls Fudds wore, but it gives off the same correctional vibe. While he's several inches shorter than Aaron, he outweighs him by at least sixty pounds. Some of that may be pudge, but I'm pretty sure that if you punched him in the gut, your hand would meet a solid wall of muscle beneath the padding.

Aaron tries to engage the guy in conversation, but it's fruitless. Miller answers a few questions about guns and perimeter cameras but never offers any info or asks anything in return. He doesn't even sit down, saying he's been driving all day. Aaron finally gives up, and Miller just stands there next to the floor lamp like he's on sentry duty, eyes traveling in a circuit around the room. They rarely land on Kelsey and linger a little too long on the rest of us. His wary expression makes it clear that he knows we're Delphi adepts, just like the kids who are still in a drugged stupor downstairs.

Magda must not have gone into much detail about our specific gifts, however. Aside from Daniel's ability, which Magda doesn't even know I have, none of us could do anything that would affect Miller. But he's on edge nevertheless, his eyes twitching our way each time one of us moves.

Taylor crosses behind the couch where Aaron and I are sitting and whispers, "Is that a gun in his pocket or is he just happy to see us?"

"Not a gun," Aaron says. "Wrong shape. Probably a taser."

Deo and I exchange a look. He received a very personal lesson on the effects of a taser at The Warren.

Taylor whacks Aaron on the back of the head and then says loudly, "Gah! You are such a dweeb, Aaron!" It seems like a total non sequitur, until I see Miller watching us.

Magda rings us about ten minutes later than we'd agreed. Aaron had planned to patch in Sam, but he phoned a little while ago saying he was stuck in traffic and wouldn't be able to make it in time. And they're running some sort of tests on Daniel this afternoon—that bit of information made Daniel cringe—so Michele said to call later and fill her in.

Magda scans the room. "I see we're all here. Did the children make the trip without any problems?"

"Yes, ma'am," Miller says. "Slept like babies. Still sleeping, actually, since the nurses felt it would be better to keep them on a normal schedule. Before we get started, though . . . can I just state that this place is going to be a security nightmare? It's isolated, but there are sliding doors in almost every room leading out onto the decks. That's going to make it really difficult to lock down, especially as others arrive. I may need additional staff."

"Understood. Do what you can, and we'll discuss this later." Magda appears even more tired than when we saw her a few days ago. She rubs her forehead distractedly before looking back up at the camera. "I'm glad to see that Taddeo is feeling well enough to join us this time."

"It's just Deo," he says. "And yes, I'm feeling much better."

"At least for now," I add, ignoring Deo's glare. "The other person who was given the amplify serum had a relapse after a few weeks. Have you had any luck locating the scientist you mentioned?"

"Yes, actually. I sent a sample to her this morning."

I wait to see if she'll volunteer anything else. When she doesn't, I push on. "So . . . did she give you any idea how long it might take to—"

"She will get back with me as soon as she has time to analyze it thoroughly." Magda enunciates each word carefully, using the same tone you might take with a child asking *are we there yet* on a car trip.

Kelsey gives me a look of sympathy, which Magda must catch, because she says, "Dr. Kelsey. We spoke on the phone during the interview process, but it's nice to put a face with the name."

I seriously doubt that this is the first time Magda has seen Kelsey's face, given the plethora of information that Magda had on the various people we interviewed at Fort Bragg and, as I'm sure she would note, the many more that we failed to interview. She's much more polite to Kelsey than to the rest of us, so maybe she's impressed by Kelsey's medical degree.

Once she's done with the pleasantries, Magda puts on her *let's-get-down-to-business* face. "How much of what Senator Cregg revealed today is accurate? I have my own ideas, but I want to get input from those of you who were at the facility. And also from Anna's—*hitcher*, as I believe you call him? Let's start with the obvious area of concern—the soldiers."

"That part is false," I tell her. "At least based on everything that Jaden and I saw. Most of them were kids and a few teens who are second-generation adepts, like me. And then there was a group of girls who were brought in from Eastern Europe, as Dacia mentioned at the press conference."

"That was Dacia Badea today?" Magda looks startled. "The person you believe to be responsible for the murders at Fort Bragg?"

"Yes," Taylor says, "it was definitely her. They've altered the images on Cregg's campaign website to hide the fact that she was working with him earlier. And they changed her appearance a bit. But we're positive it's her."

Magda nods and then looks back at me. "Continue."

"As I was saying, they tested some guys in the Eastern European countries, as well, at least at the beginning. But they had the same problems with mental instability as the recruits who were given the drug a few decades ago. Violence, suicide, and so forth."

"I find that puzzling," Magda says. "The second-generation adepts seem evenly split between male and female, based on all of the information at hand. And with rare exceptions, even the ones who make it to adulthood show few signs of mental breakdown. Certainly not to the extent of murder or suicide."

"I think I may have an explanation for that." Kelsey repeats the theory she explained to me earlier about the Delphi drug being aimed at the fusiform gyrus and unintentionally affecting the nearby amygdala, adding that the effect might be different for males and females, depending on the age at which they were given the drug. "The amygdala continues to grow in males for several years longer than females. It's larger in males, as well. Anything that overstimulated the amygdala could cause fear, anxiety, aggression, even visual hallucinations."

"Why wouldn't this affect the brain of a second-generation male adept?" Magda asks.

"Well, I have only actually encountered one second-generation male subject to date," Kelsey says, nodding toward Aaron. "So I can't entirely discount the possibility that it does affect them at some point. But it's also quite possible that the brain adjusts. Those who inherit the altered DNA have it from the time they are born, so it's less an issue of putting new pressure on the amygdala than of a brain with a slightly different layout. The two parts grow in tandem, so it has less impact. This is just a theory, of course."

Magda asks Kelsey a few clarifying questions, including whether she could test any of this if she had the proper equipment, and then she returns to the press conference. She agrees that "John" is Dillon Lentz, based on the photos in her records. She also has info on "Jane."

"Her name is Olivia Wu," Magda says, checking a paper in front of her. "I wish that her mother and the Blake woman had taken us up on sanctuary when it was offered. Do we have any clues on the identity of the children in the videotape they supposedly retrieved from the Delphi facility?"

"The pyrokinetic girl is named Svetlana. No clue about the last name, but she was clearly one of the women who was trafficked in from abroad. Jaden didn't recognize the boy. But the last girl, the one who disrupted the electrical circuits, is actually a second-gen. She's Sabrina Bieler, whose twin brother was killed at Overhills."

Magda looks surprised, but my revelation doesn't generate the sort of keen interest that I expected it would, given her repeated inquiries about twin adepts.

Aaron glances at me from the corner of his eye and then jumps in with the question I was about to ask. "The Bieler girl was probably evacuated with Graham Cregg and the Delphi staff. Based on what you've said in the past, I take it that she should be our top priority?"

Magda shrugs. "She would have been, if her brother were still alive. My goal was to learn more about their interactions, to see if there were any similarities to my own daughters. But the most we'll have now is anecdotal evidence from one side only."

I guess it's time to tell Magda about Hunter. Sighing, I shift my focus inward. Hunter is easy to find, right near the front. I don't get the sense that he has completely followed everything we've been discussing, but he definitely went on alert when I mentioned his sister.

Hunter? We haven't really talked about this, and I was hoping to keep quiet about the fact that you're . . . in here, with my other hitchers. But this lady is someone who may be able to help us find Bree. She will probably have some questions for you, either now or after we find your sister. Would you be willing to talk to her?

He agrees without the slightest hesitation, even before I finish the question.

I look back at Magda, who's staring at me. "Sorry. I was just checking on something. You may still be able to get both sides of the story. I seem to have picked up a hitcher when we were at Overhills. I didn't say anything before because he was very distraught," I add quickly, in response to her annoyed expression. "Usually when I pick up hitchers, they've had time to figure out what is going on . . . months, even years. Given the trauma and his age, I didn't know if he'd stick around long enough to help."

"And you believe now that he *will* help?"

"Yes. But only if we rescue his sister." That last bit is a total lie. Hunter would immediately answer any questions she has. Apparently it takes more than one bad woman with a gun to erase his inclination to trust grown-ups. I have far more experience with adults who don't always have your best interest at heart, however.

"Hmph," Magda says. "It sounds as though I'm being blackmailed by a ghost. When the living do that, I take the opposite action out of spite. And . . . to be perfectly frank, Anna, I'm not sure that you're telling the truth."

"I was there when she picked him up," Aaron says.

Magda raises her eyebrows. "Really? And let me guess—you saw the spirit of Hunter Bieler rise up from his dead body and slide into Anna?"

I give Aaron's arm a squeeze to let him know I've got this.

"Why would I lie about it? You're the one who wanted us to prioritize finding twins. But if you need proof . . . hold on a sec. I may have something."

This is a bit of a gamble, because Hunter's never been in the driver's seat. I have no idea if his quirk with electrical gadgets will work through me at all.

Hunter? I'm going to slide to the back, okay. You take my place.

Okay. So she can ask me questions about Bree?

No. See that floor lamp? Think you can blow it out, like you used to turn out the lights at Baker Elementary?

Yes.

I can feel his grin. It's a small one, but it's the first bit of real pleasure that I've felt from him since he came on board.

The only thing is, you need to slide right back afterward, okay? No running off with my body. Otherwise, it will be really tough for me to help you find Bree. Deal?

Deal.

Okay, then—go to the front, Hunter! And no dawdling. Head straight for the lamp.

He moves forward, and I watch as he holds my hands up, wiggling the fingers in front of his face.

"Exactly what is your point, Anna?" Magda asks.

Hunter doesn't answer. He just pushes us up from the sofa. Unfortunately, he's not accustomed to navigating a body twice the size of the one he owned, and he bumps the coffee table, sending a bowl and the few remaining chips tumbling onto the carpet.

"I'm sorry!"

"It's okay," Aaron says, giving me a confused look as he bends down to scoop them back into the bowl.

Hunter stands there, briefly paralyzed, and then remembers what he's supposed to do. We stumble toward the floor lamp.

Miller stands just a few feet away. His eyes widen, and he reaches into his pocket just as Hunter closes my hand around the lamp pole.

A sensation much like the feeling when you bang your elbow radiates from my neck through my arm, all the way down to my fingers. The pole feels hot against my palm, and then the bulb glows brighter. It fizzles out with a final pop as Miller draws his taser.

CHAPTER EIGHTEEN

Carova Beach, North Carolina
November 12, 2019, 6:15 p.m.

I'm not sure Hunter knows what a taser is, but he can tell that Miller is angry. He retreats from the driver's seat so quickly that my stomach does a one-eighty. Despite the queasiness, I quickly step away from Miller. What did the guy think I was going to do? Hit him with the lamp?

"Hey!" Aaron steps in front of me. "Put that away."

"It's nice to see that you have quick reflexes, Miller," Magda says. "But yes, do put it away."

Miller complies, but his eyes remain locked on me, even after Aaron and I are back on the sofa.

Was that okay?

It was perfect, Hunter.

Now that I'm in control of my body again, I notice the burning sensation in my palm. When I flip my hand over to inspect it, I see a line of reddened skin down the middle. It looks like I grabbed the barrel of a curling iron. I don't think it will blister, but I borrow the can of seltzer Aaron is holding to cool it down a bit.

I'm sorry. It never burns when I do it.

It's not a problem, Hunter. Just a bit singed.

"It might be wise to give us a bit of warning in the future," Magda says. "So that Mr. Miller isn't startled. Could you do the other lamp, too?"

"Probably, but I'm not going to." I hold up my hand to show her the burned area.

Kelsey heads into the kitchen, giving Miller some serious stink eye along the way. I suspect she's going in search of the first aid kit, although I'm not sure it's necessary.

Magda jots something down on the sheet of paper on her desk and then looks back up. "Are there any other secrets that I should know about?"

I glance at Aaron and then over at Taylor and Deo. We've already told Kelsey about the text messages that have been coming in from Graham Cregg, and we were planning to tell Magda tonight. But I've got serious misgivings about that after meeting Miller. He's already on a hair trigger, and I can't even imagine how he'd respond to the possibility that there's a threat he won't be able to see or hear. That the four of us could be, without our consent, transmitting information about his security precautions to the enemy.

Even without discussing it, I can see that the others are in agreement.

"No, ma'am," Aaron says. His words are clipped, and he keeps shooting angry looks at Miller. I wonder if they're left over from Miller threatening me a few minutes ago or if he's still picking up new vibes.

"Well, then," Magda says, "perhaps we should think about the next steps for finding the Bieler girl and any others they're holding."

"I've been working on that," Taylor says. "Although things would move a lot more quickly if we could narrow down the geographical area a bit."

Magda frowns. "Thought you needed a personal object in order to track someone."

"I found a shoe." Taylor doesn't elaborate, just flashes her wide-eyed innocent look, and Deo chuckles in response.

"I'm guessing your mother will be less amused than your friend is," Magda says, "since she was adamant that I keep you and Taddeo out of any direct involvement. I'll have my people intensify efforts to pin down the new location of The Warren, but given the deaths at Fort Bragg and the fact that it would be difficult to find another place to hide that many children with powers, we may need to also consider the possibility that they were all killed."

I send a silent message back to Hunter, telling him that I'm sure his sister is okay. I'm certain that he can sense I'm *not* sure, but I don't want him to lose hope.

"Then why expose the program now?" I ask as I spread some of the ointment that Kelsey dropped into my lap on my scorched palm. "Senator Cregg is opening himself up to considerable criticism for his role, and his son's role, in creating the adepts in the first place."

Aaron says, "That's true. If they've killed off most of the adepts, why take that hit, especially in the middle of a political campaign? Wouldn't it make more sense to keep covering it up and pretend it never happened?"

They toss a few ideas around, none of which seem logical to me. Finally, Magda says she's out of time and reaches forward to disconnect.

"Oh, one more thing. As of today, I officially own the two properties on either side of you, along with the Isle of View itself." Her nose wrinkles in disgust. "Which will be renamed, and I'd appreciate it if someone could remove that tacky sign from the front. If you have any ideas for a new name, let me know next time we—"

Aaron cuts her off. "How about *Sandalford* . . . like the British village, just with the first part spelled like sandals? You know, beach shoes."

Magda doesn't know Aaron well enough to know that the smile he's wearing right now isn't genuine. And she either hasn't read *Watership Down* or doesn't remember the book, because she smiles and says, "I like it! I'll have my assistant order a sign."

After she signs off and Miller retreats to the ground floor, Taylor shoots Aaron a puzzled look. "What was *that* about?"

"It's a place in a book I'm reading," he says. "I'll give it to you when I'm finished. Let's just say Sandleford Warren wasn't quite as safe and peaceful as it appeared on the surface."

"You were planning to . . ." Kelsey lowers her voice and leans forward. "To tell Magda about those text messages. I'm guessing Mr. Miller changed your mind."

"Yeah. I don't trust him not to overreact," Aaron says.

Taylor shrugs. "Yeah. He's a jerk. Although, to be fair, if Cregg has a way to hack into our minds, to figure out what we're thinking? You've got to admit that's a legitimate security concern."

I suspect this will end up as an argument, even though I could tell from Taylor's expression that she agreed with the decision when Aaron made it. Since I really don't want to listen, and since my hand is still stinging despite the salve, I leave them to it and head to the kitchen for a couple of Advil.

Deo follows. "You okay?"

"Yeah. It's minor. If I'd known to expect it, I wouldn't have gripped the damned pole so hard."

"Hunter didn't know it would burn you?"

"Nope." I find the bottle on the top shelf in the pantry and pour two into my hand. "Didn't happen when he was in his body. Maybe it's like Daniel's mind-control thing . . . harder to do when you're working inside someone else's skin."

He steps forward to grab something from the fridge. He's still more than a foot away, and he's been this close to me several times in the past few days, but when the *NNNNN* sound hits my ears, I barely have time to slide to the floor.

—idea it could be this cold. Wicked, biting cold. The snow is up to my knees, and even though I'm bundled in layers and a thick, padded parka, the wind cuts to the bone.

Our progress is excruciatingly slow, and it has to be even tougher on Aaron, with the boy strapped to his back. He only weighs about forty pounds, but climbing multiple flights of stairs with him in that pack can't have been easy. And now this, immediately afterward. At least we've reached the tree line now and aren't going uphill any longer. And the snow has stopped.

There are still a few clouds, but otherwise the sky is clear. The one good thing about the snow is that it reflects the faint light from the crescent moon, making it easier to see the path Aaron is carving through the drifts. It's the path we made earlier, but we've gotten at least another four inches in the ninety minutes or so since we hiked in.

Bree's pace slows again. I tug at her arm with my unbandaged left hand. She's bundled in a thick Star Wars *jacket, with a glow-in-the-dark BB-8 on the front. A red scarf covers most of her face, but she's still shivering.*

"Not much farther, sweetie. See the lights on the houses down there?" I nod toward two houses in the valley below decked out for the holidays. One has colored lights along the eaves. The other has white lights and a large star on the roof. "The camper is even closer than the houses, and it's nice and warm inside."

I glance over my shoulder at the bedraggled line of people behind me, most of whom are having an even harder time than I am slogging through the snow. Seeing Ashley, Maria, and a few of the older teens helping the smaller ones triggers a memory of the scene in 101 Dalmatians *where they're trying to get all of the puppies through the snow to safety.*

Although with all of this snow on the road, is the RV really—
NNNNNnnnn

Aaron's face is the first thing I see when I open my eyes. Deo is standing on the opposite side of the kitchen, as far as he can get from me and still be in the same room. They both look worried. I can't focus enough to tell them I'm okay, though, because Hunter is barraging me with questions.

> You were with Bree! How could we see her like that?
> Does this mean she's okay? Does she make it to the
> camper?

Yes, it was Bree. Daniel, Jaden—little help here please?

I leave them to explain the visions to Hunter, and stack up my mental bricks so that I can concentrate on what's happening outside my head.

"I'm okay, guys. But we need to invest in some heavy parkas."

What we really need is to try to invest in a few dozen snowmobiles or a heavy-duty snowblower to speed up our progress. But I know it won't make any difference. The stores will be sold out, or a wheel will break off the blower, or it won't start. Whatever happened in the vision is what *will* happen.

We go back into the great room with Kelsey and Taylor, so I don't have to explain the vision twice.

"You're sure that it was Ashley?" Aaron asks. "And she was helping us?"

"To be honest, if I'd only been relying on visuals, I wouldn't have known it was her. She was too bundled up, and the snow was still falling. But in the vision, I thought of her as Ashley. And yes, she was definitely helping us get the kids out of . . . someplace underground with a lot of stairs? Bree was with me. That girl named Maria, too, the one Jaden called a *Peeping Tomasina.*"

"What about me and Deo?" Taylor asks.

"You must be waiting in the RV. It's Christmastime, but I didn't get any info about the location of the place, so I'm guessing it's considerably north of here. There was a lot of snow. And I think there were mountains in the distance, although it could have been clouds."

"We've gotten some hellacious blizzards in DC the past few years, so it wouldn't have to be too far north," Deo says. "Why do you think it happens on Christmas?"

"Not on Christmas, just *around* Christmas. I saw holiday lights on two houses."

"Well, that narrows it down to somewhere north of here and sometime between Thanksgiving weekend and New Year's Eve," Taylor says, her mouth twisting. "Not a lot to go on."

"The moon. It was crescent. Waning crescent."

Everyone except Kelsey gives me a blank look, and Kelsey laughs. "A waning crescent is shaped like the letter *C*."

Aaron runs a search on his phone. "That narrows it down quite a bit. The moon will be in the *waning crescent* phase"—his tone is clearly mocking, and I stick my tongue out in response—"the third week of December. Which picture does it look like?"

I glance at the pictures of the moon on his phone. "The twenty-second. Or . . . maybe the twenty-first."

Taylor says, "I haven't had a lot of luck with the girl's sneaker. But I may try using Deo as an amp, like I did the other day when we were tracking Peyton and her dad. If I get a sketch, do you think you'd be able to recognize the area?"

"I don't know. Probably not. We were outside. The kids looked tired, so I think we may have already walked some distance from where they were being held."

"Then it's a good thing we've got some time," Taylor says. "Because we're going to need it."

Deo asks me to take over puppy duty, and then he and Taylor head downstairs. She's carrying two large bags of Doritos, so I'm guessing they're going to start trying to get a location from Bree Bieler's sneaker.

Aaron messages Magda, Sam, and his mom with the new development. Kelsey, who has a busy day tomorrow doing intake on the new patients, heads down to her office to look over the files.

"You up for a nighttime beach walk?" I ask Aaron after Ein has finished his bowl of puppy mush. "Ein could probably use a potty break."

"Outside, yes. But no beach. We have to stay close to the building—no one is allowed outside the perimeter after dark unless we clear it with Miller first."

"Ugh. No, thanks. What did Magda say about the info from the vision?"

"Basically what you'd expect. Asked me a bunch of questions that I doubt you'll be able to answer. She doesn't seem to understand that you can't just push harder and get more information."

We take Ein out and let him wander around for a bit. He has trouble keeping his footing in the loose sand and toddles around like he's had one beer too many. Aaron usually chuckles at Ein's antics, but his attention is elsewhere tonight. At first I think he's looking out at the ocean, but his eyes are unfocused and a bit angry.

"Still thinking about Miller?" I ask.

"Yeah. I'd be a lot happier if that vision of yours wasn't nearly six weeks in the future. This house is big, but it's going to be hard to avoid picking up on Miller's hostility."

We'll likely be back here, at least temporarily, even after we find Bree and the other adepts. But I decide not to mention that right now, since Aaron is already dreading the prospect of six weeks.

"Did you get something specific from him earlier or were you just pissed that he was about to tase me?"

"Both. Magda hired these guys because they're ex-military, and they're supposed to be good at keeping stuff confidential. Most of them seem okay, but Miller and one of the other guys . . . they give off the same vibe as that Pruitt woman when she was yammering about adepts being God's curse. And while most people have a violent thought occasionally, Miller is constantly running scenarios in his head any time he enters a room. Thinking about what he'd do if someone jumped him, and then thinking with graphic detail and a great deal of pleasure about what he'd do right back. He had a scenario for all of us. Even Kelsey."

"So . . . not just casing the room for security but enjoying the possibility of mayhem."

"Precisely." Aaron sighs, biting at his lower lip, and then adds, "I was already on edge, though, because when Miller saw you helping unload the truck today, he told me you look a lot like the girl that police are looking for as a 'person of interest' in connection with the murders at Overhills. He called Magda immediately, and she told him you had nothing to do with it, but I'm not sure he entirely believes her."

"Great. So we have hospital security in Maryland thinking I tried to kill Daniel and God only knows how many people thinking I go around killing little kids. What's to stop Miller from calling the police anyway, despite what Magda said?"

"Money. Probably a lot of it. Plus, he knows that the kids who were murdered were adepts, and like I said, he seems to view them less as kids and more as freaks who need to be contained. I called Sam and asked him to have a chat with Magda about Miller's . . . volatility. So maybe she'll find someone else."

"Or maybe he'll mellow out after a while?"

"Yeah. Maybe."

When Ein finishes, we head upstairs. After crating the puppy, I join Aaron on the deck. The stars aren't quite as vivid as they were the other night, and the wind has a definite chill, but it's still nice to stand there with his arms around me, breathing in the sea air, as we look out at the night sky and listen to the waves crash against the shore.

Of course, with our bodies in such close proximity, it doesn't take long for calm contemplation of nature to morph into something else entirely natural but a little less calm. Aaron pulls me away from the windows, into the shadows. He presses his lips to mine, his breath hot against my cheek, and his hands, surprisingly warm despite the weather, slip under my shirt. We stay there, lost in the kiss, until we hear the sliding glass door open.

A blond-haired boy about TJ's age steps onto the deck and takes a few steps out toward the railing. He's barefoot, dressed only in a T-shirt and white cotton briefs. A thin band encircles his ankle, black except for a tiny flashing blue light. He looks around, searching, and then stops when he sees me. His eyes are glassy, almost unfocused.

"Get thee to a nunnery."

The words are clearly directed at me, and I feel a chill that has nothing to do with the temperature. The line is from Hamlet, when he's talking to Ophelia, and it's one of Shakespeare's double entendres—a nunnery was also slang for a brothel back then. I'm beginning to wish I could erase every single bit of Shakespeare from my brain.

"Flee also youthful lusts: but follow righteous—" The boy stops abruptly, his eyes widening in terror as he backs away from us. "Where am I? Where's my dad?"

He backs up again as Aaron steps out of the shadows.

"Hey, it's all right," Aaron says, taking a few cautious steps toward the boy. "Your dad is downstairs. I think you were sleepwalking. Why don't we move away from the stairs and—"

"What the hell is he doing out here?" Miller roars from the doorway. His body is a dark outline against the light from inside the house, his face illuminated only by the red dot of light at the base of his taser.

The boy flinches and screams as he loses his balance. His arms pinwheel in a futile attempt to stay upright. Aaron reaches out just in time and snags the collar of his T-shirt, yanking him back to safety. Had Aaron been a split second slower or a few inches farther away, the poor kid would have hurtled head over heels down the stairs to the lower deck.

He's shaking now, although I suspect it's as much from fright as from the cold. And Miller is still blocking the doorway.

"You stupid idiot!" I'm in Miller's face before I remember that he's holding the taser, but at this point I don't really care. "The kid was sleepwalking, and you scared the hell out of him. Go downstairs! We'll get him back to his room."

Miller gives me a look that can only be described as a snarl, but at least he moves out of the doorway so we can get the boy inside. I grab the chenille throw from the back of the sofa and wrap it around his thin shoulders.

"What's your name?" Aaron asks.

"B-Ben." His eyes, blue with lashes so blond they're nearly white, keep darting apprehensively toward Miller. "Ben Fleck. I don't know how I got here."

"What's going on? We heard a scream," Kelsey says from the top of the stairs. A middle-aged woman who must be one of the nurses is right behind her.

I lay out the basic facts calmly, sending a long, pointed glare in Miller's direction so that Kelsey understands exactly who is at fault. "Luckily, Aaron has quick reflexes."

The other woman with Kelsey frowns, pushing forward to get a closer look at Ben. "We halved the dosage of sedative for him because he's so small," she says, looking over at Miller. "Must not have been enough. I guess his dad is still under, or else he'd have seen the boy leave."

"Why didn't *you* see him leave?" Miller demands.

"I was using the bathroom," she says with a defiant tilt of her head. "And nothing in my contract says that the children are to be under constant watch."

Miller storms off toward the elevator. My opinion of him, already near rock bottom, dips even lower. You can't get much lazier than taking an elevator to go *down* two short flights of stairs.

The nurse leans down to look Ben in the face, turning his head slightly, like she's checking his pupils. "Let's get you back to your room. I'll give you some medicine to sleep."

Ben seems torn about going with the nurse. He nods but also leans back against Aaron, as if for protection.

"Maybe Aaron could walk with you back to your room?" Kelsey says. "And if you'd like, I'll get you a cup of cocoa to warm you up first."

Ben looks relieved at that suggestion, so Aaron leads him over to one of the stools at the bar. The nurse, who is clearly annoyed at the delay, goes off to get the medicine. I follow Kelsey into the kitchen.

"So," she says as we mix up the cocoa. "I take it there's a bit more to the story than you were willing to say out there? What exactly did Miller do?"

"Scared the hell out of him, mostly. What's that thing on his ankle?"

"The tracker? One of the nurses mentioned that all of the kids were tagged with GPS locators by the school at Fort Bragg. And no, I don't like it either, but I guess they were worried about them wandering off."

"Maybe. But Aaron's picking up nasty vibes from Miller, and I'm not sure he's going to be able to take six weeks of that man's negativity."

Kelsey snorts. "*I'm* picking up nasty vibes from Miller, and I have no psychic ability at all."

"Yeah. He has one of those faces. The Germans have a word for it." I comb through the Emily files quickly and locate it. "*Backpfeifengesicht*, that's it. A face in need of a fist."

"I can't make my usual case for nonviolence, since I would have happily punched Miller when he jumped at you with that taser. How is your hand?"

I hold it up for her inspection. "The ointment helped. Thanks. There was something else I didn't want to mention in front of Miller and the nurse, though. Have you had a chance to look at Ben's file?"

"I glanced through all of the files briefly when Magda sent them over. But no, I haven't looked at his in detail yet. Why?"

"Well, if the file doesn't say he's a telepathic receiver, you need to make an addition. He just delivered a message from Graham Cregg."

CHAPTER NINETEEN

Carova Beach, North Carolina
December 16, 2019, 9:20 a.m.

"Another fallen soldier," Miranda says, showing me the empty jar of grape jelly that she's rinsing out at the sink.

"I'll add it to the list." I stash the butter and eggs back in the fridge. "Aaron and I will go into Kitty Hawk and stock up before we head north, so you won't run short while we're away. And . . . Christmas dinner? I don't know exactly when we'll be back, so we should probably get a couple of hams, since we had turkey for Thanksgiv—"

"When will you be leaving?" Miranda interjects.

I shrug. "Soon—we're less than a week out from what I saw in the vision. We're just waiting for Magda's go-ahead."

"And you don't know *where* you'll be going yet?"

"Nope."

She continues loading the dishwashers, and I add a few more items to the shopping list. Most of my time over the past four weeks has been divided between the day-to-day tasks of keeping the residents of Sandalford fed and helping the younger adepts with their online classes.

I've been glad for the work, since it distracts me from worrying over the fact that we still haven't located the snow-covered valley we'll be hiking through in four or five days for this rescue mission.

Taylor has been holed up in her bedroom most of the time, either alone or with Deo nearby as an amp, clutching Sabrina Bieler's sneaker, which is now stained with sweat and Doritos dust. I'm starting to understand why her family was so worried about Taylor's health when she was searching for Molly. She's lost about ten pounds since we got here, even though she's eating enough to feed three people.

Taylor's sketches have gotten more detailed, but they're still just a house in the middle of the woods, although recently she added a well nearby. The only unusual thing is that the room the girl is being held in appears to have curved walls. But that doesn't mean the entire house is round, and even if it was, round houses aren't uncommon enough that it helps us nail down the geographical location.

In many ways, the past month has been like being back at the group home. There are ongoing squabbles between the kids, who range in age from seven to fifteen, and who all have troubled family backgrounds. Some of the kids seem pleased at the change of scenery, but others are upset about being so far from home. Some of them cast jealous looks at Ben, who has his dad here, and at TJ and Peyton, who have their mom. The others can call and Skype with their families, but when they were at Fort Bragg, families were allowed to visit in person. Thanksgiving was especially tough, and I suspect that these kids are already thinking about the fact that Christmas is right around the corner.

The biggest difference for me is that I'm now seeing what it's like to be a houseparent. You can't manage this many people without rules and boundaries. And that's even more necessary here, given how quickly minor disagreements can heat up—and I mean that literally. One of the boys is what Jaden calls a Zippo. Overall, he's been very constrained, but he lost it when Javier—the kid who picked up Bernadette Pruitt's thought about tossing her bra in the trash—pulled a stray sexual fantasy from our resident Zippo's head and blurted it out to everyone, including the girl whose breasts the kid was admiring. The Zippo then turned Javier's lunch into mac-and-cheese flambé, torching the nearby napkins in the process, and prompting Magda to invest in a sprinkler system and additional fire extinguishers.

Once the shopping list is completed, I start chopping veggies for the pasta salad we'll be serving in a few hours for lunch.

"Why do you think Magda hasn't okayed your departure yet?" Miranda asks, and then quickly adds, "Not that I'm looking forward to the four of you leaving. After that, there will be very few adults here who don't think these kids are all *los hijos de Satanás*."

"Who knows why Magda does what she does. And I don't think they *all* believe the adepts are the spawn of Satan."

Miranda wrinkles her nose. "Maybe. But I listen when they talk between themselves sometimes, when I'm down there cleaning. They're not much better than the people Jasper saw carrying the signs at Senator Cregg's . . . speech." Her face reddens slightly, and then she turns away to wipe down the counter. "When Jasper was watching it at the bar, I mean. In Corolla."

She seems uncomfortable, like she's hiding something, but then Miranda is always a bit on edge when she discusses Jasper. As for the Vigilance people, she's right that they don't treat the adepts like normal kids, but to be fair, they *are* different and the risks are greater. At Bart House, for example, there were a few kids that the counselors knew to keep apart, because they just couldn't get along. That's true here, too, but some of these kids could be dangerous to each other without even trying. Deo, for example, can't go near the other adepts. It would be like throwing gasoline on a match if he bumped into our resident firestarter when the boy was in one of his hot moods. The girl who is an empath— much like Aaron, except she gets *all* of the strong emotions—is already overwhelmed by everyone in the house, and I'm afraid being too close to Deo might push her over the edge.

And Deo going too close to Ben Fleck might trigger more Shakespeare and biblical quotes from Cregg. One of us still gets a text at least once each week, but I'm more and more convinced that the sole non-Shakespearean text I received on my phone really was from the kid called Snoop Dogg, and that he really is trying to avoid giving Cregg anything other than superficial information. Otherwise, it seems likely that Magda's security guards would have had to fend off visitors by now.

Miranda also keeps Peyton isolated, not just from Deo but from the older adepts as well. She's simply too young for us to be sure she can control herself. One lamp has already fallen casualty to her cranky mood when bad weather thwarted her desire to hunt for seashells two days in a row, and there's a coffee stain on Kelsey's office wall and probably a few chips of ceramic still in the carpet from a broken mug.

"Be glad you get to escape for a few days," Miranda says, continuing to scrub out a sink that I'm sure she's already scrubbed.

"I'd happily trade places," I tell her. "I'm not a big fan of snow. And now that Senator Cregg has ripped the lid off the Delphi program, it's not exactly a great time to be traveling around with a bunch of adepts."

Miranda doesn't comment, so I finish chopping the veggies in silence and then leave her to her mood.

Even though escaping the chaos of Sandalford for a few days will be a welcome break, the clatter *inside* my head travels along with me, and it seems to grow louder the closer we get to D-day. Hunter knows that the rescue attempt won't happen for nearly a week, but he still chomps at the bit every time we see something on the news about Senator Cregg.

And we've seen the Senator a lot lately.

Congress voted the week after Cregg's press circus to establish a bipartisan commission to examine the Delphi Project, the Stargate program that preceded Delphi, all military and government ventures into paranormal research, and any efforts to cover up crimes, both here and overseas, that may have been committed by Delphi subjects. It's officially the Committee on Psychic Weapons of Terror, but everyone just calls them the Delphi Hearings. The committee members demanded that the military and all government contractors hand over their records on the program, including names and addresses of all persons who were given the serum. That still hasn't happened, and I'm not even sure that it will—there's a lot of talk about privacy rights and national security. But there's also a very real desire for someone to take the blame for this. At first, there was a veritable blizzard of finger-pointing, but now most of Congress has clued in to the fact that these programs spanned seven presidencies, during periods when both of their parties held control of the White House and/or the legislature.

The only ones who could really point fingers without getting blowback are the handful of senators and representatives with Unify America. UA is a brand-new party, after all. Can't really blame UA for the mess that those other guys have gotten the nation into, can we? Perhaps it's time to clean house.

Senator Cregg doesn't say any of this outright, of course. But it's implicit in his earnest expression when he gives a press conference, when he asks a question during the Delphi Hearings, and whenever he talks on one of the twenty-four-hour news shows. And if anyone alludes to Senator Cregg's family ties to Decathlon Services Group, he just deflects, noting that DSG is a huge international company and he divested years ago. Anyway, he says, his son was connected to the group that handles human resources for the company, not the research-and-development arm. And if not for his son's heroic actions at Port Deposit, many more lives might have been lost. Blah, blah, blah.

Each time Senator Cregg's face pops up on the screen or his name is part of a headline, Hunter pushes forward, hoping to get some new bit of information about Bree. Each time, there's nothing new. And each time, he asks me if I'm sure we'll be able to rescue his sister and get her home safely. I'm as honest with Hunter as possible—the visions have always come true in the past. But I can't answer the last part of his question, because I have no idea what happens to Bree after that short snippet of the future ends.

Daniel is on edge about the vision, too, although he hides it better than Hunter. And while I try not to pry, it's clear that he's wondering not just about Ashley but also about Ashley's sister, Sariah. Daniel can't be certain from the brief glimpse we got in the vision, but he thinks maybe the kid Aaron was carrying on his back, the one who was sedated, was Sariah's son. And that scares the hell out of him.

Jaden, at least, is quiet. He's fading away like Molly did, ready to move on to whatever comes after, and even though my head could use the free space, I wish he'd hold on a bit longer. It's only partly because I'm not looking forward to processing his final dreams. The dreams will be unpleasant, but I know how Jaden died. I was right outside the room, helpless to stop it. The bigger issue is that I promised to find his parents. To let him say good-bye and give them closure.

> Damn, girl. There you go with that guilt thing, again. All you promised was that you'd deliver a message for me. I don't have to be there. Yeah, I'd like to see them again, but it's not a deal breaker for me. That's not what's holdin' me here.

Then what is? Are you worried about . . . ?

I'm not sure how to finish the thought. He laughs.

> You tryin' to get rid of me?

No, I was just . . . curious.

> I'm jokin', okay? I know what you meant. I'm not hangin' on 'cause I'm scared I picked the wrong religion and I'm

gonna fry, if that's what you're thinkin'. Once you take out the self-serving bits that people add in, all religions boil down to the same thing, anyway.

Really? And what is this universal bit of wisdom?

Simple—don't be an asshole. Treat other people right. My parents taught me that, and I always tried my best to follow it. So I think I'm good. The only thing keepin' me here is just what you said a minute ago. Curiosity. I want to know how this part of the story ends. But I'm also curious about what comes next. What lies beyond, as they say. At some point, I think the balance will tip in the other direction. Until then, I'll just hang out at the back of your very noisy head and meditate.

Maybe you should teach me. I could use some Zen.

Ooh, no. Think I'll pass on that. You'd be a real challenge. Hard enough to meditate when you only have to manage *one* set of thoughts.

He's right. Kelsey and I have tried pretty much every meditation technique there is. I suck at it, possibly due to the various walls and partitions I've constructed in my head.

Seems to me you come pretty close when you're with Aaron, though. Who says peace of mind has to be a place? Maybe in your case it's a person.

As usual, Jaden's right. So, I pull on my jacket and head outside in search of my own bit of nirvana.

That Aaron has managed to stick it out at Sandalford for this long is nothing short of amazing. Two of the adepts have short tempers, and Ben's dad is perpetually annoyed at being here, although I don't know if he's actively thinking about hurting anyone. Except Miller. Aaron says everybody thinks about hurting Miller—ironically, his very offensive personality means that the guy might actually have *reason* to be worried about self-defense.

So, Aaron spends most of the day on the deck to get away from all of it. He's developed a pretty impressive winter tan on his face and arms. Some days, the deck isn't far enough, and he ends up out on the beach. This could well be one of those days, since he was already on edge from talking to Sam earlier. A family friend, Beth Wilcox, one of the women who owns the townhouse Aaron took me to that first day we met, was struck by a car on her morning jog yesterday. She's in serious condition, and they're not sure if she'll make it. The news hit Aaron hard—for the past few years, anytime Beth and Virgie travel, he's been their designated sitter for the cat and the house.

Aaron's not in either of his usual spots on the upper deck, and when I look down at the lower deck, I realize why. Jasper is here for a visit with Miranda and the kids. The lone female Vigilance guard sits on the other side of the pool, one eye on her phone and one on Jasper. It took several weeks for him to calm down about Miranda and the kids not coming back to the cabin, about not being able see the kids without supervision. He kept saying Miranda and the kids aren't safe here, which seems mind-blowingly ironic, given his recent actions.

Miranda swears that the episode that first week was one of the few times Jasper ever hit her or one of the kids. That the vast majority of the bruises she's received over the past few years have been the side effect of Peyton's telekinetic temper tantrums. And while that's actually plausible based on what we've seen, it's also a *very* convenient excuse, so I don't know whether to believe her or not.

Any meltdowns Jasper has had over the past month have been confined to telephone arguments with Miranda, after which he disappears for days at a time, apparently over at the island. He consented to family therapy sessions and has had a few individual sessions with Kelsey. She can't, of course, divulge what is said in those sessions, but I know that her eventual goal in these situations is family reunification, assuming the abuse isn't pervasive and that it's what the entire family wants.

Reunification is definitely what the Hawkins family wants. Miranda has already started hinting that maybe Jasper could move into the guesthouse out back. That way, she and the kids could see him more often, and maybe they could eventually move in there with him.

While Kelsey hasn't outright rejected taking Miranda's idea to Magda, I don't see it happening anytime soon. Everyone is still on edge when Jasper is around, especially Aaron and Deo. I'm not even sure Jasper would agree, since he doesn't like being around me. His one condition for giving Kelsey what little information he had about my aunt Rowena was that I keep my distance.

I'm perfectly okay with avoiding Jasper, so I duck back inside and take the service elevator down to prevent any possible confrontation. I snag two bottles of water from the downstairs fridge and grab a portable beach chair from the row of hooks below the deck. Cutting through the sea oats, I make my way down to the beach.

Aaron is there, reclining in one of the beach chairs as he reads on his tablet. Taylor is next to him, sprawled out on a blanket, with Ein curled in the crook of her arm. We keep Ein to ourselves as much as possible. I know that's hypocritical. We're judging these kids in the same way that Pruitt and Miller judge all adepts, and I really don't think any of them would hurt the puppy on purpose. But he's still relatively helpless, so the rule stands: they can't play with him unless one of us is nearby. Just in case.

"Sorry, Taylor," I say as I hand Aaron one of the bottles. "I'd have grabbed another, but I thought you were still in your room."

"Nope. I quit."

"Good. You probably need a few hours off."

"No. I mean I actually *quit*. Not just for today. I'm not going back into that room. Whatever you saw in your stupid vision happens, right? So why should I spend all day, every day, with that damned sneaker in my hand? I'm going to soak up the fresh air on the beach for a while. Maybe drive into town later and eat something with flavor for a change."

I ignore the dig, mostly because I agree. Something spicy—Thai, or maybe chiles rellenos. When you're cooking for twenty-six, including a bunch of kids, you don't experiment. You stick to the basics—pasta, tacos, pizza, burgers, chicken.

"So, maybe we should just *go*," I say. "Pick up the RV from the storage lot in Kitty Hawk and head out tonight. I know Magda wants us to wait until Taylor nails down the location, but maybe it would be easier if we were farther north? I need to go to Massachusetts, anyway, to deliver Jaden's message."

Aaron sighs. "You know how much I'd like to get out of here. But Magda doesn't want us driving around aimlessly anymore. That sketch the state police released based on Pruitt's description of Anna is pretty dead-on."

Taylor leans up on one elbow and gives me an appraising look. "I could fix that. Haircut, new color. Boob inserts. And we could dress you more like a girl."

I stick my tongue out at her. "I was dressed like a girl in the sketch, remember? So no thanks."

"Her hair looks great as is," Aaron says. "And she definitely doesn't need boob inserts."

"TMI, bro. And I was just trying to be helpful."

"Changing my hair might not be a bad idea."

She smiles. "We can do it once we're on the road. Maybe a deep blue to match your eyes?"

"So," Aaron says, "the two of you are saying you want to hit the road tonight? Do Deo and I get a vote?"

"Deo's been ready for weeks," Taylor says. "He said he had more freedom when we were in the RV since he can hardly leave his room for worrying that he'll accidentally amp up one of the other adepts."

That's the sense I've been getting from Deo, too, but I haven't been able to get him to say it explicitly. It's a little disconcerting that he's more direct with Taylor about this than he is with me.

"Then that makes it unanimous," Aaron says. "You know I'm ready to go. But I'm pretty sure Magda is going to veto it."

Taylor scoops up Ein and her beach towel. "Nope. Because we're going to be halfway to Boston before she knows we're gone."

❖ ❖ ❖

Clarksboro, New Jersey
December 17, 2019, 8:15 a.m.

Taylor pushes the mirror away from my hand. "Not until I'm done. Would you ask Leonardo da Vinci to show you his masterpiece before it was complete?"

"Several of da Vinci's works were left unfinished," I say. "*The Adoration of the Magi, St. Jerome in the—*"

"Don't care." Another snip of the scissors.

Deep breaths, Anna. Deep breaths.

We left Sandalford around three thirty yesterday afternoon, on the pretext of going into Kitty Hawk for supplies. It wasn't the first time that we'd all gone into town together. We'd been to see the new DC comics movie—even though Deo is a Marvel boy through and through, he's been known to cross the aisle for Wonder Woman. We also drove into Corolla two weeks ago to celebrate my eighteenth birthday, which I've been anticipating for as long as I can remember, since it heralds my official independence from the State of Maryland. It seemed rather anticlimactic, given recent events.

This time when we left, however, our backpacks were a little chubbier than usual, and we also tossed an extra bag into the truck—black with a red-and-white Vigilance logo. It contained several stun guns, a couple of real guns, night-vision goggles, various medical supplies, and syringes filled with the tranquilizer that the med staff used to keep the adepts sedated on their trip to the Outer Banks. Thanks to Daniel's intervention, two guards and a nurse have little gaps in their memories, gaps that I paid for with a pounding headache that lasted well into the night.

In retrospect, I'm pretty sure Miller was counting on the tracking device they attached to the truck to keep tabs on us. But we've played that game before. Aaron located the tracker when we reached Kitty Hawk and transferred it to a delivery truck in the parking lot outside of a Wendy's.

I asked Miranda to cover kitchen duties for the evening, claiming I needed a night off—that part, at least, was true. The only one who knew where we were really going was Kelsey. Leaving her behind at Sandalford was tough. She agreed that we needed to go, although she thought we should run it past Magda first. But I doubt Magda's answer would have been any different than it was two days ago.

And it was really hard to leave Ein. We're going to have enough to worry about without a puppy on board.

The scissors snip again, and another lock of midnight blue falls to the floor of the tiny bathroom.

"That looks . . . longer than the other pieces you've cut."

"Um, yes. That's because it *is* longer."

I close my eyes and go back to my deep breathing, but it's hard to relax when Daniel is laughing. It's the only laugh I've heard from him in weeks, so it's nice to hear, but I'm certain it's at my expense.

Go away, Daniel.

Taylor cut my hair once. And *only* once.

You're not helping.

She's improved. No blood this time. I thought my ear was going to need stitches.

Ha ha. Very funny. Are you better?

It healed long ago.

He knows I don't mean his stupid ear.

Yesterday at the beach house. When you nudged the guards. I could tell—

I'm fine, Anna. I bounced back faster than you did.

I'm not sure that's true, even though I'll admit that the headache I had for the first four hours of the trip was vicious. But as with all things Daniel, arguing is a waste of time.

The scissors snip-snip again, closer to my ear than usual, and I can't help but flinch.

"Stop that!" Taylor says, whacking my shoulder with a comb. "You're going to make me cut you. Just close your eyes until I say you can peek."

When the snipping noises finally stop, I glance up at Taylor.

"Are you done?"

She responds by handing me the mirror.

The cut is asymmetrical, just above the shoulder on the left and just below the ear on the right. I can't remember when my hair was this short, and it's never been any color other than my natural honey blonde, aside from some temporary streaks Deo applied for a Halloween costume one year.

It doesn't look at all like me. And I'm surprised by how much I like it.

Deo gives a wolf whistle when I emerge from the bathroom. Aaron's reaction is a little less enthusiastic, but I kind of understand that. If he bleached his hair and got a spray tan, I'd still love him . . . but . . .

Those words—*I'd still love him*—take me utterly by surprise. Did I actually just think that?

Yep. You totally did.

I wasn't talking to you, Jaden.

Oh, I know. But I still heard it. Pretty sure Hunter and Daniel did, too.

Hunter giggles. Daniel, however, who was so eager to chime in about Taylor's skills as a beautician a few minutes ago, remains silent.

Aaron and I haven't used that word. We've danced around it, I guess, implying it by touch and gesture, but never giving it voice. I'm not sure either of us is ready for that. The fact that I even *thought* the word, that it popped into my head so naturally, stuns me. When the hell did *that* happen?

"So, you don't like it?" Aaron asks, clearly confused by my sudden change of expression.

"Oh, no," I say quickly, reassuring Taylor. "It's great. I really . . . love it."

That word again. Totally innocuous in this context, but I still feel the blood rushing to my cheeks.

"I'm going to go get a better look," I say, although it's more a pretext to get out of the room than anything else.

I hear Aaron behind me and catch his eyes in the closet mirror.

"Didn't mean to hurt your feelings. I really *do* like it. You look beautiful. It's just . . . you don't . . ."

"I don't look like me. It's okay. I understand completely."

He starts to say something else, but I turn around quickly and silence him with a long kiss. When I eventually pull back, I say, "Don't bleach your hair, okay?"

"Okay . . ." Aaron laughs. "Another kiss like that, and I *might* be able to convince myself that what you just said makes sense."

"With pleasure."

Once our bargain is sealed, we grab some coffee and a breakfast bar to eat in the cab of the truck. Before we get out the door, however, Aaron's phone rings.

"I win!" Taylor says. "I said nine o'clock and it's not even five after."

That Magda would call around this time was a fairly safe bet, given the time difference between here and London. Miller is *probably* not stupid enough to call and wake her up in the middle of the night, and the information that we slipped his surveillance isn't something he'd want to relay by text or a voice message. Nor would he want to stay up until some ungodly hour of the morning in order to be sure Magda got the news that we were AWOL over her morning tea and crumpets.

"It's a video request," Aaron says glumly. "Which means she's angry enough that she wants to see our faces while she yells."

That's an exaggeration. Magda doesn't yell. She just scowls very loudly. It's still not pleasant.

"Hold on. Let me and Deo get into place." Taylor snatches up the grimy sneaker, along with her drawing pad and pencil. Deo sits next to her and puts one hand on her knee, her loyal amp.

"Good morning, Magda," Aaron says in a chipper voice. "We were expecting your call."

"As well you should. You are currently in possession of my truck and caravan, without permission. Supplies and weapons are missing as well. So the real question is whether you were also expecting me to report this larceny to the authorities?"

"Larceny?" Aaron's smile wavers a bit, but he laughs as though she's joking. Because she is, at least on the whole issue of calling the police. I think.

"We simply left a few days early," he says. "Taylor's actually making some headway now that we're farther north."

Taylor dutifully holds up the drawing pad. She pivots it toward the camera for a few seconds for Magda's benefit and then gets back to sketching.

"Plus," Aaron adds, "I can think of many reasons you wouldn't *want* to contact the police."

Magda raises one sardonic eyebrow at this last comment, but there's a hint of acknowledgment underlying her expression. I'm sure there are at least a dozen official permits that she currently lacks for housing children—and troubled children, at that—at Sandalford, and she quite possibly wouldn't receive them if she were to apply.

"And *I* can think of at least one reason that *you*, or at the very least Anna, might want to avoid the police. I'm not sure how much protection I can offer to her if you run into trouble. That police sketch looks very much like—"

Magda halts midsentence when Aaron turns the camera my way, and then says, "Actually, that police sketch bears only a passing resemblance to Anna now. I'm impressed."

"Taylor has hidden talents," I say.

"Indeed. You usually don't want to attract attention to yourself in these situations, but since the sketch is of a rather nondescript girl, this new look is probably a better option."

"I'm glad you approve." I smile sweetly, ignoring the fact that I've just had my usual appearance dissed by a woman who bears an uncanny resemblance to Miss Trunchbull in *Matilda*.

Magda continues to complain about our abrupt exit for a few more minutes, and we let her vent without interruption. Aaron even tosses in an apology, although if Magda is a halfway decent judge of human behavior, she realizes it's not exactly a *sincere* apology. He was as eager to get out of Sandalford as any of us, maybe more.

Magda winds down eventually. Before she hangs up, she orders us to text twice daily with our location and an update on Taylor's progress.

Once we're on the road, I turn on one of Aaron's stations, and Cage the Elephant fills the cab. Then I start work on our daily news roundup. For the past few weeks, it's mostly been me and Aaron scanning through the news—both the real news and the conspiracy stuff—out on the deck after breakfast. Neither of us is as media savvy as Taylor, but she's a bit preoccupied at the moment trying to track down Bree, and there's a lot to comb through.

It's become an increasingly disheartening task. There's just so much out there that's ill-informed and ill-intentioned. And Cregg is more than happy to exploit it.

It's the ill-intentioned types that worry me the most. The things I've been reading stirred up a memory from my former hitcher Bruno, who once had a protracted debate with another homeless guy when they were sleeping beneath the same bridge. Bruno couldn't remember the guy's name—he just thought of him as That-Jerk—but his mind would often drift back to their conversation in the years before his death.

Their debate centered around the question of what would happen when the aliens finally let everyone here on earth know that they exist. That they're watching. That they have peaceful intentions, but they're actually smarter and more powerful than we mere earthlings.

This is one of Bruno's memories that I probably got more nuance from than he did. Bruno wasn't the brightest bulb on the tree. His views on aliens were almost like a religious faith—he had his beliefs, and he stood by them, regardless of any evidence others might present. (Although, to be fair, there wasn't much actual evidence on either side.) He told That-Jerk without hesitation that everyone would welcome the Grays, with their peaceful intentions and advanced intelligence, and they would then share their technology, and soon no one would be hungry or sick. They'd cure cancer, which made Bruno happy because his mom died of cancer. And maybe they'd even take some volunteers back to Zeta Reticuli. Bruno really hoped they'd pick him.

The other guy, who was considerably smarter than Bruno, disagreed. He said that the aliens' arrival would result in an upheaval of massive, maybe even apocalyptic, proportions. Contact with the Grays would call into question the religious beliefs of many people, especially the idea that we were the center of God's focus, and that would make them angry. But more importantly, humans would have to view themselves as lesser than. Inferior to these aliens with their advanced tech. We wouldn't be top of the heap anymore. That-Jerk was convinced that things would get really nasty, really quick. There might be a few people, like that kid in *E.T.*, who could see past humanity's limitations and imagine the possibilities of cooperation. But for the most part, if the Zeta Reticulans didn't watch their scrawny gray backs, humans would end them. Humans would end every single Gray they could find.

The discussion never erased Bruno's desire to meet the Zeta Reticulans. But That-Jerk's comments did unsettle him. They gave him nightmares for weeks.

The Delphi adepts aren't aliens, but public reaction so far is tracking closely with what That-Jerk predicted. The reaction has been almost universally negative, with the exception of the people who still aren't buying it, who refuse to believe until they see proof in person with their own two eyes. A new editorial appears almost daily about the consequences of tampering with nature, with many of the authors arguing that the government must track down and tag every person who was connected to the project, along with their offspring. Most believe we need to isolate them from the rest of the public. Some say this would be for their own good. Others don't even sugarcoat it. They just say the government should lock 'em up. And on the few occasions when I've ventured down into the comments section—something I should really know better than to do—I've found that the individuals chanting *lock 'em up* are actually the *moderate* voices.

What really scares me is that I'm hearing a slightly subtler version of that sentiment from senators, representatives, and witnesses appearing in the Delphi Hearings. Many of the witnesses are simply offering objective testimony about the program. But plenty of opinions have been entered into the official record, not just by the witnesses but by the members of Congress asking the questions.

So far, we've heard from victims of the original Delphi subjects, the men whose brains were so addled from the serum that they killed dozens of people. We've heard from law enforcement officers who worked those cases, and a half dozen or so individuals who were part of the initial testing at Fort Bragg. As of now, however, none of the individuals who moved on to the next stage, when the Delphi Project became property of the CIA, have been called to testify.

The witnesses for the past few days have been more science focused—psychiatrists, neuroscientists, and physicists, among others. Some took the stand to proclaim the impossibility of psychic phenomena, and some to proclaim the opposite. A member of the latter group set up a demonstration by putting electrode caps on members of the commission to show that they could transmit short thoughts back and forth via computer. I'm still not entirely sure how that was relevant, since Delphi psychics aren't connected to wires and computers, but I guess it takes baby steps to convince some people that telepathy and other psionic abilities are possible.

The session I'm reading about now, which was held yesterday afternoon, has moved on to the psychologists who worked with the original

Delphi subjects. As I scroll down through the summary posted on the *New York Times*, a photograph pops up on the screen that startles me. Even though his hair has grayed and there are a few wrinkles at the corners of his eyes, he hasn't changed much since the pictures in the papers around the time of his trial.

Aaron glances over at my sharp intake of breath. "Something new?"

"Yeah. The Senate committee heard testimony yesterday morning from the lead psychiatrist who treats my father. The doctor who wouldn't talk to Kelsey. The chair of the commission is demanding that Pfeifer be brought in to answer questions, even though his doctor says that's a bad idea. Senator Cregg seconded that, saying that it would be—and I quote—'too taxing given the patient's mental history,' but he was overruled."

"So your dad will be testifying before the commission?"

"Looks like. But they haven't decided whether he'll testify in person. They could also do a video deposition."

I continue reading through the other accounts, sharing anything of particular interest with Aaron. The one that catches me by surprise is an article in the *LA Times* about public protests in front of three state capitol buildings demanding that those who participated in the Delphi protocol, along with their children, be included in a national registry along the lines of those required for sex offenders.

He gives me a pained smile. "Well, that escalated quickly."

"No kidding. Get this. 'Senator Ron Cregg spoke to the protesters gathered in Harrisburg late Monday afternoon, noting that he shares their concerns for public safety, and that those concerns would certainly be a key focus were he to be elected next November.'"

"How very convenient that one of these three spontaneous protests just happened to be in the Senator's home state. And how very convenient yet again that he just happened to be at the capitol building in Pennsylvania at that very hour to address them, after a busy day of congressional hearings in DC."

"I know. He's clearly using this situation for political gain. That's been true from the beginning. It's just—how can he believe that digging deeply into Delphi won't end up pointing back to his own family? There must be dozens of people who know that his own son was involved with the program after it ended up with government contractors. It reminds me of the old adage about riding a crocodile across the river."

"I'm not familiar with that one . . ."

"The point is, the croc *might* get you where you want to go. But there's an equally good chance you'll get eaten when you get there."

CHAPTER TWENTY

Waltham, Massachusetts
December 17, 2019, 6:24 p.m.

"You think they're home?" Aaron asks as we pull into the driveway.

None of the lights seem to be on inside the Park residence, a small white split-level in an older neighborhood near the center of Waltham. The house is decorated for the holidays, but the strings of lights that someone hastily wrapped around the bushes at the front of the house aren't on, and a battered air-blown snowman decoration is collapsed in a heap in the yard. An aging Honda Civic is parked in the driveway, blocking the one-car garage.

What do you think, Jaden? Is anyone home?

Yeah. They both should be. Two cars are here, or there wouldn't be one in the driveway. I can't believe they still have that Frosty decoration. Mom hates that thing. She said she was gonna make Dad throw it away last year.

You ready?

Yeah. Ready as I'll ever be.

Jaden started getting cold feet right after we crossed the Massachusetts border. I could feel his anxiety as soon as I pulled the sheet of paper with his parents' home address out of my backpack. He was the one who gave me the address, and I'm sure he was listening in when I asked Sam to run a background check to be sure they still lived there, so there was nothing new on that sheet of paper. Maybe the whole thing just didn't seem real until we were nearly here.

As we continued north, Jaden developed an entire shopping list of reservations. Was it fair to open up a wound that might have begun healing? Was it fair to take away their hope that they might find their only son one day? On the other hand, was it fair for them to keep hoping, to keep looking for him, expending resources and energy on the search, rather than getting on with their lives?

I didn't get involved. Better just to stay out of his internal decision-making, even if it was draining my ability to concentrate on anything else. He ran through the entire gamut of options several times, always returning to the belief that this was, after all, a good thing. Or at least a necessary thing.

It didn't stop him from worrying about his mom, though. She's the one with the military background. She lived in Maryland for a while, too, so he's not sure whether her involvement continued after the CIA took over the program. Jaden doesn't want her to feel guilty about what happened. But then she probably already feels guilty. She must realize that Jaden's psychic abilities were connected to her time in the program, even though she never talked to him about it.

Aaron walks with me to the front door, although I guess I should say walks with *us*. Jaden is waiting near the front, and I plan to slide back and let him take over once I've explained why we're here. This is

351

his good-bye. Not just his parents' chance for closure, but also his own, and I don't want to get in the way.

No one answers the first time I ring the doorbell. Jaden thinks they could be down in the basement, so I give it thirty seconds and ring again.

This time, the door opens. I can see the man's face through the chain lock, and my first reaction is that he looks a lot like Jaden.

Yeah. My mom always said . . .

Jaden's thought trails off when his dad flicks on the porch light and we see his face more clearly. It's red and puffy, especially around the eyes.

"Can I help you?" Mr. Park's voice is quiet, drained of all energy. "I'm guessing you worked with Mi-Sook. Thanks for stopping by, but . . . I'm just not ready to talk to people yet."

Jaden, who has never been pushy, zips to the front.

"What happened?"

Mr. Park winces. "I thought you must have seen the details in the paper. We were coming out of that little pizza place she likes downtown on Sunday night, and . . ." He stops, shaking his head. "The shot came out of nowhere. I guess it was a drug thing. Didn't even see a car nearby. One minute she's standing next to me, and then she's . . ." Another headshake, followed by a long silence. "Visitation is tomorrow from five to seven. We're asking that people give to Reading is Fundamental instead of flowers."

"She'd have liked that." Jaden's voice is flat and faraway. It barely sounds like me. "She was allergic anyway."

"That's right," Mr. Park says with a sad smile. "Always said she didn't want to be sneezin' at her own funeral. Maybe I'll see you there tomorrow, Miss—?" His voice goes up at the end, and I realize we never gave him our names.

Jaden can't find his voice for a moment. Then he clears my throat. "It's Anna. Just Anna," he says as he begins backing down the steps.

Aaron takes my elbow and says, "I'm sorry for your loss, sir." Then he turns us back toward the truck.

Jaden starts apologizing before I can get my seat belt on.

> Couldn't do it. I'm sorry, but not like that. Not when he just . . . the words . . . I couldn't find them.

> *Oh, God, no! Don't apologize. Of course you couldn't. I'm so, so sorry, Jaden.*

Once we're pulling out of the driveway and Mr. Park closes the door, Jaden and I change places.

He huddles in the back, much like Hunter did when I first picked him up. I feel waves of sympathy from both Hunter and Daniel, and my first thought is that I'm glad he's not alone. That he's with people who understand loss.

I'm so struck by the utter absurdity of having an entire therapy group within the confines of my skull that I half laugh, half sob.

Aaron reaches over for my hand. "Are you okay? Is Jaden okay?"

"I don't know."

"I'm . . ." Aaron shakes his head in anger. "I'm not buying that it was an accident. You said Jaden's mom was the one in the program, right? She gets shot, and we have Beth lying in a hospital in Silver Spring after some asshole swerves off the road to hit her."

"I didn't know Beth was connected to Delphi."

"Yeah. She wasn't one of the subjects, but she worked there. We met her and Virgie through my dad, although I didn't really get to know them until after he died. I'm pretty sure she's the one who funneled information to him when he was planning to blow the whistle. Two women suffer accidents in the same day, and both of them were among the maybe fifty employees connected to Delphi when it was under Graham Cregg. I can't see that as a coincidence. Can you?"

"No."

Aaron calls Sam to give him the news about Jaden's mom and to check on Beth. She's still in critical condition. We're quiet after that, both thinking about the implications of these attacks. Are they eliminating everyone who worked with the Delphi program? Or simply everyone who has knowledge of Graham Cregg's role in the later stages of the program? If so, that includes the four of us, Kelsey, Porter, Aaron's entire family, Jasper Hawkins and his family, Magda, and maybe even some of the security guards, depending on how much information Magda has given them.

It also includes my father. If what Jasper Hawkins told me is true, Scott Pfeifer and Graham Cregg were basically partners. Is my father safe in the psychiatric hospital? For that matter, how safe is Daniel's body, even with his former police colleagues watching him?

We arrive at the campground much earlier than anticipated, given that we were at Jaden's house all of five minutes. Taylor and Deo aren't in the main cabin when we enter the RV. Music blares from the back area where they've been working. Initially, they'd each used their earbuds because Deo was not a fan of Taylor's music and she was not a fan of his. But they seem to have found a compromise they can tolerate.

Aaron puts the pizzas we picked up on the counter. I push the door open quietly, hoping to signal to Deo that there's food waiting while trying to avoid interrupting Taylor's concentration.

Neither of them notice me. Deo's eyes are closed. I can't tell if Taylor's eyes are open, because her body—her very bare body on top of *his* very bare body—faces the other direction, toward Deo. They are both far too distracted, too caught up in each other to even hear my gasp. I step back, bumping into Aaron as I pull the door shut. One look at his face tells me that he saw the same thing I did.

TAYLOR!

Okay. That means Daniel saw it, too. It takes every bit of effort to shove him back and keep him from taking control.

Let me out. I'm going in there to kill the little son of a bitch.

Oh no you're NOT. Back off!

As much as I hate penning Jaden up with Taylor's vengeful oldest brother right now, I have no choice but to stack the mental bricks. Daniel needs to cool off. And I need to get *out* of here. I need bleach for my eyes. Or holy water. Which is beyond hypocritical, since Deo has seen me in the same bed as Aaron.

Of course, we had *clothes* on.

Without exchanging a word, Aaron grabs the pizzas off the counter. We exit the RV in full stealth mode, almost as though we're in a silent film running backward, and get back in the truck. Aaron drives to the far end of the campground, maybe half a mile away, before he stops and looks at me.

"I thought Deo was . . ."

"Bi. He's bi. Which is what I told Taylor weeks ago when she asked. *Oh my God!* She's so much older than he is! How *could* she—"

"Um. Don't yell at me, okay, because I'm just as horrified as you are. That's my baby sister in there. And . . . there's less of an age gap between Taylor and Deo than between you and me."

"But that's different! Deo is just a kid."

"Oh, no. No, no, no. I had a very clear view, and I can promise you he's *not* just a kid."

His lip quivers, holding back a laugh. I stare at him for a moment, and then join him, even though there's a part of me—and not just the part that is occupied by Daniel—that wants to storm back into the RV, yank her out of that room, and . . . and . . .

Ask her intentions?

"I don't even know if Deo has protection. I mean, we've discussed it. And I'm sure he's talked about sex with Kelsey, but . . ."

"Yeah. Probably not an issue. I don't think it's Taylor's first time at the rodeo. She had a steady boyfriend last year. They dated for about eight months until she got bored with him. I made sure she was . . . safe. I'm thinking Mom did, too."

That prompts another roar from behind the walls.

"Daniel seems to be saying that is *not* the decision he'd have made regarding Taylor's sex life."

"Yeah, well, I'm her brother, not her parent. Same goes for Daniel."

And even though Aaron doesn't add it, I know what he's leaving unsaid. I'm not Deo's parent, either.

We sit there for a moment, and then Aaron says, "Do you think they're done?"

I lean back against the seat and take a few deep breaths. It's partly to keep Daniel at bay but also to keep myself from erupting into nervous laughter again.

"Deo's fifteen," I say. "I think it's a pretty safe bet that they're done."

"Good point. They've probably already started again."

"No! Stop that!" I punch him on the shoulder, and we both laugh as he pulls me close. "It will be hard enough to erase that visual without you talking about sequels."

"So . . . do we say anything to them?"

He's shaking his head even as he asks the question, and I join him. *Nope, nope, nope, nope, nope.*

As it turns out, it's a moot point. They're both in the main room when we come in. It's instantly clear from Deo's slightly sheepish expression and Taylor's totally defiant one that they know we know.

Taylor finds the pizza with anchovies and grabs a slice. "Hmm . . . it's kind of cold. What took you guys so long? Did you stop and make out on the way back?"

Deo rolls his eyes. "Really, Taylor?"

"No. We were back early as I'm pretty sure you're aware. But . . ."

I stop and take a long look at Deo. He's probably six feet tall now, but in my mind's eye, he will always be the eight-year-old boy who tried so hard to be tough, to take whatever life dished out. Who looked at me like I was a hero when I stood up for him, when I stopped someone older who should have been protecting him, not hurting him. That wasn't something he expected from a stranger. It wasn't even something he expected from his family.

"But that's between you two. None of my business. And we have other things to worry about."

We fill them in on what we learned about Jaden's mother and Aaron's concern that this might be part of a larger operation by the Creggs.

Taylor's face falls. "God, that's awful. If only we'd gotten here a few days earlier. But, hey . . . at least we have some *good* news. I found where they're keeping Hunter's sister and the others. That's . . ." She stops and gives Deo a sly smile. "That's what we were celebrating. Earlier."

Deo blushes. Taylor obviously likes teasing him, which makes me kind of want to smack her again.

"Really?" I say through clenched teeth. "That's great. Where is it?"

"Upstate New York. *Way* upstate. Close to the Canadian border. I'm positive I've got the right area, but there are four or five houses nearby. I'm still nailing down exactly which house is the one over the pit."

"The *pit*?" Aaron says.

"Well, to be more accurate, it's a silo. That's why I kept seeing round walls. Some company renovated a bunch of old missile silos a few years back. Turned them into doomsday bunkers. There are rooms below, and that's where they're keeping the kids. But the house on top

ary looking. And I still need to get a better sense of the
he bunker."

"I don't like the sound of that word," Aaron says. "*Bunker.* How the
hell are the four of us supposed to break into a bunker?"

"No, *kemosabe.* Anna's flash-forward showed the two"—Taylor
forks two fingers at me and Aaron—"of you. *Not* the four of us."

Aaron gives her an unamused look. "Taylor, as always, you are a
ray of sunshine."

We dive into the pizza. And when Taylor goes over to the fridge to
grab a drink, I follow.

"Remember what you said to me about Aaron a few months back
at Kelsey's beach house?" I ask in a low whisper.

Her eyes narrow slightly, but she nods. I wait, raising my brows to
indicate that I want her to actually *say* the words.

"I *remember*," she hisses. "I said not to hurt him."

"Exactly. That goes double for you with Deo. Understood?"

❖   ❖   ❖

Waltham, Massachusetts
December 18, 2019, 6:49 p.m.

Jaden has control when we approach the coffin at the front of the
funeral parlor. It's closed, adorned with a single wreath of white roses.
Small white candles flicker on the low tables in front of the coffin. The
air is heavy with the scent of sandalwood. Soft music combined with
the sound of birds and falling water plays in the background. Next to
the casket, propped up on an easel, is a large family portrait. I'm guessing it was taken at least five years ago, since it shows a slightly younger
Mr. Park and an awkward-looking adolescent version of Jaden, standing
behind a small woman with neat dark hair and a round face. None of

them look comfortable in their formal clothes, but they all smile dutifully for the camera.

We waited until the end of the visitation period, hoping that friends
and colleagues would have come and gone. And for the most part, they
have. Two women—Jaden's aunts—continue to hover around Mr. Park,
who looks like he's very ready for this day to be over.

Although I wish we could give Jaden real privacy, that luxury isn't
exactly easy to come by inside my head. At least we're quiet, though.
Hunter picked up on Jaden's mood and is subdued for the first time
since Taylor announced that she'd located his sister. Daniel has calmed
down, too, possibly realizing that there are more important things to
worry about right now than his sister's chastity. But this is also the first
time in the past few weeks that I've spent more than a second or two
back here in the peanut gallery with him, and I realize there's something
deeper going on.

Daniel has faded in the past few weeks. Not a lot, but he's definitely
diminished, less *present* now.

It's a subtle change, but I pick up on it quickly simply because I've
seen it happen with my other hitchers. I'm currently watching it happen
with Jaden. In the past, though, it has been a good sign. A *necessary* sign.
It means that they've made their peace with death and they're moving
on. But in Daniel's case, it's most definitely not a good sign. It's avoid-
able, or at least I hope it is, and the timing truly sucks.

Daniel can clearly tell what I'm thinking, and I expect to see anger
or denial on his face. What I see instead is fear, coupled as always with
obstinance.

We wait, Anna. We wait until you get those kids back to
Sandalford. After that . . . we'll talk.

I want to argue with him that we still have a few days, that his
body is only a six-hour drive to the south. But Jaden doesn't need this

argument running through the back channels of his mind when he's saying his final good-bye to his mom. He deserves better.

Later, Daniel. We will discuss this later.

Jaden runs my finger across the woman's face in the photograph. A tear slides down my cheek, and then I feel a large hand on my shoulder.

"It's Anna, right?" Mr. Park says. "And let me guess. You were one of her Park Readers."

I have no idea what he means, but Jaden must, because my lips curl up in a smile. "Yes, sir," he says. "She pointed me toward some very good books when I was younger. They changed my life."

"What was your favorite?"

"Oh, that's a tough one. There were so many. She gave me this one called *The Tao of Pooh*. Some stuff by Neil Gaiman. And there was a book by Mark Twain that—" Jaden stops abruptly, aware that he's probably said too much.

He probably *has* said too much, because a question flickers in his dad's eyes. "Maybe you knew my son, Jaden, from school? Though he'd have been a few years older than you. I just wondered because . . . he liked some of those books, too."

Air rushes into my lungs as Jaden pulls in a deep breath. Decision time. We came here not knowing if he would say anything to his dad, unsure if his dad could take a second blow so soon. Yes, there are some questions that it would be nice to have answered, but the main goal was to let Jaden say good-bye to his mom.

"Yes," Jaden says. "I knew him. We had a couple of classes together. Not at Eastbrook, but later. Before he got so . . . sick. We talked about books, mostly. Books that Mom, I mean, *his* mom had recommended. I know he loved her a lot." We turn then, and he looks directly at his father. "Loved *both* of you a lot."

Mr. Park bites his lip and looks back over at the photograph. "I know. And she knew that, too. It's the oddest thing . . . She held out hope for so long that we'd find Jaden. Or that he'd find his way back to us. We even hired a detective. But then a few months ago, Sookie sat across from me at breakfast and said Jaden was gone now. That we should stop looking. And she always had a way of knowing that kind of thing, so I accepted it. Made my peace with it. I don't know what comes after this, but maybe they'll find each other. And maybe I'll find them too, eventually."

He smiles then, and even though his eyes are still red-rimmed, he does look at peace. "Thank you again for coming. It means a lot to me, and it would have meant a lot to Sookie and Jaden, too. Maybe you could think of them occasionally when you curl up with a book. That would be a good way to remember them."

"I'll do that."

Mr. Park pats me on the shoulder again and then goes back over to his sisters.

Jaden rests a hand one last time on the coffin. "Sorry," he says softly. I'm not sure if he's talking to his mother or to me. Then he slides back, and I feel the cold wood beneath my palm.

> I couldn't do it. Not now. We'll call him later. Maybe when I—or at least you—can tell him that *gaesaeki* has paid for what he did. Not just to her but to everyone.

The tone is very unJaden. I've never heard him this bitter, this vengeful. Which is pretty amazing when you consider that I picked him up only minutes after he was murdered.

Aaron gives me a questioning look as I approach the back pew where he's been waiting. I shake my head, signaling that this is not a good time to discuss the matter.

Jaden doesn't ask, but I turn around when we reach the door, giving him one last look at his family. His aunts are talking to his dad, seemingly at the same time. But Mr. Park doesn't appear to be paying attention. He looks confused, probably trying to remember whether his wife ever mentioned a girl with dark-blue hair who liked the same books as Jaden.

I close my eyes when we get back to the truck and focus inward. Daniel is gearing up for the argument we postponed earlier, but I'm ready for him.

> *It's a six-hour drive to Baltimore, and we have at least a few days before this rescue happens. We need to get you back to the hospital.*

No. Not yet. I've seen the sketches Taylor made of the place, and you *need* me. First off, I know how Cregg's security people work. I was part of that team. They may be in a new location, but their patterns, their personalities, will be the same. And second, you're going to need me to nudge them.

> *No way. I've seen how that drains you. How it drains me, for that matter. We have the weapons we snagged from the Vigilance guards. Plus the sedatives. Once we get closer, Hunter thinks he can contact Bree, and maybe she can give the others a heads-up.*

You're counting on a lot of things falling into place.

> *Yes. I am. But I already know that it works, somehow, because I saw us leaving. I'm going to talk to the others tonight. We'll take a vote.*

No. The only vote that counts on this is mine. But I *will* compromise. You're right. I'm almost tapped out in terms of influencing anyone. I'll stick to helping you with logistics only. And once you get the kids to safety, I won't argue. We'll head right back to Baltimore and see if you can shove me back into what's left of my body.

They've been doing physical therapy, Daniel. Your mom says they have you on these machines—

What about my brain, Anna? Is there physical therapy for whatever damage it suffered?

Waiting doesn't feel right, Daniel. It's too risky.

Doesn't matter. I can promise you that if you drive back to Baltimore now, I will fight you. I'll refuse to leave. I'll grab onto your cerebellum or one of these filing cabinets and you won't be able to evict me.

I huff in annoyance, not realizing I've made the sound out loud until I see Aaron's face from the corner of my eye.

"Something wrong?"

I shake my head. "Not really. Just tired. And ready for this to be over."

We reach the RV park a few minutes later. The lights are on inside, and I see Taylor's silhouette through one of the windows, so at least we don't have to worry about interrupting another make-out session. That's a relief.

Aaron laughs when he catches my expression. "It's weird, isn't it? Last year, when Taylor was dating that Seth guy, I came home early one day, and they walked out of her room together. He was still pulling on his shirt. It was hard for me to reconcile the image of my little sister playing with her Disney Princess dolls with the idea of her being . . . um . . . involved with him in that same room. See? I can't even say the words."

"I know. But . . . it's really less the sex side of it for me and more that I'm worried about somebody getting hurt."

I don't add that the specific person I'm worried about getting hurt is Deo. Taylor is older. She's been in a relationship before. Deo has kissed exactly three people prior to Taylor. And one of those was in a game of seven minutes in heaven, so he says it really didn't count.

I also don't add that it's annoying that Taylor and Deo are getting more action than we are. They occasionally get time to themselves, *without* chaperones.

❖ ❖ ❖

Waltham, Massachusetts
December 18, 2019, 9:49 p.m.

The sketches of the various layers of The Pit, as Taylor has dubbed it, are more detailed now, and Taylor has pinpointed where the house above it sits on a long private drive. Judging from the satellite map, it's an average-sized ranch house. Taylor located some photos from a real estate company that had the place listed for sale until a few months ago, when it was pulled from the market abruptly. No record of a sale or rental, just no longer on the market.

Each of the five belowground levels is stacked on top of the other. There may be levels below that, as well, but Taylor doesn't think they're occupied. Some of her drawings of the occupied levels are just roughly sketched rooms within a circular frame, but the fourth level down is drawn in much more detail. Bree is in the third room to the right after you enter from the staircase.

"What's in the center area?" Aaron asks.

"A guard, maybe?" Deo says. "Or at least a monitoring station."

"Great," I grumble. "Even if we take out the guards on the ground floor, we'll still have to fight our way down five levels, each of which could have its own guard."

Aaron pushes the pages aside. "It's probably useless to plan this out until we get closer tomorrow and see if Hunter can contact his sister. And then maybe she'll be able to . . . somehow . . . get word to Ashley."

"That shouldn't be a problem," I say. "I saw Maria in the vision, and she's one of the group Jaden calls The Peepers. No secrets in a place like that. Daniel and Jaden both are certain that if we can get the message to Bree, Maria will know, and then so will anyone Maria chooses to tell."

"If that's true," Taylor says, "then Maria must know what the guards think. And you said some of these kids can also start fires. So, why haven't they jumped the guards by now? Why haven't they escaped on their own?"

I don't have an answer to that, but Jaden does.

Some of them are kids. Just kids. And the rest of them—they've got nowhere to go. Like I said before, I would have loved to get a message out to my mom and dad, but until things started going bad, and Cregg's people started "disappearing" the few adult wabbits in the place, I was happier at The Warren than I'd been anywhere else. It was the only place I didn't feel like a freak. And I was one of the lucky ones who could go back to my family if I'd gotten out. The kids they've pulled in from Eastern Europe . . . they don't have a way to get back home. If their families had enough money for travel, they wouldn't have signed up for those jobs in the first place.

As I'm conveying what Jaden told me, my phone buzzes with a news alert. The last one was another protest, this time in Washington by a group calling itself Mothers Against Psychic Predators, who are terrified that psychics could be peeking inside their children's minds, or maybe planting thoughts. While I totally understand their concern, some of them also seem happy to have a scapegoat—anything you don't like about your child can now be explained away. Johnny won't do his homework? Must be those Delphi psychics. Suzie might be gay? Subliminal messages from the psychics, obviously.

This time, the headline is *Massive Outage Leaves Millions in the Dark*. I nearly click to close it, but then I see the subheading—*WOCAN Splinter Group Claims Credit for Attack on Texas Power Grid*.

The freeze-frame of the video is a group of maybe twenty people. They're dressed in black, wearing ski masks designed to make them look like bears. Judging by their size and build, they're all adults—most of them male, but there are definitely also a few women in the mix. Several of them are holding WOCAN flags—with the California bear in the center and logos for the other three states across the top.

The video is silent—just quick flashes of these "bears" at a variety of locations. Most show a fenced area behind them, some with strands of barbed wire across the top. All of the locations are brightly lit, a few almost blindingly so, with an array of metal boxes, pylons, and wires.

I pause the video on one of these images—a guy in a bear mask, moving his gloved hand toward a large gray box. A sign on the box says *Texas Electric Cooperative*, above a cartoon version of an electric plug wearing leather chaps and a cowboy hat. On the right side of the frame is the lower portion of a body—just work boots and a few inches of denim—lying on the concrete.

"You guys need to see this. What's the box he's touching?"

Aaron squints at my phone. "Best guess would be a power transformer. Who's that supposed to be?"

"Apparently a member of a WOCAN splinter group." I push play again, and the man's hand touches the top of the transformer. A bright-blue glow appears beneath his glove, and then the entire screen goes dark.

The next clip is the same scene with minor changes. A different transformer. Someone else in a bear mask, same blue glow, and then pitch black.

"How is that possible?" I ask.

The others shake their heads, but it's Daniel who provides the answer, with a strong second from Jaden.

> It's *not* possible. Someone may have taken out the Tex-as power grid, but it wasn't a bunch of adepts in bear masks. I doubt they're even adepts. That's just the diversion.

Another transformer blinks out. And another, and another, until I lose count. All wearing the stupid bear masks, dressed in black, wearing gloves—

"Hold on," I say, running the video back a few seconds. They're all wearing gloves, plural, except for one. She's dressed in formfitting black leather, and the small hand on the transformer is gloved. The other hand, however, is not. I very clearly remember the sensation of those nails clawing my skin and, even worse, the sensation of her psychic claws raking through my memories.

"Hmph," Taylor says. She reaches over to expand the picture on my phone, and peers closely at the screen. "I think we've found a Dacia Bear."

CHAPTER
TWENTY-ONE

Lyon Mountain, New York
December 19, 2019, 8:10 a.m.

As usual, Taylor is the first one awake. She's tearing open a packet of instant oatmeal when I slide my tablet across the counter toward her. "If I had any doubts that you locked on to the right location, this erases it."

She looks at me instead of the screen, her eyes narrowed.

"I said *if* I had any doubts. Not that I actually had them."

Mollified, she reads the headline and makes a noise that's half snort, half laughter.

"*Cult of Alien Worshippers Gathers in Adirondacks.* You need to stop reading this garbage, Anna."

"Oh, I'm going to. I'm going to stop reading anything except escapist fiction, if we ever get out of this mess. Cozy mysteries. Maybe a little shifter romance now and then."

"Any more on the bear attacks in Texas?"

"Nothing beyond what we heard yesterday. A lot of speculation. A few experts noting that there's no way that the entire grid for Texas could be taken down by damaging a few dozen substations, that it's more likely the grid's computer system was hacked. No one is listening to them, however—I mean, we saw it with our own eyes, so it must be real, right? A lot of political posturing, especially by those in the congressional hearings, and, of course, repeated denials by the WOCAN group."

"Yeah," Taylor says. "Did you see the interview with the WOCAN spokesman? He was literally in tears talking to the reporter, saying that they'd never do something like this. That people die during major outages, and they're committed to nonviolent change."

"Can't help but sympathize with the group. They're getting a false rap same as the adepts, and it's not—"

My phone rings. It's Kelsey. I can tell from her tone that something is bothering her, so I pull on my jacket and take the call outside. "What's up?" I ask as I brush the top step of the RV clear of snow.

"Nothing major. I just wanted to hear a friendly voice, more than anything. Miller is making me crazy. He wants to run this place like a prison camp. What's the point in Magda paying for a house by the ocean if we're not even going to let the kids run on the beach?"

This is Kelsey's ongoing battle with Miller. The eventual compromise was that the kids can go with her in groups of two, one group per day, as long as she convinces two of his guards to walk with them. One of the guards is almost always willing, but finding a second has proven tough. Most days, the kids end up exercising on the volleyball court.

"Miller's an ass," I agree.

"He is. Hopefully things will improve once Magda arrives and sees for herself that he's simply not a good fit for this position."

"Magda is planning to visit Sandalford?"

"She didn't mention it to you?" Kelsey seems surprised. "Contractors showed up yesterday to get the other house ready for them."

"Oh. So . . . I guess that ends Miranda's hopes that Jasper could stay in the guesthouse."

"What?" Kelsey laughs. "Oh, no! Not the guesthouse. You've seen Magda's London house in the video meetings. Do you really think she'd even consider living in that tiny cottage? I meant the big yellow house next door."

That makes a lot more sense. While nowhere near the size of Sandalford, that house is still huge, and there are several acres of land between the two so that Magda could maintain a bit of privacy.

"And Jasper's not around anyway. He's missed his last two therapy sessions. We're not sure where he is. Miranda even went over to that island yesterday, the one where he was keeping Peyton after her episode, but he's not there. I don't think she believed he would be really, since the truck is missing instead of the boat, but she had to check. She's been downplaying it to the children, but she's actually quite upset."

My chest tightens. I don't like Jasper Hawkins, but I definitely don't wish him dead. And given the recent spate of accidents happening to people connected to Cregg and the Delphi Project . . .

"You haven't mentioned anything about Jaden's mother to Miranda, have you?"

There's a long silence on the other end before Kelsey responds. "No. I hadn't even made that connection until you mentioned it."

"Mrs. Park isn't the only one. A car swerved off the road to hit a friend of the Quinn family, someone who worked with Aaron's dad. Pretty much the same MO as the van that tried to sideswipe me and Deo."

"I'm not going to mention any of this to Miranda yet," Kelsey says. "It will just worry her."

"That's probably a good idea."

After we hang up, I sit on the steps, taking in the view. It's beautiful here—a vivid blue lake in the valley circled by evergreens. The entire scene is capped with a light dusting of snow that's supposed to melt away by afternoon, and according to the weather forecast, that's all the snow we'll see for the week. The big storm on the horizon will miss upstate New York almost entirely, dumping the bulk of the snow—a foot or more—farther to the south.

Of course, I know that's a total crock. We're going to get well over a foot of snow here, and I'm going to have to hike through it. We stocked up on winter gear yesterday at a department store just off the interstate. I'll admit I was tempted to skip that step since I know that we have those things in the vision. Since nothing can change, our winter clothes and backpacks would have to magically appear even if we didn't go shopping. Right?

But the first thing I saw on the rack when we walked in was a kid's padded jacket with BB-8 on the front and back—the same jacket I saw on Bree in the vision. Before that moment, it hadn't even occurred to me that the kids wouldn't have jackets. But if Cregg didn't let them aboveground at The Warren, I seriously doubt he's doing so at this new location. We bought a few dozen jackets, scarves, hats, and gloves in an array of sizes, along with two extralarge backpacks—one regular, and one for hiking with a toddler. Taylor also insisted on buying two yellow plastic sleds, which I suppose might come in handy even if I didn't see them in the vision. And then we spent three hours waiting for a technician to install a snowplow on the front of the truck.

Aaron had to put the snowplow on his Quinn Investigative credit card, because Magda insists it won't be necessary. Her security team is on standby at their offices in New York City. If Hunter contacts Bree, she'll give the team the green light to head to our location. Under no circumstances are we to move in without that security team. They will do the actual rescuing. We're in charge of reconnaissance only. Her team will have weapons and four-wheel-drive vehicles to transport the kids back to the airport, where her jet will be waiting to fly everyone to Sandalford.

She has reiterated this over and over. Kelsey, Sam, and even Aaron's mom joined in to reinforce the point about us not going in alone. And I know it makes sense. *Of course* it makes sense. But no matter what they say, no matter how much I may agree with them, there *was no security team* in my vision. It was only me and Aaron, leading the others out through the snow.

This is the closest campground we could find, but it's still nearly twenty miles from where they're keeping Bree. Deo and I—or to be more accurate, Deo and *Hunter*—spent the last few hours of the six-hour drive yesterday in the back room, trying to link with Bree. We had absolutely no luck, and by the time we got in last night, we were too tired to keep pushing.

The plan is to try again from here, and if it still doesn't work, we'll unhook the truck and drive closer to The Pit. And, as reluctant as I am to hand my body over to a six-year-old again, we might as well get started.

Taylor is rummaging around in her bag for clean clothes when I go back inside.

"Is Deo still asleep?"

"I wouldn't know," Taylor says archly. "Just because we're having sex doesn't mean we're *sleeping* together. Those bunks are too snug."

There's no response when I tap on the door, so I push it open. The ozone smell hits my nose instantly, stronger than it's been in weeks. It increased a bit as soon as we were back in the camper with less circulating air, and it was back full force yesterday, but I assumed it's just stronger when he's working as an amp.

Deo's on his side, huddled against the wall under two blankets. A bottle of Tylenol is open on the shelf next to him, along with a partly empty glass of water and the thermometer. I stare at the thermometer, unable to pick the damn thing up and check the history. It's been nearly *eight* weeks. Way beyond the three weeks when the other amp relapsed.

He has a cold. Or the flu.

"Something wrong?" Taylor asks from the main cabin.

When I don't respond, she pushes past me, resting the back of her hand against Deo's neck.

"No." She curses softly. "He was *fine* yesterday. Not sick at all."

Her voice breaks on the last word, jolting me out of my shock. I step inside and grab the thermometer from the shelf, but the humming noise hits me and I'm forced to move out of the room to read it. The display shows 104.2, taken three hours ago. I push the history button and see that reading is down slightly from 104.8, taken at around two thirty this morning.

"Damn it, D. Why didn't you wake someone up?"

I moisten a towel from the kitchen and bring it back to the bedroom, tossing it to Taylor. She presses it against his forehead, and he stirs, mumbling something I can't make out.

"It's the flu," Taylor says, her tone indicating that there will be no argument. "It's been *too long* for it to be a relapse. It's. The. Frickin'. Flu."

It's possible that I could sit out here in the cabin and Deo's ability would still boost Hunter's signal, but I don't know whether Deo using his amp ability weakens him. And it's not like this is something I can look up on WebMD. If there's any chance it might make him sicker, I'm not risking it.

"Listen, I'm going to wake Aaron up so he can drive me closer to the silo. Call me if there's any change, okay?"

Taylor nods, pulling another blanket from the closet, and crawls into the too-snug bunk next to him.

"Is that a good idea? I mean, if it's the flu—"

"It *is* the flu, which means I've already been exposed. In fact, I'm starting to feel like crap. Close the door behind you."

Near Lyon Mountain, New York
December 19, 2019, 2:24 p.m.

The sky is crystal clear, with just a few wispy clouds. Despite my worries about Deo and about our upcoming jailbreak, it's nice to be in the fresh air. It's cold, though, and I'm glad for the thick jacket and gloves.

Aaron is behind me. He reaches around and puts the binoculars to my face, turning me slightly to the right. "That's it. The one with the wraparound porch. The other houses appear empty."

"I see it." The house is downhill, maybe 150 yards away. From here, it looks like a perfectly ordinary house. You'd never guess it was hiding a missile silo. A passenger van is parked on the far side, and beyond the house is an open hangar that wasn't on the satellite map. Inside the hangar is a small helicopter, like the ones you used to see reporting on traffic until most cities turned that task over to drones.

"Do you think this is close enough?" Aaron asks.

"Hunter thinks it should be. He once contacted Bree from school when she was home sick. That was nearly a mile away."

Of course, neither their elementary school nor their house was encased in six feet of steel and concrete. We have no idea how that might interfere with their mental telephone. But there's only one way to find out.

Aaron and I park ourselves on a blanket beneath a large pine, and I brace myself to change places with Hunter. I'm more nervous about it than I was last time, mostly because it means letting my walls down. I think the odds of Dacia being in that house are pretty slim, given that she was in Texas thirty-six hours ago, playacting with her fellow bear terrorists. But Dacia wasn't the only one at The Warren who could read minds—Jaden says she wasn't even the best of the bunch. I think we have to assume that the boy called Snoop Dogg is among the kids at this place, although I'm not convinced he's entirely against us. But that's the real problem—I don't know *who* is on our side here.

You taking me with you this time?

Startled, it takes me a moment to place the voice. I've only heard her speak once before, in the cafeteria at The Warren.

Maria?

Yes, it's Maria. If you take me with you, then I'm on your side. But you already know this because you saw me in . . . Oh, wow! That's Jaden in there with you! We miss you, Jaden! You got one of the Fudds too, don't you? The cute one. How many people you got in that head of yours?

Too many.

Apparently, we've been planning this all wrong. I thought we'd have to transmit a message, but Maria is like one of those robot spiders on the internet, crawling through my head and snagging information. It's not pleasant, but her intrusion carries no malevolence like Dacia's did. Just rampant curiosity.

Including curiosity about things that are very *personal* and absolutely *none of her business.*

She takes the hint.

This Aaron is cute. Not as cute as the Fudd in your head, though. Me and Pavla had the biggest crush on that one, I tell you. But we can talk sex stuff later. What do you need?

I have no intention of talking sex stuff with her, so I decide it might be a good idea to lay down the ground rules.

Aaron is with me, Maria. No peeks inside his head or at his tush. You got it?

It's joke, okay? Anyway, the *zadek* game is no fun since they took Pavla.

Pavla? Who took her? She was your friend—the one who scribbled the note on my mirror, right?

Only half of us made it here after The Warren burned. But she got out. I hear this from the guards. She is with the other group.

The group that Dacia is with?

Ha. Daciana Badea is not with any group. She does her own thing.

I am tempted to dive down the rabbit hole and ask her everything she knows about this other group and Dacia. But I need to stay focused, something that isn't easy with Maria.

How many guards are inside The Pit—the silo house?

Ooh. The Pit. I like this. Good name. There are six right now, not counting Snoop. He has uniform, but is not really Fudd. Two are the . . . *medici* . . . the nurse guards. Like Ashley. But day after tomorrow, there are only four. The *zloduch*—the crazy man—will go to hospital in Albany for his checkup.

Um . . . do you mean Cregg?

Yes. The creepy man with fingers in a box. One nurse and one guard—well, two if you count Snoop, but I don't—will go with him. So then there are only four here, counting Ashley.

Cregg needs to go to the hospital because of the burns?

No. For the cancer. Although the burns heal slower because he was taking the chemo.

Cancer. Okay, that explains things like the weight fluctuation—he was thin when I last saw him in person but heavier in some of the photographs online. It also explains the Senator's vague reference to his son's ongoing health problems.

How often does he leave to get treatments?

This is the first time since we left The Warren. And it's not clear . . . I am thinking maybe no chemo? Maybe just checkup to see if he needs more chemo later. I would know more, but I don't go inside the *zloduch*'s head. One minute he is fine and normal. And then his mind turns to a snake nest, and you are seeing pinky fingers in a box. So gross. But I know the schedule for tomorrow from the Fudds.

So . . . that will leave four guards overnight?

Yes. One stays up in the house most of the time because down here he gets the clusterphobia, although he doesn't tell the other Fudds that. Another is Ashley. She is always on bottom floor where they keep Caleb—

you remember him, the boy who told you to run at The
Warren? And the other two Fudds, Kokot and Hlupák,
float between the floors. Kokot is usually at the monitor
so he can watch everything. Well, except me. I sent him
a little message about watching me.

The memory of Jaden calling her a Peeping Tomasina runs through
my mind, even though I try to stop it. But she laughs.

I can't help what I see. It's like locker room or painting in
the gallery. This one, though, he has nasty thoughts, like
Lucas. We were glad that you and the dead girls killed
Lucas. Why do you call them Furies?

Maria's stream-of-consciousness style of speaking is making me a
little crazy, although I guess it could be my own stream-of-consciousness running through her head?

Sorry. This happens because . . . too much info. Hard
to stay on the topic when new thoughts come in, you
know? Maybe we kill Kokot and Hlupák too, like the Furies did with Lucas?

No. Our goal is to get out of here without killing anyone.

You have misplaced sense of justice. These are not good
Fudds. Well, except Ashley. She has to act bad sometimes, though. Otherwise they kick her out, and she has
reasons to stay. But the rest are bad.

If it makes you feel any better, I doubt that the security people Magda is sending in are going to be worried about keeping things nonviolent.

Pfft. Her security men, they won't get here in time. The snow will stop them. You already know that. I see it in your head.

Okay. Fine. Can you give me a tally of how many people are being held inside? And how many of them will leave with us without a fight?

All of us will go. Every one.

Her absolute certainty worries me a little. I mean, it's nice that we won't have to evade any of the adepts, but Maria seems so certain that leaving with us is an unadulterated *good*, and I'm far from convinced that Sandalford will be a permanent safe haven. I don't want Maria or any of them to be under the illusion that this move will signal the end of their problems.

This new place we're taking you isn't perfect. There are guards, and—

This place is *peklo na zemi*. A hell pit in the ground. I think even Snoop would go, but he will not be here to decide. The *zloduch* keeps Snoop on short chain in case he picks up some bit of info on his little radio.

It takes me a moment to realize she means his mind reading. Her tone is dismissive. I'm not sure whether it's because she doesn't think this Snoop Dogg's gift is useful or because the kid is colluding with Cregg, and she doesn't pause long enough for me to ask.

> All of us will trade this hole for your not-perfect place. I see the picture in your mind, you know. It has sunlight. And Jaden isn't only one who sees things from the future—we have our own Fiver in here. There *will* be more of us soon, and we will gather at that sunny place in your head. We will be strong and ready to fight the bears when the time comes.

There are entire pockets of that speech that I don't understand, but Maria seems to be getting annoyed with me, so I don't push for clarification. I really don't want to piss off the girl who will be, for all intents and purposes, command central of this entire mission.

> I'm not pissed off. But we have been waiting for you to show up, almost from time we arrived here. We have been planning this escape on our own. So yes, if you want, I will tell the others about your . . . concerns. But I *know* that we will all go with you.

Okay. I believe you. How many total?

There's a long pause. I can almost hear her tallying up on her fingers.

> Fourteen of us, and Ashley.

What ages? How many little ones? And what can they do? Are there any that are especially . . . volatile? I mean, other than Caleb?

Caleb is youngest and the most trouble. Not
Too little. Too strong. Ashley will sedate hi
Peepers, but none as good as me, and none who can
also send. They only see. Two seekers . . . people who
find stuff. Two movers. One is strong, *really* strong. The
other is . . . meh. One person like your sexy Fudd and
the *zloduch* who can push minds, but this one can only
do a little. One Zippo, but he can control it. Also we have
two Fivers—seers, I guess you'd call them. Like Jaden.
And one blocker, she's only eight—

What do you mean, a blocker?

A signal blocker. Like you do sometimes, except she is
always blocking. Can turn it off for a few moments, but
not long. And then Bree. She is next youngest to Caleb,
but you know what she does.

Hunter perks up at his sister's name. He's ready for us to stop talking so that he can finally speak to her. But Maria puts the brakes on.

No, no, no. That is a very bad idea. You will not be able
to hide that you are . . . passed on. Your sister will see
it in your head. And maybe then she wouldn't fight so
hard to get out of here to safety. You don't want that, do
you? You can't be alive, but you want *her* to stay alive,
no? You will talk to her soon, once she is safe and warm
and we have a chance to let her know what's happened
to you.

Hunter doesn't respond to Maria but simply slides to the back, trying to fend off a fresh wave of grief. Logically, Hunter has known that

he's dead for some time. But a little part of him has been clinging to the irrational hope that if he could just find Bree, everything would change. That it would be a magical reset button, and they'd both go back home to their mom and brother and *everything would be okay.*

Maria's words were the pin that burst his fantasy bubble. If we're lucky enough to rescue Bree, he'll be able to tell her good-bye and know that she's safe, but that's the extent of Hunter's happy ending. And without her brother, Bree's happy ending will be bittersweet, at best.

❖ ❖ ❖

Lyon Mountain, New York
December 21, 2019, 4:15 p.m.

I dump two cans of chicken noodle soup into a pot at Taylor's request. She still insists that she and Deo both have the flu. On the few occasions that Deo has been awake long enough to talk coherently during the past two days, he's also said it's the flu.

Or maybe it's strep. Or tonsillitis. Definitely not a relapse. Taylor took a photo of his throat, and yes, it does look red.

I'd be more convinced if not for the fact that the air in the room feels . . . charged, so full of that ozone smell that Aaron and I can't even get close. It doesn't appear to affect Taylor—in fact, she says that Deo gets that ozone smell any time he sweats. Since I don't want to follow *that* line of inquiry any further, I drop it. I have no idea how this works, so yeah, I suppose simply running a fever could be increasing the ozone odor instead of being a sign that he's relapsed.

I'd also be more convinced if I thought Taylor was actually sick. Despite dosing both herself and Deo with NyQuil and refusing to eat anything other than soup, she looks healthy. But I can't fault her. She seems determined to create a reality where they are both sick with the flu by the sheer force of her will.

She promised to watch Deo's temperature carefully. If his fever tops 105, we're getting him to a hospital, regardless of what is causing the spike.

Magda's security team was due to arrive at the airport in Plattsburgh an hour ago. That would have put them here by five o'clock at the latest, at which point we were supposed to go over the logistics for tonight's operation with them. But their flight still hasn't left JFK.

As late as last night, the local weather service continued to insist that this storm would veer south. I think it did—but it's a much larger system than they'd predicted. They've gotten six inches in New York City, and while both airports are still open, there are significant delays. Flurries began here around two p.m., when we had our last chat with Magda before she left for the airport in London. They're reporting three inches on the ground at Plattsburgh, and it's coming down steadily, so I'm doubtful that Magda's plane will be able to land. That means we're going to have a whole bunch of adepts crammed into this RV by eleven p.m. tonight. And it's entirely possible that the RV, like the planes, will also be snowbound.

Aaron comes up behind me and massages my shoulders. "We need to get into place. You know, just in case they don't make it on time."

I laugh at the sarcasm oozing from his last line. Magda may doubt the accuracy of my flash-forwards, but the rest of us know better.

Still, I have to say it.

"We could postpone. Tell Maria to hold off. Wait until the security team arrives. Even if it means dealing with two extra guards."

"Except it also means Graham Cregg," Aaron reminds me. "What if he forces Magda's security team to turn their guns on *us*? And even if that Snoop kid isn't sharing critical information—and I have to admit I'm not entirely convinced on that point—he could be a liability, too."

"I know, but maybe we could . . ."

There's no point in finishing the statement, so I don't. We're going in tonight, without Magda's team. After all, I've already seen it happen.

Forty minutes later, we back the RV into the long unpaved drive we scouted out when we were here day before yesterday. It stretches for over half a mile through the woods, and will cut about a half mile off the distance we have to hike through the snow. Driving a camper in reverse, even in a straight line, is not an easy task, however. It takes Aaron nearly fifteen minutes to back the trailer to the very end.

We toyed with the idea of just parking on the main road, but someone might be concerned enough to phone the police if they see seventeen people, mostly kids, stumbling out of the woods and into an RV. This gets us as close to the house as possible, without driving straight to it, and it seems like the safest option overall.

Aaron and I spent several hours in the woods near here yesterday, working out a plan with Maria, Ashley, and the others, using Maria as our go-between. I wanted to challenge Ashley, to ask why she followed Cregg's orders and pulled Daniel's life support. Daniel was adamant that this wasn't the time or the place. Personally, I wanted a little more assurance that Ashley is on our side, that she's not planning to rat us out to Cregg, before we included her in the plan, but Daniel's right—I saw Ashley walking out with us. If she turns traitor, it will be after we escape.

Of course, *after the escape* is exactly when she turned traitor last time.

The plan we worked out with Maria isn't complicated. Our optimal window to act is between ten and ten thirty at night. Ten is lockdown for the adepts. Once everything is quiet, the second-floor guard, who Maria calls Kokot, usually goes down to chat with Ashley. This job has cost him his girlfriend, and he seems to think Ashley should be her replacement. Ashley disagrees. She has happily agreed to deal with Kokot, leaving the other two guards to us.

The second guard, Hlupák, usually takes a bathroom break between ten and ten fifteen before he scans the monitors to make sure that the adepts are actually in their beds. Once he's in the toilet, Bree will put out the power, disabling the lights and the monitoring system. That will momentarily disorient both the guards and the adepts, but the adepts will know it's coming.

This is the one part that worries Hunter. Bree is terrified of the dark, and she'll be alone in a pitch-dark room, without even a night-light, until Ashley unlocks her door. But Bree assured Maria that she can do it. That she *will* do it.

The first blackout won't last long—a backup generator located behind the house will kick in quickly. From what we've read in the online manual, there's a timer and then an engine crank cycle, giving us maybe a minute and a half to reach the generator and disable it. The manual suggests that we should be able to simply cut it off, but I'm guessing something goes wrong there, and that's when we'll have to use Hunter's ability. I remember my right hand throbbing in the vision. It wasn't debilitating, but it wasn't fun, either. My only question is why I would use my dominant hand, instead of my left, for something where either hand would do.

Maria insists that everything will run like clockwork on her end. She knows the guards. She knows the adepts. She knows their patterns of behavior, how they think and react. And she can send us whatever intel she picks up.

The problem is that she can only monitor one mind at a time, two, if she really pushes it. That means she'll have to skip around rapid fire as she monitors the guards, Ashley, and the adepts. Plus, she'll be "off-line" briefly whenever she's relaying information to us. So, while having Maria as our eyes and ears inside The Pit is an incredible advantage, it's not foolproof.

I reheat some of the soup, which is long since cold. Aaron and I manage to get down a few bites, but we're both too nervous to really eat. Magda calls as we're clearing the dishes away. She is still a few hours out, but her security team has landed in Plattsburgh, where they are currently waiting on the two four-by-four passenger vans she reserved.

They expect to reach the campground by nine thirty. Nine forty-five at the latest.

"We're already in place," Aaron says. "I'll send you a location pin."

There's a long silence, and then she says, "You are not to enter that property prior to the security team's arrival, even if they are delayed. There's absolutely no reason we cannot wait until midnight or whenever the team arrives to do this. I'll let you know when my plane lands."

He gives her a quick, "Yes, ma'am," and shoves the phone back into his pocket.

"So," he says, "what's your guess? Road closure between here and Plattsburgh? Or maybe the company won't rent vehicles in this weather?"

"I'm guessing road closure. The other one is a problem that Magda could make go away by throwing money at it."

We wake Taylor, who does look kind of ill at this point, to let her know we're leaving. Deo doesn't budge. His fever seems to be holding steady around 103, sometimes spiking a bit higher when the Tylenol starts to wear off, so while I'm worried, I've stepped down a notch from frantic to mild panic.

When Taylor joins us in the main cabin, Aaron says, "Okay, I'm rerouting my calls to your number. So you're now Magda's point person. If her security people ever show up, give them our GPS coordinates from your phone. And . . . remember. Drive the trailer back and forth, at least halfway down the path, every half hour, to keep it clear of snow. It would be better if you can go all the way to the end."

She glares at him. "Don't push your luck. And don't blame me if you come back and find the damn RV tipped over."

Aaron spent several hours this morning showing Taylor how to use the snowplow and drive the RV in reverse. She's going to have to keep the path at least partially clear, otherwise we might not be able to move the trailer at all, even with the snowplow.

We're about to head out the door when Taylor calls us back. She gives Aaron a tight hug. *"Be careful."*

I'm surprised when she pulls me into a hug as well. "You, too. And not just because you're carrying my other brother."

"Lovely," Aaron says. "You make it sound like she's pregnant."

My legs sink to midcalf in the snow when we step outside. The hike to the ridge overlooking The Pit took a little over five minutes last time, but it takes us nearly three times as long tonight. It's not just the snow, which is coming down in big, fat flakes. This time we're also dragging Taylor's sleds with our backpacks stuffed with winter jackets, weapons, and assorted gear.

We finally reach the tree line at nine fifteen, and Aaron pulls the binoculars out. As soon as he raises them to his eyes, he curses and lowers them again.

"What's wrong?"

"The van is still there."

"Okay, so . . . maybe his appointment was canceled?"

Aaron scans downhill again. "Nope. It wasn't canceled. They just decided not to drive."

He hands me the binoculars. Sure enough, the van is still there. The helicopter, however, is missing.

"It won't matter, though. Right? They can't fly in the snow."

"Not *when* it's snowing, or at least not when it's snowing heavily." He glances up at the clouds. A snowflake catches on his eyelash, and he brushes it away. "But you said the sky was almost clear in the vision. They can definitely *land* on snow, and it would only take, what? An hour and a half to fly back from Albany. If that."

I sigh. "Well, Magda was wrong. It looks like there *is* a reason we can't wait until midnight."

CHAPTER TWENTY-TWO

Lyon Mountain, New York
December 21, 2019, 9:37 p.m.

Aaron takes a seat on his sled. I join him for a few minutes, and we wait for Maria to contact us. But it's not even ten minutes before I'm up again, pacing. I need something to do. We've already packed our jacket pockets with wrist restraints, pepper spray, duct tape, hydrogel burn pads, and a roll of gauze. All that's left is waiting.

I hate waiting.

It's partly my own nerves. But it's also Hunter's nerves. And Daniel's. Daniel has kept a fairly low profile for the past few days, storing up his energy, and now he's a bit more like the caged-tiger version that paced around my head just after I picked him up. Even Jaden seems on edge, but it's not the same as the other two. He's more . . . disinterested. As though he's watching a movie.

Hey, I'm *interested*. Like I said before, I need to see how this part ends. Be nice to see Maria and the rest of them get out of there.

But . . . after that?

I'm thinkin' maybe after that I need to catch up with my mom. I can take it on faith that you guys will eventually make those bastards pay for all this.

"You okay?" Aaron asks.

"Yeah. It's not Maria yet. Just chatter inside my head. And nerves. I'm not cut out for this spy stuff."

Aaron smiles. "Relax. I'm not picking up any vibes. I think these guards might just be in it for the paycheck."

"Or maybe that's only the one on the top floor." I sit down next to him, huddling closer for warmth. "You said you had a tough time reading what was going on in The Warren. And I doubt it was anywhere near as heavily reinforced as a missile silo."

"True . . . although I think you're borrowing trouble."

I smile at that, wondering if he'd be pleased or dismayed that he's just reminded me of an octogenarian former hitcher.

He looks up. "The snow seems to be tapering off, surprise, surprise."

He's right. The occasional clump still falls from the trees above us, but it's intermittent.

I sit back and close my eyes, trying to conserve my energy. Then Aaron jumps up so suddenly that he nearly knocks me off the sled.

"What? Are you getting something?"

"What the . . . ?" He looks over both shoulders and then relaxes a bit, although his expression is still annoyed. "*Maria*. A little warning would be nice."

She's still laughing when I pick up her voice in my head. It seems a little quieter than last time.

> Just telling him hello, Anna. Not peeking at his thoughts. Well, not *much*. I see you find the helicopter is gone. Those two Fudds were not happy. They wanted their day away from the crazy kids. But no. Change of plans.

Cregg's not staying away overnight?

> No. The guy who likes to stay on the top floor, Bazlivetz, he just got a call that they're leaving Albany in about twenty, maybe thirty, minutes. The flight is a little over an hour. I will let you know when Ashley has taken care of Kokot. And give you countdown for blackout and diversion.

What diversion?

But I'm talking to air, because Maria is gone. I begin relaying what she said to Aaron, but he stops me.

"I caught a lot of it. Not your answers, but what Maria said. I guess that's why she gave me that blast at the beginning. Conferencing me into the call." He shakes his head. "So, did Cregg hire a bunch of European guards? The names are kind of unusual."

Daniel laughs.

> Those have got to be nicknames. I don't know what the first one means, but I heard *kokot* a lot at The Warren. Even had it yelled at me once or twice. Pretty sure it's slang for a part of the male anatomy.

Aaron chuckles when I explain it to him, but then his face turns serious. "That . . . that thing with Maria. It would take a lot of getting used to. Someone who can hear your thoughts. Transmit her thoughts back. How can you . . . I mean, that's pretty much the end of privacy."

We sit there in silence for a moment, letting that one sink in. Because he's right. Jaden seems to think Maria is benign enough, and I get that sense as well. But what about someone who can do this who has bad intentions? We already have a pretty good idea what that feels like, constantly wondering which of our thoughts are being handed over to Graham Cregg. So, even though the angry, pearl-clutching moms currently storming the statehouses tick me off, I have to admit that they've got reason to be concerned.

> Stop it. You can't think about the bigger picture right now. We need to focus on getting those kids out. Get me the binoculars, okay?

Oh, great. Emperor Daniel is back.

I'm only half annoyed, however. It's actually something of a relief to have him engaged again.

What are we looking for?

Cameras.

Okay, but we're taking out the power, so . . .

The camera could be battery operated.

Yes, but the computers would be—

You ever seen those backup battery systems people use at home? Even if you take down the power and the generator, they keep ticking.

That's the kind of thing that might have been useful to share when we were planning all of this . . .

Didn't think of it earlier. Look near the corners of the porch, just below the floodlights.

On each of the three visible corners there's a small box just under the lights. I hone in on the corner facing us and see what appears to be a lens with a blinking light just below.

"They've got cameras," I tell Aaron. "Cameras that may be battery operated. And Daniel just pointed out that the monitors may have a backup battery separate from the generator."

"Damn. He's right. Why didn't I think of that?" He begins digging in the other backpack and pulls out a pistol. It's not his usual gun—I'm pretty sure that one is in his shoulder holster—but rather one that we grabbed from Vigilance. A silencer is attached to the barrel. Another few seconds of rummaging around, and then he pulls out a small scope.

"We'll have to take the cameras out first. Or at least the ones facing our way."

"Do you have another gun?"

He raises his eyebrows. "Yes. I grabbed three from their gun locker. But I thought you said back at Overhills that you don't know how to use one?"

"I'm not asking for me."

Aaron takes a deep breath. "Okay. But I only have one scope."

I listen to Daniel for a second and then chuckle softly.

"What?" Aaron asks.

"You won't like it."

Aaron just stares at me, holding the gun back until I answer.

"Daniel says *you* might need a scope, but he doesn't."

He rolls his eyes and pulls out a second pistol, identical to the first except for the missing scope.

"Is the safety on?"

"*Of course* the safety is on."

I still don't like the way it feels. Cold, even through the leather gloves I'm wearing. Heavy. Ominous. I leave it on the sled next to me while we wait for Maria.

When we hear her voice again, she sounds frantic.

> Wait. Do not go yet. The guy on top floor. They called him to say he should clear a path from the landing spot for the *zloduch* so he don't have to walk in the snow. Is putting coat on now. Watch for him!

"Clearing that path is going to take a while," Aaron says. "If we time it right, maybe it will work in our favor. Once we take out the cameras, I'll go around the back of the house and take him out, too. In a nonlethal fashion, if at all possible. I've already got one kill on my conscience. I don't want another."

"Okay. But . . . if it's him or you—"

"Then it will be him," Aaron says, digging around in his backpack again until he locates a couple of small plastic bags. He tosses me one. Inside is an all-too-familiar-looking portable anesthesia mask. I shudder, having been on the receiving end of one of these. It wasn't exactly unpleasant aside from the first jolt when Dacia smashed it into my face—just a faint vanilla scent, and then I was out. But I had a vicious headache and felt like barfing when I woke up.

"This will only buy us fifteen or twenty minutes, depending on how big a guy he is."

"You sure? I was out for a lot longer when Dacia . . ."

"They must have injected you with a stronger drug once you were knocked out. We have something like that too, but I'd rather avoid it if we can. This way he might get back inside before hypothermia sets in."

I stash the mask in my pocket. A few moments later, the guard comes through the door onto the porch—a short, stocky guy in a jacket, scarf, and one of those hats with earflaps. He stomps around the corner, pulling on his gloves as he goes. Maybe thirty seconds later, he's back, pushing a snowblower in front of him. He lowers the machine to the ground and then hops off the porch. It cranks on the first try. The guard clears the area around the steps and then turns away from us, inching the snowblower toward the floodlights on the hangar, maybe forty yards away.

"He's going to realize something is up when those floodlights go out," I say.

"Yeah, but if we go too soon, we run the risk of alerting them before the others are in position." Aaron shakes his head. "When Maria gives us the countdown, we go. It won't give us long, but it's better than nothing."

"Agreed. I'm . . . I'm going to go ahead and switch places with Daniel. Just so you know."

"Wait." He pulls me in for a quick kiss and then looks into my eyes. "We'll rendezvous inside on the first floor. *Be careful.*"

"You, too."

He straps the empty kid carrier to his back and shoves my pack behind the tree. As much as I'd love to have the kids' jackets down there, I'll be lucky to get myself to the house undetected without the bag, which is stuffed like Santa's sack. It's not *that* far from the house to the tree line. Hopefully they can survive a few minutes of arctic blast until we can reach our gear.

As I shift places with Daniel, Maria's voice fills my head.

One minute. Be ready!

Aaron grabs the gun on my sled, swapping it out so that I—or rather, so that *Daniel*—now has the one with the scope. Then he grins and pushes off, hurtling down the hill on his sled.

Daniel mutters a curse, then scoops the pistol up, belly flops onto my sled, and careens down the slope. We pass Aaron just as he spins his sled sideways to stop, crouches down into a drift of snow, and takes aim at the closest camera. There's a *pfft* sound and then a ping as half of the camera flies out into the snow.

As my sled slows, Daniel pivots around so that my arms point at the camera to the right. It barely even registers that my hands are holding the gun, especially with the gloves and the unfamiliar fur-lined sleeves of the parka in my line of sight. It's more like the first-person shooter game I played with Deo a couple of times until we both decided we'd be happier if he played it with someone else.

This camera doesn't fly off like the first one but remains partially connected to the wall. It is, however, now pointing straight down at the porch. As soon as the gun fires, however, I'm tossed off my sled into the snow. Daniel's long string of curses runs through my head, most of them aimed at my "weak-ass" arms, which couldn't take the recoil as well as his manly ones. Because it couldn't *possibly* have been that he just doesn't know how to control this body.

Aaron quickly takes out the third camera. The guard continues moving forward, snow shooting out in arcs, left and right, in front of him—oblivious, thanks to the silencers and the noise from the snowblower.

We're still a good ten yards from the generator. Daniel takes two steps through the snow, frustrated that the legs currently at his disposal belong to a body that is nearly a foot shorter than the one he's used to operating. He's clearly planning to remain in charge, but I tug him back. And the fact that I *can* tug him back so easily tells me that his claims that he's doing just fine are seriously overstated.

I've been operating this body for eighteen years, and right now, we can't afford clumsy. I can do this part. Save your strength until we need you to do something I can't.

Okay. Just . . . put the safety on the gun. No . . . there. *That's* the safety.

Once I figure it out, I shove the gun inside my jacket sleeve, handle first, and snap the closure at the wrist. It's clunky, but at least I have my hands free and it will be easy . . . or, at least, easy*ish* . . . to grab the gun if Daniel needs it again. Then I climb back onto the sled and begin pulling myself across the snow toward the generator with something equivalent to a butterfly stroke. The ground is fairly level, but I'm still able to move at a faster pace than slogging through knee-high drifts.

As I reach the generator, I hear Maria.

Go, go . . . Oh. You *already* go. Okay.

And then the lights cut out.

I wish I could see Aaron, to tell whether he made it to the snow-blowing guard before the power outage alerted him. But he's now beyond my line of sight. I try not to worry, reminding myself that he should have at least a split second of warning courtesy of his spidey sense . . .

Damn it, Anna. Find the switch!

The generator begins to crank up at the same moment that Daniel yells at me. From what we read online, that means I've got about ninety seconds. Assuming this is the model we thought it was. I feel around the back, hoping to find the off switch, trying to keep count in my head so that I'll know when I have to resort to letting Hunter step forward and singe my hand.

My fingers locate the hatch to the power box—it's closer to the top than I'd thought. I pry it open and flip the switch. The noise continues for a few seconds and then sputters to a stop.

That's when I hear the beeping. It's faint at first. I inch my way along the outside wall of the house toward the bushes lining the porch. Just as I reach the corner, a screen door swings open and bangs against the wall. The beeping is louder through the open door—then I hear a woman's voice saying, "Fire. Fire."

"Weeks?" Footsteps echo across the porch, and then the man bellows a second time, straining to be heard over the snowblower. His voice sounds familiar, but I can't place it. "Weeks! Cut that damn thing off and get in here! We got a situation on Level 3."

The snowblower falls silent as the door slams shut.

Where the hell is Aaron? I peer through the bushes, but all I can see in the dark is the man behind the snowblower, moving this way, with something slung across his back.

The alarm continues. *Fire, Fire. Beeeep, beeeep, beeeep.*

It's not until the man reaches the edge of the porch that I realize it's not the guard. It's Aaron, in the guard's hat and jacket. He slips his arms out of the kid carrier, props it against the bushes, and then mounts the steps to the porch.

"Anna?" he whispers as I pull myself up onto the porch. "Or Daniel?"

"It's Anna," I answer. "For now. Where's the guard?"

"On the other side of the snowblower. Threw the sled and my jacket over him."

We enter the house and begin moving toward the sound of the alarm, but we're only a few feet inside when the alarm halts abruptly midbeep. The fact that the alarm has stopped and that everyone is still downstairs has me very worried.

As we continue into the house, I realize exactly how much light was reflecting off the snow. I pull on the night-vision goggles. Aaron does the same and then nods toward an opening at the back of the room.

Finally, we reach the door and see stairs that circle downward. Aaron reaches into his pocket, pulls out one of the chemical lights, and snaps it in two.

That seems like a mistake.

The man calls from below. "Weeks! Get your ass down to Three. Little freak set his bed on fire again."

I place the voice when he says *freak*. That's what he called us back at The Warren, too, and while it's not exactly an original label for Delphi adepts, Timmons says it with an extra sneer in his voice.

A pale-yellow glow comes into view as we move downward. I lower the goggles. Aaron stops so abruptly that I smash my nose against his back. At first, I think he's just noticed the light, too, but his body goes rigid. He's picked up a vibe.

And then I hear Maria.

We are out of our rooms, but trapped on Level 3. Door locks from outside. Hlupák saw the body you left in snow.

How? We shot out the cameras, except for the one at the back.

Is camera at hangar, also. Hlupák is holding two kids—Bree and Maggie—on Level 2. Not Level 3, like he says. That is trick.

His name isn't Hlupák, is it? It's Timmons.

Yes. But Hlupák fits much better. Listen to me. Maggie is the blocker I tell you about before. I can't read Hlupák now. Or Bree. They are like brick wall. And I can't talk to Maggie either until her shield is down.

But she knows we're trying to break all of you out. And she approves?

Oh, hell yes. Maggie would bite him if he wasn't holding that taser. I told her to release the block when she sees you or when you put those lights out. You'll have four, maybe five, seconds.

Timmons only has a taser?

What? No! He has a gun, and he can shoot your friend. Just can't use it on a kid. Or on you, for that matter. Cregg told him that when you were at The Warren. That man has plans, and you're part of them.

Yeah. I pieced that much together. He seems to think that if he can pack me up with enough skills, I can be his personal psychic Swiss Army knife.

Maybe . . .

I nudge Aaron with my elbow and tap my ear. He nods. I really, really hope that he heard what Maria said, because even a whisper will likely echo in this place. Every footstep I take sounds like it's made by a full-grown elephant.

We halt a few stairs above the second level. The light seems too diffused to be handheld. Since Timmons was able to see the feed from the hangar, Daniel's prediction about the backup battery appears to be correct.

As long as Timmons is holding the girls, our window to act is really narrow.

Hunter moves forward tentatively.

> Doesn't matter if it's on a battery. If you touch any part of the circuit, I can put the light out. It's probably gonna burn you, though, like before.

> *Um. It will burn you, too. You're going to feel it.*

> Not for long. I'll be back here in your head, and you'll be stuck with it.

> *It's okay. We'll do what we have to, right?*

"Weeks!"

I squeeze Aaron's hand as tight as I can and push past him, trying to signal with my eyes that he should stay put.

"No," he mouths.

Daniel echoes that sentiment.

> What the hell are you doing?

> *Winging it. Be ready, both you and Hunter. Hell, Jaden, too—I might need his tae kwon do again.*

> At least get the gun out.

> *No. Aaron will handle the gun. Timmons needs to think I have something even more powerful.*

I turn back to Aaron, tapping first myself on the chest and then him. I motion forward with both hands simultaneously. *We go in together.* Then, one finger up. *But wait for it . . .*

These are almost certainly not the standard hand signals for any sort of covert operation, but Aaron seems to get it.

I take a steadying breath and then call out, "You know this isn't Weeks, Timmons. Let's cut the pretense. There's a way for you and the other guards to get out of this alive, but only if you listen to me."

"Who the hell are you?" he yells back.

"The name is Anna. We met at The Warren. I'm surprised you managed to escape after I set your boss on fire. Too bad about your buddy Lucas." I snort. "Nah. We both know I don't mean that."

He calls me a few unflattering names. Then he asks if I'm alone.

"You know I'm not alone, Timmy. You saw the video feed. And please watch the language in front of the kids."

We move down one more step. "Remember how I picked up Jaden Park and his visions after Lucas shot him? And remember all those *other* people who were killed in Lab 1 before him—Will, Oksana, and the others? I sucked them up like a vacuum cleaner, exactly the way your boss thought I would. They're all here with me, too. They don't like you much. And I also picked up a girl named Sonia. She's what they call an amp."

Timmons has no way of knowing how much of that is true. For all he knows, I could be carrying around an entire psychic arsenal.

"Sonia has come in really handy. She helps me focus my powers. Which means I don't have to set this whole place on fire. I could just start a tiny fire at the base of your brain. Or your optic nerve."

"Not scared of the voodoo crap, freak."

"Oh, I know. You think you're protected. Such a brave man hiding in there behind little girls. But here's the thing—I'm pretty sure my *amp* is more powerful than your *suppressor*."

Another step down to the bottom stair. I press my back against the cold concrete of the circular wall and glance up at Aaron, a question in my eyes. He nods. *Ready.*

Daniel. Once we see them, you're on.

I hold up one finger, two, three, and then Aaron and I pivot around the corner.

And . . . nothing. This is the second floor. There's even a big *2* on the wall across from us. But the room we've stepped into is a ring around the wide column that encloses the stairwell. And Timmons isn't waiting at the opening.

Um. Anna?

What, Maria? It's not a good time unless you can tell me where Timmons is and what he's thinking?

No. Still blocked. It's just . . . fire's out, but we still have smoke. Ashley has kids on the floor to breathe better, but . . .

Got it. We'll hurry.

Aaron motions with his head, and we work our way to the right, our backs against the center column. We stop when we spot shadows, hyperelongated so that I can't get much info from them. And, unfortunately, we're running out of blank wall to press against. There's an obstruction—a metal table with a bank of computer monitors—directly ahead.

Fortunately, the table also marks the beginning of the strip of lights that illuminates that side of the room. The strip runs parallel to the floor around the column. I pull Aaron back and signal for him to put on his night-vision goggles again. Then I take off my right glove, because if I turn to use my left hand, I'll briefly present more of a target. Timmons might not be *supposed* to shoot me, but it doesn't mean he won't, so I'll have to take the burn on my right hand rather than my left.

> *Okay, Hunter, you're up. And then Daniel, immediately after. Whatever you can do to incapacitate him.*

I slide back, wincing as my hand connects with the strip of lights. It's not as quick as destroying the lamp. The small lights pop rapidly one by one like a pack of firecrackers as Hunter struggles to keep my hand in place and not cry out. It's only a matter of seconds, but it feels much longer. Then there's a loud crackle as the battery itself is fried, and I feel myself slink down against the wall.

And then Hunter changes places with Daniel.

I'm not sure whether Daniel was planning to say something different, but the pain from my palm seems to have made the decision for him.

> Your hands are on fire!

I'm not even sure he says the words aloud, but the sound is so loud inside my head that I flinch. So does Hunter. Jaden, however, seems somewhat oblivious.

The only light now is the glow stick that Aaron pulls from his pocket and flings toward the opposite wall as Timmons begins to scream. Then the girls start screaming, too.

Daniel increases his volume, so loud it makes my head ring, even rattling Jaden this time.

> ON FIRE, TIMMONS. YOUR WHOLE BODY IS ON FIRE.

It must have the desired effect on Timmons, because the scream on the other side of the room rises to a shriek, coupled with scuttling noises and a sudden loud pop. Sparks briefly light up the dim room as the keening noise continues.

Daniel pulls my body to standing. He starts walking forward, but it's more of a stagger.

Get back, Daniel. I've got this.

He'd like to argue. I'm certain of that. But he doesn't have the energy. My body crumples to the ground before I can take the driver's seat, but then I'm up again, hurtling around the bend to see what has happened.

Timmons is on the ground clutching one hand, which is burned far worse than mine. A taser lies on the floor next to him, still smoking. Bree hunches against the wall, staring at Aaron, who is pointing his gun at Timmons.

He's not the only one, however. A girl of around eight, who must be Maggie the Blocker, has Timmons's gun in her hand. And the muzzle is pressed directly against the guard's temple.

CHAPTER
TWENTY-THREE

Near Lyon Mountain, New York
December 21, 2019, 10:33 p.m.

"I don't have to shoot him, do I?" The girl's voice is high, breathless, almost at the point of panic.

Timmons has now realized that he's burned but probably not about to spontaneously combust. He turns his eyes toward Maggie, and seems to be weighing his options.

"No," Aaron tells the girl. "Because if he so much as twitches a muscle, *I* will shoot him. Hold there for just a minute, though, okay? Can you do that?"

Maggie nods.

"Anna," Aaron says, "do you have the other mask?"

I pull the anesthesia mask he gave me earlier from my pocket and rip it open with my teeth to avoid using my singed hand. Which might be a little more than singed, judging from the pain, but I don't have time to think about it. A whiff of orange hits my nose.

Timmons is following Aaron's orders and hasn't moved. But he's clearly planning something.

"I can tell what you're thinking," Aaron says. "It won't work. Move a single muscle, and I *will* shoot you, *kokot*."

He's using the wrong one of Maria's decidedly unaffectionate nicknames, but it reminds me that Maria and the others are still breathing in smoke. We need to hurry.

Moving forward on my knees, I smack the mask against Timmons's face to break the seal. I probably smack it a little harder than strictly necessary, but this is the guy who tased Deo back at The Warren. Who covered for Lucas when he came to my room planning to assault me. His eyes widen in pain, and I realize I'm pressing so hard that the jerk might not be able to breathe in the gas. I pull back the tiniest bit and watch as Timmons's capacity for violent thought—for any thought, really—floats away on an orange-scented cloud.

"Give me the duct tape," Aaron says. I fish it out of my jacket pocket and toss it to him.

"Can you take us to the door to Level 3?" I ask the girls as Aaron hastily wraps Timmons's wrists and ankles.

Maggie gives Aaron the gun and reaches for Bree's hand to pull her to standing. I follow them back in the direction we came.

"You were very brave," I tell Maggie.

"Bree, too," she says. "She's the one who blew up his taser."

A few steps beyond the opening to the stairwell that goes to the surface is a second metal door set into the concrete pillar. Aaron has caught up with us by then, and he shoves down on the long red handle, which groans and then clicks open. As he tugs backward on the heavy door, smoke billows out into our level.

"Stay here," I tell the girls and then call out, "Maria? Ashley?"

Aaron pulls his scarf over his face and heads down the stairs. I follow, going against the surging tide of teens half carrying younger ones up to the next level. I lean against the wall, cradling my burned hand against me, to let them pass. Everyone is coughing and wiping their eyes, and soon I am, too.

I spot Maria near the bottom. "Is that all of them?"

She nods just as Aaron yells, "Anna! Stay back."

Maria sighs. "All but Ashley and Caleb, yes." Then she tacks on a mental message.

> Ashley won't shoot. She's just scared. But you know that. You see her with us in the snow in your vision.

I bite back a curse. "Get everyone to the top floor. Keep an eye out for the other guard. There's a backpack carrier in front of the house. Have one of the older kids bring it back down."

"No need for the carrier," Ashley says. "Just get the kids moving, Maria. I'll be taking Cregg's van with Caleb."

The air is beginning to clear a bit, and I see Ashley at the bottom of the stairs. She has a cloth wrapped around her nose and mouth. A boy with wispy blond hair is asleep near her feet, and the gun she's holding is pointed at Aaron.

His gun is pointed right back at her. With the lower half of both their faces covered against the smoke and their guns out, this looks like a Western shoot-out between two masked bandits.

"Pick Caleb up," she tells me. "Carefully. I don't want him breathing in more smoke."

I scoop him into my arms, being careful to avoid my injured hand. The boy is slack, totally out, and feels heavier than he looks.

"Upstairs. Both of you."

We comply, and when we reach the second level, Ashley tells me to put the boy down next to her.

I back away after placing him on the floor. Ashley shifts her aim briefly toward me and then back to Aaron, making it clear that she doesn't trust either of us. "I don't want to hurt anybody," she says. "But

I obviously can't leave here with you. I've got a responsibility to Caleb. I can't end up in jail."

Aaron shoots me a confused look, and I'm pretty sure he's thinking the same thing I am. Neither of us had even considered turning Ashley over to the police. It's entirely possible that Taylor has the authorities on speed dial, waiting for us to get back to the RV, but it's not something we've discussed with her, and she's smart enough to know it would be hard to hand Ashley over to them without drawing attention to ourselves.

I shake my head. "Put the gun away, Ashley. We're not planning to turn you in."

"Maybe *you* aren't. But this guy came down the stairs pointing that gun directly at me."

"Because I knew you had the gun out! That you're trying to muster enough anger to use it if you have to. You can't leave in Cregg's van, Ashley. It's totally snowed in. There's probably eighteen inches out there." Aaron stops, looking around. "Where's the other guard?"

"Locked on Level 5 in Caleb's room," she says. "He won't get out until someone lets him out. Did you take care of the other two?"

"Temporarily. I'd say twenty minutes for Timmons. Maybe fifteen for the other guy . . ."

"Then you need to go now. Get those kids to safety. I'll use the snowblower and . . ." Her lower lip starts to quiver, and I'm pretty sure she's realizing that her only path out of here is with us.

"Maria thinks Cregg could be back by 11:15," I tell her. "You won't have time."

Daniel moves forward, his voice weak but insistent.

Let me talk to her.

Do you really think that will make things better? Right now, she's assuming she's wanted for attempted murder. If she knows you're in here . . .

I'll explain, Anna. Just let me talk to her.

I tap Aaron's arm. "Swapping places for a sec."

"Okay . . . but we don't really have much time."

"I know."

When I slide back, the first thing I see is Hunter, sitting against Molly's file cabinet. His fists are clenched. Seeing Bree and not being able to say anything to her seems to have just about pushed him over the limit. I flash him a sympathetic smile—*not much longer, be patient*—but I need to keep my focus on what's happening on the outside.

"Where is Sariah?" Daniel asks. "Did he . . . did he kill her anyway?"

Her eyes narrow, and the gun is definitely pointed at me now. She's pretty much forgotten Aaron is even in the room.

"Ashley, it's me. It's Daniel. I'm not dead. I don't even know if I'm really in a coma. It's . . . complicated. Sariah's favorite song is 'Bohemian Rhapsody,'" Daniel continues. "The two of you always do a truly horrible duet when it comes on the radio. She eats deviled ham out of the can, which is disgusting. You told her that it leaves her with cat food breath."

"You're not Daniel. You just have his memories. I know you pick up ghosts—do you think I don't remember that?"

"Hey, um . . ." A tall boy is standing two stairs up holding the kid carrier. He glances at the guns and says, "I'm just gonna leave this here and . . . go."

"It's okay," Ashley says in her nurse voice. "Just a misunderstanding."

The boy nods, but he doesn't turn his back to us as he retreats up the stairs.

Once he's gone, Daniel says, "Okay, you're right. I can't prove it. But, damn it, Ashley, you need to listen. Sariah ended up in this mess because she tried to save the kid on her own. It's not a job for one person. That kid requires a *team*. He may require an entire village. You *need* us. And the other kids, plus the ones we have back in North Carolina, could use your help. So give me the damn gun, and let's get out of here before that son of a bitch comes back and we all die in this hole."

She doesn't respond.

"I know you were acting on Cregg's orders. That you were trying to protect Sariah. And if she's not here with you, he double-crossed you. He killed her anyway."

Again, Daniel's emotions flood in as he speaks. There's still a splash of the red-orange of his fear, but behind that is the deep black of grief. Despair.

I feel his energy fade even more, but he pulls in a shaky breath and says, "If you don't come voluntarily, Ashley, I'll have to nudge you. Or at least try. I'm not sure I have another push left in me after Timmons. I think that might end any chance I have of getting back to my body, and I'll be dead just like Sariah."

"I don't *know* if she's dead," Ashley says. "Probably. When he learned that I failed . . . he didn't call me back. And his assistant won't return my calls."

Aaron looks over toward me, clearly feeling as confused as I am. Daniel is confused, too, and I feel my mouth form a soundless *what*.

Another second passes before Daniel says, "But Cregg was *here*, right? You could have talked to him . . ."

"*Graham* Cregg, yes. But it's *Ronald* Cregg who had Sariah. He's the one I was talking to at the hospital."

For a moment, we just stand there trying to process what she's just told us. And then Aaron snaps us out of it. "We need to get moving."

Daniel doesn't argue for once. He slides back without a word, and I find myself staring at Ashley's pistol with my undamaged hand stretched out toward her. She grimaces like this decision is the bitterest pill she's ever had to swallow and gives me the gun.

❖ ❖ ❖

While Ashley and Aaron get Caleb into the carrier, I take a minute to apply the burn bandage. After a few seconds, the hydrogel starts to take the edge off the pain. I hastily wrap the gauze around my hand and then help Ashley grab blankets from a supply closet.

When we reach the top level, I do a quick head count. Then I call Taylor to make sure the path is clear for the RV and to fill her in on Cregg's change of plans.

"Yeah," she says. "I didn't make the last snowplow run. There was a truck parked out by the road, and I didn't want to raise any suspicions."

"Are you sure it wasn't Magda's security team?"

"Not unless the entire team is in a dirty white truck. Anyway, Magda says the security team is delayed. An eighteen-wheeler tipped over on Route 3 just out of Plattsburgh. The new ETA for the security team is, oh . . . about twenty minutes from now. She wants you guys to call ASAP."

"Is Deo—"

"Yes. Deo is okay. He ate some soup. Fever is down to 102. *Both* of our fevers are down."

"Good. Stay put. I'm guessing fifteen, maybe twenty, minutes."

I glance at my phone—it's 10:52 already. I'm really hoping we haven't cut things too close. Cregg's chances of locating us once we're out on the highway are slim. But if they see us struggling to make it out of a nearby snow-covered private drive as their helicopter is coming in for a landing? And then find three Fudds knocked out and the wabbits missing? I'm guessing they'll call in an anonymous tip to the local police to be on the lookout for an RV full of missing children.

Maria has already sent someone ahead to grab the backpack with the winter gear, and kids are rummaging through it. Bree found the BB-8 jacket, but it's a little tight, and she's having a tough time zipping it. I help as best I can with my one working hand. Aaron is helping one of the others bundle up.

I tell Aaron what Taylor just said. "Do you want to call Magda, or shall I?"

"I'll do it," he says. "But let's get out of here first."

Once we're outside, Ashley piles the extra blankets on the other guard, Weeks. Part of me wonders if leaving the guards alive is doing them any favors. Cregg doesn't strike me as a compassionate boss, and the three of them have just failed miserably.

Then we start trudging through the snow, up the hill toward the tree line. I follow behind Aaron, who is now on the phone with Magda, and tug Bree along in my wake, trying to create enough of a path that she and the other kids can follow.

Hunter lurks at the front of my head, to the point where it's hard to focus on where we're going. If he was in charge right now, we'd probably trip and fall, because he'd keep my eyes pinned on his sister. She looks a lot like him. Her hair is longer, and she's taller, but then my mental image of Hunter is based on a photo that's probably a year old.

Bree's eyes are wary, though, like there are questions she wants to ask but doesn't think she should. She's one of the only second-gen adepts who hasn't asked if they're going home. The older ones are mostly first-gen like Maria, and so far, *none* of them have asked. That makes me wonder how much they know about the current political climate for our kind. I doubt they've been reading or watching the news, but who knows how much Maria has managed to pluck from the minds of the guards.

It takes a bit longer to walk uphill than it did coming down on the sleds. Bree and I reach the top shortly after Aaron and wait for the others to catch up.

"What did Magda say?"

"You mean after she stopped cursing and ranting about how she'll have to pay the security team anyway? We're to meet her near Lake Placid. It's about an hour away. They couldn't fly into Plattsburgh, so they're headed for a small private airport there. They're getting the jet ready now. She was a little worried about seating—her jet only has room for twenty-five, and there's seven in her party already."

I run the tally in my head. "Should be fine. Taylor and Deo can go with her, and we'll drive the camper back. We need to get to Baltimore as fast as possible, and I'd rather not have to explain that side trip to her."

"Is Daniel okay?"

I shrug. "It's hard to get a straight answer out of him. But you heard what he said in there. I didn't get the sense he was bluffing. Blasting Timmons like that took a lot out of him. As soon as we hand the kids over to Magda, we need to head for Baltimore."

Once everyone reaches the top, we continue at a faster pace. Ashley is right behind us at first, keeping a close eye on Caleb, but she begins to slow down, along with several of the others, as the hike continues. I'm guessing this is the most exercise any of them have had in the past month.

It may be the first fresh air they've had, too. Despite the cold and despite being clearly winded, most of the kids are actually smiling, tilting their faces up occasionally to look through the trees at the sky.

The temperature has dropped even further, though, and the wind is wicked enough that I doubt their good mood is going to hold for long.

Déjà vu hits full force as I watch Aaron forging ahead with Caleb on his back. I glance up at the moon, remembering when I saw it before, but still somehow noticing for the first time that it's a crescent. Being glad that the clouds have cleared and that there's still some semblance of the path we made on our hike in. Seeing the Christmas lights off in the distance. Pointing them out when Bree falters, telling her that the camper is even closer, looking back at Maria and Ashley and the others helping the kids—almost like the puppies in *101 Dalmatians*. Wondering if the road will be clear enough for the RV.

When we reach the end of the events foretold in my flash-forward, I'm suddenly nervous. Before, I could be confident, certain that we'd at least make it to this point in time.

Anything at all could happen now. We're in uncharted territory.

As I suspected, the pace slows, and I start hearing grumbles from behind. But once we spot the RV up ahead, everyone starts moving a little faster. A few of the older kids seem skeptical, asking how we're all going to fit inside.

"It's bigger on the inside," I tell them. "Anyway, if we're squeezed in tight, we'll warm up faster."

Aaron huffs. "Might be a tighter fit than it looks, since Deo is in the back bedroom. I think we should probably keep Caleb in the truck, even if he's sedated, to separate him from Deo and his amp ability. And speaking of . . . how long can she *keep* Caleb sedated?"

"I don't know." The boy still seems completely out, his little head slumped forward, bobbing gently with each step Aaron takes. "What if Maggie and Deo were in the same room? Maybe they'd cancel each other out?"

"Or maybe it would be like mixing matter and antimatter and the entire RV would explode."

"Hmph. You are *not* funny, Aaron Quinn."

Bree tugs on my arm to stop me when we're almost to the RV. "What's wrong?"

She grabs the front of my coat and pulls with more strength than I'd expect from someone her size. When I crouch toward her, she reaches up with one ungloved hand and touches the side of my face. A faint static shock runs through me, and then she says, "Hunter."

Just the one word, and then she starts backing away from me, fear and sadness filling her eyes.

I'd really been hoping to delay this, at least until we were out of the cold.

"Bree, you can talk to him. Let's just get inside. We need to—"

"Hunter's in your head. There's a monster in there with him. I saw it!" She takes another step backward, stumbling into a pile of snow. *What did you do to him?*

It takes Ashley and two of the older kids to get her into the camper. Every time I move toward her, she screams again. And inside my head, Hunter curls up into a small, dim ball on the other side of Molly's cabinet and whispers his sister's name, over and over.

❖   ❖   ❖

Near Lake Placid, New York
December 21, 2019, 11:53 p.m.

Aaron's shoulders relax when we turn onto the main highway. This section of the road must have been salted, because it's relatively clear, unlike the slushy side road we just left. And even the side road was an immense improvement over the trail where we'd been parked. Aaron had to back up twice to get enough momentum to push snow away for the last hundred yards or so, and on the second try, the camper nearly skidded into a tree. There was no sign of the truck Taylor mentioned when we reached the end of the trail.

I point toward the intercom screen. "Will this distract you? I want to check in, see how they're getting settled."

"Sure. Go ahead."

There was no time for planning when we got to the RV. We just piled Ashley and Caleb into the back seat of the truck, and the rest of the kids, including the kicking and screaming Bree, into the camper.

Taylor answers, and I can see a few kids in the main cabin behind her.

"Just checking in," I tell her, keeping my voice low. "GPS says we've got maybe fifteen minutes before we arrive at the airfield. Are things going . . . better?"

Taylor nods, although I can tell she's a little uneasy. "Maggie has calmed Bree down a bit," she says. "And Maria has been trying to explain about Hunter. Maria was a big help with the others, too. She already knew about Deo and why we need to keep the more volatile kids at the other end of the trailer. And she's *trying* to use the normal mode of conversation, but . . ."

Her voice drops almost to a whisper on the last sentence, and her mouth quirks downward on one side.

"Yeah," Aaron says. "We both know what you mean. It's a bit unnerving."

"Just a heads-up that there will probably be potato chip crumbs in your bed. The rest of them are back there, playing some sort of game. Maria says this is the first time some of them have seen each other since they left The Warren. Mostly they were kept in their quarters."

Behind her, I see Maggie lean over and whisper something to Bree. The younger girl shakes her head, still not looking up from the floor.

"Deo's temp is up again," Taylor says, sensing my next question. "Only a degree. It's nearly time for more Tylenol, so . . . could be normal fluctuation."

"And how is *your* fever?" I ask.

Taylor stares at the screen. I can't tell if she's sad or scared or angry, but she's obviously fighting some sort of internal battle.

Her expression eventually lands on *angry*, and she says, "Same as it's been the past two days. Ninety-eight-point-frickin'-six. It's not the damn flu, so stop pretending. The only question is what we're going to *do* about it."

The screen goes out. "Your sister is a lunatic, Aaron. You know that, right?"

"Yes," he says. "Always has been."

Hunter is very close to the front, and he's not happy the screen was turned off.

Turn the TV back on. I want to see her. You need to let me talk to her!

Once we get to the airport, okay? We'll try to find a quiet spot. Right now, I don't think she would listen. Don't think she even can listen.

That scares him. He both wants to talk to her and dreads it, which is perfectly understandable.

She will talk to you, Hunter. Once she's . . . calmed down. And your mom can come to Sandalford to see her real soon. I'll talk to Magda, and we'll make it happen.

Hunter doesn't respond, just slides away. I don't follow, sensing that he needs some time alone. Or what passes as that, for anyone stuck inside my head.

I glance in the rearview mirror at Ashley and Caleb. We didn't have a car seat, so she propped him up on the backpack, working the seat belt to hold it in place. The boy is sleeping soundly, and he looks absolutely angelic, tendrils of blond hair framing his chubby cheeks. A crisscross of white medical tape on the back of his hand holds a tiny catheter in place. It's hard to reconcile the innocence in that face with the things that Daniel and Jaden said as we were leaving The Warren. But it's also hard to imagine that this small child could alter the physical structure of the door to Room 81—or did he simply make me think that happened? I'm tempted to ask Ashley, but her eyes are closed, her head resting against the inside of the cab. While I doubt she's asleep, she's clearly not interested in conversation.

Looks can be deceivin'. Just because he seems innocent don't mean he's not dangerous.

I think Jaden is going to leave it at that, but then he laughs.

But it's hard to convince people of that. Hunter's sister is pretty freaked out right now. Bad enough to learn her brother died and now he's hangin' out in some strange lady's head without also having to look at an extra from *The Walkin' Dead*.

She'll get past it.

Yeah. She would, in time. Hunter was freaked out to begin with too, but we're buddies now, ain't we?

Hunter either nods or says something I don't catch, because Jaden laughs again.

Yeah. She would eventually get past it, but there's no need to put the kid through that. And I don't know if I'm takin' up space or energy or whatever in here, but resources ain't ever infinite, and I think maybe Daniel could use the bits I'm takin' up. Like I said before, I'm ready . . . and I'm getting curious about what's next, you know?

Tears sting my eyes, and I bite my lip to keep from losing it. I don't cry when my hitchers go. This is good news for Jaden. Crying would be selfish.

You're worryin' about the dreams, aren't you?

A little. But mostly . . . mostly I'll just mi

Well, damn, girl. That's the nicest goin'-aw~,
anyone ever gave me. Maybe the only one, come ι∪
think of it, but still . . . You take care of yourself. And take
care of my roommates in here. Oh, and let up a little on
the guilt, okay?

My head fills with the light of a thousand tiny candles. They flicker gently, and I'm surrounded by the scent of sandalwood and the gentle music from the funeral parlor. The only thing missing is the sadness that hung in the air like a dense fog. In its place is a sense of peace, acceptance, and joy. Two bright-gold threads meet, intertwine, and vanish. Then the candles, like the fireflies in Peyton's video game, blink out one by one.

For a long time, I sit with my eyes squeezed tight. Breathing. Letting go. When I finally open them, I catch a glimpse of something on the road behind us. We're rounding a curve—one of many on this mountainous highway—and I get a brief look at the vehicle.

"You okay?" Aaron asks. "Thought you were asleep for a minute."

I shake my head. I'll tell him about Jaden later, when we're alone.

"Just resting. But . . . there's a white truck behind us. Like the one Taylor said she saw earlier."

Aaron looks in the rearview mirror. "You sure it's white?"

"Yeah, pretty sure."

He shrugs. "Probably nothing to worry about. There are a lot of white trucks on the road. And I'm not sensing anything. But keep an eye on it."

I do, confirming at the next bend in the road that it's indeed white. But that's all I can tell, especially since it's dropped back a bit.

A beeping noise from the back seat startles both of us.

"What's that?" Aaron asks.

Ashley pushes her blonde hair out of her face and then digs in her coat pocket. "It's midnight," she says, turning off the alarm on her phone. "Are we going to be stopping soon? I need to give Caleb another dose of the sedative at twelve twenty. I'd rather not do it while we're moving."

"We'll be there in less than ten," Aaron says. "With any luck, you'll be all set up inside the plane by then."

We ride along silently, and then something occurs to me, and I turn back toward Ashley. "Whose phone is that?"

"Um . . . *mine?*" she says, with the distinct implication that it's a stupid question.

"No. I mean, is it a personal phone or a *work* phone?"

"Personal. I know what you're going to ask next, and no. I've checked it thoroughly. There's no way he's using it to track us. But I can toss it if you'd like."

I glance in the mirror again.

"The truck is still there," I tell Aaron. "What do you think?"

"Not sure it matters," Aaron says. "We're, what—three miles from the airport? If Cregg's got a tracker app on that phone, I think he'll be able to figure out where we're headed."

"There is no tracking app on the phone," Ashley says. "I'm not an idiot."

When we spot the sign for High Peaks Regional Airport, we turn. I watch to see if the truck turns, too. It doesn't, and I breathe a bit easier as we continue down the narrow road.

The airport is tiny, and mostly dark. There are only two cars in the lot. Off to the left, behind the fence that extends on both sides of the terminal—which I guess is what it's called, even when it's this tiny—are two large hangars and a few other outbuildings and open shelters. Four small planes are parked near the end of the row, along with some heavy equipment and a few trucks. Magda's large silver jet is in front of the second hangar. It looks decidedly out of place.

Aaron parks near the fence and then taps the intercom. When Taylor answers, he tells her to hold tight until he talks to Magda.

We don't have to wait long. Before we can even get out of the truck, a section of the fence is rolled away, and a luggage cart moves toward us. The driver, an older man, pulls up near the truck, with Magda on the passenger side facing Aaron. A younger guy sits on the rear of the cart. I can tell instantly that he's private security—he looks us over carefully, and then his eyes start scanning the parking lot and surrounding area for threats.

"You made it," Magda says. She's annoyed, but there's also a bit of grudging admiration in her expression. "I suppose I shouldn't have questioned your vision, Anna—or, for that matter, your obstinance. I assume the children are all okay?"

Aaron nods. "They're okay." And then, just as I'm opening my mouth to say it, he adds, "But Deo needs a doctor."

"As you told me earlier. It's fortunate that I happen to have one with me."

I feel an odd combination of relief and worry. "Does he . . . I mean, is he aware . . . ?"

"Dr. Batra is my personal physician. He's cared for my daughters since we returned to London, so . . . yes, he's aware of the circumstances. Perhaps we could get the adepts into the jet first, where there's a bit more room. Bring them through the gate. Then the doctor can examine Taddeo and determine whether he's healthy enough to travel."

The cart drives off. There's a security guard standing next to the gate, but he seems out of it, ready for this to be over with so that he can sleep.

"Wow," Aaron says. "Just walk through. No standing in line for ID checks and security pat downs when you own the jet. Yet another benefit to being disgustingly rich."

He starts to get out of the truck, but I hold back. "You might want to get Bree on the plane first, and then I can help with the others. I don't want to upset her further."

Hunter doesn't like that idea.

If Bree goes on the plane, I want to go, too.

We'll see, okay?

I'm gonna be lonely in here now that Jaden is gone, and Daniel . . . he's . . . I think he's sick.

I know. But Bree is terrified of me, and, unfortunately, you and I are a package deal right now. I'm not sure that the pilot or anyone else would be comfortable if your sister screams the entire flight.

For now, I don't address Hunter's point about Daniel being sick, because it's a strong argument for us not going in the plane with the others. I just push the boy back as gently as possible and wait for Aaron to tell me the coast is clear.

"Do you trust this Magda person?" Ashley asks from the back seat.

"I guess? This is the first time I've seen her face-to-face. It's been video meetings before. And she's certainly put a lot of resources into setting up a place for these kids to stay—a place that isn't a pit below-ground. I don't get the sense she has any desire to exploit them. She wants to find a cure. So—yeah. I don't entirely like her, but I guess I trust her."

A tap on my window startles me, and I look out to see a dark-skinned man in his early thirties. He appears Indian, or maybe Pakistani. When I open the door, he extends a hand and introduces himself, in a crisp British accent. He's dressed in jeans and a white shirt and has a large red bag slung across his shoulder.

"Dr. Rajpal Batra. I'm Mrs. Bell's private physician, and I . . ." He frowns, peering into the back seat. "Is that the patient? I understood him to be older."

"No," Ashley says. "My nephew isn't ill. He's heavily sedated. And for everyone's safety, we need to ensure that he *stays* sedated."

Dr. Batra blanches slightly but gives her a nod. "Very well." His eyes turn back to me. "I have a few questions about your brother's symptoms and medical history."

As I answer the doctor's questions, the adepts begin to cross in front of the truck on their way to the plane. I'm still telling Dr. Batra about Deo's otherwise unremarkable medical history when Aaron gives the all clear for me and the doctor to enter the camper. Then he begins helping Ashley move Caleb to the jet.

Dr. Batra sniffs and wrinkles his nose as soon as the RV door opens.

"Yes," I say. "That's one of the symptoms. The first one I noticed."

Deo is semicoherent when we enter the room. Taylor squeezes past, joining me in the main cabin to give the doctor some space. She looks as exhausted as I feel.

I can't just sit here waiting, but there's little room to pace in the RV. So I splash some water on my face in the tiny bathroom. Run a comb through my hair. And then I sit on the bed and pray that the doctor says it's the flu after all, and Deo just needs rest and fluids.

There's a tap on the door. Taylor sits down next to me, leaving the door open so that we can keep watch.

"I hate waiting like this," she says. "I know he's only been in there a couple of minutes and I know Deo's not in any more danger right this minute simply because he's seeing a doctor. If anything, he's in less danger. But it feels like when we were waiting after Daniel's surgery. Like his fate is hanging in the balance. Like it's either a reprieve or a frickin' death sentence."

"I know."

"Aaron called while you were in the bathroom. Magda knows about our side trip to Boston, and she's cornered him for a debrief. Apparently, Jaden's mom and Beth aren't the only Delphi personnel who have been targeted. Two others, that they know of. And he says Bree is hysterical because she's decided yes, she does want to talk to you after all. Magda says to come get her before she drives everyone on the plane completely—"

Taylor stops when the door to Deo's room opens. Dr. Batra emerges, setting his bag on one of the barstools. He seems perplexed, and that starts my heart pounding again.

"Your brother is showing signs of cerebral edema," he says. "The symptoms are oddly similar to the severe altitude sickness that mountain climbers get sometimes. Definitely not something we should see this close to sea level. I've given him an injection of dexamethasone and also acetazolamide. They should reduce the swelling. The drugs won't take full effect for several hours, however, and I'm afraid I can't clear him to fly. That would most likely exacerbate the swelling."

"That's okay," I tell him. "We have to drive the camper back anyway. As long as he's stable . . ."

"I believe he will be," the doctor says. "I left additional syringes on the shelf, with instructions."

I shudder. While I'll definitely make myself do it, the needle phobia I inherited from a former hitcher is strong.

But Taylor is all business. She nods and then asks, "Is Deo's fever causing the inflammation of his brain? Or vice versa?"

"I really don't know," Dr. Batra says. "I've worked with Mrs. Bell's daughters for several years, and I still can't explain their condition or do anything more than treat the symptoms. And that's the only thing I can really do for Deo until we hear back from the team that Mrs. Bell has working on a cure, or at least a more comprehensive treatment for all of these patients. If his fever continues after we reach our destination,

I'll give the nod for an MRI and possibly other tests as well, but for now, let's not beg trouble." He gives us a reassuring smile and then pulls the bag over his shoulder. "There are a few individuals Mrs. Bell feels I should sedate before travel. I'll pop back in before we take off."

As much as I hated seeing the kids come into Sandalford drugged up, Magda probably has a point. They won't let you smoke a cigarette on an airplane, and someone who can ignite things with just a thought seems like a far greater risk.

Taylor and I walk over to check on Deo. He's asleep, although I'm not sure if that's due to the injections or to him being sick. I scan through my memories of Arlene, my hypochondriac hypodermaphobic hitcher. I'm able to place dexamethasone as a corticosteroid, but Arlene must not have had occasion to take the other drug.

"You should get moving if you plan to talk to Bree," Taylor says. "Magda wants to take off as soon as possible."

I pull on my jacket and head back outside. The wind has picked up again, whistling noisily as I walk through the gate and onto the tarmac. I glance around for the guard, still feeling like I shouldn't be able to just walk through without telling anyone. But he's inside the main building now, talking to the two men who were with Magda earlier. The lights are dimmed inside, and there's a cluster of tables near the back, with chairs piled on top like we always did when I closed Joe's deli for the night. I seriously doubt that this airfield is normally open for business at midnight. How much did Magda have to pay to allow for this flight?

As I approach the plane, the door opens. Maria stands in the doorway. Bree is next to her in the BB-8 jacket, still crying, but at least she doesn't scream when she sees me.

Bree has calmed down now. Not happy, but she understands. I explain about Jaden, too, so maybe he will not scare her so badly now?

I think we'll be okay on that front. Jaden is gone.

Gone . . . ? Oh. Okay. Maybe that is best. Magda says talk to her out here. We have enough trouble inside with the others. One of The Peepers realized the doctor was giving her friend a sedative and they're all a little worked up about that.

Okay. I'll take her back to the camper.

It would have been much easier if Bree had decided to speak to me before we moved her over to the plane, but she's six and she's just had a shock. A little inconsistency is probably to be expected.

Maria walks Bree halfway down the stairs and then says, "They need me inside. You will be okay?"

It's somewhere between a statement and a question. Bree nods, still watching me warily.

"Want to come back to the camper with me?" I ask.

She shakes her head.

"It's too cold and windy to chat right here. Wouldn't you rather be warm?"

Another headshake.

I look around for other options and notice an open shelter on the other side of the plane. "Maybe we could at least go inside there?" It won't be much warmer, but it will cut some of the wind.

She hesitates for a moment and then starts walking toward the shelter. I follow. It's empty, aside from a few small pieces of equipment. At the far end, beyond the fence that encloses the airfield, a lone truck is turning around in the circular drive.

It's white.

But then so is another truck parked near the outbuildings, and, as Aaron noted, a good quarter of the trucks on the road.

I could *still* be imagining things. Either way, Bree and I need to make this conversation a quick one. I'll feel better once she's back on the plane and I'm back in the RV.

A wooden bench stretches along the wall. I move toward it and motion for Bree to follow.

> *Hunter, are you listening? We don't have much time. Let Bree know it's really you and that you'll see her in two days at Sandalford.*

> Okay. She already knows it's me, though. I just need to let her see I'm . . . safe.

There's so much irony in that statement coming from someone who is dead that even a six-year-old can't miss it, and he gives a hopeless little laugh at the end.

"I don't want Hunter to be inside of you," Bree says. "He doesn't belong there. Hunter belongs with me."

"That's not really something we can fix, Bree. But . . . I'm going to let him talk to you, okay? You just need to remember what Maria told you. Hunter can't stay with us. He's here to tell you good-bye. Hold on . . ."

We start to switch places, but before I can move to the back seat, I'm startled by another gust of wind, much stronger than the others. A can of some sort scuttles through the front of the shelter and across the floor, coming to a stop against the far wall. The wind is so fierce that I hear Olivia Wu's voice in my head for a second, saying a tornado was headed for *Tuthcalootha*.

And then I hear Aaron's voice *outside* of my head, screaming my name.

The sound of gunfire.

Landing skids appear and hover above the ground.

Not a tornado.

CHAPTER
TWENTY-FOUR

Near Lake Placid, New York
December 22, 2019, 12:24 a.m.

The spray of gunfire starts even before the helicopter reaches a complete stop. Magda's security guy is the first one out of the terminal. He's down before the door closes behind him. The man who held the gate open for the kids earlier is right behind him. He goes down, too, but then manages to pull himself back through the door and inside the building. I don't see the older man.

My view of the plane is blocked from here, and I don't see Aaron either. I can only hope that he was able to get the airplane door closed before the shooting started.

I pull Bree farther back in the shelter, where the shadows are darker, and we crouch against the wall. She hasn't made a sound, except for a brief gasp when we first heard the gunfire.

Two men exit the left side of the chopper, which is still running, and head toward Magda's plane. They're both dressed in the same tan uniform that the guards wore at The Warren. One of them is short and stocky, and I'm almost certain it's the guard that Timmons called Weeks. The third man keeps his gun trained on the terminal building.

Another two people get out on the far side of the helicopter, and then a wheelchair is lowered to the ground. One man maintains his position near the helicopter door, but the wheelchair moves toward the nose of the chopper, followed by a guy who is a lot younger than the others. He has dark hair that hangs down into his eyes, and he's wearing a Fudd uniform, like the rest, but he doesn't look any older than Deo.

I don't recognize the boy, but the man in the wheelchair is Graham Cregg. He's lost at least ten pounds since I last saw him, and his cheeks have the sunken look of a cadaver, but it's definitely him. I scan the dirt floor around us for something to use as a weapon. The only candidate is a large wrench about a yard in front of me, but grabbing it will require me moving out of the shadows.

And if Cregg gets into my head, any weapon I'm holding could be turned on me. Or on Bree.

That brief thought pushes Hunter into a panic.

Daniel. You need Daniel. He has to wake up!

I think back to what Daniel told Ashley earlier—that using his ability again could end him. I'd love to believe that was hyperbole meant to convince Ashley to come with us. But the fact that I've heard nothing more from Daniel, the fact that Jaden was worried enough to take an early exit to free up a little extra mental energy for Daniel's use, the fact that Hunter is screaming inside my head and Daniel still sleeps on? All of those things tell me it wasn't an exaggeration.

And what could he even do against Cregg? Their ability is basically the same. And I'm guessing that right now Daniel is the weaker of the two, especially since he'd be working through me as an intermediary.

I don't stop Hunter from trying to wake him, though. Bree is in danger, too. And if I don't make it back to Baltimore, Daniel doesn't make it back to his body.

But he will be my option of last resort, and not simply because he's ill. The more immediate reason is that Daniel can't nudge anyone from behind my walls. And I can't risk leaving them down.

I stack the mental bricks as quickly as possible, walling Daniel and Hunter inside, but more importantly blocking Cregg from getting in. And once I have the wall in place, I start on a second row.

Cregg's wheelchair passes the shelter and continues toward the terminal building, prompting the guard stationed on that side of the plane to abandon his post. The guard is yelling something at the boy, but I only catch smatterings of what he's saying over the noise of the propeller.

". . . saw movement inside the building . . . take him inside the shelter until we get the area secured!"

Cregg doesn't look particularly concerned, but he pivots the chair and heads back this way, stopping only a few feet from the wrench I'd thought about grabbing. The boy follows. Neither of them appears to be armed, but they have several men with automatic weapons who will no doubt come running if they call. And Cregg, of course, is a weapon all by himself.

"Gellert's probably right." The boy's voice is high and thin, almost comically so. "I thought I saw someone, too."

"And you all know, security is mortals' greatest enemy," Cregg mutters. It's another quote, although the boy doesn't seem to be paying attention. *Hamlet*? No, I think it's *Macbeth*.

"I can't believe Timmons and Gellert let them get away," Cregg says. "It's going to take four or five flights to get them all back to the silo, since we don't exactly have a place to land that plane."

The boy nods and then says, "We could steal the camper out fr—" He stops suddenly, almost as if his breath is cut off. At that same moment, Bree clutches my arm with a viselike grip. Between the hydro-gel and the painkillers, I've barely noticed my burned hand in the past hour, but now it throbs again. I don't pull away, though. I barely even breathe.

"Someone is in here," the boy says. "Two people, I think? One of the kids. And someone else, though I can't get a good reading. But it's not the girl you're looking for, the one we messaged."

He falls silent, and I hear voices beyond the shelter, but I can't make out what they're saying.

The boy's face is slack, and when he speaks again, his voice is robotic. The words gush out in a single beat, without any inflection. "Don't let him find me I don't want to go back you're going to die you son of a bitch I want to stay with Hunter send you to hell I can't breathe Anna you're squishing me you're—"

The boy stumbles backward as he sucks in air. He sits cross-legged in the dirt, holding his head in his hands, rocking back and forth.

Some of the thoughts he just plucked out of the air were clearly Bree's. But he must be picking up from someone else, too, since most six-year-old girls don't curse quite that fluently. And it wasn't me—while I generally favor the idea of Cregg going to hell, I wasn't thinking about it just now. At least not explicitly.

"Anna!" Cregg says as he looks around. "So you *are* here. And exactly who is it that you are *squishing*? She was thinking about someone. Hunter, Hunter . . . why is that name familiar? Oh, yes. That would be Sabrina Bieler's brother. One of the children my father had murdered."

Bree whimpers and slides a few steps away. I follow, keeping myself between her and Cregg.

"This doesn't need to involve anyone but you and me, Anna. Jeffrey, why don't you take Sabrina to the helicopter?"

Jeffrey, who I'm pretty sure is also known as Snoop Dogg, breaks rhythm slightly at the sound of his name but continues rocking. Cregg sighs.

"It seems we'll have to wait a moment for him to reboot," he says conversationally. "You'll be okay, Jeffrey. Just breathe. It will pass."

Cregg turns his attention back to me, rolling closer. "If you think your actions are keeping Sabrina—or any of them—safe, Anna, then think again. You would have been wise to answer my messages, instead of trusting a wolf in sheep's array. Assuming you would like to keep the adepts alive, you and I have a common goal and a common enemy. Magda Bell will turn on you in an instant if it is in her interest to do so."

He's no longer moving, and his eyes are fixed on mine. Last time, I remember hearing a noise almost like a hum when he was trying to break through my defenses, but if it's happening now, I can't tell over the noise of the rotor. I'm pretty confident that my walls will keep him out, but, unfortunately, they can't stop him from influencing Bree. The only thing that might help on that front is distraction.

"You say you want to save these kids. That it's your father who's the murderer. Is that what you tell yourself when you're forcing people to snip off their fingers, Graham Cregg? When you're forcing them to kill? How many kids died at The Warren?"

"You think in such simplistic terms, Anna. It's a shame. I suspect you're capable of much more. And I'll admit I may have pushed Daciana in Molly's case, but if you believe that anyone is forcing her to kill now, you'd be very, very mistaken. She has developed a taste for it. That's one reason she's with *him* now, and not with me."

As he speaks, Cregg's voice remains calm, his eyelids barely open. His body is perfectly still in the wheelchair. From past experience, both mine and Molly's, I know that means he's focusing, amassing his strength for an attack. I should jump out and tip the chair. Disrupt his concentration. The boy, Jeffrey, is still huddled on the ground, and I don't think he'd be of much help to Cregg. It's possible that he doesn't even want to help him. But the other guard could be within shooting range in only a matter of seconds. All it would take is one scream from Cregg.

Instead, the scream comes from me, barely a second later, when Bree sinks her teeth into my wrist. It's not a gentle nip, and her teeth rip my skin as I pull away. It could have been worse—if not for the gauze holding the hydrogel pad in place, she would have gotten a solid chunk of flesh.

I shove Bree away, hoping the physical motion will break Cregg's control. It does, briefly, and I take the opportunity to grab her from behind, pinning her arms to her sides. She can still kick, but it eliminates her arms and teeth as weapons.

Not that it matters. As I expected, one scream was all it took to draw the attention of the guards—not just one, as it turns out, but two. The first Fudd moves inside the shelter, pointing the gun at me, and I feel like a total coward for holding her in front of me. Anyone watching would assume I was using the poor kid as a shield.

The second guard hasn't quite made it inside the shelter, however, when the helicopter, motor still running, skids backward toward the runway. He hurries toward the chopper, waving his arms, and the other guard's attention is also pulled away. For a moment, Cregg's attention is even on the chopper. Only Jeffrey seems oblivious, still rocking on the floor.

I take advantage of the momentary reprieve to back farther into the shelter with Bree, but I've taken only two steps when something rustles behind me. I want to turn and look, but taking my eyes off the Fudd with the gun seems like a very bad idea, especially now that he's decided to ignore whatever drama is happening with the helicopter.

"Put the girl down," the guard says. "Or I'll—" A dark spot appears on the man's forehead before he finishes the threat, and he falls backward into the dust.

I do look behind me then, just in time to see Jasper Hawkins fire twice at Graham Cregg.

Both bullets catch Cregg in the chest. Behind him, the helicopter is now listing to one side, spinning on a single skid, almost like a pirouette.

Cregg's wheelchair jolts backward from the force of the bullets, but then he begins moving this way. His eyes are fixed on Jasper, and his look of shock morphs into a tiny smile.

I remember that expression. It's the same one Cregg was wearing as he forced Deo to point the gun toward his own temple back at The Warren.

Something hard and cold crashes into my head. Once. Twice.

I fall to the ground, and so do my walls. Bree grabs my wrist, still slick with blood from her teeth. She's screaming Hunter's name as the wheel of Cregg's chair hits my thigh. I raise one hand, hoping to push the wheel away, but connect instead with the side of Graham Cregg's foot.

An odd sensation, almost like an electrical current, flows through me from one arm to the other, filling my body. My head.

A child—Hunter? Or is it Bree?—speaks a single word.

Yes!

And then everything goes black and silent.

❖　❖　❖

Something is poking me in the stomach. It's small and sharp. I want to move away from it, but moving makes my head hurt. Which is unfortunate, because the entire bed seems to be shaking.

It takes a few minutes, but my eyes finally begin to adjust to the light. Small fragments of memory start falling into place.

Jasper shooting Cregg.

The helicopter spinning out of control.

Something bashing me in the head.

Aaron's face, as he kneels over me.

And then another face. Dr. Batra.

Needles. I remember needles. Ugh.

Slowly I work my hand up to my head and feel a bandage. The movement causes the pointy thing to jab my stomach again, so I reach underneath me and grab it. Orange, sharp. It takes a second to place it as a broken Dorito.

"Oh. Sorry," Taylor says as I drop the chunk onto the floor. "Thought I got them all. If you're going to move, you should probably do so slowly."

"I'm not going to move."

"Good call."

I open my eyes a bit more, but the room is too bright for that to be comfortable. "What time is it? And where are we?"

"A little after seven, and hell if I know. Pretty sure we're still in New York, though. Aaron is hopped up on Red Bull and 5-hour ENERGY, but he's starting to fade. He's looking for a place to stop now. We all need sleep."

I start to protest that I just woke up, but my brain is so foggy that I could easily fall asleep again. "Deo. How is—"

"I thought you said you weren't going to move!" Taylor says as I sink my head back into the pillow. "Deo is better. A lot better. I gave him a second set of injections about an hour ago. His fever is a little over a hundred. The doctor said we'll treat the symptoms for now, and hopefully whatever is causing the problem will resolve over time. Do you want something to drink?"

She brings me back some water. When I finish, she asks, "How much do you remember?"

"Jasper shot Cregg. Is he dead?"

"Yes," Taylor says. "Along with three of his guards and one of Magda's security people."

"Something hit me after that. It was . . . I'm pretty sure it was Jasper's gun. Why?"

"Good question. Jasper says he wasn't in control when that happened. That it was Cregg. And Maria poked around in his head a bit. She thinks he's telling the truth. Do you remember coming back to the RV? Getting stitches?"

"I have a vague memory of needles. There were gunshots outside. And the helicopter . . . was spinning out of control."

Taylor shrugs. "I wouldn't say it was out of control. It just wasn't under the control of a *pilot*. Moving the thing took a concerted effort on the part of two of the adepts, but it provided a useful diversion and knocked out one of Cregg's men."

I have many more questions about that, but I push them aside for now. "Bree. The other kids. Was anyone else injured?"

"None of the kids. The guy who runs the airfield took a bullet in the thigh, but he's okay. Magda had already paid him a good bit to open the place, and I'm pretty sure that she had to sweeten the pot considerably to get him to forget all of this."

"But . . . they'll have to call the police, right? There were bodies. Cregg."

"An agreement was reached," Taylor says. "Magda will handle her guy. And two of Cregg's guards were allowed to leave, as long as they took Cregg's and the guards' bodies back to The Pit with them. I guess they'll bury them there. The younger guard went back to Sandalford with the others."

"Snoop?"

"Yeah. Spying piece of . . ." Taylor huffs and shakes her head. "Anyway, Magda called a few hours ago to say they'd gotten all of the adepts to Sandalford safely."

"A few hours ago? I thought you said it was a little after seven?"

"She still seems to be on London time. Deo got a text from Kelsey, checking on you, so I'm guessing Magda has her up too, getting the new adepts settled."

My eyelids are growing heavy, but Taylor's voice pulls me back from sleep. "Aaron told me what Daniel said when he was trying to get Ashley to leave with us. That using his power again might mean—"

"He didn't use it at the airfield. I'm not even sure he was awake."

"Is he . . . ?"

I turn my attention inward, which isn't exactly easy with my current state of brain fuzz. It's almost like I'm looking through a fog.

Once my vision begins to clear, I see that my mind cottage is a mess. Bricks are scattered everywhere. Apparently having something crack my skull had a similar effect on my walls. The file cabinets are still there . . . the plain gray-green ones near the back. Molly's purple cabinet near the front. And a new addition—deep forest green—next to it for Jaden. I'm glad to see that my subconscious has given him a nice cabinet, maybe to make up for the fact that he had to hang out looking like a victim of the zombie apocalypse for so long.

Myron's corner is still walled off, although, like the rest of the place, it took some damage. Most of the warning signs that I posted there to keep Daniel away are now scattered on the ground along with chunks of brick and powdered mortar. I want to put the signs back up, to patch the cracks along the foundation, but I don't have the energy or the focus.

Daniel's still here. I can sense him, so I move farther back and call his name. He doesn't exactly answer—it's more of a groan. But he's here.

I pass that news along to Taylor and then go back to look for Hunter. There's no trace of him. Even though he only had a brief moment with Bree, it must have been enough just to know that she's safe now. There's no file cabinet for him yet, but then, I've never lost two hitchers in a single day before. Maybe the subconscious is having trouble keeping up with checkouts at the Hotel Anna.

I wish I'd had the chance to tell Hunter good-bye.

❖   ❖   ❖

I hate this room. It's too white and too cold, and I know what's gonna hap-
pen because it's happened already over and over in my vision. The duct tape
tugs at the hair on my arms.

Will is seriously freaked. Oksana just looks drugged, but then she most
always looks that way. The kid at the end keeps staring at me. I just hope
he remembers to tell that Anna girl what I said about picking me up first.

When the door opens, Lucas walks in, holding the gun. Beyond him I
see Cregg and the girl.

They both look this way, and Cregg's face morphs into someone else. It's
wider now. His hair grows longer, as the hairline recedes.

Myron.

And then back to Cregg.

I jolt awake and hear a whimper. It takes a moment to realize that
the whimper came from me. My head didn't appreciate the sudden
movement.

"Anna? Y'okay?" Aaron's eyes are barely open.

"Yeah. Just . . . a dream."

"I thought they were over?"

"The Molly dreams are over. But Jaden left last night. Hunter, too."
I very carefully shift my body toward him, moving my head as little as
possible, and curl one leg around his. "Go back to sleep. We'll talk in
the morning."

I close my eyes and drift off again.

Good night, sweet prince.

Sleep, perchance to . . .

❖   ❖   ❖

Silver Spring, Maryland
December 24, 2019, 2:31 p.m.

Sam Quinn looks like he's going to burst into tears as soon as he spots us inside the small café. He hurries over to our table. Aaron and Taylor get up to meet him, and he wraps them both in a long bear hug.

"You shouldn't be here," he says. "I'm damn glad to see you, but things are crazy right now, especially this close to DC. And if anyone spots . . . Anna . . ." He catches sight of me for the first time and laughs, shaking his head. "Okay, so maybe you've got that covered."

It's mostly the hair, but I'm also wearing a pair of costume glasses. A fake nose ring. A skirt of Taylor's, plaid leggings, and a pair of boots that Deo would actually wear if he could squeeze his feet into them.

Deo has taken the opposite tack. He's in a pair of plain denim jeans, a flannel shirt, and a NASCAR cap. The only way I convinced him to leave the RV dressed this way was to say this is our substitute for the Halloween we missed. And even then, I still had to promise him candy.

Aaron has a cap, too. Taylor has a hoodie. Hopefully if anyone is still watching, we'll slide under the radar.

"So," Sam says, looking between me and Deo. "Both of you are feeling better now?"

"Yes, sir," I say.

Deo, whose mouth is full of waffles, just nods.

Taylor squeezes her grandfather's hand. "I'm a very good nurse, Popsy. You should see me giving Deo his injections."

Deo half chokes and then takes a gulp of his orange juice to cover. Which makes me wonder exactly *where* she's giving those injections. And then I immediately wish my brain hadn't gone there.

"Well, that's nice to know," Sam says. "Won't be too many years before I'll probably need a good nurse."

Taylor smiles back at him, but I can see that his comment rattles her. I'm not sure if it's the idea of her granddad getting older or the juxtaposition of that with the whole sexy nurse thing she and Deo have going.

We spent all of yesterday recuperating at a campground outside of Poughkeepsie. As much as I hated waiting an extra day, my head was still pounding and I was fighting dizzy spells as a result of the concussion. Aaron and Taylor needed the rest, too. Deo was actually the most alert of all of us by last night, since his temperature has dropped to just a smidge above normal, and he slept pretty much nonstop while he was sick.

"Does Mom know we're here?" Aaron asks.

"No," Sam says. "One, I knew she'd worry and say you shouldn't be here, just like I did. And two, I thought since you ignored me and came anyway, we might as well give her a little Christmas Eve surprise."

The waitress comes over and pours Sam a cup of coffee.

"There hasn't been much change with Daniel," he says, stirring some milk into the cup. "We keep hoping for some sort of miracle, but now that he's out of the trauma center, they've started talking about long-term care options with your mom."

We had mixed feelings when we called yesterday and learned that Daniel had been moved. On the one hand, it's less likely that security at the new hospital would recognize me. On the other hand, the security probably isn't as tight, which means Daniel could be at greater risk. His old police department still has someone watching him, but we have no idea how much longer they'll continue.

"The new hospital is a couple blocks over," Sam continues. "Might make more sense for Anna and Deo to wait here. They'll only let two visitors in at a time, but Michele can step out for a minute so you and Taylor can see him."

"Um, no," Aaron says. "Actually, Anna and I need to go in first. Taylor and Deo can chat with you and Mom in the lobby. It will only be for a few minutes."

Sam's clearly confused, especially when Taylor doesn't argue. Because he knows that normally Taylor *would* argue.

We pay the tab and step out onto the street. The weather is still brisk, but the sun is out, and the air has the familiar, if not entirely pleasant, scent of the city. Gray slush is piled up against the curb, a sight that is pretty much the definition of winter for me.

"Home sweet home," Deo says with a wink.

He's right. The group home where we met is less than a mile away. I could walk from here to Kelsey's office. Two months ago, I'd never been outside the state of Maryland. Now, after so much time on the road, it's nice to be back in a place that feels like home, even if it's only for a brief visit.

"Yeah," I tell him. "I kind of miss it too. Although the beach smells better."

"True. Don't you wish we could hop in a cab and go grab one of Joe's cheddar-jalapeño bagels?"

"You're kidding me. That plate of chicken and waffles was bigger than your head."

"Okay," he admits. "I'd have to save the bagel for later. But it would be nice to see Joe."

"It would." I give his arm a squeeze. "We'll make it back eventually. If not back here, at least back to a normal life."

It's a struggle, but I manage not to add the words *I promise.*

He grins. "Doesn't have to be normal. I'd be happy with neither of us being suspected of murder or being called the spawn of Satan by hordes of middle-class moms."

We catch up with Aaron, Taylor, and Sam just outside the hospital. Sam asks Taylor one last time if she's sure she wants to wait. And then Aaron and I sign in at the visitors' desk. I sign in as Elizabeth Bennet, and have the ID badge from Magda's fake law firm at the ready. But the nurse at the desk just waves us through.

"Not sure if that's good or bad," Aaron whispers once we're in the elevator.

"Good for now," I say. "Worrying in the long term, though."

His eyes are concerned as he looks at me. "Are you ready for this? I mean, I'm sure you're ready to get rid of him, but . . ."

"I'm nervous. What if it doesn't work, Aaron? Daniel seems so weak, and I've never done this in reverse. What if I can't do it?"

Aaron tips my face up toward his. "Then you'll have done your best. You will have done everything you could to save him."

"Except getting here sooner. We could have—"

"Shh." He leans down and silences me with a kiss. A short one, because the elevator door then slides open and a middle-aged couple boards. The woman gives my outfit a quick up-down and sniffs dismissively. Despite my nerves, I have to fight back a giggle.

The guard outside Daniel's room is reading something on his phone. Aaron introduces himself as Daniel's brother, shows his ID, and is about to vouch for me. But his mom must hear his voice, because she's already opening the door.

"Oh my God! Aaron!"

She hugs him tightly and then looks at me, confused. "Hi, Anna. Is Taylor . . . ?"

"She's waiting down in the lobby, Mom. Anna and I are going to step in and see Daniel real quick, and then Taylor can come in with you when we're done. That way, she can spend a bit more time with you. She's been kind of homesick."

This arrangement actually makes a bit of sense when he puts it that way, and Michele's eyes begin to water. She gives me a quick hug and then squeezes Aaron again. "I've missed you guys so much. This needs to be *over*. All of it."

After she heads down to the lobby, Aaron and I step inside the room. Daniel is hooked up to some of the same equipment as before but with fewer wires and tubes. The monitor that showed a flat line moments before I picked him up as a hitcher now has a steady, repeating pattern of hills and valleys, although I have no idea if that pattern is normal. What strikes me most, however, is that Daniel looks smaller. Diminished, in almost the same way he seemed inside my head earlier.

I sit in the chair next to his bed, pulling it a bit closer to his body.

Closing my eyes, I breathe deeply several times, then turn inward to look for Daniel. I find him exactly where he was last time, sleeping in the back rows of my mind.

Daniel? You ready for this?

I don't really expect an answer, and I don't get one. But at least he's still here. His presence in my mind is so weak, so faint now, that I know it may not survive the attempt to transfer him back to the shell in this hospital bed. On the other hand, he certainly won't survive if he stays on as a hitcher. So we might as well get it over with.

Kelsey's theory about my hitchers has always been that they're similar to what Jewish mystics call an *ibbur*—basically a benevolent soul tethered to this earth by an unfinished task. She thinks the tether is one of their own making, some regret or question that they simply cannot leave without resolution. My job, assuming I want my head free of lodgers, has been to help them finish the task. Find their peace. Move on.

In some sense, this was true for Daniel, too. He had a task—he was determined to get Caleb and the other kids away from Graham Cregg. Those kids are now safe. And Cregg, the man Daniel believes was directly responsible for his father's death, is no longer alive, no longer able to use his power to harm others.

If Daniel is too weak to return to his body, I hope all of that is enough to give him peace. Enough that he can actually move on without remaining here. He didn't like being cooped up as one of my hitchers the first time. I don't think he'd be happy repeating that experience.

As important as that sense of peace is, however, it's not what I want him to focus on right now. Instead, I turn my thoughts to all of the reasons he has to live. All of the unfinished business. Unfortunately, many of his reasons for living are tied up with anger and revenge. But I focus on the positive side of those emotions. The righteous anger of correcting an injustice. The desire to ensure that evil doesn't win, that innocent kids don't end up in the cross fire of Senator Cregg's political battles. The desire to find a way for the adepts to coexist peacefully without being used or mistreated.

These are all positive goals, and they'll be so much easier to achieve if Daniel is with us.

So, with those things in mind, I reach across the railing of the bed and take Daniel's hand. I expect it to be cold, but his skin is warm and dry.

> *It's time to go home, Daniel. Back to your body, back to your family, back to running the show. You can do this.*

But the only thing I feel is resistance. Almost like he's following through on the threat he made before, to latch on to my cerebellum and refuse to go.

> *We had a deal, Daniel. The kids are safe. Cregg can't hurt them anymore. You need to go. While you still can.*

There's a long pause, and then something whooshes through my head, as turbulent as the wind from the helicopter at the airfield. The movement is agitated, almost frantic.

This is definitely not the way I'd imagined the transfer happening. When I thought about this moment, I'd envisioned focusing on the positive and feeling a gentle flow of power from my hand to his.

Instead, a bolt of pure fire runs through me. My eyes fly open, and I press my lips tight to keep from crying out.

Aaron is at my side immediately, worried. Asking if I'm okay. But I can't answer him until I know what happened. I close my eyes and focus on the corner where Daniel has been for the past two days.

I don't see him. I don't hear him. I don't feel him.

Daniel's *ibbur*, his ghost, his psychic echo. Whatever you call it, it's no longer here.

"Anna? What happened?" Aaron is shaking me gently, trying to get me to respond.

"I'm okay."

The chair is now several feet away from the bed. I don't know if I pushed myself away from Daniel, or if Aaron did that for me.

My head aches again, not like the roar the morning after the attack at the airfield, but more of a dull throb, similar to the one running down my arm.

"What happened?" Aaron asks again.

"I don't know. Daniel's not in my head anymore. I'm certain of that. But . . ."

We can both see that there's no change to the body in the bed. The machinery continues with the same gentle hum, the same readings. Daniel doesn't move, doesn't blink. The only thing that's different is his blanket, which I apparently managed to untuck when the transfer jolted me backward.

"Just because we can't see anything, that doesn't mean it failed," Aaron says. "He's been immobile, unresponsive, for a long time. It may take a bit for body and brain to reconnect."

"I know. I didn't expect . . ."

And that's kind of true. I didn't *expect* there to be an instant reaction.

But I hoped. I really, really hoped. Especially after that intense jolt, which was nothing like the odd slipping sensation I get inside my head when a new hitcher comes on board.

"We should go," I say. "Let Taylor see him."

We've only been in here five minutes at most, but Aaron says, "Sure."

He steps back over to the bed, and I follow, looking down at Daniel.

"I hope you're in there," I say. Then I tuck the blanket back around his body and squeeze his hand gently. "I hope you're safe."

Daniel's hand doesn't move.

Except for his thumb, which grips my fingers against his palm with surprising strength. He holds it for a moment, releases, then squeezes again.

I look up at Aaron, tears springing to my eyes. "Did you see that? He squeezed my hand, Aaron. He's in there! He's really in there."

"Are you sure?" he asks.

"I'm positive. It happened twice."

He sighs. "I hate to get Mom's hopes up, but we probably need to tell them."

I nod, but reach over the rail to try again before we go downstairs, squeezing his hand tightly. "Come on, Daniel. Give us a clear sign. Show us you're in there."

Aaron is watching this time as Daniel squeezes my fingers, his grip firm enough that the knuckles stand out against his skin.

Even though Daniel's expression hasn't changed, the spikes on the monitor seem a bit more distinct now. He continues to grip my fingers, but this time, he raises his forefinger to give the back of my hand three short taps, followed by three slightly longer, harder presses. Then three more short taps. After a moment, he repeats the pattern.

Three short, three long, three short.

And again, three short, three long, three short.

I don't even have to dig through Abner's memories of Morse code to recognize that one.

Aaron knows it, too. "He's signaling SOS."

"We should call the doctor—"

At that word, Daniel's eyes flutter and he groans, a muffled version of the huff he makes when he's frustrated. It's a familiar sound, one that I've heard frequently over the past two months any time he thinks I'm being unreasonable or stupid.

Daniel's grip tightens on my hand again, and he repeats the SOS pattern. But this time, at the end, he raises his finger upward and holds it there.

He's pointing directly at me.

ACKNOWLEDGMENTS

There are often bits of truth mixed in with even the wildest fiction, and in my acknowledgments for each book I write, I like to take a few minutes to separate the purely fictional from the bits and pieces that have a basis in reality. Unlike the CHRONOS Files, which pulled in many historical figures and events, most of the Delphi Trilogy is fiction. Several of the settings and situations are, however, real.

- The Delphi Project is obviously my own creation, but predecessor programs like Stargate and Project MK-Ultra are very real. The military's remote viewing program has been well documented, and numerous reports claim that one of its leaders really did think you could create psychic soldiers capable of walking through walls.
- Overhills Lake is located on Fort Bragg in North Carolina. There was once a posh resort on the premises, owned by the Rockefeller family. While I haven't gone exploring there in person, others have, and I stayed fairly close to the posted images in my descriptions. Links to images of Croatan Cottage and the other buildings at Overhills can be found on my website at http://www.rysa.com/overhills.
- If you're looking for someplace to wait out World War III, there are several companies that have converted old missile silos into

heavily fortified housing. My descriptions of the bunker where Cregg is holding the Delphi adepts is based in part on the various online images of these renovated buildings.

- The Outer Banks of North Carolina are obviously real, and gorgeous, and you should go if you get the chance. You might even encounter some of those wild horses if you venture up toward Carova. (You might encounter me, too, depending on the time of year.)

One reason that I've usually chosen, as a writer, to blend fact and fiction is that I find it easier as a reader to accept the fantastic elements of a book if the rest of the story mirrors the real world. If I had possessed an active CHRONOS key earlier this year, however, I'd have jumped back to my Writing Cave in the fall of 2015 to caution my slightly younger self about the perils of setting a book in a near-future based on our own reality. I'd have told her to seriously consider setting the Delphi books in a distant future, or in a galaxy far, far away, because less than a year later, fiction about politics and conspiracy theories would have a difficult time topping the stories on the nightly news.

But while I have several CHRONOS keys, I lack the gene to use them. As a result, my research for this second book in the series took me down quite a few dark and scary rabbit holes. I truly appreciate the family and friends who listened to me screech and bang my head against my desk during the research phase. Pete, Ian, and Ryan—you deserve medals for your patience, your understanding, and above all, your ability to determine whether my shriek of frustration was a plea for a hug, for caffeine, for wine, or for holy water to cleanse my eyes. (Frequently, it was for all of the above.)

My support team at Skyscape has been incredible, as always. Courtney Miller, my managing editor, is a rock star. Special thanks go as well to Adrienne Procaccini, who stepped in to keep the ship afloat while Courtney was away managing a very special (and adorable!) side project. Amara Holstein, my developmental editor, again offered stellar advice, most of which I took, and even more of which I probably *should* have taken, but like most writers, I'm stubborn when it comes to killing my darlings. Thanks as well to the behind-the-scenes crew at Skyscape who do so much to get my books into the hands of readers.

Mike Corley has created another beautiful cover, and I'm delighted to have his artwork as the "face" of this series. Virtual hugs and kudos to my incredible narrator, Kate Rudd, for breathing life into my characters—I am so grateful to once again have you as part of my team.

Writing can be a somewhat solitary occupation, but thanks to social media, I'm surrounded with friends even when I'm in the Writing Cave (and really should be working). If you're among my friends on Facebook or in one of my online author groups, thanks for keeping me informed and entertained when my brain simply wasn't ready for work. My beta readers deserve a special mention for their excellent advice: Cale Madewell, Karen Benson, Chris Fried, Karen Stansbury, Hailey Mulconrey Theile, Billy Thomas, Meg Griffin, Kristin Ashenfelter, Shell Bryce, Fred Douglis, Jen Gonzales, Dori Gray, Donna Harrison Green, Susan Helliesen, Stephanie Johns-Bragg, Christina Kmetz, Jenny MacRunnel, Trisha Davis Perry, John Scafidi, Antigone Trowbridge, Jen Wesner, Dan Wilson, Jessica Wolfsohn, Tracy Denison Johnson, and Becca Porter. (Apologies in advance to the person I've forgotten . . . because there's always at least one!)

Finally, thanks to my family for everything you do and for simply being you. And thanks to Griffin for sharing my snacks and keeping my feet warm this winter.

ABOUT THE AUTHOR

Photo © 2014 Jeff Kolbfleisch

Rysa Walker is the bestselling author of *The Delphi Effect*. *Timebound*, the first book in her CHRONOS Files series, won the 2013 Amazon Breakthrough Novel Award—Grand Prize—and was the Young Adult Fiction winner. Her career had its beginnings in a childhood on a cattle ranch, where she read every book she could find, watched endless episodes of *Star Trek*, and let her imagination soar into the future and to distant worlds. Her diverse path has spanned roles such as lifeguard, waitress, actress, digital developer, and professor—and through it all, she has pursued her passion for writing the sorts of stories she imagined in her youth. Now living in North Carolina, she is focusing on the final book in The Delphi Trilogy. Discover more about Rysa and her work at www.rysa.com.